The Last Resort

RANDOM HOUSE 🏠 NEW YORK

The Last Resort

A MYSTERY

Carmen Posadas

Translated by Kristina Cordero

This is a work of fiction. Names, characters, places, and incidents are the products of the author's imagination or are used fictitiously. Any resemblance to actual events, locales, or persons, living or dead, is entirely coincidental.

English translation copyright © 2005 by Random House

Published in the United States by Random House, an imprint of The Random House Publishing Group, a division of Random House, Inc., New York.

RANDOM HOUSE and colophon are registered trademarks of Random House, Inc.

This work was originally published in Spanish as *Cinco moscas azules* by Extra Alfaguara SA, Madrid, Spain, in 1996. Copyright © 1996 by Carmen Posadas

Library of Congress Cataloging-in-Publication Data
Posadas, Carmen.
[Cinco moscas azules. English]
The last resort: a mystery / Carmen Posadas; translated by Kristina Cordero.
p.   cm.
ISBN 0-375-50886-4
I. Cordero, Kristina   II. Title.
PQ8520.26.O72C5613 2005
863'.64—dc22   2004061434

Printed in the United States of America on acid-free paper

Random House website address: www.atrandom.com

2 4 6 8 9 7 5 3 1

First U.S. Edition

Book design by Lisa Sloane

To my brother Gervasio,

and also to the memory of Ana Wickham

To die like you, Horacio, of sound mind,
And just as in your stories, isn't so terrible;
A timely thunderbolt and the festival is over . . .
Let them talk.
(. . .)

'Every hour wounds us' so it goes,
'but the end is what kills us.'
A few minutes less . . . who can blame you?
Let them talk.

Fear rots far more, Horacio, than the death
That goes behind people's backs.
You drank well, and then you smiled . . .
Let them talk.
(. . .)

"To Horacio Quiroga," Alfonsina Storni

$\mathcal{C}$ontents

PART ONE

London

A Lunch Date at Drones

THEY HAD GIVEN HIM A TABLE SHOVED INTO A CORNER BY THE STAIR-case, shrouded in a profusion of greenery. When he leaned to the left, the branch of a kentia tree lightly caressed the nape of his neck as a motley assortment of aromas—*chile con carne,* gnocchi with four-cheese sauce, mandarin soufflé—wafted up the shaft of the spiral staircase. At least they had not condemned him to the arctic zone, the downstairs dining room, or, in other words, the shadowy underworld where the maître d' normally sends pariahs.

Molinet leaned back a bit in his chair. He had arrived ten minutes early, as was his habit, and he allowed his eyes to wander about the restaurant in search of a familiar face. There wasn't a single one. It had been years since he'd last lunched at Drones, and he was pleased at how little the place had changed. The same black-and-white-tiled floor, the same red chairs, even the maître d' seemed familiar—an old waiter. The walls were the same as ever, which was just as well, since they were, after all, the main attraction at Drones. Years earlier, when David Niven, Jr., had taken over the restaurant, he had decided to decorate it with a rather curious collection of photographs. The photographs' subjects looked like nothing more than a bunch of anonymous children, but the waiters were quick to explain that the youthful faces were actually those of actors, starlets, well-known beautiful people, and many of old Mr. Niven's Hollywood colleagues and cronies. There were large photos, small photos, color photos, and black-and-white photos, and they all served as entertainment for the neophytes, who would either study them and try to guess who was who or else use them as conversation fillers when the chitchat waned. Molinet gracefully unfolded his napkin. He had never fallen prey to that temptation, not even with the dullest of companions. He considered himself a sterling conversationalist, and even when desperate, he never permitted himself to stop something so trite.

Now it was different, however, for he was alone, and so he decided to take a look at the photographs closest to him. He couldn't identify a single person in them until, finally, he thought he could make out . . . was that Sophia Loren in her First Communion dress? Yes, that just might be her, a homely little girl whose lovely eyes were not quite able to distract the viewer's attention from her rather disproportionate-size mouth.

Seven years. Seven long years away from this world, thought Molinet. Too long, he thought, to have been so far removed from all this. It was a relief to see that all these worldly things had remained more or less the same—pleasures, after all, change very little. That was precisely what he admired about London: A man could really believe in a city where five, ten, even fifteen years could go by and the same restaurant would still be in fashion. This thought, however, was just a momentary digression, and Molinet immediately decided to abandon this line of thinking. The last few years had been a parenthesis, a black hole to which he did not wish to dedicate even five minutes of his luncheon, for he had returned to the land of the living—in fact, he had even organized a little excursion to celebrate his return, and right then his only concern was Fernanda and her imminent arrival. It was one-thirty on the dot and he was beginning to get hungry.

He realized that at least twenty years had gone by since he'd last heard from his niece. He had been quite surprised when she had called him. Could this possibly be Fernanda's first trip to London, in all this time? Probably not, but it might very well be her first trip without her husband, which would explain why she had come to call upon her old uncle.

For certain women, he mused to himself, traveling alone always begins with a little flip through the date book: charter flight, budget hotel, and then a glance through the very last pages of the book, which is where the old addresses pile up. These old addresses— obsolete as they may be—are copied down year after year, from date book to date book, on the off chance they might be useful sometime. As on this occasion.

Molinet wondered if he would even be able to recognize his niece's face, for she belonged to a scattered, foggy past that he generally referred to as "my relatives in Madrid"—family members he felt connected to by an affection that was, in all honesty, more abstract than real. But they nevertheless shared a bond, one that translated the occasional seasons greetings over Christmas and inspired them to write occasional letters that kept everyone abreast of only the most essential news, such as deaths, marriages, and the obligatory scandal.

Molinet signaled to the maître d', who chose to look directly through him with that selective blindness so typical of restaurant employees. Finally, after a very long while, Molinet managed to catch the attention of a young waiter passing by as he performed a balancing act with a tray piled high with plates and spoons that clinked away against the china. At long last, he ordered a sherry.

"I'd soooooo love to see you," Fernanda had said to him over the phone. His reply had been very cautious so as to avert the possibility that she might invite herself to stay with him.

"Darling, I would simply love it if you could stay with me at Tooting Bec, but things aren't quite the way they were when Mama was alive," Molinet had replied. "You see, I'm dreadfully far from the center of London, and in fact I'm going away on holiday. Morocco, if you can believe it, a little vacation." He didn't think it necessary to offer any more details: that he had spent seven long years taking care of his mother day and night, for example. That after she died he had spent a month and a half in a hellhole, a terribly expensive hellhole at that, called the Cedars of Lebanon Mental Hospital. That he now rented two miserable rooms in a neighborhood on the outskirts of town. That the last thing he wished to ponder was exactly how he was going to get his life on track, and that the very first thing he had done was reserve a hotel room in Morocco for two weeks. After that, God would provide for him. Why bother going into all of it? Surely his niece knew at least half of the story—the hospitalization, the depression . . . sordid tales do travel the fastest, after all.

"Don't you worry about a thing," Fernanda had said to him, adding that she was coming to London on business and had no intention of staying at his house, even though she would "be thrilled to see you even if it's only to have lunch. You know, I would have come with Alvaro-husband, but at the last minute he didn't come through, as always, and no . . . no, don't worry about me, really, I'm perfectly happy at the hotel, it's an adorable little place, right in the center and everything . . ."

And so they had agreed to see each other on Friday. Fernanda would be through with her professional appointments by around twelve-thirty, and she could take the Tube to be at Pont Street at about one, one-thirty.

"Yes, yes, it would be really grand if we could meet straight at the restaurant. I'm here for the Ideal Home Exhibition, you can't imagine how boring it is—for the past two days I've talked about nothing but casserole dishes. But, well, what's the use complaining?

This is what has become of my life ever since I decided to become a domestic worker . . ."

Molinet hadn't had the easiest time understanding some of Fernanda's ironic turns of phrase. His visits to Spain were very infrequent. It had been years since he'd last been there, and his childhood summer vacations in San Sebastián, at the home of his maternal relatives, were vague memories. Also, he considered himself neither Spanish, like his mother, nor Uruguayan, like his father, who was also from no place in particular, having lived here, there, and everywhere. For this reason Molinet spoke Spanish with the ambivalence that comes from feeling no particular claim to any one nationality; he was the kind of person who had learned so many different languages that he peppered his speech with words and expressions from all of them, stealing and adapting them to fit his own, very idiosyncratic kind of Esperanto. Rootless people such as he, people who have learned to speak in the family home and not out in the street, at work, or in school, end up speaking in the most outmoded fashion, using expressions that have long since become obsolete, and are always ignorant of newer, more contemporary terms.

Even so, after his telephone conversation with Fernanda, it hadn't been too terribly hard to figure out that his niece belonged (as did he) to that illustrious social class known as the New Poor. From what little she had said, he was able to deduce that she had been forced to supplement a meager household budget ("Alvaro-husband is a landscape architect, so you can just imagine how this little recession is treating us") with the help of a personal catering business.

"To put it bluntly, darling, I am what you might call a high-class maid," she had explained to him. "I'll do anything from a cocktail party for two hundred people to some rich old lady's afternoon tea party, with watercress sandwiches and mango infusions. That pretty much sums things up for us right now."

By the time the waiter finally brought him his sherry, Molinet was already thinking about other things. It was fifteen minutes past

the hour they had agreed to meet, and though he was more than accustomed to female tardiness, he nevertheless had the limited patience of a man who was not terrifically charmed by the opposite sex.
After another sip of his Dry Sack he patted about the inside pocket
of his jacket, to make sure that the plane ticket he had just picked up
was still there. Yes, giving himself that little gift had been a truly
marvelous idea. "Relaxation," the advertisement had proclaimed,
drawing him in like a spider weaving a web: "Relaxation, silence,
and nothing but pure luxuriant bliss." Truth to be told, it was a vacation that was far beyond his financial means, but two weeks in
Morocco—at L'Hirondelle d'Or, a magnificent hotel according to
Tatler magazine—couldn't possibly make him any more bankrupt
than he already was. Such an extravagant Eden seemed to be the
perfect place to visit after seven long years of (somewhat) voluntary
captivity.

All of a sudden, this last thought reminded him that he should
not drink another drop of alcohol if he didn't want to disobey the
recommendations—or orders, depending on how you looked at it—
of his shrink. This was how he referred to Dr. Pertini, a psychiatrist
who had studied at the University of Chicago and who also happened to be a somewhat rootless Latin American. Dr. Pertini insisted that Molinet call him his "therapist," but Molinet figured that
if Woody Allen (and every other rich New Yorker, for that matter)
could call his therapist a shrink, so could he.

As Molinet took a long sip of sherry, he looked through the gob-
let and the golden-colored liquid in it and his eyes were met by the
vision of his niece Fernanda. From the very first moment he knew it
was her. In reality, he realized this not because they shared any kind
of family resemblance but because of the clothing she wore.

During the long, dark years of tending to his mother (and also
during the last month and a half, as the occupant of a very tranquil
room at the Cedars of Lebanon Mental Hospital), Rafael Molinet
Rojas had developed a special talent for guessing the nationality

of certain people based on the way they dressed. It was all in the details—things that would be missed by the casual observer but highly revealing to someone like him, who had so many hours to kill in a day. During his stay at the mental hospital he had become quite adept at examining the many photograph-laden magazines he regularly purchased—*Paris Match* and *¡Hola!* primarily, *Tatler* and *Der Spiegel* only when a copy somehow found its way into his hands. This was how Molinet had honed his very peculiar talent for recognizing people—and not just famous people. For Molinet, star-watching was a pastime for doormen and chambermaids. No, no. His particular gift was an uncanny ability to identify the origins of the incidental characters who appeared in those gossip-magazine photographs— the person standing behind Luciano Benetton at a regatta, for example, or some random person laughing away next to Arnold Schwarzenegger at a hotel in Gstaad. Over here, for example, an English-born Greek shipping tycoon; over there, a third-rate actress from Texas trying to rub shoulders with the rich and famous; and just a bit further down, a Milanese financier. Very rarely did he make a mistake.

This talent was precisely what helped Molinet recognize his niece at first glance, and he stood up to greet her like a father welcoming home his prodigal son.

"Fernanda darling, it's you . . . I'm here, right over here. My, how lovely it is to see you!"

On this typically drizzly October day Fernanda had dressed up like a real English lady, complete with gabardine raincoat and cashmere scarf draped rakishly across one shoulder—only her bulky Loewe purse, misshapen from overuse, gave her away as unmistakably Spanish. Of course she would never have guessed how her Uncle Rafael had managed to pull off that bit of extemporaneous long-lost-relative identification.

How Would You Like to Hear the Story of a Murderess?

MOLINET AND FERNANDA TACITLY DECIDED TO DEDICATE THE APPE-
tizer period of their lunch to a discussion of family members. Old
relatives. Dead people. Children. And in the final fifteen minutes,
once all blood relations were exhausted, Fernanda did her best to
stretch, as far as she possibly could, the topic of casserole dishes, thermal blenders, and other startling innovations she had just learned of
during her visit to the Ideal Home Exhibition.

Good girl, he thought, duly noting her efforts to be sociable.
Even so, he was not too concerned about livening up the conversation, simply because he was not the kind of person who felt the need
to maintain constant small talk. And anyway, a perfunctory conversation had its advantages: He could let his mind wander off, do a bit
of idle speculation, concentrate on other things. On her, for example.

The first thing that occurred to him was that Fernanda most
definitely was something of a health nut. That much was obvious
from the food she had ordered: lots of herbs, sprouts, and watercress,
not to mention the collection of pills that she very quickly arranged
in a little line on the tablecloth. But then again, who knew? Nearly
everyone had become some kind of health-food addict these days. In

anticipation of more significant hints, Molinet decided to review her external appearance, which was much easier to classify.

Fernanda was thirty-five years old, but she had an adolescent air about her, the kind that made people think her much younger than she actually was. She had a wide face, clever eyes, and a mouth that smiled often enough to reveal a row of teeth with just a few too many gaps. None of her features could be called perfect in the strict sense, but the overall result was not at all unattractive.

He knew that face of hers, for he had seen thousands like it before, in magazines as well as in real life, where the passage of time always seemed to manifest itself so remorselessly. It was the kind of face that always reminded him of Mickey Rooney. Masculine or feminine, it was a face with adorable chubby cheeks, a snub nose, and smooth dimples that lasted well-past age thirty, when, little by little, wrinkles would etch their way into the skin before time erased those childlike features and turn her into an elderly-looking elf.

Fernanda, however, had not quite begun to pay that steep price for her seemingly eternal youth. Also, she seemed to have a predisposition for seeing everything in life as a kind of amusing joke—she had a dispassionate way of speaking and wasn't afraid to laugh at herself from time to time. In this manner she regaled her uncle with the details of her life, in the very best manner of the relative one sees on very few occasions.

By the time Fernanda decided it was time to get her uncle up-to-date on her present life, Molinet was already thinking about other topics—the trip he was taking the following day, for example. As such, he only registered bits and pieces of his niece's storytelling. He vaguely heard something about Fernanda's children, three big boys of various ages, none of which he could remember, and about how they took lots and lots of classes.

"You can't even imagine all the classes: piano, judo, tennis, horseback riding, karate, and God only knows how expensive it all is. It's a nightmare, I'm telling you . . ." From there, his niece then found it necessary to go into a detail about the Ideal Home Exhibition that had brought her to London with the intention of purchasing some kitchen utensils for the catering outfit she ran, something called Paprika and Dill—or was it Cayenne and Dill? In any event, all of a sudden, she leaned in toward her uncle to tell him something in a most conspiratorial tone of voice:

"Listen, Rafamolinet—" That was how she addressed him, saying first and last name all together in one long tongue twister. "Listen: how would you like to hear the story of a murderess?"

For a moment, he felt a shiver run up his spine, but he quickly shrugged it off, certain that he knew what the question was leading up to. He squinted his eyes and then patted his pockets for his glasses. Of course, the explanation was right in front of him: Surely she was referring to one of the actors' photographs on the wall. *What a melodramatic way of changing the conversation,* Molinet thought, with a touch of displeasure. Maybe he was a bit behind the times when it came to social habits, this banal chitchat used for passing the time, but from his point of view, their conversation had not sunk so low that they had to turn to the hopelessly unimaginative topic of the star photos lining the restaurant walls.

"Darling, really, I would much rather you tell me more about your children," he was about to reply as a way of redirecting the conversation when he realized that Fernanda's eyes were not at all glued to the lineup of celebrity photographs. Gazing just a bit to the left of him, peering in between the pillars along the staircase, Fernanda seemed to be spying on someone downstairs in the lower-level dining room.

"Did you hear what I said, Rafamolinet?" she repeated. Molinet then assumed that she always chirped first and last name like that, all together in a powerful phonetic blast, because she went on to pronounce another name in the very same manner.

"Look at her right there, Isabellalaínez," she said. Then, leaning back to allow her uncle to see who she was talking about, she flicked her chin to indicate some indeterminate location in the downstairs dining room.

"If you lean a bit to the right, you'll see her. No, no—down there, silly, in the dining room for the nobodies, in Siberia. Boy would she be furious if she knew that I came here and saw where they sat her."

Molinet looked, entirely skeptical, toward the spot Fernanda was pointing at. His angle of vision wasn't very good; it was awful, as a matter of fact. The plant that swished against the nape of his neck from time to time covered a fair amount of the space between the pillars along the staircase, and he found it annoying to exert such an effort to follow his niece's instructions, despite the information she had disclosed. A murderess. Come now, he thought, truly gruesome stories never start off that way. But he relented and dutifully steered his gaze downstairs. All he saw was what looked like a married couple with a considerable age difference between them, sitting at a table and eating in silence.

"Who are they?"

"Darling, I thought that in your spiritual withdrawal from the world you spent all your time devouring gossip magazines."

"I have never seen those two in my life. Though I sense they are a married couple despite the age difference. Am I right?"

"Yes, a marriage maintained through eight years of mutual boredom. Do you want to hear the story or don't you?" she asked, signaling vaguely for the waiter to remove the salad she had barely touched. "I have never met anyone more immune to high-society gossip than you, Rafamolinet."

Molinet didn't bother to explain that he was an old dog. He wasn't insensitive to gossip, far from it—he simply did not trust clever conversationalists and their theatrical attempts to liven up otherwise boring conversations. *Coffee time chitchat,* he thought, and his face indicated that yes, he was familiar with her little trick— exaggeration can sometimes be very effective.

"So what do you have to say?"

Molinet shrugged his shoulders without saying anything. The waiter had just arrived with the second course, a cheese soufflé that was listed as an appetizer on the menu and which he had long since learned to request as a main course, since it was quite filling and inexpensive, to boot. "The story of a murderess," Fernanda had said in that very conspiratorial tone a person uses just before tearing someone to shreds. He looked downstairs. The woman seemed attractive enough to interest him for another ten minutes, at least. Maybe even half an hour, he conceded. *She has something of a contradiction about her. She seems like such a good girl.*

Molinet paused for another moment to study the husband and then he turned his gaze back to the woman before admitting surrender. *What a shame I have no idea who these people are,* he said to himself. *No matter how intriguing it may be, a story is never quite so fascinating when the protagonists are two illustrious people you don't know.* Distracted, he took a little sip of the sherry that an imprudent waiter had not seen fit to remove from the table. Then he added, to himself again, *I do hope that Fernanda is not one of those insufferable types who take an eternity to tell a completely idiotic story.*

Terrible Things That Happen Only to Other People

FERNANDA'S FIRST VERSION OF THE STORY OF JAIME VALDÉS'S DEATH was told amid a fit of giggles, combined with a confusing tale about two friends and her description of a man who listened to Silvio Rodríguez songs, as well as two or three additional anecdotes that Molinet could make neither head nor tail of. It was now painfully clear that his niece was not someone who could speak and eat at the same time. And to make matters worse, as she talked on and on, the little arabesques she drew in the sauce of her scorned fish grew more emphatic. Once she had laid out the basics, she sat up straight in her chair, waiting for some kind of a response.

"Fernanda darling, I haven't understood a single word of what you just said."

She leaned in toward her uncle once more, her fork pointing toward her sauce, threatening to begin a new set of designs, but he stopped her with a halting hand gesture.

Holding out his fingers to reveal a set of fingernails that were not quite as well tended as the rest of his person, he began to enumerate with his pinky: "First of all, there is no way she can possibly hear you. Second, from what I can see, there is nobody in the vi-

cinity who might interrupt us, and third, neither my ears nor my
sensibilities will allow . . . *des chuchoteries,* my darling. So, please,
start from the top and tell me that . . . terrible story with the same
level of detail you use when you tell me about our dearly departed
relatives. Better yet, try and do it slowly. With serenity," he said, and
immediately congratulated himself for having used such a word.
"Serenity" sounded good. It was a word that he had not used or
thought of in quite some time.

"All right, fair enough. But don't go telling me now that I talk
too much. Have you ever thought about how bad girls always seem
to have better luck in life than us saints? Well, that is what this story
is all about."

Molinet was able to endure this little digression without losing
his patience. It was the kind of digression that often serves as a prelude to a frivolous gossip tale, and he took advantage of the moment
to sneak another peek at the two restaurant patrons sitting at the
only occupied table downstairs. Drones had emptied out little by little. A group of noisy Italians were still jabbering away at a table
nearby, but on the downstairs level the only people in sight were the
two that Fernanda had pointed out. In silent boredom, they alter-
nated between taking sips of their coffee and staring out at nothing
in particular, and their faces had that ventriloquist's-dummy look of
unhappy husbands and wives who think that nobody is watching
them. The man was sixty-something, rather short, and had the curious habit of jerking to attention in his chair every so often, as if to
stop himself from nodding off. Now he sat upright once again, took
a long sip of coffee, and allowed his gaze to settle on the wall in front
of him, as if he was scanning it or waiting for something or someone.

*Apart from a pair of unusually alert eyes, there is nothing out of the
ordinary about him,* thought Molinet. *He may just be a man who is extremely bored, although I would say he has a certain air about him . . .
What would be the right word? Self-assured. Yes, that is what it is, the
kind of self-assurance that comes from having held countless glasses of*

champagne at countless gala benefits where he is always something of the outsider.

Then he turned his gaze to the woman, who was easily twenty-five years younger than her husband. Even from that distance, he was duly impressed with her angular face, which changed depending on whether you looked at her face-on or in profile. It was fickle in the way that some Magyar faces are, with high cheekbones and very dark eyebrows. Her medium-length hair, on the other hand, was very light—an inconsistency. Pulled back, it rested softly against the nape of her neck to reveal her very tiny ears.

"Now, you might think I'm old-fashioned, but I am going to start this story by telling you what Alvaro-husband thinks of our friend Isabella," he heard Fernanda say.

"He thinks Isabella is a bitch. Well, actually, that's what he thought of her until the day the two of them ended up in the same Golf Clinic at the Puerta de Hierro Golf Club. 'Oh, Alvaro!' she kept saying. 'Oh, I'm sorry! I'll just never get the hang of this club!' And that was all it took to change his opinion—radically change, I might add. But you know, don't you, that men's moral judgments can be so . . . fragile when it comes to pretty women. They fall to pieces with a simple little flutter of the eyelashes."

As Fernanda laughed, Molinet noted that his niece's eyelashes were not exactly paralytic, either.

"That should give you a fair idea of what kind of person we're dealing with. In any case, and all joking aside, one thing is for sure: Isabellalaínez—and take a good look at her, now—came very close to getting herself in a big old mess, thanks to her personal charms.

"It's the oldest story in the world," she continued. "I could tell it to you in two words. But I don't want to do that. I think it would be much more fun to first describe all the personalities involved. Tales of adultery are so boring if you don't accessorize them a bit. Even this one, which ended up in the Almudena."

"The what, my dear?"

"In the cemetery, darling. Forgive me, I a-a-always forget how foreign you are," Fernanda remarked. And as she said "a-a-always," Molinet thought he saw her emphasize this on the table with one of the colored pills that had not met the same fate as their brethren. He couldn't be certain, however, for he was wearing his distance glasses—he needed glasses for both distance and reading, a double curse that somehow made everything blurry in the end.

"She," continued Fernanda, tilting her head in the direction of the couple, "is called Isabella Laínez, née Isabel Alvarez. She acquired the Italianesque 'la' and the less-common last name of Laínez through her first marriage. I suppose you have heard about the very convenient nature of last names in Spain: If you're a woman you can practically pick yours. Some women keep their last names. Others— the sharp cookies—adopt the last name of a dead husband, while others choose to mooch off their new husband's last name. It all depends on the convenience of the pedigree."

"What about the man with her?" asked Molinet. "He doesn't look terribly Spanish."

"Jewish. From Tangiers. Rich, though nobody knows exactly what he does. I mean, just picture it: a house in La Moraleja filled with Boteros and Warhols, a Doberman that answers to the name of Kaiser, and tons—I tell you tons—of money . . . enough to whitewash his own shady past and hide Isabella's as well. Because she is, after all, from Madrid and she does still have a number of, say, inconvenient relatives in neighborhoods like Ventas . . . or is it Embajadores? Something of the sort, anyway."

Molinet smiled. He was decidedly in favor of this more venomous facet of Fernanda's character. "Everybody has a darker side, it is just a question of drawing it out," as he always said. *Plus,* he told himself. *This is what everyone is going to be like when you get to the hotel in Morocco—divinely superficial, every last one of them.*

"The story is as follows," Fernanda began. "Eight or nine years ago, our friend Isabella Laínez suddenly appeared on the scene in

Madrid—out of nowhere, it seemed. As if she'd dropped down in a parachute from somewhere. Even before marrying Steine (he calls himself Steine, by the way, so that nobody has the slightest doubt as to his background—Jean Jacques Steine is his full name), she was already all over the place, never missing a single party. She dated all the single men in the city at one point or another, but she had to get herself remarried and was not interested in wasting her time with professional bachelors. No scandals. No bed-hopping (or at least she had a very wise and discreet way of dealing with that). With these tactics, she managed to cultivate a reputation for being something of a prude. Now, believe it or not, that, coupled with a pretty face, works miracles for a woman. And one fine day she turned up married to Steine. It was a smart move on her part; he was the perfect stepping-stone for her. And let me tell you," Fernanda continued, barely stopping to catch her breath, "Steine had a reputation for being a total bore, but he liked to have a good-looking woman on his arm, and he liked to be 'in the know' about things. Beauty and money are not a bad mix, plus Isabella is very sociable—right away she cast her net, to fix things so that she could rub shoulders with— oh, I love this expression—'the right people.' At first she had a tough time, as you can imagine, but after the first few snubs and a couple of other fiascos, our friend decided to use an infallible method for opening the most exclusive of doors: the old oxpecker system."

"The what?"

"Come now, Rafamolinet. Listening to you, anyone would think it's been centuries, not years, that you've been away from the madding crowds. The oxpecker: a very old trick for clawing your way into high society. I don't know how you call it in French, or in any other language for that matter, but you know the routine, I'm sure you do. If you want to be accepted by the flock, the best thing you can do is stick like glue to the biggest of the bunch—just like those giant brown birds that pick lice off of the backs of cattle. Just find the biggest and fattest of the sacred cows and follow that cow anywhere and everywhere. Those are the laws that govern the animal kingdom, and they work just as well for humans. You just have to be a little crafty and patient, and you have to be prepared to put up with a lot of shit. And those are all virtues that Isabella possesses. I have to say she did an excellent job of choosing her cow—her sacred cow, as it were. Marta Suárez is her name. Perhaps that doesn't mean much to you, but if I were to add a few more details, I'm sure you would get the picture: fifty-something, a big name with certain committees and charity organizations. You know the type—one of those pillars of society who can say anything, even the stupidest little thing, and everyone goes around repeating it as if it were gospel. Have you ever noticed this phenomenon? Strange, but true. It usually comes out sort of like, '*Marta* says' or '*Marta* swore to me' and also 'my dear, I was just talking to *Marta* the other day . . .' Everyone just loves to drop names."

Fernanda paused for a moment and then continued, deeming it unnecessary to go into more detail about such obvious social mores: "Anyway, as I was saying, she was a very well chosen sacred cow, because Ma-a-a-arta"—and Fernanda elongated the 'a' in Marta's honor—"Ma-a-a-arta loves to launch new social stars into the stratosphere, and as coincidence would have it, Isabella was the ideal student: attractive, intelligent, and seemingly submissive, and her husband was more than willing to pay for the debut. What more can you ask for?"

Fernanda broke off for a moment, turning aside so that the waiter could take away her plate and rapidly clear the tablecloth of any offending breadcrumbs before serving dessert. Once her coconut ice cream had been delivered, she continued telling her story.

"All right, so now we have Isabella on the road to stardom, but first—just so you can see the impressive level of work the sacred cow put into this metamorphosis—I am going to tell you about a conversation I heard a few months before Isabella became Marta

Suárez's willing pupil, so you can get an idea of where we're coming from. The conversation took place at a wedding—I don't remember whose, but it was one of those really swank events. Guests flew in from London, Rome, who knows where else . . . Anyway, at a certain point, Alvaro-husband and I happened to walk near the Steines; we ended up right behind them, in fact. Isabella looked just beautiful, I have to admit, and Alvaro just stood there gaping at her. Oh no—I know what you're thinking, but no, no, it didn't bother me, not at all. Because if he hadn't been looking at her like that, we never would have heard this little gem: 'J.J.,' Isabella said to Steine, 'J.J., isn't that the Remy-Davraises? Come on, sweetie, do something so that we can meet them, please, please, please, sweetie, I heard they have the most colossal *gateau* near the Loire!' "

  "Now, I know you are not going to believe me when I say this," Fernanda continued after allowing time for a conspiratorial laugh for the malapropism. "You won't believe it, but in the space of three or four months, Marta Suárez worked a miracle. A total and complete transformation: In one fell swoop she eliminated every last 'sweetie,' 'honey,' 'J.J.,' and other words of the sort. Nothing. There was absolutely nothing about her eager pupil's speech or diction that would suggest she had studied anywhere but an Irish convent school. Since then, naturally, Isabella has had plenty of time to learn other essentials about the subtleties of language—nuances, intonations, and a number of the more typical mistakes that the more careless social climbers almost inevitably make. And now she never misses an opportunity to let us all know that she knows, for example, that the ladies who lunch never spend their time doing *petits pois*—how ghastly! *quelle gaffe!*—*petits pois* is what one eats with roast beef. And she also learned that children can be *mischievous,* not 'mischeev-ious,' and that one wears *jewelry,* never ever 'jew-lery,' because that sounds perfectly horrible. To make a long story short, the bella Isabella learned, in record time, all the ins and outs of speaking like the worldly woman she aspires to be. She had already worked over her appearance and clothing, but those things, after all, were the easiest to get down. With Marta's guidance she developed an indefatigable finger that was ready and willing to make the thousand, two thousand, however many phone calls were necessary, just to be able to talk to certain people and say things like, 'How are you, my darling? Are you feeling better now? Everyone was telling me that you've come down with the worst cold . . .' Her skin grew thicker than a hippopotamus's after all the feminine slights she had to put up with, and at the same time she learned how to charm the pants off all the men, so that in the end, Isabella Alvarez Laínez Steine—or whatever you want to call her—managed to get every last door in Madrid to swing open for her, even those doors that were considered to be double- and triple-locked to someone like her. You know how these things work, Rafamolinet. Once you've reached certain heights, they simply adore you. They take you in just as if you'd been sharing beach umbrellas with them since childhood. Anyway, the fact is, they take you in and they adore you until it isn't convenient for them anymore. But that's another topic entirely."

"So the scene is set then," Molinet interrupted.

"What?"

"For the lover to enter the picture. From what little I understood of your initial explanation, that is what you were leading up to. And if there was some sort of murder, I would imagine that the dead party is . . ."

"You are so impatient, Rafamolinet. Things are not that simple. What do you want me to do, rip apart the story just so that I can get to the end?"

At that very moment Molinet felt an old social instinct, only a trifle rusty, kick in. Even before Fernanda had begun to discreetly signal that he was to shut up immediately, Molinet knew that the Steine couple was about to walk past their table. He sensed this from the light tickle he felt on the nape of his neck. And from a very lovely perfume that wafted up the spiral staircase, growing stronger and stronger until Isabella Steine materialized, along with her husband, at the top of the stairs.

She looked at them and then approached Fernanda in the friendliest manner, just as Fernanda called out, "Hello, darling! I mean, really, to run into you here when I never, ever see you in Madrid!"

And Isabella, in response, said, "I know, I know. And tomorrow we'll run into each other on the Portobello Road, of course. You go all the way to London and you run into everyone you know from Madrid, isn't it crazy?"

A brief moment went by, not long enough for introductions, and Molinet took advantage of the lull to admire the very tall woman, who threw her shoulders back, as do all women who know they are beautiful. There was only one small detail that disconcerted him slightly: When the smile that lit up her face faded, he could see that she had extremely thin lips that a well-outlined lip pencil had failed to conceal. *Greek lips,* thought Molinet. Before he knew it, the Steines were making their way between the tables and Fernanda was back on track with her story, as if the fleeting presence of the Steines had only corroborated the accuracy of all her previous comments.

"Now that you have the background information down," Fernanda announced, "we have now arrived at the topic of the . . ."

"The lover?"

"Please, do not make me rush through this: For the moment, we have Isabella attending all the little parties in Madrid, pursued by all, everyone telling her how beautiful she is, giving her thousands of reasons to realize that her husband, poor old Steine, is really just a bore who can't keep up with her—and this, of course, is her own fault. Because she very innocently married the first acceptable male that crossed her path, when in reality she could have done a whole lot better. And then, suddenly—abracadabra—the right man appears: Jaime Valdés, who is, of course, the husband of a very good friend."

"Typical."

"I know, I know, but just let me describe this new character. It's a shame you never met him, because Jaimevaldés was one of those types that you would have just loved to dissect. He wasn't handsome, exactly, but he definitely had a way with women. He must have been . . . forty-seven—somewhere around there. He went to the same elementary school as my brother Miguel. The Colegio del Pilar, in Madrid. We didn't know him all that well, but he was a pretty popular sort of a person. Aside from being a real ladies' man, he always hung around with the successful crowd, if you know what I mean. The kind of people who try to position themselves with the in crowd every chance they get—showing up everywhere with them, going to all the parties, etcetera . . ." Fernanda sighed, looking at her uncle. "Honestly, I will never understand why some people are so obsessed with being part of this in crowd. It's so much *work:* First you have to freeze your ass off at, like, fifty fox hunts a year. Then you have to start playing golf. And then destroy your knees on the paddle-tennis courts. And be 'beeeeest friends' with so-and-so even though they put you right to sleep. And when someone 'forgets' to invite you to dinner, you have to casually call them up and ask how they are, for God's sake. And then? And then, oh yes, you have to listen to opera day and night—even Wagner!—and swear that you absolutely adore it. All the classic tricks of social acrobatics . . . but anyway, enough with all these weaknesses. Suffice it to say that our newfound hero suffered through all these social requirements. But there is one other point I wanted to make: Jaimevaldés was an intelligent man: intelligent, a womanizer, and fatally flirtatious, I would say . . ."

The Italians at the table next to them had asked for their check, which the maître d' delivered right away, sending a crystal-clear message by carrying it directly over the heads of Fernanda and Molinet.

"Perhaps you ought to get back on track, Fernanda dear. These British restaurants don't have much patience for our Spanish-style post-meal chats."

"And it's a shame," said Fernanda, sighing again. "Because that means I will have to give you the official version, which is much shorter than my own."

"There are two versions of the story? I'd prefer the real one."

"All right, but please do let me just finish painting a picture of our dearly departed. Now, Valdés was married to a very good friend of Isabella's, a good friend of mine too, for that matter. Her name is Mercedes Algorta. She is from Bilbao, a dyed-in-the-wool native of Bilbao." Fernanda emphasized it as if it were some kind of special achievement. "Oh yes, I could tell you plenty about my friend Mercedes, plenty indeed. But I'd better just quickly tell you what happened that fateful day before they kick us out of here."

Molinet looked at his watch. It was twenty to four. As he signaled to the waiter for the check, he took advantage of the moment to ask Fernanda to speed things up.

"Brevity, darling, does not mean going off on tangents."

"Oh, whenever I think of poor Valdés, may he rest in peace," she said, a bit more hastily now, "I imagine him just as he was: wearing a soft khaki Bel jacket, some kind of light-colored shirt. The tie . . . hmm, I don't know, maybe pistachio-colored, with little teakettle designs on it . . . something like that. He was always very up-to-the-minute that way. The pants, gray . . . yes, gray. Very possibly, this was what he was wearing the day of the races. Why not? The point is, as you can surely understand, that what I am about to tell you is the very cornerstone of the story—are you certain that you don't want to hear the version I heard through the maid connection? It's much more intriguing, because, you see, it presents a number of additional tidbits that . . ."

"What on earth is the maid connection?"

"Darling. It is by far the best way of learning about indiscretions and unspeakable secrets. Through the hired help, naturally. That is the maid connection. My maid tells your maid, who tells it to so-and-so's maid . . ."

"I don't want backroom gossip," said Molinet, unaware of the decorous and somewhat-rusty masculine instinct that had suddenly come to life inside of him. "I have always found servants' gossip rather sickening."

"Oh, you're ruining my story . . ."

"I'm interested in the facts. We've been on this for almost two hours," he protested.

"I know, I know, but I'm warning you now, it's not half as intriguing," she said bluntly, her tone of voice suddenly changing. For a few moments, before she was once again suffused with the drama of her tale, Fernanda narrated the sequence of events like someone reciting a list of Visigoth kings. Setting (colon): a country estate that the Valdéses had just bought in La Adrada, some sixty miles outside of Madrid (semicolon); a very charming country house, no ugly Boteros or Warhols on the walls, like in the Steine home.

"Fernanda, are all these details truly necessary? Can't we skip the *House and Garden* description?"

"The details, my dear, are to give you an idea of precisely how abnormal Mercedes and Isabella's friendship was. We're talking about two people who have ab-so-lute-ly nothing in common. But of course as you well know, one of the golden rules of the human condition is that when a woman—or a man, for that matter—attempts to steal someone's mate, the first thing he or she does is become the inseparable confidante and soul mate of the future cuckolded spouse. Isabella had her eye on Valdés, and then all of a sudden the two couples began doing everything together, the women putting together little outings and events, sharing the most private secrets—I invite you over to my house, you invite me over to yours, etcetera. And as it turns out, our four protagonists decided to spend the weekend together. Until now everything was perfect. But at this point, on that very Friday, it turns out that Valdés was feeling ill. Not so ill that he had to cancel the weekend date—the opposite, in fact. He actually thought some fresh air—listen closely, Rafamolinet: fresh air!—would do him some good. Now, Mercedes couldn't get out to the country until the following day, so Valdés invited Steine and Isabella to go with him. The three of them were to leave Madrid at about eight in the evening and Mercedes, who had some things to take care of in town, would arrive on Saturday morning. Everything clear up to now?"

"Yes, everything is clear. I just don't see why it is so hard for you to—"

"Just pay attention, because if you miss even the smallest detail, the story will lose all its meaning and I will be forced to tell you the version I heard through the maid connection."

"Fernanda! I beg of you!"

"They reached the country after dinnertime, and the only person in the house was a Moroccan maid named Habibi—incidentally, very good friends with my housekeeper, who talks. Boy, does she like to talk." Molinet executed a few imperious coughs, and Fernanda continued.

"Now, if Valdés was a bit out of sorts that day, it was because he always suffered in the springtime—allergies, sneezing fits, and so on. Now comes the interesting part."

"Finally," said Molinet with a sigh of relief.

"Well, as it happened, the poor man, may he rest in peace, suffered from asthma. Now, being asthmatic is really the most distinguished kind of ailment." She let out a sigh as she said this, as if she too were a chronic sufferer. "Whenever spring rolls around, people who have asthma become incredibly languid, and they talk in a kind of gaspy, a very, very . . . oh, how would I put it? A very Don Corleone way, kind of a cross between threatening and sexy. Apparently,

given how repulsive pollution is these days, the air appears to be full
of new fumes, terribly dangerous ones—just look at poor Valdés—
Russian fumes, Rafamolinet, extremely dangerous stuff."

"I've never heard of anything so preposterous."

"Don't you read the newspapers?"

"Is that why you take all those multicolored pills, dear?"

"Don't be so old-fashioned, Rafamolinet—melatonin and an-
tioxidants and selenium pills are for staying young and fit, they have
nothing to do with Russian fumes. Russian fumes only affect asthmatics, and their effect is so severe that asthmatics are advised to
take very special precautions with regard to changes in temperature
and climate, and they are supposed to carry around a special, rather
bulky inhaler at all times, to use in the event they begin to feel sick.
Nobody does it, of course, especially not in a situation like the one
our friend found himself in. Because, I mean, can you possibly imagine a romantic rendezvous with an inhaler, Rafamolinet?"

"What do you mean romantic? Romantic with whom?"

"With Isabella, who else?"

"This story makes absolutely no sense to me. Just now you said
that the dead man's wife wasn't able to go to the country that night
but that Isabella's husband was most definitely there with them."

"A husband of a certain age, who falls asleep on the couch in the
middle of a conversation and who, that night, went straight to bed
upon arrival."

"Ah, I see, I see. Now we seem to be getting somewhere. So
there was a romantic tryst between Isabella and Valdés."

"May he rest in peace."

"Yes, may he rest in peace. You said that before."

"And I will say it again. Maybe it sounds provincial to you, you
don't have to remind me, but there's no need to tempt the spirits. It
is a very important precaution, according to my Tarot card reader,
especially when one is preparing to discuss certain things about certain dead people."

"Fernanda, for the love of God . . ."

"All right, all right, I'm finishing up. The point is, Steine goes to bed, quiet as can be, at about eleven, eleven-thirty. Valdés and Isabella claim they are not tired and stay on in the living room for a nightcap. Risky, you might say, to take advantage of such a dangerous opportunity for a little roll in the hay or, to put it bluntly, a fuck. It would have been much easier, and much more comfortable, to wait a day or two and go to a hotel together—how far could they go with this, after all? But their relationship, if you look at it carefully, was in the very early stages. They were in that very romantic phase in which both of them must have been feeling, *Ooh! Anything is possible. Let's use whatever excuse we can come up with to be alone.* And so they say to each other: 'Shall we stay here a bit, have another drink?' 'Of course, why not? I'm going to put on an album you are going to love. Do you know Silvio Rodríguez?' 'Silvio Rodriguez? No, no—who is he? I don't think I've ever heard anything of his . . .' A blatant lie, of course, but that doesn't matter—any old excuse will do at the dawn of a new relationship, so that the two bodies can inch closer and closer together, first the heads, all very careful, let's just huddle together to look at the song lyrics. And then, 'Oh, look, look! Read this—what do you think he means, this bit here about *you are my blue unicorn* . . . what fascinating lyrics!' And this goes on for a while until, surprise surprise, the passion suddenly bubbles up after a fortuitous brush of the skin. Of course. But anyway, I don't have to bother describing the ritual to you—you certainly know it well enough. Everything deliciously slow, because what makes these early encounters so very perfect, so very thrilling, is when they are played out like this in slow motion. 'Can I pour you another drink? Are you hungry at all? There's not much to eat around here. All I can find are some almonds; would you like some? and then . . . I tell you about my hopes and dreams, you tell me about yours . . . we laugh a little, with the devious knowledge, of course, that all of this seems so perfectly normal. And that, more or less, must have been the atmosphere in that house that night. But given that these things take time, we have to assume that by now it had gotten late, it had to be about one in the morning, and Steine had long since been snoring away peacefully in the guest house in the garden. That was when Habibi, the cook, who was the only other person in the house, suddenly heard noises coming from the living room. Valdés had given her strict orders not to come downstairs, that he would take care of their guest. For this reason Habibi was hesitant about checking in on them—that is, until the music suddenly stopped. Then Habibi heard a thunderous noise, like the sound of something breaking, like a piece of furniture. This was then followed by 'a lot of very hoarse panting. Just awful. It sounded as if it was coming from a sick animal,' according to Habibi. That noise, she said, was what convinced her to go downstairs—she was rather frightened, of course. And when she reached the downstairs vestibule, she says, she heard a woman's voice, followed by the sound of a door creaking—the door that opened onto the garden. Someone was leaving the house. She ran into the living room, and when she walked in, all the lights were out, which led her to believe that she was the only person in the room. When she turned on a lamp, she saw the overturned table. And next to the table there was something else, too, something very interesting that I heard about through the maid connection. Now, are you sure you don't want me to . . . ? All right, all right, just the essential and substantiated facts, fine. Well, the fact is that Habibi found Mr. Valdés lying on the floor, but she didn't dare move him."

"Because he was bleeding, naturally . . ."

"Bleeding? What are you talking about? Why on earth would there be any blood anywhere?"

"When his head struck the . . . the table, or whatever it was . . ."

"No, no, nothing like that happened. Habibi did not dare move him, because he seemed gravely ill. His breathing was very labored. He sounded as if he was choking. And then, just when the poor woman was simply desperate, at that very moment the door flew open and suddenly—guess who appeared?"

"Isabella, who had gone out for help."

"That is a logical guess, isn't it? Well, no, actually. The person who suddenly appeared was Valdés's wife, whom nobody expected to see until the following day. Appeared out of thin air. And right behind her—ten minutes later, however—Isabella and Steine turn up, both of them in their bathrobes, as if they've just crawled out of bed. Habibi was calmer by now, because Mrs. Valdés was there to take care of things, so she breathed a sigh of relief. If only we could say the same thing for poor Valdés, whose face had suddenly turned a ghastly shade of blue, according to those present. The next thing Mercedes did—now, listen closely—was this: She asked everyone to leave her alone with her husband. She wanted to call for an ambulance, one of those mobile ICUs. But it was all for nothing, because poor Valdés died long before any help could arrive."

"Now I get it . . . the man was a real womanizer, and so you think he was having a tryst with Isabella when he suddenly had an asthma attack, which is why she up and left at the most incriminating moment of their little get-together. Really, *c'est très typique.*"

"No, no, no. That isn't what happened at all. Just simmer down for a second and then you can draw your own conclusions. When they found him, Valdés was completely dressed. He even had his dinner jacket on—a little pretentious, if you ask me. And now I am going to tell you what happened next. I am not going to go into what the gossipmongers have said. I am going to tell you exactly what Mercedes herself told me, and then I will add a few of my own conclusions, because, after all, Mercedes is from Bilbao."

"And what does that have to do with anything, for the love of God?"

"It has everything to do with this story, silly, because people from Bilbao are so reserved, they never tell you anything at all. They

never embellish their stories enough, and this story must be embel-
lished because the Truth—and I mean 'truth' with a capital 'T'—is
a terrible bore, don't you think?"

"Fernanda, can't you just leave well enough alone?"

"Just wait until I get to the end. You're going to like it, because
despite everything, this seems to be what really happened: Valdés
and Isabella were listening to music, nibbling away at a bit of food,
all very innocent, when Valdés, in the middle of his seduction,
preening like a peacock . . . Now, can you guess what happened?"

"Something ridiculous, clearly."

"The worst thing imaginable: He chokes! You can't whisper
sweet nothings and swallow whole almonds at the same time, Rafamolinet. The two activities are totally in-com-pat-ible, especially if
you are an asthmatic. The least little scare and there goes one of your
bronchial passages—it just closes up something awful."

"Fernanda, for heaven's sake already!"

"I am telling you, that is exactly what happened. A little almond
went down his windpipe and then his nerves kicked in and his
bronchial tubes closed up." Fernanda coughed a couple of times and
then raised her hand to her mouth to add a bit of realism to her story:
"Just picture the scene: It was one disaster on top of another, one
long chain of rotten luck. A lover who gets frightened and leaves,
then the Russian fumes, and then Valdés, out of pure idiotic vanity,
doesn't have that special inhaler with him. It's all very logical, Rafamolinet, because we never think that these things, such ridiculous
things, can ever happen to us—'Oh, that bizarre kind of thing only
happens to other people,' we always say. And that, Uncle, is what happened to Valdés. Just picture it. Why, I can practically hear him saying, 'Oh, it's nothing. It can't be anything serious—I just coughed up
a bit of almond. I'm fine, really I am. It's nothing, nothing at all.'
And then he waits a few seconds to see if he can breathe a bit better . . . once, twice, three times, and then: 'Oh dear, this isn't going
away. My throat feels as though it's closing up . . . oh no! This is turn-

ing into something serious,' and he loosens his pistachio-colored tie and tries to breathe again: 'Oh, oh, how can this be happening? I feel awful. Good God, someone help me . . .' But Isabella has long since left him—and not exactly to go looking for help, either—only to return to the scene later hanging on the arm of Papa Steine."

"Darling, all I can say is that you have an imagination that could be put to far better use. Why would she do something so foolish?"

"Because she is a petty, frivolous woman. And because she was frightened. Forgive me for saying so, Rafamolinet, but you would make a terrible detective." After tilting back in her chair to assess the effect of her revelation, Fernanda leaned forward once again to say:

"Uncle Rafael, how can you not realize, at the very least, the irony of the story I have just told you? That night, everything that happened was perfectly ri-di-cu-lous. Death has such a strange sense of humor, don't you think?" When Fernanda saw that her uncle was not following her train of thought, she decided to conclude her tale in a more light-hearted tone. "Well, anyway, that's that. Now that you know the grim story of Isabellalaínez, I suppose we can go. It must be awfully late."

She got up from the table and Molinet followed suit.

"Is that it?"

"That's it."

A hush fell over them for a few minutes. A waiter, now dressed in street clothes, opened the door for them with an exceedingly professional smile despite the fact that it was four-thirty in the afternoon. Back out on the street it was cold and still drizzling. Without another word, Molinet took his niece by the arm and guided her toward Sloane Square, where he would wait for the bus to take him home.

"That is the most inane bit of gossip I have ever heard," he said as they stopped on the tiny bridge that led to Knightsbridge. "There was no sex, no mystery—there wasn't even money involved. And what are we left with? A flirtatious Casanova who chokes on a cocktail almond. How appalling."

"Well, in Madrid it's the topic of the moment. Everyone is totally fascinated by the story. Did you really find it that silly?"

"Absolutely."

"And you don't think that if thoughtless Isabella, instead of going to her husband in her moment of despair, had done something to help Valdés, he might be alive today? What do you have to say about *that*?"

"People do irrational things in moments of stress, Fernanda."

"If Isabella is irrational, darling, then I am a nun."

"I can see why it occurred to you to start your story by calling that poor girl a murderess. Murderess! Women just love embellishing *petites histoires* so that they come off sounding as scandalous as possible. From the very beginning, I knew I was in for something farfetched, some kind of exaggeration."

Fernanda, her raincoat wrapped tightly around her body, clung to her uncle's arm even more tightly and laughed.

"Well of *course* it's an exaggeration, but what did you expect, Rafamolinet? That we would spend the whole meal talking about dead relatives? You have to admit, at least, that I kept you in suspense for a good little while. Now didn't I? But in all honesty, most people think that one person and one person only is to blame for Valdés's death: Is-a-bella!"

"The story of a murderess! So that's what they're all calling it . . ."

"The problem, Uncle, is that you have insisted I tell you the strictly official version of the story. That was a very foolish error on my part. Now I know for next time: One should never recount a story according to what witnesses say, even if they swear up and down. Nobody ever believes those official versions. Even if they do happen to be true."

"Mysterious allergies, men who choke on a tiny almond sliver— do you really find it such an extraordinary story, my darling?"

"Oh, it's all your fault, Uncle. You were in such a rush that I didn't get a chance to tell you what some other people think. There are some very imaginative interpretations, let me tell you . . ."

"No, no. Please, for goodness' sake, don't go into them. I can't bear this nonsense one second more." Molinet loosened his grip on his niece's arm and pointed across the square. Two or three buses were pulling in.

"Oh look, one of those must be the 137," Molinet exclaimed. "That will take you straight to Park Lane. If we hurry we might be able to catch it."

"But I still have one little tidbit left to tell."

"My dear, it's starting to rain buckets. You wouldn't want to wait another half-hour in this weather for the next bus to come around, would you?"

Fernanda, a bit grudgingly, quickened her pace. "Whatever you say," she replied. "But there's something else, something I heard about through the maid connection, and I am sure you will find it very interesting. It has to do with a certain bracelet. All right, all right. I will only say one thing about it so that I can leave you with a bit of intrigue to ponder during your trip to Morocco. Would you believe that foolish little Isabella actually thought that nobody would ever find out that she had been right there when everything happened, and she actually turned up at the funeral, blasé as can be? And, of course, since the church was filled with photographers—only complete nobodies have funerals without paparazzi—my poor friend Mercedes is now being hounded day and night by the magazines, all of them begging her to tell the sad story. And let me tell you something else: I am a perfect saint for telling the most innocent version of the story, because there are two or three other hypotheses out there that are plenty more interesting. In one hypothesis, the wicked witch is Isabella, naturally, but in another, would you believe, the bad girl is the widow! Because, now, you tell me," Fernanda added, with the sauciest little smile. "Didn't you find it extremely odd that the wife just suddenly appeared like that in the middle of the night, out of nowhere? A bit strange, wouldn't you say?"

"Darling, that only proves that she trusted her friend about as much as she would a poisonous viper."

"So much hearsay. So many conflicting accounts. I don't know what to say," Fernanda said, shrugging her shoulders. "I suppose that is the price of being rich and fascinating. At least, *I* will never suffer from such problems. Poor Mercedes Algorta . . ."

"Who the devil is Mercedes Algorta?"

"The widow, Rafamolinet. My God, to hear you talk, it's as if you haven't heard a word I said. Oh—is this my bus? Are you sure it goes to Park Lane?"

They said good-bye with a hasty kiss on the cheek. The last few words they exchanged involved family members, hugs to all, and the like.

"If I come back to London, I'll be sure to give you a call."

"Yes, yes, please do." And they looked at each other, smiles frozen on their faces. That was precisely when Fernanda leaned forward toward her uncle, as if to tell him something. Stuck between all those people, hanging from a pole, she looked like a little schoolgirl in her blue raincoat.

"You know something, Rafamolinet? Curiosity is the virtue of the wise," she said at the very last moment. And perhaps she would have added a thing or two, but the din of the city had already closed in on Molinet. It was almost five o'clock.

Kellogg's Corn Flakes

EVEN BEFORE MOLINET CROSSED THE SLIVER OF SIDEWALK SEPARATING the bus stop from the entrance to the Sloane Square station, Fernanda's story was already long gone from his mind, replaced by more domestic concerns. It was dark, and the rain reminded him of the socks he had left hanging on the clothesline outside his bathroom window, and suddenly he noticed how ruthlessly the cold weather penetrated his feet, so poorly protected by the Italian moccasins—made of Moroccan leather, incidentally—that he saved for special occasions.

He ascertained that his pants' hem as well as his shoes were looking very shoddy indeed. Without realizing it, he must have stepped in a puddle somewhere, though he couldn't recall when. A long gray line snaked around the circumference of each shoe, threatening to turn white if not dried off immediately. Molinet tried rubbing his shoes against the hem of his pants. They looked a bit better now, he thought, and continued walking. Of course, he would have no choice but to treat them with a coat of his expensive shoe polish the minute he arrived home if they were to be in tiptop shape for his journey to Morocco the next day. Perhaps they had not been the best choice of footwear for such dismal London weather and such a ridiculous lunch date, but they were most definitely ideal for a night on the town in Fez, paired with a dark suit. Nobody would ever guess they were more than ten years old.

Prompted by the thought of Morocco, he patted his jacket pocket once again. To his relief, the plane ticket he had picked up earlier that day at the travel agency was still there: October 10, 8:30 P.M., a charter flight from London to Rabat, returning two weeks later, £250, not including airport taxes. And who knew? Perhaps he wouldn't even need to use that return ticket, but it was always much cheaper to travel round-trip—the mysteries of modern travel, he mused . . . and of the financial trials suffered by poor souls like himself, living on shoestring budgets.

"As of tomorrow, everything will be different," he suddenly said. "Welcome back to the world of the living." He said it out loud—a little habit he had picked up during his many years of living alone. Very occasionally he would spontaneously talk to himself, in public places even. But he didn't care. Nobody gave a damn about him, anyway—to them he was just another nut who talked to himself in the Tube. The usual gust of people at that hour of the day blew down the stairs, onto the platforms and through the deepest underground tunnels.

After passing through the turnstile, he caught up with some schoolboys in plum-colored trousers, and two of them turned around to observe the old man who now proceeded toward the stairs with a grandiose air. He, however, did not notice them at all, because he was too busy staring at the massive advertisement for Kellogg's Corn Flakes that covered the wall on one side of the escalator. The dirty glass pane protecting the ad allowed passersby to catch a glimpse of their reflections on the long escalator ride down to the platform. Molinet peered into the glass, running his hand through his hair. In

general, he always tried to peer into only the most forgiving mirrors, the dirtiest windows, those opaque surfaces that erased wrinkles and softened facial lines enough to reflect the image of a person who, long ago, had been quite attractive. He took a moment to straighten a stubborn lock of hair that was rather miraculously still black, but he scarcely bothered to look at the rest of his body. He never looked anymore, not unless it was absolutely necessary, because even the most distorted glass reflected the very deplorable manner in which time had taken its toll on him, transforming his features until they bore a remarkable resemblance to those of his father. And never were two people more different than Molinet and his father. As the years went by, it seemed that this resemblance was yet another cruel irony of old age. In the early stages of this metamorphosis, Molinet peered into every mirror he saw, just to watch the phenomenon repeat itself again and again in so many different ways: the slackening of his facial muscles, the way the wrinkles had set in around his lips. All these changes in his facial features seemed like some sort of conspiracy to revive a person whom he had believed to be dead and buried for many years, a person whose death he had never felt the need to mourn.

As the scent of the underground tunnels grew stronger and stronger, a mouthful of thick air forced him to wrap up his examination, and in the last few seconds of his descent, he confirmed, much to his relief, that the rest of his figure was more or less the same as it had been during other, happier, moments in his life. For a few more brief moments he was able to look into the glass and catch a glimpse of his very stately bearing, as well as the condition of his gray overcoat—a bit frayed at the edges, yes, but the astrakhan collar still retained every bit of its prewar dignity and glory.

"As of tomorrow, everything will be different, Rafael Molinet," he said to himself, out loud again. And then, prompted by the noise of swiftly approaching trains, he began to elbow his way forward through the crowd. After a few seconds he successfully made it through the swell of heads bobbing up and down, everyone in a terrible rush—brunettes, blondes, with hats or with Rastafarian dreadlocks—racing together toward the deepest tunnels of the London Tube.

The Remains of the Shipwreck

MOLINET PLACED THE KEY IN THE LOCK, TURNED IT TWICE, AND THEN inhaled deeply as his feet navigated through a patchwork of gray linoleum. Advancing down the long communal hallway at top speed, past the fireproof glass doors and through two more corridors, he finally arrived at the door to his apartment. Holding his breath, he entered and rapidly made his way to the sitting room without bothering to turn on the light. He knew exactly how his furniture was laid out and easily dodged the old leather easy chair and the side table. He was still holding his breath when his hand finally located the solid, age-old bronze lamp and turned it on. Only then did he allow himself to inhale deeply, for the danger had been successfully averted: Once more he had skillfully eluded the wall of unforgivable odors that wafted from the neighboring apartments.

Long before settling into these two rooms, in a sad house on the outskirts of London, Rafael Molinet had known how dismal such squalid living quarters would be. However, the person who had actually articulated this thought and put a name to the feelings was Dr. Pertini.

"The worst, most repugnant thing about poverty," his shrink had said during one of their last sessions, "is how awful it smells."

For Molinet, this had been something of a revelation, and ever since that moment he had repeated the phrase thousands of times whenever he thought back to the many experiences he had lived through over the past few years. Every squalid house had its own particular stench, and his own present lodgings seemed to take pride in a tenacious odor that was a combination of boiled cabbage, pine-scented Mr. Clean, and cat urine, an aroma that had a way of clinging to the pituitary gland with all the conviction of life's cruelest realities. It was as if they conspired to remind him again and again: *You are bankrupt. You are a nobody. You are nothing but a destitute old man.*

Ever since his release from the hospital a few weeks earlier, he was determined not to let the hallway wreak its havoc on him. His two little rooms formed a true oasis, a sacred haven in a land of infidels, and it smelled of absolutely nothing except, on occasion, the Floris room deodorizer that he had pocketed from Harrod's and now stored in one of his night-table drawers. Now and then he would add a bit of water to the bottle to extend the product's shelf life a bit, and whenever he was feeling especially low he would very generously spray the potion around the apartment so that for a few brief minutes, at least, his home might be suffused with the indulgent aroma of opulence amid "the remains of the shipwreck," which is how he referred to his home that overflowed with all the mementos he had hung on to following his mother's death. Every piece of furniture had been down the same path in life as he (splendor, stupor, decadence, and disaster).

Any mental digressions from the practical matters at hand could be very dangerous for him. Just yesterday, for example, a few minutes after his niece had called him to confirm their date at Drones, he very innocently bumped into one of his favorite pieces of furniture—his mother's favorite ottoman—and was suddenly reminded of his

mother's last pain-filled days. Certain memories were suddenly too much for him to bear: the shape of his mother's head; the fragile neck that sank so deeply into the pillow; the bright white lace appliqués, as white as the sheets that he had changed every day and washed every night, with the same care and attention he devoted to everything in his mother's environment—the last stop on her very eventful journey through life. About when he turned fifty, he had begun to care for his mother, his only source of company, in their rambling old house near Holland Park. Unfortunately, the costly upkeep had forced him to take in boarders, horrid as they were, and little by little he had had to sell off all the paintings, the dining room set, and much of the living room furniture to pawnbrokers and secondhand shops. He couldn't have cared less when the paying guests complained about the lack of creature comforts, the cockroaches, the chill in the austere, curtainless rooms, and a thousand other annoyances, but his mother's room was untouchable, unaffected by the passage of time. He went to great pains to ensure that the room was exactly as it had always been, so that when she opened her eyes, the whites whitened by all the sedatives he gave her, she would see exactly what she had always seen in all of the houses they had lived in together: the blond-wood armoire that went so well with the queen-size Indian mahogany bed bought in Havana; the mirror with the silver handle that sat on top; the clock that no longer told the correct time—not because it was broken, but because one day his mother had decided that it should always be set at ten minutes to five. And then there were the photographs. Very close by, almost within arm's reach, was the little table where his mother had kept her collection of silver frames, filled with photographs arranged in rather idiosyncratic order. They were something of a walk through her life and began with a large, magnificent portrait of her at a party in Biarritz as an adolescent; it was signed by Cartier-Bresson himself. Next to this photograph sat a cluster of smaller frames that constituted the River Plate series: the house in El Prado where her husband had been born; a group of people dressed in white at a picnic; and finally, his mother in her wedding dress, standing alone at the door to the house in all her regal beauty.

There were also two other oversize frames. The one closer to the bed featured a very young Molinet in a raw linen suit and Panama hat on a ship's deck. This photograph was occasionally moved from its spot—not because of any intrinsic virtue or flaw it possessed, but because its placement on the table blocked another frame whose fate waxed and waned depending on the ailing woman's mood. Whenever she said to him, "Rafael, I want to see your father today," he understood exactly what she meant and would quickly turn around the one photograph that was normally condemned to face the wall.

These memories came rushing back into Molinet's mind all because of a clumsy brush against a footstool upholstered in petit point. The experience very nearly prompted him to call Dr. Pertini, but he decided against it. He had to learn to live without Dr. Pertini.

"From now on, whenever you start to feel nostalgic, dear Molinet, why not write to a friend, get your feelings out on paper. It is, after all, far less expensive than Kleinian therapy," Pertini had said to him as he sent Molinet on his way at the end of their last appointment. "Sending him on his way," of course, was not quite the same thing as "declaring him cured," even though the result was the same. It meant he was on his own now, without a penny to his name and still plagued by the same nightmares that led him to the doctor in the first place. Following his comment, the doctor had written out three or four prescriptions on an elegant red notepad before ceremoniously walking Molinet to the door in his white, probably custom-made, robe:

"Here you are," Dr. Pertini had said to him. "A muscle relaxant, some vitamins, and these sleeping pills. But, please, don't abuse them, because if you do, they might start causing you more nightmares. And think, my friend. Think that you are cured, that you have emerged from your depression, that there is nothing more that science can do for you."

Science, Molinet knew, can do precious little for someone who hasn't the wherewithal to pay his psychiatry bills. Even so, Pertini accompanied him to the door like a true professional. "If you need anything, you know where we are," he said, using the well-practiced good-bye speech, which very obliquely indicated that Molinet needn't bother calling him again, although he was kind enough to suggest that little bit about writing to a friend to unload his cares—Dr. Pertini was *so* polite.

That was when Molinet was struck by the splendid idea of reserving a room at a fabulously expensive hotel, far away from the real world, not to whittle away his time writing letters to friends— he had none—but to ingest every last pill that Dr. Pertini had prescribed in one fell swoop, and end his days as a gentleman in an amenable environment.

"Write, Molinet. Write to a friend," Dr. Pertini repeated in that soft monotone so often used by doctors. He sounded as if he were reciting items off a very long list.

"But you are the only friend I have now," Molinet exclaimed, trying his luck with one last bit of flattery, but Pertini didn't take the bait. Instead, he just slipped his arm around Molinet and gave him a couple of reassuring pats on the back.

"Come now, don't be concerned. Why, anyone would be thrilled to receive a letter from you filled with stories like the ones you've told me. I assure you, Molinet, you are a walking novel, especially your childhood, your adolescence . . . my goodness! Now, why don't you go and take a little trip somewhere?" he suggested.

"That marvelous caftan you wear to our therapy sessions deserves a better climate than the London fog and mist," the doctor exclaimed. "Why don't you go to Morocco for a few days? They say the weather there is absolutely brilliant."

Certain ideas need a bit of time to grow after they have been planted. As he left Cedars of Lebanon, Molinet would never have dreamed that he would soon be spending night after night plotting his very theatrical departure from the world, an idea that had unexpectedly occurred to him while chatting with Pertini. But a few days in Tooting Bec was all he needed to realize what the future held for him if he did not take drastic measures. "The worst thing about poverty is how awful it smells," the doctor had said to him. And yet Molinet knew of a fate even worse, even more tragic: growing accustomed to the smell of boiling cabbage, finding himself actually enjoying the fresh scent of Mr. Clean mixed in with the smell of cat pee, losing the ability to react or escape—even if escaping meant ingesting an entire bottle of sleeping pills. But then again, why not? Only fools fear death more than squalor.

The minute he made his decision, everything around him seemed to brighten up somehow. He actually felt a kind of pleasure as he planned all the little details: buying the plane ticket, selecting the best hotel. Even seeing his niece and listening to all that inane gossip was like an amusing general rehearsal of sorts.

Now he had two weeks before him in which he would, quite literally, throw his life out the window and say good-bye, *ciao, au revoir,* dying exactly as he had lived: beyond his means, Oscar Wilde *dixit.*

And now, on the eve of his departure, he had to take care of all the final details: so many little things to remember. As such, he could not allow a stupid little footstool or some other family heirloom to come between him and his plans and ruin the delicious ritual of packing his suitcase.

Molinet looked neither left nor right.

It was almost seven o'clock. His white caftan sat neatly on top of his bed, along with a number of other articles of clothing: a pair of lambskin slippers, a linen suit, the least threadbare of his dinner jackets, a Panama hat . . . everything seemed ready to go. Now, all he had to do was muster up a bit of resolve and put certain sad (and use-less) thoughts out of his mind.

"Mr. Molinet! Sir!"

He had just entered the bathroom to collect the bottles of pills Dr. Pertini had prescribed him and was still hunting for them when he heard the voice.

"May I, Mr. Molinet? May I?"

The young man had entered through a window, bumping into and overturning the little basil plant that he himself had deposited on Molinet's windowsill not two days after the men first met. He was so lithe, firm, and young that he had already jumped over the verti-cally sliding window and was standing in the middle of the living room by the time Molinet's head had popped out from the bath-room.

"Hello, Reza. Hellllo, Reizzzah," he intoned, as would a Persian aristocrat accustomed to the customs and idiosyncrasies of the age-old court of the Blue Peacock. "Reizzzahh darling, I have told you a thousand times to please use the front door."

"Excuse me, chief. You know I try to use the door whenever I come to bring you your dog, but he's sleeping right now, and . . ."

"Is he still running a fever?"

"He's fine, just cries a little bit when we touch the paw. But that's normal after a vaccination."

Young Reza, his next door neighbor, had the odd habit of always speaking in the plural whenever he spoke of dogs and cats, as if the sustained contact with animals of all shapes and sizes had somehow granted him that very paternal authority assumed by so many physi-cians. In the back pocket of his tight jeans he usually carried some instrument of his chosen profession: a pair of scissors or a metal-tipped comb. Ever since they had met a few weeks earlier, it was the rare afternoon when Molinet, with some excuse, did not venture out to see how skillfully his neighbor handled things in the back room of his canine beauty parlor, hypnotized by the movements of those lustrous arms, exposed by the carefully rolled up sleeves of a cotton shirt. He would watch him slip his fingers in between the paws of the animals he tended. And Molinet reveled in the sight of those muscles as they grew tight under the sheath of his youthful skin, especially when they were busy handling his dog.

"Relax, Gomez. Relax, darling," Reza would say to the dog before giving his coat a healthy comb-through. Reza would then flip up his ears in search of some nonexistent parasite, whispering all sorts of sweet nothings in Persian mixed in with a little bit of lower-class French slang that, to Molinet's ears, was a song of pure bliss. The dog had, as do all basset hounds, a long, sad face, and broad ears that flopped down over a set of stumpy, bowlegged paws that were utterly incapable of conferring him even the tiniest shred of dignity. And calling the dog Gomez was an exercise in pure vengeance, for that had been the name of a certain majordomo that Molinet's father had brought with him to Europe from America. And, no, it wasn't that the dog actually reminded him of Ceferino Gomez, that vulgar, ridiculously loyal houseboy who looked like a dockworker and whom his father always addressed by last name only in one of his many attempts to Anglify the un-Anglifiable. No, that wasn't it at all—he just liked how ludicrous the name sounded. Molinet would have called him Bertie, in memory of the man who sired him, but he sensed that he might actually start to feel some affection for the pup. Of course, the real reason Molinet had succumbed to the extravagant purchase of a pet was to have an excuse for sitting down every so often in the canine coiffeur's back room as Reza worked his magic on the various animals that entered his shop.

"Things are a bit of a mess around here, chief, aren't they?" Reza said. "I see you're cleaning house."

Three open suitcases indicated travel, not housecleaning, but Reza just scratched the back of his neck, apparently thinking of other things. Perhaps he was thinking of Gomez, who had remained in his care during Molinet's lunch with Fernanda. Or perhaps he was thinking about his business or some nighttime escapade or something else entirely. But never of Rafael Molinet.

"Reizzah darling, I wonder if you might do me a little favor. Nothing important, just *une petite chose.*"

He was sitting back in his easy chair, with young Reza standing very close by, just a few paces away. If he looked straight ahead he could see only Reza's bottom half, clad in jeans so tight that it became rather difficult to look any higher.

"Whatever you say, chief," young Reza said, smiling.

"Listen, Reizzaah. I am finally going to go on the little vacation I mentioned to you the other day. And I would be so grateful if you'd look after Gomez while I'm gone. It will only be for two weeks."

"To Morocco?"

"Yes, to Morocco."

Young Reza had knelt down and was now straddling the arm of the sofa, so close that Molinet could have reached out and touched the knee trapped in those piercing blue jeans.

"I also have to ask you a favor, chief." And those Persian cat eyes shone with a brilliance that was not unfamiliar to Molinet.

"How much money do you need?"

Reza's hand, the same hand that so assiduously stroked the bodies of domesticated animals, the hand that delivered such skillful caresses, had moved perilously close to Molinet. It slid across the back of the sofa and Molinet watched as it came to a stop near a tiny speck of dust resting against his neck. Only once before had Reza's hand come this close to him. It had taken place a few weeks earlier, when they had met for the first time following Molinet's arrival at the flat. Reza had been kind enough to help him arrange his furniture, and when they were finished, Molinet had felt obligated to give him a tip— twenty pounds, a fortune—but he was such a very friendly neighbor.

"You know what, chief? I think it will do you very good to leave this dump for a little while. Really. Tooting Bec is no place for a gentleman like you. Take it from me."

"How much money do you need, Reza?"

The young man shrugged; his abusively green eyes answered the question.

"Twenty, thirty pounds? I can't give you any more than that, but you know I am your friend, Reza—I told you so the other day. I don't want you to have to go around asking other people for money. What is it this time?"

"Nothing serious. I owe a friend some money."

It was always the same story. He had heard it a thousand times, from so many other Rezas. The only thing that changed was the name and the country of origin. The blue-eyed René. Gustavo. Gianfranco. Timothy, the waiter with the strong hands. He was never able to save them from danger, and only rarely did they ever truly acknowledge his friendship, for which he requested nothing in return. Occasionally, of course, one of these boys would compensate him with an ambiguous, careless brush of the hand or, if they were feeling generous, perhaps a couple of pats on the lower back. Nothing much, but after all, a destitute, dirty old queer couldn't really expect much more than a few crumbs of affection. He had a special weakness for macho types, exceedingly masculine queers, and with each and every one of them he would relive his old, worn-out dreams, as he did now with Reza. But Reza seemed different from the others. He really did. He loved animals, didn't he?

"Thirty pounds. Not much, but it should do."

Molinet handed over the thirty pounds, and Reza reciprocated with nothing but a pat on the arm, dry and manly.

"Wait, don't go just yet. Now, would it be all right for me to leave Gomez with you?"

"I'd love it, chief—you know how I adore that little pup—but I can't do it. My boyfriend is coming down this weekend. I told you about him, didn't I? He lives in Liverpool, he's got a laundromat there. Oh, he's such a good boy. You know how it is, chief. There's no way. Mohammed hates my animals."

"What happened to your other friend, Reza? The one that was so good-looking? Don't tell me you've already . . . ?"

Reza fidgeted slightly, but Molinet paid no mind.

"You know who I mean. He's Italian, isn't he? I saw him leave your apartment the other day. Now, he looked like a real gentleman. I'm good at noticing certain things, Reza, and you would be smart to notice them, too, instead of wasting your time with boys named Mohammed who run laundromats. You're not going to be young forever, you know."

"You're not going to be young forever, you know," he had said, as if he were the screenwriter of a bad Italian soap opera, *porca miseria*. And he knew that it came out sounding like the advice of a maiden aunt to the nephew she has always been in love with in the most incestuous and inappropriate way, but Molinet didn't give a damn. He also knew that young Reza did not take kindly to his recommendations, but he nonetheless remained in the apartment, pacing about the sitting room as if waiting for the moment to object—or perhaps provoke Molinet further. He chatted, he laughed, but most of all he took special care to strut around in front of Molinet like a cowboy, splaying his legs so that the metal-tipped comb peeking out from his back pocket shifted positions: First it bristled against his ass, then it tilted diagonally, always erect, always provocative. And he chatted away about Morocco as if he actually gave a damn about Molinet's trip. What did he care? Such a stupid concept, Molinet said to himself. Nobody gives a damn about anyone.

Reza finally left, but his scent hung in the room for a long while afterward. Molinet hadn't quite ascertained the nature of his aroma—it was a mix of disinfectant and the aggressive, cloying sweetness of young skin. Reza's love for animals, however, was entirely undetectable, which was a good thing, for it would not have produced a very felicitous olfactory blend.

Reza's scent was still present in the room when, suddenly, he returned—this time through the front door—to give Molinet his dog. He didn't even cross the threshold. Nothing more than a brief farewell, a few words, and that was it.

As Molinet watched him retreat down the hallway, he called out, "Good-bye, Reizzaah, don't get into any trouble, now." And as he hugged his little dog, running his hand through all the little nooks and crannies of his warm body in search of elusive tenderness, he thought about what Dr. Pertini had said: "Whenever you start to feel nostalgic, dear Molinet, why not write to a friend, get your feelings out on paper. Why, anyone would be thrilled to receive a letter from you. Your life is like a novel . . ."

Like a novel! Dr. Pertini could rot in hell for all Molinet cared, Dr. Pertini and the rest of those goddamn doctors at Cedars of Lebanon. Who did he think he was kidding? His life was the most typical, commonplace soap opera, and it could be summarized in all of three lines: He was nothing but an old queer who hadn't been smart enough to take advantage of his beautiful flesh in his youth—flesh that had once been as young and beautiful as Reza's, and much more willing for that matter. That was why he had ended up old and decrepit, cast aside by all. And so, in his old age he had turned to his mother with an adoration that was equaled only by his hatred for his dead father, the person he blamed for everything, even though, of course, it was far too late to do a damn thing about it. That was his story. It wasn't even original.

Molinet stood at the door to his flat for some time, which was rather remarkable given that the hallway was filled with all of its usual abominable odors. Gomez was squirming about in his arms, his young body searching for a comfortable position, when the phone rang.

Molinet did not move. Two . . . three . . . four rings. He waited for the answering machine to pick up, because the phone was not usually a harbinger of good news, and he silently prayed that it wasn't some obnoxious creditor demanding to speak with him.

After five rings, the telephone stopped to recite a friendly message that Molinet had recorded in his most sophisticated voice. Following the beep, a female voice rang through the air:

"Rafamolinet, it's me. Are you home?"

Fernanda most definitely *was* the kind of person who thought that "it's me" was a universally effective mode of identification, but Molinet decided not to pick up the call. He let her go on speaking.

"I just called to say that I hope you have a wonderful vacation, Uncle, and to thank you for lunch today. And don't go thinking that I am calling you out of obligation, because I am not that kind of person, you know. I just wanted to tell you how lovely it is to know that I have an uncle in London who . . ." That was where her message got cut off. His machine allowed fifteen seconds of aggravating, undesirable messages before cutting off the caller. Now, however, Molinet was wondering if perhaps he ought to call his niece at her hotel to see if she had anything else to say. But then he decided against it. Fernanda was delicious only in small doses. Even so, her voice on the answering machine was like a tonic, for it was a cheerful call, bless her little heart. And this tiny reminder of the world to which he had once belonged was enough to make him think far more pleasant thoughts, such as: *Tomorrow, finally, everything will be different.* He repeated this over and over again, like a mantra. Then he let go of Gomez so that he could focus on more practical matters, such as packing for his trip to Morocco.

All his things were in a jumble on the bed that had once belonged to his mother: his medicine, his clothing, his shoes. Now he had to ask himself which of his Bermuda shorts he should take with him: the blue ones? The leaf-green ones? He was undecided. Far more important, however, were the three bottles of pills that Dr. Pertini had prescribed, which he would ingest all at once on the day of his choosing, at L'Hirondelle d'Or, a fabulous hotel for only the wealthiest of vacationers, a most tranquil little hideaway.

Little by little, with the aid of this positive thinking, he began to formulate a plan of action. He had always believed in the importance of the mise-en-scène, and it seemed exceedingly obvious to him that death would be far more pleasant if experienced in luxurious, expensive surroundings and not in the squalid little room that had been witness to all his failures.

He paused for a moment in front of the armoire mirror, and before forming any opinion about his appearance or the state of the bedroom (which, for him, was utter chaos), he lifted his white caftan off the bed and put it on over his street clothes. He had selected this article of clothing precisely because it contrasted so divinely with his dark, distinguished looks. And right then he felt certain that not even Truman Capote in his golden years, the fabulous queer and darling of Lady Luck, had ever cut such a grand figure as he did right then dressed in that impeccable white linen sheath.

"God bless frivolity, for it puts everything in its proper place," he said to himself. Prompted by this sudden thought, he began to speak to Gomez. In reality, he had never been very fond of lap dogs, but the presence of Gomez, a previously unwanted dog, somehow helped him mold the persona that slowly had begun to take shape in the mirror, a persona that was not at all unattractive.

"What do you think?" he said. "As I look at the two of us, it occurs to me that perhaps before ending it all with a theatrical finale, I might just try my hand at a few long-forgotten techniques—like mooching off rich people, for example." After all, he reasoned (not out loud this time, since he was not given to chatting with dogs), it should be easy as pie to find some rich old matron desperate for company at a hotel like L'Hirondelle d'Or. Elegant places are always filled with lonely people.

"What do you think, Gomez?" he said, out loud this time. "Wealthy old ladies are not exactly my specialty, but . . ." He wasn't very well versed in the art of mooching off wealthy old men, either, tricking innocent fools, or taking advantage of hapless tourists. In the past, he had tried all those methods, with rather pathetic results. The truth is, he was a sorry disciple of the arts of Arsène Lupin, and it was a shame, because they really would have come in handy at so many junctures in his life.

"None of this is my specialty, no, but we shan't forget what the prophet has indicated," he said, and he was suddenly overcome by a wave of laughter as he saw how quickly he had grown into this new persona he had fashioned.

"Yes, Gomez, the prophet to whom our dear neighbor Reza entrusts his soul every night says that victory belongs only to the man who is prepared to lose everything. Very wise, wouldn't you say? Especially in my case, because I have *nothing* to lose, absolutely nothing. I mean, think about it: Before saying good-bye to this world, why shouldn't I have a little fun, play whatever role strikes my fancy? Who knows? Make myself out to be an eccentric, meddlesome old busybody, for example, or perhaps a gambler. I'm not so bad at gambling, and who knows, maybe I can even win a little money to sweeten my two weeks at the hotel." He sighed, and then paused for a moment.

"Well, that is that. Whatever I do, whatever I dream up, no matter how extravagant, will be just perfect. And that, *mon cher,* is the advantage of being almost dead. And now, *viens,* my darling little dog," he said in the worldliest, most sophisticated tone. "It is time for dinner. No matter what happens in these next two weeks, the one thing I can promise you is that this will be our very last night living in squalor."

PART TWO

The Book of Worldly Customs

If spitting chance to moove thee so
Thou canst it not forbeare,
Remember do it modestly,
Consider who is there.
If filthiness or ordure thou
Upon the floore doe cast,
Tread out and cleanse it with thy foot,
Let that be done with haste

"BOOKE OF DEMEANOUR," RICHARD WESTE, 1619

At the Hotel
L'Hirondelle d'Or

65 MILES FROM FEZ, MOROCCO

(FAX RECEIVED AT L'HIRONDELLE D'OR AT 11:45 A.M., AND DELIVERED *to Mercedes Algorta in the solarium just before the 12:30 Pimm's*)

Dear Mercedes:

Sweetheart! You can't even imagine what I have been through trying to track you down. Finally, I got hold of your sister Carmen who gave me this fax number (L'Hirondelle d'Or, Fez, Morocco . . . where on earth are you??). Anyway, I am herewith sending you the proposal we discussed last week over lunch. As I said to you before, I do hope that our newfound friendship will inspire you to at least consider the idea. As you can see, it is a very flexible project that can be developed in any number of different ways, and I also have to say that after everything you've been through in the past few months, a light distraction like this would do you a world of good. On that note I also must reiterate my admiration for the aplomb and class with which you have handled your situation. To lose a husband, and in such circumstances, must have been doubly painful. With all the opportunists out there, I imagine someone has already tried to convince you to tell your story, to write about everything that happened. Because, after all, a well-known, classy woman like yourself who has endured what you have endured really makes for quite an interesting story. But don't you waste any time thinking about them, sweetheart, because they are all vultures.

Now, I am writing because I would like to propose an idea I am sure you will absolutely love. What we are interested in is an elegant book filled with worldly advice on customs and traditions. And now, I mean real customs, not a bunch of jokes for people to laugh about around the water cooler. To give you an idea of what I'm talking about, the Baroness of Rothschild in France has written two or three books of this type and they have been runaway bestsellers. When you're back in Madrid I'll send them over to you. One is called *The Baroness Will Return at Five,* and the other, *The Art of Savoir-Faire.* They're classy books, the kind that are worthy of such an important woman. For the moment, take a look at the outline I've drafted for you here, and when you get back we can talk further. How does that sound?

Following the letter was a three-page outline as to how the book might be structured: "How to react in an embarrassing situation," "How to receive guests," "The proper way to conduct oneself at a variety of social occasions: baptisms, weddings, gala dinners, funerals . . ." And so on. The last page ended with a two-line postscript:

Don't say no, darling. You'd be great for this. Let's get together when you return—and don't stay in the sun too long, it's terrible for the skin. Hugs and kisses from your friend,

JP Bonilla

When she finishes reading, Mercedes takes off her Giorgio Armani glasses and takes a long sip of her Pimm's. She peers into the glass and fishes out the cucumber garnish (peel and all) and pensively nibbles. Suddenly, she spies a basset hound, his head cocked a bit, observing her from nearby and she motions for him to come over. She offers him the tiny slice of cucumber, but the dog trots away in the opposite direction. The silence is total and unbroken except for the sound of the dog's paws clicking very faintly against the clay floor. The two are inside a glass-walled solarium with a hot-water pool. Outside, the sun shines down rather weakly, but inside it is hot, and a sticky sort of steam casts a shadow on the yellow of the walls, the red of the floors, and the bright green of the giant plants and trees, which veritably engulf the surrounding environment.

The Story According to Mercedes, Part One

I SUPPOSE I OUGHT TO START OFF BY SAYING THAT I AM NOT A GREAT fan of small hotels in the middle of nowhere. But then again, this thought—and many, many others, for that matter—would never have even occurred to me a few months ago. The truth is, I knew very little about what I liked and didn't like back then. Stupid, I know, and ludicrous if you consider that my passport says I am forty years old—two years younger, in fact, than my real age. But I must admit that L'Hirondelle d'Or is a far cry from your average hotel, and it is exactly as the brochure described: "One of the most exclusive luxury spa hotels in the world, a haven in the middle of the red lands of Morocco, where guests come to rest, eat well, exercise, and escape from all worldly distractions." I doubt I will actually run into "... Martin Amis, finishing his latest novel in quiet solitude, or Mick Jagger, unwinding after his tour with the Rolling Stones" as the pamphlet attests. Something tells me that at this time of year I would be hard-pressed to "bump into Isabelle Adjani indulging in the spa's legendary restorative mud treatments," and as of yet I still haven't seen a single "... pop star sharing confidences with the crème de la crème of the English aristocracy near the buffet table by the pool," but I can easily imagine that this would be ". . . the kind of place where one might cross paths with Italian signoras who are devotees of exquisite, healthy cuisine, French men utterly taken with the notion of 'clean living,' and people from all over the world who absolutely insist on conducting their private lives in the most rigorous solitude."

All of this is straight out of the hotel's promotional brochure, which is designed as soberly and seriously as this elegant hotel, printed on vellum paper with blue ink-drawings—no photographs, God forbid. Strictly drawings—this isn't the Holiday Inn, after all. One thing is true, however. For the moment, at least, I haven't bumped into a single person from Madrid, and that fact alone divests me of any guilt over paying 700 euros per night for my tiny room at the southern end of the hotel, called the *chambre pistache,* according to the little plate that came along with my key. Here there are no room numbers, of course.

Right now I am sitting by the winter pool, and my sole companions are two or three senior citizens who are strolling past me now, bundled up in giant terry-cloth robes, silent, pleasant, discreet . . . foreign. What a splendid idea it was to come here. Before this trip I had never traveled alone, but a hotel catering especially to people wanting to eat well and exercise is the perfect place: Lots of people come to L'Hirondelle wanting to diet. Nobody thinks it at all odd when they come alone. And anyway, if anyone did happen to find it strange, I don't believe it would bother me in the slightest, because that is what this trip is all about: From now on, I plan to do what I want without thinking twice about it. Someone else, I don't remember who, once said something to that effect—that solitude is only an unpleasant synonym for the word "freedom" and that one must learn to enjoy it. Very well; that is exactly what I intend to do.

Not long ago I was widowed, in the most unexpected fashion. W-i-d-o-w-e-d. As I write it for the first time, it seems so strange. Painful, too, I should add, but I have recently discovered that grief is a slow sentiment compared with other, more instantaneous feelings one goes through, such as shock and bewilderment. The emptiness takes a while to set in, but I suppose that is a good thing, for it gives a person time to sort things out.

This is the first time I have spoken—or, rather, written—about what happened, and I can't decide if this is a good or bad idea. I'd like to think it is good, because if there is anything I have learned in recent times, it is that life's experiences become real only when you put them down on paper.

Not long ago I was widowed in such a ridiculous fashion that people have jumped to the wildest conclusions about my situation. There it is. I've said it and everything is perfectly fine. I have written it down and made it real. Now, I suppose, I might consider adding a few pertinent details. I might describe the people present when everything happened, and explain that my husband died a rather undignified death: He choked on an almond. My God, how humorous our misfortunes sound when we write them down so succinctly. But that is exactly what happened to him; I swear it is just as I said. Absurd, isn't it? Tragic too. And nevertheless, absurdity and tragedy are apparently not enough for some people—this has become extremely obvious to me, given all the wild speculations my situation seems to have inspired. As I know all too well, people have been saying the most preposterous things about what happened that evening: Some people claim that Jaime was in bed with another woman when it happened, while others insist that he had financial troubles and that his blood pressure and stress were really what killed him, and there are others who say that he died from some mysterious allergy— to what, I can't even imagine. There are so many unbelievable stories, so many, that I wouldn't be surprised if one day someone came out and said that I, tired of all his philandering, was the one who pushed him to his death, although I hope people wouldn't actually go that far. No, no . . . that would really be too far-fetched. My God, the ridiculous things that a person thinks of . . .

So then why am I writing all this, if my goal was to talk of the present and only the present, not a word about the past? Ideas . . . memories . . . It feels a little silly to let them all out, because they are all still such a giant jumble in my mind, and after all, the reason I came here was specifically not to spend my time thinking about those things. So there it is. Enough with my musings. They are of no interest to anyone anyway. And now I shall go back to what I was explaining earlier about this hotel, because that was my original intention when I began to scribble these lines, sitting here in front of the pool.

NOW, I HAVE no desire to act as a travel guide of any sort, but I do feel it necessary to mention that L'Hirondelle d'Or is a hotel some sixty-five miles from Fez, and it is run like a very exotic country home, a place people go to under the pretext of taking care of their bodies and resting their minds. It is a sanctuary, a monastic retreat, in the form of a luxurious red building that rises up in the middle of nowhere. And I am serious when I say this: There is nothing anywhere near this place, just dusty tracks in the dirt everywhere. But once you get here, you quickly forget that you are practically in the middle of the desert. L'Hirondelle is like a world unto itself, different from anything I have ever seen—I've never known anything like it. Everything is organized, from the morning workouts to the massage sessions to the skin treatments to the food, which is of course delicious. As far as the decor goes, a few palm trees here and there serve as a kind of homage to the African landscape, as do the outfits of the waiters and the ubiquitous spearmint aroma which emanates from the bath towels, the afternoon tea, the lamb, even the couscous. Everything else, however, especially in the area of creature comforts, is very European . . . although now that I think about it, nothing is quite *exactly* as it appears—the tea, for example, isn't plain tea, it is a highly sophisticated infusion of concentrated herbs; and the minute you bite into the lamb, you can instantly tell that it is completely fat free, light as a feather. And the couscous? Well, maybe the couscous is made from semolina, but I would bet that it is made in the USA, as they say.

The amenities here are also very European—like the little golf course, for example, so green I don't even want to think what the upkeep must cost. And then there are the two pools: a summer pool, which is closed at this time of the year, and the indoor winter pool, which is where I am right now. And then there is the bath or spa area, which, they say, draws its mud from some old Roman hot springs in the vicinity. The other glass-enclosed building just to my right is where we all spend hours and hours indulging in various treatments according to the recommendations of the very efficient spa staff. Efficient and almost invisible. That is another of the more surprising aspects of L'Hirondelle d'Or: You never see anyone. Yes, it may seem odd, but beneath its exotic veneer, everything at L'Hirondelle d'Or functions with the precision of a Swiss clock—and in fact, the secret powerhouse behind this place is a real-life Swiss clock by the name of Miss Guêpe. I have never seen her in person, though, because she only communicates via telephone. It is easy to see how this efficient management style works in the day-to-day operations, but it is even more apparent in what you might call the exceptions to the rule—like the little accident out on the golf course yesterday, for example. One of the guests (a Swiss man, in fact) almost electrocuted himself on a fallen wire. It was all quite frightening, really, a case of truly rotten luck. But wouldn't you know it, nobody around here is even *talking* about it today. It almost seems as if there is some kind of tacit agreement that we are all bound to uphold: silence, discretion; everything is fine; we *are* on vacation, after all.

This is a world apart. Really and truly. Just consider my first day here. The hotel jeep picked me up at the airport and drove me down an endless labyrinth of dusty roads until we finally arrived at what felt like a real-life oasis. And I am not just saying that: from the start,

L'Hirondelle makes you feel as if you are the guest of a mysterious, highly discreet host whom you never see but who very quietly makes sure that everything runs like a well-oiled machine, with the most sublime hospitality. Even speaking with the other guests somehow seems in poor taste. All of this was rather strange at the beginning, but you do get used to it very quickly, and now I would even go so far as to say that it is possibly the best thing about the hotel. After all, why on earth would any of us want to encourage that horrendous camaraderie that one must always confront on package tours:

> *"Hi, my name is Erik. I'm from Göteborg, Sweden, and this is my wife, Greta. I'm thirty-four years old, and we have a daughter named Ingrid . . ."*
> *"Pleasure to meet you, Erik. My name is Pierino de Rimini, from Italy, separated twice, three children, Paolo, Carla, Gigi. Would you like to sit at our table for the next twenty-five days?"*

Twenty-five days! Thank God nothing like this is expected of the guests at L'Hirondelle, and may God bless the person who dreamed up this haven for lonely hearts, whoever he may be.

Speaking of lonely hearts, here comes the Marquis de Cuevas again. Actually, I have no idea what his real name is, but he reminds me of that famous Chilean heir who was all over the gossip magazines a few decades ago. They are so amusing, these guessing games. Observing the various people at this hotel, from a prudent distance of course, is the perfect pastime. First I try and imagine who the person is, and then I craft a personality that seems to suit his or her appearance. And this Marquis de Cuevas is a very typical case in point: sixtyish, good-looking, in fine health, although he doesn't seem like the type of person who would be especially interested in the hotel's therapeutic treatments—not that one is obliged to partake in them, but still. . . . I have had my eye on him for some time now, and I have watched him walk back and forth past the winter pool, his eyes gazing out toward some faraway point in the distance—but far away in time more than space. I can't quite explain it, but it's almost as if he were looking out at an entire decade—say, the 1950s. He wears a white caftan with a little sprig of mint sticking out from the first of a long line of little buttonholes. And caramel-colored slippers. And a hat that looks like a straw-colored Frisbee. To top it all off, he actually brought his dog with him, although this particular dog doesn't quite fit the look. Normally, characters like Mr. de Cuevas have little poodles, or maybe dachshunds if they're the serious type. This man, however, is the master of a little basset hound, a chubby, long-eared, sad-eyed creature, the kind of dog that belongs to a mischievous little boy.

What a delicious afternoon. The man sits down on a nearby lounge chair.

"*Viens ici, Gomez, viens.* Bad dog . . ." Gomez? What is he talking about? Does he mean the dog? And is it possible that he speaks Spanish? What an odd coincidence . . . Well, who knows, maybe my hypothesis is correct and he *is* the Marquis de Cuevas, a throwback from another age entirely. But I don't know, I think I'm making him out to be a much more romantic character than he really is. The world seems to have run out of rich, decadent heirs with Chilean (or Bolivian or Peruvian or Uruguayan or Argentinian) passports. So where did this man come from? My thoughts drift back to Juan P. Bonilla and the fax he just sent me. How my little friend Bonilla would die if he saw all this.

"Now, what you need to do, honey, is go off somewhere by yourself and get some rest. You have had a terrible time with all this. These past few weeks have been just awful for you," he said to me the other day when he took me out for lunch at Casa Lucio to talk business, or so he said.

"Go, go, forget about everything. Take the advice of a friend who adores you." Sometimes he says "adore" and other times he says "a-dore," but it's not a speech impediment, I'm positive; it must be some kind of affected phrasing I can't quite put my finger on.

"Your friend who absolutely adores you is going to make you the most indecent proposal. Now, don't go getting scared, sweetie. I just want you to write a book for us, for our popular nonfiction section, something light that will give you a chance to laugh a little at all those silly beautiful people who say they're your friends and now look where they are. Take my advice. Take a few days for yourself, you and no one else, and go off somewhere. I'll make sure you get the proposal. We're a very eclectic publishing house, and we'd really love to have an author like you."

Just today I was thinking about that conversation—that's why I put it down in writing, along with a few of my own reflections—but I don't know what made me do it. It was just a little idea that floated into my head. Now that I have his fax in hand, I realize that I can hardly even remember what the proposal said, outside of the basic idea that they wanted me to write a guide to good manners. What on earth made J. P. Bonilla think that I would ever agree to write a guide to good manners? People come up with the most bizarre ideas. If I were to write anything, I would love to be talented enough to write about what happened to Jaime that ludicrous night—now, *that* would be interesting. The blow-by-blow story of Jaime Valdés's death. Not a bad title, eh? How odd, how really and truly odd, because now that I think about it, if I could write the story of everything that happened that night (and everything that has happened to me since) with the sufficient level of irony . . . now, *that* would be a real story about the meaning of "good manners." And J. P. Bonilla would eat it up, no doubt about it. Of course, it wouldn't be very publishable, I'm afraid. Absolutely unpublishable, I'd say. And anyway, I don't have the slightest idea of how to write. I'm awful at it, perfectly awful. Just look at what a mess I've made of these notes.

"Gomez, *chou chou,* you stay right where you are."

I look up and there he is, lying on that lounge chair nearby with a very serious look on his face. His foot seems to be tapping to the beat of an invisible melody: one-two-three, one-two-three.

What is happening now? The dog (And did I catch that right? Is he really called Gomez?) has escaped from his master and is trotting toward me with his head cocked to the right. I wish I had something to offer him, something he might like, even just a potato chip. All I have is my glass of Pimm's, thanks to the diet regime here. I offer him the little sliver of cucumber swimming in my glass, but he doesn't want it, of course. Who ever heard of a vegetarian dog? And so he very regally trots away from the pool.

"*Viens ici,* Gomez, bad dog, bad dog!" the Marquis de Cuevas repeats. It must be a combination of the heat and the alcohol that has put me in such a good mood.

So here I am at L'Hirondelle d'Or, far from Madrid. I can stay here as long as I please—a month, two months if I can bear it, for I am in full possession of my time, and my money, too . . . but most of all I am in full possession of my freedom. And that is the most important thing of all.

The man is looking at me. Under his straw hat I can make out an olive-toned face, that isn't very distinguished, really, a mixture of European and . . . perhaps indigenous South American.

And yet he has such determined, precise mannerisms. How he moves his hands, for example, and the way he flips through the pages of a novel I know he isn't reading. It takes years and years of boarding school in Switzerland for a person to move like that, even if that person is dressed in a caftan and a pair of bedroom slippers. And I suddenly begin to think about what it is, exactly, that makes a person elegant—or not elegant, for that matter. Some people are completely hopeless when it comes to clothes and yet they always look perfect. And then there are others who may insist on only wearing Armani—like J. P. Bonilla, for example—but they just don't cut it; it's something you can tell from a mile off. My God, if I had to ex-

plain this in a book about good manners, I wouldn't know where to
start . . . but then again, do I have anything better to do this afternoon? Or tomorrow? Or in the next forty years? This is the perfect
setting for enumerating the virtues of being a snob, isn't it? Now,
let's see. Where shall I begin? Oh no, no. I should drop it right here.
The truth is, I feel completely inept when it comes to writing—
of course, when one finds oneself in an environment as picturesque
as this, one does feel the desire to emulate, I don't know, Somerset
Maugham. Besides, it's much more fun to describe all the things I see
here than to think about putting together a book about good manners, like Bonilla wants. It reminds me of a book my grandfather
had, a late-nineteenth-century Russian novel intended to be a kind
of manual of the social habits of the day. It was absolutely hilarious,
but so affected. The author began each chapter with a bit of worldly
advice regarding a specific topic and then went on to describe how
that topic manifested itself in the real world. And of course the advice shed absolutely no light on the real-life part, because life is the
polar opposite of what you read about in guidebooks about good
manners. What was the name of that novel? *Greek Lips,* I think. According to some Armenian proverb, the best liars have the thinnest
lips. Or maybe it was *Greek Mouths* . . . ? Anyway, it doesn't matter
much. We all know that the tightest lips and the tightest mouths are
those that belong to the biggest liars of all, and we don't need Armenian proverbs to teach us that. The one thing I do remember
from the novel, though, is that each chapter was dedicated to a specific social occasion, like "the baptism," "the wedding," and "the funeral." Things like that.

The Funeral

FOR TWO YEARS FOLLOWING THE FUNERAL, THE WIDOW SHALL remain in mourning. The great, most austere mourning shall last one year . . . and during the last six months the following variations are permitted: black lace edging, silk, and embroidery (only in jet black).

During the last three months, the widow may wear white and black petticoats, the colors gray, mauve, aubergine, and lilac (to be observed strictly in this order). And finally, when the mourning period comes to a close, she must observe a transition period before beginning to dress as the rest of the world does. This period shall begin with neutral tones, and the jewels may slowly and discreetly emerge from their boxes. She may adorn her hair with a chrysanthemum (of any color), because it is the flower of the widow.

—Baroness Staffe, *Usages du monde: Règles du savoir-faire dans la société moderne* (1890)

A Widow Is the Very Best Thing a Woman Can Be
(The Story According to Rafael Molinet)

A few yards from Mercedes Algorta, two lounge chairs away, there he was.

It was terribly hot, but his face hardly shone at all, because sweating is not very distinguished. His eyes, on the other hand, shone with an owl's acuity, the kind of owl that knows it is only a matter of time before some hapless little mouse comes walking by. However, the physical appearance of this particular guest at L'Hirondelle d'Or might best be described by plagiarizing Truman Capote's observation of Jean Cocteau:

Rafael Molinet was a walking laser beam with a sprig of mint in his buttonhole.

That, at least, was how he thought of himself. And this lounge chair was the exact spot where, ten days later, he recounted the full story of all that had come to pass during his stay at the hotel. On that day, October 23, he would go back to the morning of October 13 and begin his story; he even imagined himself telling his tale aloud to somebody, who would no doubt be very surprised to hear it—to his neighbor Reza, the canine coiffeur, for example, or perhaps he would tell it not to one person but to many, an entire audience of choice listeners. And, yes, maybe what he had to say was nothing but an old man's prattle, a compendium of idle gossip, but it was so very colorful. He had also discovered—far too late in life, unfortunately— that he had a singular talent for embellishing stories and a very refined way of retouching (or sometimes inventing) certain characters, including his own. With this in mind, he would stop for a moment before embarking on his narrative.

"So how would you like to hear the story of a bad girl?" he would ask his audience. And then, without waiting for an answer, he would say to himself:

"For heaven's sake, for heaven's sake, no names, no names—
that would be in terribly poor taste."

The audience, he thought to himself, would not take long to
react: chairs would creak, bored ears would suddenly prick up to attention, and then, following a few seconds of well-calibrated silence,
Molinet saw himself bring the tips of his fingers together, just as his
beloved Capote often did, before plunging into the tale of all that had
happened at L'Hirondelle d'Or during those two weeks in October—
exactly as if he were reliving it right there in front of his listeners. And
so Rafael Molinet began to tell his story:

HAD IT NOT been the middle of October, a perfectly insipid month
of the year, or had the hotel been filled with truly important people,
I might never have taken such a keen interest in the story of Mercedes Algorta. Had the situation been different, I might never have
thought to ring up my niece Fernanda in Madrid and she, in turn,
would never have had the chance to expand upon the two or three
bits of common gossip she had fed me in London, gossip that had
made a certain impression in this keen old head of mine. In short,
had things played themselves out differently, perhaps I would not be
telling you this story right now.

The story of a bad girl. That is the story I propose to tell, but
don't go running to any premature conclusions, for the most obvious
details are never quite what they seem, and we shall have to go a bit
further back and begin at the beginning, as they say—or, rather, at
the moment I first laid eyes on the widow.

It was the thirteenth of October. I remember it well. At the time
I scarcely even knew that sanctuaries of this type even existed—
grand old hotels that have caught on to this new (and very com-
mendable, I am sure) trend of health and fitness. From the moment
you arrive, you can see they have thought of everything. Back prob-

lems, sir? A bit of rheumatism? Varicose veins? Put yourself in our hands and we will take care of you, body and spirit . . .

I seem to be the only rebellious client who has decided not to avail himself of a single therapeutic treatment, because all the other guests here are wrapped in yellow terry-cloth robes and walk about the place with a very determined air: mud application from nine to nine-thirty, stationary gymnastics in the pool at ten-fifteen on the dot, and then massage, restorative body treatments, the sauna. How exhausting it all seems, even if it is in the name of *mens sana in corpore* . . . In any event, that is the way things are here.

From the outset, the most startling aspect of this hotel is that nobody exchanges a word of conversation. I suppose using all that mud has a way of encouraging introspection, because each and every one of the guests here seems to be preoccupied by extremely transcendental concerns requiring a strict vow of silence. During my first few days at L'Hirondelle d'Or, moreover, there were very few of us, which made the silence seem even more bizarre. The only people here were me, the widow, and the Beaulieus—a highly boring Belgian couple not worth describing.

The girl, on the other hand, was extremely interesting. We happened to coincide down by the pool, and if I was staring at her a bit, it was most definitely not because of the story my niece had told me a few days earlier over lunch in London. No, it was something indescribable that—laugh if you must—suddenly made me think: *A widow is the very best thing a woman can be.*

My poor mother always said this, and for some reason it suddenly struck me that this awfully thin young girl ("girl," so to speak—*naturellement;* I would wager she's past forty) two lounge chairs away from me looked a bit like my mother. Physically, they were completely different—Mama was much more striking; there's no comparison—but this girl did have an air about her. The same blond hair, the same subtle highlights, and the kind of wide, angular jaw that tends to age so much better than the narrow kind. The eyes were different, of course. Mama's eyes were a divine, highly unusual shade of blue, whereas this woman's eyes were gray—but hers had their own appeal, too, don't get me wrong. I have never liked women with ordinary eyes. I also noticed that this woman had very long fingers, the second thing that caught my attention. That, and the fact that she wore two wedding bands, one on top of the other, as widows often do. She also wore—and I couldn't help but be slightly shocked—a thick bracelet, very 1940s, though I can't be sure, for I am hopelessly nearsighted. An interesting piece of jewelry, to be sure, but . . . at the pool? *Que c'est drôle,* I said to myself. In any event, news flies as fast as *hirondelles* at this hotel, for there is always some loquacious waiter who is all too willing to be completely indiscreet, sometimes even for free. No, the vow of silence in this beautiful place is not taken very seriously by the sons of Allah. And so, shortly after spotting the lovely lady down by the pool, I had a complete dossier on her: She had reserved a room for—get this!—forty days; she was from Madrid, childless, and had recently been widowed. *Very well,* I thought. *May he rest in peace, whoever he was.* What more could I say?

Now, to be completely honest, I have never had very much money, but I do try to spend what I have with style—on this occasion, at least, this is what I was trying to do. I should also mention that on more than one occasion I have been lucky enough to come into some extra earnings. And though it may be unseemly to say so, I happen to have a great talent for the gaming tables, especially for backgammon, which, coincidentally, is the preferred game of both playboys and novices, and some of them happen to be very rich. Even before arriving, I had a sense that L'Hirondelle d'Or might be the ideal hotel for this sort of activity. Expensive, discreet, silent . . . Although I was there for three whole days before any truly interesting people showed up, people whose bank accounts I might have had the pleasure of lightening up a bit. Who knew? A rich guy might enable me to earn some bonus cash.

"Gomez, *viens ici,* chi-chi. Don't bother the lady." My dog was sniffing around her now, and she was very clearly pretending to be distracted by other things, behaving exactly as I suspected she would: Good girls never strike up conversations with strangers. Though what was she writing with such fervent determination? Something relating to her estate, for sure. She looked extremely well-off. Who knew? Perhaps the dead man had been an old rich guy. What had the funeral been like? I wondered. How did they do them in Madrid? What was the mourning process like? Very different, I supposed, *Dieu merci,* from what I lived through way back when.

It was inevitable. That last thought sent me straight down memory lane: Mama in Madrid, dressed in black, Mama sitting silently at the funeral mass for Bertie Molinet (*"Is that what you call your father, Rafael? As if he were some sort of stranger?"* People always ask me that, and, yes, that is what I have always called him. It would be pointless to fake it, for Bertie and I despised each other, no doubt about it.) There she was in my mind's eye. It was sometime in the early 1960s and we were all as stiff as the ace of *piques*—broke, that is. Mama was very pale, dressed completely in black, with no accessories whatsoever aside from her marvelous eyes, so dignified. Nobody understood her decision to return to her place of birth like a real lady to honor the dead Bertie, as if she hadn't been forced to live the previous three years in a sad house in the *dix-septième* in Paris. All of this, of course, was long before we moved to London to fulfill our final and very dismal fate.

Had upper-class funerals in Madrid changed over the years? I wondered. Were they really as crazy as they appear in the magazines, where it looks like the importance of the dead person is measured not by the number of Mercedeses and BMWs at the door to the church but rather by the number of paparazzi, scavengers positioned at the door to the church, photographers *partout,* turning their backs to the sacraments so that they can hover by the pulpit to capture the painful expressions on the faces of the mourners? Was that what the scene had been like at the funeral of this woman's husband? And, no, that was not the moment the little lightbulb went off in my head, sparking my interest in the young widow. After all, what did I care about that woman? For the moment, at least, she did not seem to be all that intriguing a character, although I *was* certainly intrigued by the very ostentatious bracelet on her left wrist. And she *did* remind me so very much of Mama.

In any case, that was how everything began, out of sheer boredom. The afternoon of October thirteenth went by with no contact at all among the guests beyond the officious nods that we exchanged each time we ran into one another in the corridors: "Good morning," "Good afternoon," etcetera. *Good Lord,* I remember thinking. *If only there was someone I could chat with, about nothing at all— just some simple company.* Maybe the rest of the guests were happily engrossed in their therapeutic mud treatments, but I was really running out of things to do. Any more of this and I was going to end up talking to myself, like a character out of some sad Chekhov story or exchanging witty repartee with my dog. Of course, I do adore animals—they have so much more common sense than human beings. But this isn't the time to discuss animals. I don't want to stray too far from the topic at hand. Anyway, as I was saying, more guests began to arrive. The first ones to show up were a group of Germans, but they were too young for me. Trying to snow-job twenty-year-olds is a bit of a drag; it makes one feel like such a *clochard.* This particular bunch was from very southern Bavaria, I believe, and magnificent-looking—the men, that is. *Que les femmes sont laides!* Not even the most miraculous muds of these hot springs could do much to save them. The men, on the other hand, with their frayed jeans, Calvin Klein T-shirts, and round tortoiseshell glasses, seemed both incredibly distinguished and also so, so . . . oh, how to describe them? So very *Thurn und Taxis*. That was it.

Unfleeceable, mon cher, I said to myself. I knew it right away. Skimming money off these fresh-faced brats would be harder than drawing gold out of the rocks in this desert. A quick process of elimination led me to think I could perhaps try my luck with the widow, *alors.* It couldn't be too hard to earn myself a little spending money off her, I said to myself.

And that is precisely what I set out to do. There was no artistry or skill about my decision. Had there been other, more approachable people around, I surely would never have gotten myself mixed up in the affairs and unspeakable secrets of the little Spanish widow. But that is how things always happen, in the most banal way imaginable. The facts were: She reminded me of Mama; my niece in Madrid had a penchant for high-society gossip (she had demonstrated as much a few days earlier); and I had a restless, horribly frivolous finger that was completely unconcerned about the high price of international phone calls from hotel rooms. And, quite frankly, there weren't many other things to do in that heavenly African oasis. Heavenly, silent, and perfect. Like an Egyptian tomb.

At L'Hirondelle d'Or, you see, indulgence is the name of the game: exquisitely appointed tables piled high with delicacies, exotic fruits, and all those beautiful flowers that some invisible hand replaces constantly so that they are always new, always fresh. And we, the guests, were here together, but we kept to ourselves. Bored but smiling, we moved about the place like shadows. Here, everything is always all right, even when nothing at all is all right. It's true: The worst things often happen precisely when it seems that everything is totally copacetic. Mama, for example. And once again I recall the day of Bertie Molinet's funeral. Apparently, nothing at all was unusual, for those are the benefits of good breeding: Everything is always all right. During the funeral service, there were neither tears nor heartrending scenes, but that was to be expected: Good breeding means not revealing your pain. Falling to pieces and breaking down in sobs like a Sicilian mourner has always been thought of as extremely low-class, although . . . although now that I think back, there was a little drama at my father's funeral. But there was an explanation for that, as strange as it may sound. And that is because among this type of people, outward demonstrations of grief are often inversely proportional to the fondness they feel (or felt) for the dead person in question. Now, nobody felt terrifically fond of my father. And when nobody feels anything, when the people who *should* care about the dead person actually feel nothing, a bit of acting is required, because that is what seems appropriate and right. But what happens is that when people start acting, they inevitably get a little carried away. And that is why, very frequently, the funerals of the most despised people can often be real tear-jerkers. Ah, the paradox of good breeding . . .

Even so, Mama, the lady of the lilac eyes, was never once seen crying, nor was she ever spotted averting anyone's gaze. Not even when her Spanish relatives approached her one by one, the same ones who gossiped in low voices about her life during those last few years before Providence, merciful lady Providence, made her a widow. "Elisa?" they said, not caring if I heard them. "Elisita? Yes, she always lived abroad somewhere, in Paris or London for many years, and in the early days it was first-class all the way. Oh, did they know how to spend money before the war, those rich South Americans—and that's exactly what Elisa was married to, you know. A Uruguayan, the kind that live all their lives in France and send their children to Swiss boarding schools until one day they suddenly go bankrupt. And then they become a terrible burden to their wives. They come home again and again after who knows how many extramarital affairs. Oh, but what were you saying? You really don't know how Bertie Molinet died? Well, let me fill you in a little first about the macho man of the River Plate who just passed away in his home in Montevideo, to everyone's relief . . ." Those were the things they said after my father died.

It is very possible that all this jumping about is confusing to you, but this is exactly how the story began to unfold in my mind. This was precisely the train of thought that led me to think that perhaps I would tell the little widow on the lounge chair that I was half-Spanish—remarks like that always help to break the ice a bit—half-Spanish, half-Uruguayan; or half-Hungarian and half-French. This type of thing was always very useful for fraternizing. Fortunately, I decided against it and chose instead to observe the prevailing vow of silence, at least until I could ascertain a few basic facts about the woman through Fernanda, who knows everything that goes on in Madrid and is so very up-do-date on these sorts of trivialities. And I definitely did not harbor the least bit of suspicion that the lovely lady lying by the pool had anything to do with the story my niece had told me in London. No, no, I just wanted to know a bit more about her tastes, her habits—one needs a few basic facts, after all, to embark on a proper conversation: "Good afternoon, how are you? There isn't much to do here, is there? I don't suppose I could tempt you with a game of backgammon?" That was what I thought of saying to her, and there was no doubt in my mind that this could be the start of a very . . . let's say *fruitful* relationship.

Now, I am not a writer, nor am I a psychologist, nor am I a playboy in the strict sense of the word, but at that moment I did get the feeling that it would be very much worth my while to keep my eyes and ears open. And I am happy to say that I was not mistaken. Everything I am about to tell you happened as if Providence herself had wished to stage, for my exclusive viewing pleasure, one of those incredible stories that always befall the very best of families—a story complete with dirty laundry, subterfuge, betrayals . . . oh yes, this story had everything. Naturally, I am not going to describe it exactly as it unfolded before my eyes, for then my story would be far too er-

ratic and confusing. Insofar as it is possible, I will try my best to leave
out the little details and I will intersperse the various situations,
combining more recent ones with older ones, mixing in Fernanda's
information with some of my own conclusions . . . after all, isn't that
what writers do? They are so very devilish. And I can do it just as
well as they do. The writer always has the upper hand, after all, because he knows the ending of his story. And I too know how this
story ends, which makes it easy for me to make all the pieces fit,
every last one, unlike the way things happen in real life. Real life,
after all, is nothing but a succession of random stories that never
really come to a close until you die. And then, of course, you aren't
around to tell how the stories end, and who really gives a damn
about them, anyway? But enough with all this mystery. Let us now
go back to our starting point, so that we may begin the story in a
logical fashion. As I was saying just before, on the morning of October thirteenth, Mercedes Algorta and I were alone by the pool, and
my dog—a very sociable dog, I must say—approached the lady with
the most innocent air.

  "Viens ici, chou chou," I immediately called out to him. This did
not seem an appropriate moment for introductions. I wanted to
wait, so that I could speak with Fernanda first.

IT WAS IN this tone, with a sophisticated sort of detachment that
seemed quite appropriate to the situation, that Rafael Molinet Rojas
began to tell the story of all that happened during his stay at L'Hirondelle d'Or. And it went more or less as follows . . .

The Dinner

October 14: The First Dinner

She had decided to dress for the occasion: black pants, white silk shirt with three pleats in the middle, very little jewelry aside from two small pearl bobby pins that were far more valuable than they appeared, and a gold bracelet. Tucked under her arm was a book, *Les malheurs de Sophie*—not because she was especially interested in the

childhood misfortunes of the Countess of Ségur but because the
hotel library, to which she had repaired in the hopes of finding a
book-shield to bring with her to the table, had a rather meager selec-
tion. In any case, if dressing for dinner alone in a restaurant could be
considered an art, it was one that Mercedes Algorta had mastered in
very little time. There was nothing about her appearance that
seemed to say "I'm bored," much less "I'm available," even if it was
true.

Be that as it may, nobody in the dining room of L'Hirondelle
d'Or that evening seemed even remotely capable of jeopardizing the
lady's virtue, and Mercedes was almost relieved when she noted this.
The dining room decor could only be described as faux-country:
The floors were laid with baked-clay tiles, and the walls were
painted in a lavender hue that, depending on the intensity of the
flickering candlelight, seemed almost indigo in the darkest corners
of the room. The tablecloths and the glassware did their best to add
to the country-rustic ambience, but the overall design scheme came
together in that special way that seems like casual, serendipitous harmony on the surface but in reality is a highly painstaking, meticulous, and expensive decorating feat. Mercedes had arrived early, and
she picked out a table next to the window. After studying the menu,
in that conscientious if slightly forsaken manner of someone steeling
herself to eat her entire dinner alone, she decided to go for the prix-
fixe dinner option, a total of 803 wisely distributed calories that consisted of two endives, a grilled turkey breast, and a frozen-yogurt
confection—all of this, of course, presented in a very haute cuisine
manner. She felt a sudden urge to open the book she had brought
with her so that she wouldn't have to bother focusing her eyes on
some faraway point on the horizon, but she wasn't certain that it
would really be the proper thing to do, especially at dinnertime. At
all costs she wanted to avoid falling prey to the kind of behavior so
often exhibited by people who dine alone. She had observed them
before, on various occasions, and she invariably found them pathetic.

Either they were too conscious of their status as loners, and made a very concerted effort to look neither left nor right nor anywhere around them, or else (and perhaps these were the more veteran solo diners) they would promptly forget that they were alone at all and looks up as their thoughts wandered. And while the former group seemed uncomfortable, the latter was even more conspicuous. After another moment, Mercedes decided to open *Les malheurs de Sophie* and read a line or at least scan the page, even if she didn't manage to retain a single word.

The room was scarcely lit but for a series of short, stout candles that seemed to pop out of the most unexpected nooks and crannies, and their light cast a ripple throughout the room: red on the upholstery, yellow on the tablecloths. Everything was blurry and silent, including the waiters who came and went, serving the three tables that were occupied by patrons. Mercedes did spot, sitting at the table farthest from her, the Belgian couple with whom she regularly exchanged a slight nod of the head in the massage room or by the pool. A bit further down, however, she was amused to observe the entrance of some newcomers, a group of Germans. But they seemed too young to interest her for more than a few moments at the most. She had met so many like them at other times in her life, on fox hunts with her husband. They had the inimitable air of those people born with a "von" between their first and last names, as if that little three-letter word were as obvious an attribute as their manner of speaking in such obviously loud voices or their uninhibited, extremely healthy appearances.

For that reason, she did not stop to observe the fact that the men wore very informal attire whereas the women had dressed up in evening gowns that were far too sophisticated for a rustic country retreat like L'Hirondelle. The only person missing was the individual she had seen down by the pool, the one who reminded her of the Marquis de Cuevas. It wouldn't be long before he came down to the dining room, though; this was made clear by the half-filled bottle of red wine sitting on a table close by. Perhaps when he entered they would exchange the same greeting that she had already exchanged with the Belgian couple: a slight inclination of the head, a smile, and nothing more. Mercedes leaned back in her chair, allowing her shoulders, which until that point had remained erect and alert, to rest in a more comfortable position. *What luck,* she said to herself. *What luck that everyone present is so very innocuous.* There was nobody in the dining room who interested her in the least, nor was there anyone who could possibly be capable of altering that tranquil atmosphere that others might mistake for tedium and which she suddenly found utterly and deliciously indulgent. Smiling, she pushed the book away. She would not need to use it as a shield—not tonight, and not on any other day or night for the rest of her vacation, all alone at L'Hirondelle, far, far away from Madrid and everyone there. *Bless you, October,* she thought to herself, *for being such a dreadfully boring month of the year.*

TWO VERY SIMILAR interruptions suddenly broke the reverie at either end of the restaurant. Both doors to the dining room opened at the very same time, invasions that prompted Mercedes to turn, ever so slightly, to see the man she thought of as the Marquis de Cuevas enter through the door to the garden. *He's like a man from another time,* she thought. You didn't see people like him very much. His figure was entirely amusing and utterly appropriate for a night just to the south of Fez, Morocco. She entertained herself by studying him, not bothering to look at the other door to the dining room and certainly not noticing the four people who walked through it at that particular moment. This was because she was far too busy wondering where this man was from (*Spain? No, definitely not, even if he does have a dog with an eminently Castilian name,* she thought) and where he had dug up the tailor who had created that gray suit with such incredibly wide lapels. It was made of a fabric that looked remarkably like—whale skin, yes, that was it. A flat gray color just like the skin of a whale, with a few bright white specks of dust that revealed the penumbra of the dining room to be every bit as fake as that rustic ambience someone had tried so hard to achieve. Someone had hidden a series of ultraviolet lights in various spots around the dining room, the kind of lights that bring everything white into bold, glowing relief, especially those things that are not supposed to be seen, like faces. And teeth. And the whites of certain people's eyes, so very translucent that they suddenly resemble the eyes of a monster that has suddenly emerged from a very dark and sinister corner.

The Art of Correspondence

WITH RESPECT TO FRIENDS, ACQUAINTANCES, OR HABITUAL purveyors, one need not possess the talent of Fenelon or the Marchioness of Sévigné to write a proper letter. All that is required is a command of one's language and impeccable spelling. . . .

Recently, however, it has become quite chic to slip in one or two words in English, or some other language, when writing to friends. Preceding the signature, for example, many people include something such as "yours," but such a practice is only recommended when writing to one's very closest confidantes.

—Baroness Staffe, *Ladies and Their Correspondence* (Paris, 1890)

The Arrival of a Fax from Fernanda

The following fax was delivered to the room of Rafael Molinet just as he was getting ready to go to dinner. At first, he thought of bringing it with him to read as he ate, but then he decided it would be much wiser to give it a quick once-over on his way down to the dining room. There would be plenty of time later on to study it calmly and in greater detail.

PAPRIKA AND DILL
Cocktail parties, dinners, and other social occasions
(Excellence Need Not Be Expensive)

October 14

Dearest Uncle Rafael,

I have come down to the office to send you this fax (speaking of which, you might want to consider modernizing your lifestyle and embracing new technologies—faxes are so passé!) because Alvaro-husband is so maniacal about the telephone. My God, if I were to call Morocco from home, he would simply throw a fit. You can't imagine how he gets with these things.

Well, my dear, I see that you and I are two peas in a pod after all: a couple of scullery maids! So you want me to tell you all about Mercedes Algorta, do you?

Fasten your seat belt, darling, because the world is nothing but a fishbowl, everybody knows everybody it seems. Now, do you remember that very intriguing story I told you about in London? The story about Isabella and Jaime Valdés, her little friend who choked to death in the most ridiculous way? Well, if you had been paying a bit more attention, you would remember that Valdés's wife's name was none other than Mercedes Algorta. I know that you get all the Spanish last names mixed up, but I told you—in Spain people pick them à la carte and Mercedes has always been Algorta, not Valdés. How hilarious that you have run into her in the middle of nowhere! It isn't really like Mercedes to go off on her own to a hotel. I suppose she wanted to get away from everything for a little while. Madrid is a pit of vipers and everyone will keep gossiping about her and Isabella until some other, more interesting scandal rolls around, so she was very smart to disappear like that. And since she's loaded, she can indulge herself if she wants—Valdés, when he was alive, cheated on her night and day and made her life a living hell, but he left her a fortune. Your poor niece, on the other hand, is back at home, disgusted with life, and chained to a kitchen.

But that is the way things go, and anyway, I can't get carried away. I've got way too much work to do. If you want more information, call me at home—try me in the morning; that's when Alvaro is out. He would never believe me if I told him that I spent all day talking to my long-lost uncle, and knowing him, he'll think you're some little boyfriend I've started seeing on the sly . . . although now that I think about it—let him think I've got a boyfriend! A woman should always keep her husband on his toes, don't you think?

All right, Uncle Rafael, have a grand time, and if you see Mercedes send her my regards.

Hugs and kisses,
Fernanda

P.S. I enclose herewith a little article from one of the gossip magazines featuring your friend Mercedes with Valdés and Isabella, the three little lambs all together. I don't know if it will come out in the fax, but at least it will give you an idea about what the dear departed Jaime Valdés (may he rest in peace) was like. The photo was taken at a party just a few months before he died. And by the way, can you make out the bracelet on Isabella's right wrist? There's a story behind it: solid gold, from Cartier. Mercedes had spotted it at a Christie's auction, but Isabella beat her to the punch and got old Papa Steine to give it to her as a Christmas present. Looking at it just now I remembered the story right away. Mercedes told me all about it when it happened; she was absolutely furious at Isabella—I mean, Isabella was supposedly her friend, and look what she went and did. Don't you see? It was like an omen of sorts: The Isabellas of this world, they start off stealing your bracelets and end up stealing your husband.

More kisses, F.

This was the fax, as jumbled as I expected, but it was enough to give me an initial idea of who my characters were. It really is fascinating when the pieces of a puzzle begin to fit, one by one, and with this bit of additional information I was able to get a basic idea of what type of person the girl's husband was, for example. Nevertheless, I didn't focus on him first. I am very methodical about certain things, and I wanted to concentrate my attention on the bracelet that Fernanda had mentioned. Unfortunately, that part of the postscript came out a bit blurry in the fax. You couldn't see much of anything at all. So I then turned to study the figure of Valdés, which had come out much clearer. Of course, I was thrilled to discover that he was very much as I had imagined him. One of those suave, attractive types who look the other way when they know they're being photographed. Tall, big-boned, holding in his stomach in an attempt to hide an incipient curve that, *malheureusement,* would never be allowed to degenerate into a series of fatty folds. Photographs of dead people, even blurry ones like this, always have something of the cruel antithesis to them, I think. There he was, the poor guy, two or three months away from death, worried about the spare tire around his waist. And he could have saved himself all that trouble, all those pains he must have taken to look younger than he was: the vegetables without salt to control his cholesterol, the hair tonic for premature balding, the gym—deadly boring, if you ask me. And then all sorts of pills and vitamins . . . and look where Jaime Valdés ended up. He would never have the chance to become a handsome fifty-year-old or a sixty-year-old fretting over his prostate, and yet there he is sucking in his gut in a blurry photo, his arm around the waist of his wife, with Isabella apparently smiling at him over her shoulder. All of it so pointless, so stupid.

I folded up the clipping, and as I made my way down to the dining room I took a few moments to recap the information I had gathered. Mercedes was the widow in that convoluted story Fernanda had told me in London. Strange, unexpected, but it was still little more than a bit of common gossip, a *petite histoire* that could not even be considered adulterous. In the end, what were the facts, who were the characters? Two couples who had decided to spend the weekend together in a recently purchased country house on the shores of a river in Spain. There was a dead Don Juan character, victim of the most ludicrous sort of death, but then aren't all deaths ludicrous somehow? Then there was the issue of the wife who wasn't at home but who appeared on the scene precisely when her husband suddenly fell ill, and the other woman, who was present when Don Juan started feeling ill but who nonetheless disappeared on the double. All of this, of course, was the story according to Fernanda, who, let us not forget, had a rather peculiar way of accessorizing her tales so that they sounded more "fun"—that, I believe, was the term she used. "Oh, who cares about accuracy, anyway?" she had said. All I had really cared about was making a little backgammon money as a bit of a diversion. Society gossip, in these situations, usually only serves to describe the characters, and give you a bit of information—nothing more.

I set off down the hallway, prepared to greet Mercedes Algorta a bit more effusively than before in the event that we bumped into each other in the dining room. It's odd, but when you get to know a person through "classified" information, you inevitably—and unwittingly—begin to feel they are more familiar, closer somehow. Yes, that's it, closer. And I knew that the minute I saw her my smile would be wider and my very Japanese nod of the head would be a bit less stiff than usual. That was to be expected.

What I did not know was that when I finally reached the dining room, I would not have the time to concentrate on such details. How could I have possibly known that after taking the shortcut through the garden, I would open the door to the dining room just as another door opened at the opposite end, introducing a whole new set of characters to the story? Have you ever noticed that when one very strange coincidence occurs, it never takes long for even stranger ones to materialize? Well, that is precisely what happened that night. If I were a more superstitious man, I would almost venture to say that everything during those two weeks seemed to be the work of a very capricious Lady Luck, who had dealt the cards of fate and then, suddenly, had been inspired to throw a few more jokers into the game . . .

Some Notes Regarding Men's Attire

A MAN WHO ASPIRES TO BE ELEGANT — AND THIS IS A VERY DESIRABLE aspiration, as long as it is always within the bounds of reason—would never wear the same clothing in the country as he would in the city, for the riding coat, the black trousers, the low-cut vest and the stovepipe hat are entirely superfluous in the city. And in the morning hours, the elegant man would never dress like a notary called in to draw up a last will and testament, for he knows that the frock coat and top hat are inadmissible until the afternoon visiting hour. Bearing in mind these and other sensible recommendations, anyone in the world may achieve the appearance of a true gentleman.

—Baroness Staffe, *The Obligations of a Gentleman, Great and Small*

The Well-Dressed Man

If we could somehow freeze the first impression we generate when we lay eyes on someone for the first time, and then if we could save that impression in its purest state, preventing it from becoming clouded by rational judgments, or snobbery, then we would be very wise indeed.

The reason I mention all of this is so that you may bear *in mente* my first impressions of the new arrivals in the dining room, and I suppose it is also to justify the seeming inanity of the comments I am about to make. But, believe me, these observations are precisely the kind of assessments that turn out to be startlingly accurate.

I had just entered the restaurant through the door to the garden. At first, until my eyes adjusted to the light, the room seemed terribly dark to me, almost darker than outside, where at least there was a sky full of shining stars.

To determine whether your hotel belongs in the "extremely exclusive" category, all you have to do is study a restaurant's lighting. L'Hirondelle d'Or was certainly extremely exclusive. The candlelight made it virtually impossible to tell whether the sauces one ingested were red or green, tartar or curry: Discretion was clearly more important than gastronomy, and darkness has a way of confusing the eyes even more than the palate. This lighting scheme successfully eliminates the chances that a guest might choke on his pepper steak upon seeing an unexpectedly familiar face precisely when he has come to the ends of the earth so as not to run into anyone at all.

The awful thing about rich people is that even when they seek anonymity, their mode of operation is the always the same. They all perform the same exhaustive amount of advance research, take great pains to select their vacation destination ("where it will be just you and me, alone, darling, surrounded by Germans or Belgians, nobody we know . . ."), arm themselves with the Michelin guide, and then they all end up at the same isolated hotel in the middle of nowhere.

That, no doubt, was exactly what happened to the quartet of Spaniards who very unfortunately turned up at L'Hirondelle d'Or wanting only to relax, smear themselves with restorative muds, and maintain as low a profile as possible. I should add that the massive amount of information I now possess regarding their lives was culled with infinite patience and acute observation, because, for a few days at least, I kept my distance from my protagonists and simply watched them in action as they staged their three-ring circus. And, like a spectator sitting comfortably in his seat at the theater, I watched them stumble, fall, and make complete fools of themselves. I had little trouble spying on them, because the quarters were close in that hotel and the guests were all there—quite conveniently for me—to focus on themselves and the needle on their bathroom scale rather than on their fellow vacationers. But it is a trifle early to be going into all that right now. For the moment, let us return to the beginning of the evening—that is, the moment when the recent arrivals, the four new characters in my little puppet theater, entered through the north door just as I did the same through the garden door.

As I walked through the restaurant, taking care not to stumble in the semi-darkness, it is possible that I may have missed one or two significant expressions on their faces as they bumped into one another. *Good God,* they must have thought. *You, of all people, here at this hotel!* And Mercedes Algorta must have thought the very same thing, because all five of them surveyed one another from a distance at first and then you could just see them thinking, *Oh Christ, we have to say hello. How can we not . . . ?* Which is exactly what they did next. The four newcomers approached Mercedes, who couldn't stop tugging at her shirtsleeve, as if she was suddenly trying very hard to make her hand, her wrist—or both—disappear. This entire exchange occurred so providentially close to my table that I was able to hear each and every word they exchanged while I remained shrouded in my anonymity and certain in my knowledge that Spanish people, whenever they travel, inevitably speak in horribly loud voices, thinking that nobody can understand them anyway.

Like our four recent arrivals in the dining room, for example. *Ah,* our four newcomers must have thought as they surveyed the terrain to see if, like Mercedes, there were any other Spanish ears that might understand their conversation. *All right . . . let's see who else we have here!* Yes, that is most definitely what they must have thought. As they all hurried over to say hello to the widow, I could see them shooting furtive glances around the restaurant in an effort to assess the outfits of the other guests. A very prudent but ultimately useless measure, for I can just imagine the kind of conclusions to which they arrived. So simple. And so very dangerous. After rapidly scanning the other tables, they seemed satisfied by the fact that there were no green quilted hunting jackets or Tyrolean-style outfits anywhere in sight and they clearly said to themselves, *Oh thank goodness, no Spaniards here,* and then began to talk in the loudest voices possible. Spaniards of a certain social class seem to have a secret compulsion to dress up like Austrian game hunters when they go on vacation. They are like perfect little Tyroleans, especially when it comes to outerwear—they always seem to wear hunting jackets, usually khaki green, as if camouflage were hardwired into their souls, *que c'est bizarre*. I must remember to mention this to Fernanda one of these days.

The four newcomers were two men and two women, and they were not very difficult to assess. Even if I hadn't heard a word they said (and I heard plenty from my neighboring table), I could have figured them out. I had the audacity to look straight at them, without the slightest modesty, but since I don't happen to cultivate the olive-green look, they clearly took me for another innocuous foreigner. Just like the boring Belgian couple sitting at the table next to the window. Or the group of self-involved Germans. (Oddly enough, by the way, neither Germans nor Austrians ever dress in the olive-green Tyrolean attire so favored by Spaniards; they prefer to dress up like Bostonians on a weekend away in Martha's Vineyard.) As such, there is no confusion possible—not even for amateur observers like my four new friends.

But let us return to the story at hand. Digressions are not good for the momentum of the story.

As I was saying, my four new characters were two women and two men. And if I have chosen to isolate my first reactions to them it is only because of the extremely distressed expressions that came over their faces as they greeted Mercedes, which left very little doubt in my mind: These four people were two couples . . . or *non-couples,* as my mother might have called them. She was always so delicate with her euphemisms. I would have just called them adulterers, or secret lovers if you prefer, but in the end the names are all the same. In any event, I began my examination with the leader of the pack, for there is always a leader, and he is very easy to distinguish. This one had a blonde hanging off his arm as he walked through the front door, but he very quickly set her loose as soon as he caught sight of Mercedes. Well, to be more precise, I would have to say that *both* of them jumped up as they spotted the widow, executing a lovely lateral *ciseau,* just as if they had been bitten by a poisonous scorpion. His clothing did not interest me (and it requires little description, because it consisted of the same green quilted jacket I mentioned before, on top of a gray executive-type suit), but his persona did. From far away he almost looked, oddly enough, as if he were sitting down, even though this was obviously not the case, because he had just walked through the room with enviable agility and grace. Perhaps this was because he had far too big a chest for far too small a pedestal. If he had been sitting on a sofa, for example, I am sure he would have seemed downright formidable with his great big head of unruly salt-and-pepper curls. He had broad temples and very light eyes which were framed by an intelligent-looking pair of eyebrows that for some reason made me think of George Orwell's Big Brother. His mouth also struck me as rather intriguing—he had very thick lips that seemed somewhat bare without an enormous, smoldering Cohiba between them. Something was missing, let's put it that way. His trunk was every bit as imposing as the rest of his upper body, but from there on down the effect dissipated entirely. This great man was held upright by a pair of legs that simply did not do him justice. They were short and slightly knock-kneed and, though I can't say quite why, something about him made him look like a walking torso, a beautiful sculpture left unfinished because the artist ran out of money.

I spent very little time studying the blonde who hung from his arm. She looked like one of those typical clones who turn forty with such great fear that as soon as the candles on their birthday cakes are blown out, they go running to get breast, lip, and cheek jobs. And now those lips were very coincidentally dissolving into a smile for the benefit of Mercedes.

"Daaarling, what a surprise. How fabulous to run into you. My God . . ."

Her collagen-implanted lips swelled up to the point of near-explosion and her expression very clearly revealed what she felt: *Son of a bitch, what the fuck are you doing here? You always turn up where you're not supposed to. And now what? How the hell am I going to explain what my married lover and I are doing on a romantic getaway together?*

Yes, that was precisely what she was thinking, without a doubt. Blond clones are so transparent, and love foul language, too.

I don't know if she and the leader of the pack actually attempted a friendlier greeting with Mercedes; perhaps they did. The problem was, there were so many things going on at once that I couldn't take it all in. And unfortunately, I had already turned my head a few degrees to study the other couple. The man's name was Antonio Sánchez López—in point of fact, I didn't find that out until the next day, when I was able to send Fernanda a fax requesting information on each of them (and, by the way, I was right about everyone; my theory regarding first impressions never fails). Mr. Sánchez was escorting a second blonde, who seemed much younger than she of the astonishingly plump lips, I don't think she was much older than thirty. As it turned out, Ana Fernández de Bugambilla was her very original and flamboyant name, and she had the frightened air of a novice in the art of illicit affairs. To tell the truth, I have known very many Ana Fernández de Bugambillas in my life. I have observed them at hotels and house parties, petrified guests wishing they could disappear, dissolve into the background, evaporate into thin air. Fernanda's explications would not be necessary, nor would I need to do too much observation to understand what her issues were. From the very first moment, they were written all over her face, as clear as a bell. A trip with a newly minted lover, a virtual stranger, is what lay behind that expression, a combination of bewilderment and fear, which seemed to say, "Good Lord, how did I let myself get caught up in this? How the hell did I get mixed up in this mess—or this bed, to be more precise?"

What a terrible waste of time, I said to myself. Such good upbringing, such delicacy, and for what? To end up as the little weekend tart of a man like Antonio Sánchez López? All you had to do was look at Sánchez López (or just plain Sánchez, or on occasion Antonio S., as Fernanda indicated) to see that he was a horse of an entirely different breed, a man who belonged to that exceedingly ambitious elite that I don't quite know how to describe. "From another world," as my mother would have said—she always had such a sweet way of identifying social differences. Short in stature, he had a fairly large head. In fact, just about all of him could be summed up in that head, which was attached to his cylindrical, compact physique like a little canister of gas. His outfit was very similar to that of the herd leader, except that his parka was a far more intense shade of hunter green, the quilting far more expensive, and the suit underneath was very well cut and exceedingly urban. No sporty attire for him—no, no. Everything about his outfit seemed to scream out to the world, "Now, I want you to know, goddamnit, that I have gone straight from the office to the plane—I haven't got time for things like changing clothes. I'm far too busy for things like that."

If you studied him closely, the man's outfit was truly perfect, but tackiness has a way of showing up in the least conspicuous accessories. Socks, for example. And in the case of Sánchez, it was a pair of thin nylon knee-highs that revealed just what kind of a man he really was. It is a crying shame, but social climbers do tend to take an awfully long time to correct the sock problem. And so, despite the darkness, Sánchez's socks sang out *La Traviata*—or perhaps *I Pagliacci* would be more appropriate—given that they were sheer and highly flammable, like the cheapest DuPont products.

I made a little bet with myself right then, and I knew I wouldn't be wrong. This man was a journalist. A fashionable journalist, the kind who earns a fortune by destroying everything that moves. Later on, thanks to Fernanda, I learned that he was actually a radio personality and not a journalist per se but rather one of those famous ayatollahs of the airwaves—on average, four million ears hung on to his merciless diatribes every week.

Nevertheless, according to some additional information that my niece included in the third fax she sent (or was it the fourth? I've lost track, there were so many flying back and forth that week), our hero was much higher up the food chain than I might have guessed judging by his sock choice. I had a lot of fun reading Fernanda's version of Antonio S.'s romantic résumé: She had a terribly funny way of setting it up and recounting his various adventures. It seemed that this Sánchez was quite the man about town in Madrid, someone who elicited very mixed reactions: disdain, fear, and a substantial amount of hypocritical admiration. I'd better just summarize what Fernanda told me, though, because the love life of Antonio Sánchez López is so typical that it doesn't deserve more than one or two lines.

Apparently, after dumping the saint who had protected and cared for him during his leaner years, Antonio S. hooked up with a wealthy Catalan girl, the daughter of a baron and something of a black sheep herself. All very convenient for this radio announcer. And so the two set up housekeeping together. Because he was such a modern sort of a guy.

Now, according to Fernanda, this rich Catalan girl was the eldest of her brothers and sisters, and thanks to a little law granting women the right to inherit noble titles, Sánchez might have been able to crown his stellar career by adding a tiny heraldic shield to it, a shield that he could have had embroidered on his custom-made shirts had he so desired. But being the elegant man he was, he chose not to marry the girl. Because he was still such a modern sort of a guy.

Sánchez was a man whose destiny was not marriage—his destiny was to open the eyes of his People, for they were incapable of seeing the Truth. They needed someone to tell them what to think, someone to explain things to the masses, if you will—a person who could tell you why this or that VIP's position was reprehensible, a person who was not afraid to call someone a thief or a charlatan, a person who could make the airwaves tremble with the irrefutable truth that all of them out there are crooks, *et tout ça, et tout ça.*

As the years rolled by—the frivolous eighties, the nineties, and then the new millennium—it seemed that people were yearning more and more for someone who could tell them what to think about the scandals and trends of the moment, and naturally Sánchez was on hand to fulfill such an illuminating (and lucrative) mission. He proceeded along in this manner, interrupting his diatribes only to insert a brief plug for Pepsi or J&B—or any other brand-name product, as long as the properly exorbitant per-minute sum was paid. This is how he became a crucial element of this very holy crusade. There are more nuances to his story, however, and they emerge when you look at it from a psychological point of view, which to me is ultimately the most interesting one. As it turned out, once his need for iconoclasm was satisfied, once he had become rich, famous, and properly feared, Sánchez suddenly discovered—Ali Kazam!—that what he really wanted was to do *precisely* all the things he had so harshly criticized when he was little Mr. Nobody (*que j'adore ça*). And that is the most infallible social rule I know. For that reason, Sánchez now played golf with the masters of the universe. For that reason, Sánchez now wore a quilted jacket just like all the other pretty boys of Puerta de Hierro. And if on this trip (and many others, I imagine) he had left the baron's daughter behind in Madrid in favor of a timid little blonde, it was no ordinary case of marital infidelity, no, no. The reason for this (*Fernanda dixit*) was that following his unstoppable rise to the top, Sánchez had realized that the baroness had some serious drawbacks: She was a bit too *much* of a black sheep, it turned out. Way too black for such a fashionable man. Because instead of playing tennis like all the other ladies, or giving *sevillana* classes, or embarking on some other respectable, sensible activity that was appropriate to a woman of her class and stature, it seems that the baroness decided to take up jewelry design. Very avant-garde jewelry: necklaces that looked astonishingly like strings of melons, earrings in the shape of penises, *des choses horribles* that, to make matters worse, she insisted on wearing to the very elegant parties (including royal receptions) that, more and more, the Sánchez couple was invited to attend. For the baroness, however, this was not satisfying enough as an expression of her artistic talents and so she had recently taken to doing things like dying her hair lilac and painting her lips green, things that were not nearly as amusing to Sánchez now as they might have been at another time in his life. Conclusion: Of late, Antonio Sánchez, who had worked so very hard to represent the implacable conscience of Spanish society, found himself forced to seek solace in other women, bored to death of squiring this horrible woman about town.

Whether he had found his solace in the timid blonde or not no one would ever really know, given the manner in which the vacation ended. Until now, however, nothing irrevocable had happened. The encounter between these four people and Mercedes Algorta at L'Hirondelle was unfortunate, because all of them knew one another far too well. It turned out, for example, that the leader of the pack (Bernardo was his name, followed by one of those last names that has resounded imperiously in the world of banking, finance, or industry) was married to Mercedes's first cousin, and the blonde clone (named Bea) was the ex-wife of one of Mercedes's second cousins. The other blonde, for her part, was separated from her husband, and though she had very little relation to my widow friend, she was a very dear friend of Isabella, the bad girl I had heard about from Fernanda at the restaurant in London. This was all very simple and very cozy, because with people like that, adultery tends to be very incestuous.

Nevertheless, this new road map of sorts took a while to fall into place before my eyes. Until I was able to piece together a conversation that began only after Mercedes had stood up and left the restaurant ("Good-bye, good-bye, lovely to see you all . . ."), all I really thought when I laid eyes on the recent arrivals was: *Oh, thank God. More guests, finally.* Now I had four more candidates to choose from in my search for a backgammon partner who might help me while away the time at L'Hirondelle. And despite the vow of silence that still prevailed over our hotel, I figured that the moment would come when I would be able to tempt one of them into a game. Between one mud wrap and the next, between the sulfate baths and the therapeutic water jets, I knew that all good intentions regarding clean living couldn't last much longer than two or three days. And that was when I would approach them. I even had my victim picked out. Would Sánchez be well versed in the rudiments of backgammon? Surely he would. And yet, as things turned out, I never did have the chance to roll the dice with him. Very soon—immediately, you might say—my interest in parlor games began to take a backseat to other matters. When I describe what I heard next, you will understand exactly how and why all board games and gambling were suddenly unimportant. And that is because another pastime, far more interesting and amusing, had suddenly opened up for me.

How to Wipe a Bloodstain from a Table Covering

BLOOD ON A TABLE COVERING, WHICH MAY BE THE RESULT OF an accident with a carving knife or even murder, need not be a source of concern. Nor should one have to trouble one's guests by changing the tablecloth as people did years ago, if one treats the affected fabric immediately by rubbing it very forcefully with warm water that has been steeped in Brussels sprouts.

—Notes from the kitchen of Leonardo da Vinci (1483)

Bloodstained Tablecloths

"So how would you like to hear the story of a bad girl? Oh, don't worry now, Bea, I'm not talking about *you,* darling. Everybody in the world knows about you, sweetheart. No, I mean a real witch, you know the kind, a real bitch, trust me . . ."

Have you ever noticed the terrible assaults on syntax you witness when eavesdropping on other people's conversations? Utter monstrosities. Other people's conversations, especially when heard from a nearby dinner table, always sound so perfectly dreadful.

"One of these days . . ." continued the man, in a loud, clear voice, "you will learn the real story about Mercedes Algorta, and it will knock you on your ass, trust me. Bernardo, all of you—the pillars of what the great unwashed refer to as 'good society' will tremble to their foundations. Trust me on that."

Antonio Sánchez was sitting with his back to me, and it is always difficult to understand people's conversation when you can't see their eyes. But his voice rang out loud and clear. It was no doubt extremely well honed thanks to the thousands of radio tirades he had delivered in his career.

Since I was unable to look at his face, I decided to inspect the back of his neck. He had a little ring of baldness at the very tip-top of his head, a pasty surface that began at the very center of his cranium. When viewed head-on, Sánchez's head seemed blessed by a good, very full mat of hair, but when viewed from behind, an unexpected shock of bare skin exposed a sheaf of rosy-colored wrinkles, just like an accordion, whenever the conversation grew intense.

"Listen to me, Bernardo, forget about it. If you're worried that she's caught you and Bea *in flagrante* here, I'm telling you, forget about it. Our little Mercedes has plenty of reasons—more than you know—to keep her little mouth shut. Trust me on that. I know what I'm talking about."

This, I believe, was when I was first disturbed by the way he used diminutives: little Mercedes, little mouth . . . There are some people whose friendly diminutives always come out sounding crueler than their insults. But I still had a bit more listening to do.

"Shit, Sánchez, if you have something to say about someone, just say it already. I can't stand the way you people 'in the know' go around talking about people as if you knew all their secrets and then, when it comes time to talk, you go and act all mysterious. If you want to tell us something, tell us, and if not, then just be quiet. Nobody is in the mood for it. Trust me on that, all right?" That was Bea, the blond clone, imitating him.

I was able to see Bea because she was facing Antonio S. and thus looking straight at me—or rather straight *through* me like the incorporeal being I was, her eyes firmly fixed on a neighboring wall. She looked extremely annoyed, and just as she buried a ring-laden hand in her left cheek, I jumped up a bit in my chair. I don't know if I mentioned this before, but she was one of those new, inflatable-looking women, the kind you don't ever want to touch for fear of puncturing them and causing an explosion of silicone or oil or plastic or some other synthetic material.

"What exactly do you mean, a story about a bitch? What bitch?" she asked, sighing and looking up at the ceiling as three rings dug mercilessly into the flesh of her cheek. "Make it entertaining at least, will you? Because we all know it's going to be a bunch of lies anyway ..." And just when it seemed she was about to finish off her sentence with some kind of final comment, she pulled her fingers away from her cheek. Her thoughts must have wandered onto another, far more interesting topic, because she seemed to be weaving a series of ideas together.

"We all know it's going to be a bunch of lies. Shit, this is serious, very serious ... and you, Bernardo, some brilliant idea you and your friend had to go looking for an 'out of the way' hotel—well, just look at this place. It can't be out of anybody's way if the first person we run into is a woman we've known all our lives!"

"That's right, all our lives," echoed the other blonde woefully.

"Oh, stop it with the 'all our lives!'" That was the leader of the pack. "You never even see each other."

"We have known one another all our lives—same school, same coming-out party, same everything. Of course, maybe that doesn't sound like much to you!"

At this point I was one sigh away from losing all interest in the conversation. All the defects of human communication seem to proliferate in the most tedious manner when one is an outside observer. And I'm not just talking about syntax—syntax is the least of it. I'm talking about far more reprehensible defects: repetitiveness, conversation fillers, annoying tics, not to mention tacky, tacky comments and blatant lies. Ridiculous.

"Come on, Bea," Bernardo was saying, newly engaged in the conversation. "In your case at least, how much do you really care what Mercedes Algorta thinks of you? You're separated, aren't you? You're a free woman."

"Yes, but you aren't," said the shockingly swollen lips, spitting out the "you."

"Oh, who cares? Anyone would understand your situation—or do you think Mercedes Algorta is Santa Maria Goretti?"

Antonio Sánchez's crown suddenly furrowed into a plethora of tiny folds, identical and symmetrical, just like one of those accordion gates that grocery stores use to protect their wares at night.

"Oh, the things I could tell you . . ."

"Enough already, Antonio, for God's sake. You're really starting to get on my nerves."

"Well, you don't even know what I'm talking about. Of course I don't have anything personal against her, but I can assure you that that lady"—and he raised his chin toward an indistinct spot on the wall, as if the ghost of Mercedes Algorta were there, *corpore insepulto*—"is not going to tell anyone that she has seen us. Trust me on that one. Not if she knows what's good for her. Trust me."

When all the heads at a table of four come together in a spontaneous huddle, it is because some very interesting information is about to be divulged. I have seen it on many occasions. It always happens the same way: The bodies huddle in silence, drawn together by a magnetic force of complicity or the anticipation of ripping a fellow man to shreds.

I pricked up my ears, for these situations tend to play out in hisses and whispers. It turned out, however, to be unnecessary. Sánchez's radio-announcer voice came out loud and clear.

"So do you all know the story of our little Mercedes?"

"By heart," retorted she of the astonishingly swollen lips. "I've known her all my life, darling."

Antonio Sánchez pretended not to hear her and turned to Bernardo instead. In group situations, men have a way of directing certain information toward the other men rather than the women. A little ploy to get the girls more interested.

"Now, what I am about to tell you is strictly confidential, of course. On my radio show, you see, we really don't pay much attention to this type of story—society gossip, you know. We have more serious issues to tackle," he said in that tone of voice one uses to dismiss trivial matters. "But the story does have its appeal, of course, because the people involved are very well known. Still, though, I don't think it can be released as a strict news item, because we don't have conclusive proof."

"As if that ever made a difference to you! Since when have you needed conclusive proof to crucify someone?" That was Bea.

Sánchez continued, with infinite patience, which made me wonder what kind of pact existed between him and Bea. Why did she have such carte blanche to speak to him that way? Had they had a roll in the hay long ago? Had she been a rung on the ladder of his climb to the top? Call me an unforgivable snob, but the Antonio Sánchezes of this world always have some or other ladder to climb on their way to the top, and they never quite manage to kick themselves free as easily as they would like. Such a sticky business.

"Well, you all know what happened to Valdés, Mercedes Algorta's husband, the very bizarre way he died—or supposedly died, because nobody knows for sure what happened."

"And who the hell cares?" the blonde clone interrupted. "God, I am getting so sick of this craze of making front-page news out of people's private lives, down to what brand of underwear they wear."

Sánchez, sticking to his tactic of addressing only Bernardo, did not feel it necessary to interrupt his discourse.

"It really is a shame that I lost interest in these little stories, because this one does have its sizzle, trust me. There's something fishy about Jaime Valdés's death. Trust me."

"I, for one," piped up the timid blonde, delighted with herself for being able to contribute to the general conversation with a first-hand account, "know exactly what happened that night. As it turns out, my maid, who is from the Dominican Republic, is the dear friend of a Moroccan girl who happens to be Habibi's sister. Habibi, of course, is Mercedes's cook, and she was the one who discovered poor Valdés turning blue on the floor. And she says that her boss was having sex with Isabella Steine when he suddenly had a fit of some kind. And that is what happened: The two of them were all alone in the living room when suddenly—I think he was choking, yes, like a fish out of water. Can you imagine it? He was so young. And then suddenly, out of nowhere, Mercedes turned up. Luckily. And what do you think? Did she know what was happening? Don't you think she would have slapped Isabella a couple of times after coming home to that? I don't know, to tell you the truth. For that you'll have to ask Habibi yourself. What I *do* know, however, is that Mercedes was very calm about everything—that's what Habibi said—and that Mercedes was the one who was with Valdés during his last few minutes. You see, nobody was expecting Mercedes to arrive until the next day. But as Habibi says, she arrived that night, out of nowhere at all. First she sent everyone out of the room so that she could properly tend to Valdés, and once she was alone, she called for a . . . oh, what do they call those ambulances, the ones that have all that life-saving equipment on them? Antonio?"

"Mobile ICU, darling," said Sánchez.

"Yes, that's right. A mobile ICU unit. She called for a mobile ICU unit, which took forever to get there, and of course it was all for nothing, because the poor man died before they could even get to him. A real tragedy. Although, according to my Dominican maid, there is another story, a rather strange story involving a bracelet that they say Habibi spotted on the floor lying next to Valdés when she first entered the living room. After the ambulance left, it was gone. Nobody knows what happened to it. No, don't look at me like that—I know what you're thinking. My maid swears Habibi didn't take it. Good Lord. You people . . . you are all so prejudiced. Poor Habibi, she's as honest as the day is long."

NOW, I AM a very methodical man, and right then a notebook would have really come in handy for jotting down bits and pieces of all that disjointed information, but of course I had no notebook on hand. I did, however, have Fernanda's fax with me, as well as a pen, which I put to use right away. With extreme caution I wrote down a few words so that I could reconstruct things later on. First, I wrote "Habibi (Moroccan maid)," and then "missing bracelet." After that, I turned my attentions back to the conversation.

Bea, the blond clone, had launched into her version of the incident, which was somewhat different from the previous interpretations, for it introduced several new plot elements that did not seem entirely implausible.

"Ana, darling, we all know that you are a perfect saint and that you believe everything people tell you, but I have to warn you that those of us who no longer believe in Santa Claus were not at all convinced by Habibi's story. It makes no difference at all to me if Valdés was putting the moves on Isabella or if Isabella was sleeping in old Steine's arms, as Isabella herself insists is the case. Who cares? And as far as that mysterious bracelet is concerned, well, it belongs to Habibi now—that is the most obvious and logical conclusion one can draw. But, listen. None of that matters in the least. The real issue is *why* it all came to pass in the first place, and that is what I am going to explain to you now. Do you want to know the truth? It's much simpler than you think. Things don't happen just like that—allergies, choking, come on! If the guy had some kind of fit it was because he was stressed-out. Can't you see what is happening to us, to everyone? It's terrible. We're all about ready to crack, and that's exactly how these things happen. I don't need to tell you what the business world has come to these days. Just look at all those golden-boy yuppies—you know, the ones who thought that getting rich was as easy as winning a Monopoly game. Just ask Bernardo. He knows a few of them himself. Stressed-out, darling, that's what Valdés was. He wasn't going bankrupt, exactly, no, no. The opposite, actually. He had more money than God, but the more money you have, the more complicated things get. And then what do you do? You just get deeper and deeper into it: more deals, more traveling, more problems, more lovers, until one day you just fall to pieces. Look, the way I see it, everything that went down that night was one terrible, cruel joke: There was no mad passion—they didn't have time!—no mysterious death. Seriously, it was pure, unadulterated stress that did him in. He certainly isn't the first person to choke on something and end up dead from trying to be Mr. Macho."

"So you mean you actually *believe* those people who say that Valdés suffered some kind of heinous allergy attack and then choked to death?" asked Ana, the timid blonde, her hand fluttering up and resting on her throat in a way that reminded me of Fernanda prattling on about Russian fumes.

This was followed by a flurry of confused whispers and one or two assertive coughs issued by the leader of the pack. The only thing I managed to discern from all of this was that the allergy story held the least weight among my four subjects.

"Well, what do you make of Isabella? She could have helped out a little, don't you think?"

"Yes. She was in the house, there's no doubt about that, but we're not talking about death à la Rockefeller Junior, darling. I'm sorry to break it to all of you who eat up these soap opera stories about cheating wives and hapless husbands, but the truth in this case is so ridiculous that it has been completely blown out of proportion. People love stories of intrigue: You know, the ladies' man, the wife who was fed up with all his philandering and lies . . . what more do you want? People make this stuff up themselves, the wilder and crazier the better, and what I'm trying to say is that nothing inappropriate happened that night. Don't forget, it was a coincidence that Mercedes turned up when she did."

"A bit too much of a coincidence if you ask me," said Sánchez, furrowing his brow in a very unbecoming manner as he cocked his head to one side.

Bea, however, was on a roll, and was not interested in other people's opinions. I think she actually thought that Sánchez's last comment was intended to support the timid blonde's hypothesis that Valdés had died in the arms of Isabella Steine. I must be right, because Bea now chose to ignore Sánchez entirely and direct her conversation toward Bernardo, precisely to make him feel invisible—a very disdainful and extremely useful tactic that I myself have used from time to time.

"Your friend," she said, not even glancing over at Sánchez, "cannot help himself. All of this is too much for him, for he simply cannot resist these stories about rich people, especially when death is involved. I know him too well—right now he is telling us that this story doesn't interest him in the least, that we should remember he is a serious journalist. But in a few days, just you wait—we will suddenly hear his voice ring out on the airwaves with 'The Tragic Story of how Jaime Valdés died.' I'd put money on it."

"Oh, Bea, I can't be bothered with those things. You know that."

" 'The Bizarre Death of a Wealthy Man,' " Bea continued, ignoring him, tracing a huge invisible headline in the air with her ring-laden hands. "No, no, better yet: 'Death by Love' or 'Death in the Arms of His Young Mistress'—that means Isabella, darling," she said, turning toward Ana, to make sure that her *petit sarcasme* was not lost on the timid blonde. Then, with renewed brio, she resumed her commentary, directed as before to the leader of the pack. "That is exactly what our friend Antonio S. plans on doing—I'd put money on it. You'll see, and after the shocking headline, he will tell his version of the facts as if it were the most important story of all time, important enough for a coast-to-coast broadcast. Who the hell gives a damn about the life and death of Jaime Valdés, you might ask? Well, he was in the public eye, and that alone is enough to turn his death into something marketable." At this, the leader of the pack coughed a little more and Sánchez's left hand grew a rosy purple color, but Bea kept on talking.

"I can already picture the sermon: Without mentioning any names, our hero will preach out over the airwaves. 'The sins of the rich,' he will say, to make it all the more interesting, and he wouldn't even have to lie very much, because Valdés's death does have all the ingredients anyone could ask for: a well-known figure, who also happens to be something of a womanizer, a beautiful woman with an old—ergo, clueless—husband, and some very strange circumstances. The ingredients are right there. All Sánchez needs to do is mix them up in the most titillating fashion, come up with the 'revelation' that he will try to sell us, including the bit about 'the story of a real bitch,' which is based, I would imagine, on the fact that Isabella was with Valdés when he choked and didn't do a damn thing to help him. Shit, Isabella just got scared—that's why she acted so stupidly. All of you know I am not terrifically fond of her, but to say she could have killed Valdés . . . even I can't go that far." Bea finished off her sentence with a long sigh that clung to the walls of the restaurant for a few moments. Then she turned back to Bernardo to say, "Don't you get the irony of it all? Before, we had priests, and now we have to put up with journalists working night and day to expose our sins. Shit."

Bea was getting more and more aggravated, and the leader of the pack now cleared his throat in an obvious, imperious attempt to get her to shut up: By the third or fourth cough you could see that he was surprised at her refusal to heed his warning. Bea rolled her eyes.

"Look, Sánchez. Now, seriously. And, Bernardo, sigh all you

want, I don't care. Just save yourself the trouble of doing all that research—or so-called research—because everyone in Madrid already knows what happened to Valdés. And I mean *everyone.*"

I watched as Sánchez's crown expanded for a few seconds and furrowed back into place in an oblique set of folds.

"The tragic outcome of that night," Sánchez said, "had nothing to do with financial distress, or surreptitious lovers. No, no, it is something far more disturbing than that. Of course, if you'd rather discuss something else, Bernardo . . .

"Now let's get one thing straight," he continued, and I could just barely see him positioning his improvised chess pieces, moving glasses and other random objects around the tablecloth, but my field of vision was blocked by his back. "I do not plan to use this story for my radio program, because I happen to be above this sort of boudoir gossip. But if you want to know what *really* happened that night and why Valdés died the way he did, just listen to me, Bernardo. Now, I want you to picture the dying man as if he were the white king. Very well, here we have Valdés, the white king, at the end of the game. Let's see. What other pieces do we have here? A white queen, a black queen, and Habibi the Moroccan maid, who we will say is a black pawn. Do you follow so far?"

The leader of the pack nodded with an air of intense concentration, while Bea smoked a cigarette and stared straight through me to the wall at my back, ignoring her friends entirely. She seemed to have lost all interest in the story, unlike Ana, Our Lady of the Innocents, who couldn't tell a bishop from a rook. She suddenly piped up with a question that, at least to my ears, sounded incredibly stupid:

"All right, Antonio. But if Valdés is the white king, who is the white queen and who is the black queen?"

Sánchez was perfectly delighted by this question—you could tell by the way the long, straw-like hairs on his neck plunged into his shirt collar as his body tightened, keen as a bloodhound about to pounce on a rabbit.

"That is the first time anyone has asked me the million-dollar question. Who is the black queen? You tell me. Is it Isabella, who everybody knows—" As he emphasized "everybody," he looked straight at Bea, and I was truly chagrined that I could not see the expression on his face, but I suspect it was defiant, "—who everybody knows was with Valdés and did nothing to help him? Or is it our little Mercedes, who took advantage of the little predicament to free herself from her annoying and very rich husband, who did nothing but go to bed with all her friends?"

EITHER MY LUCK was worse than usual that day or else it is extremely difficult to be a good spy. To my great dismay, the Germans at the table next to the window suddenly decided, at this extremely delicate point in the conversation, to get up and leave the restaurant, all of them chattering away at the same time like a swarm of giant flies. First they moved to the right, then to the left, making it difficult to predict quite where they would land, but somehow I knew they would end up directly in front of me.

I believe I mentioned before that there were four of them: two women and two men, but at that moment the group seemed much larger, and if they made me think of a swarm of flies, it was because of the very loud buzzing noises—some high-pitched like mosquitoes, others deeper, like black flies—that suddenly descended upon the space between me and the party I was so intently studying. They had gotten up en masse and advanced toward us talking up a storm, with that mindless chatter of people who feel that having fun means they must be utterly hilarious at all times, even as they say good-bye and go off to bed for the night—flies with mosquitoes, or flies with flies, or however they paired themselves off.

For the love of God, I prayed, silently begging them not to come to a halt stop in front of my four Spaniards, not to suddenly pipe up with some comment that would make them all stop in their tracks.

But they did. They stopped, and a tall man with round tortoise-shell glasses said exactly what I feared he would: "By the way . . ."

And then, to make matters worse, he strategically positioned himself in the spot that most obstructed my view. The girls walking behind him, with their fat hands and massive hips, also chose that moment to stop, and they stood there readjusting their short skirts (far too short for their Bavarian legs, if you ask me) as they laughed in their very Bavarian laughs. Due to this unfortunate bit of timing, all of Sánchez's comments were intermittently drowned out by a most unwelcome flurry of German chitchat.

"Now, let the record stand: The problem is not that Valdés choked on anything that night or that he suffered from some kind of fit or whatever you want to call it. That can happen to anyone. The problem is that *after* it happened they just sat there and let him die like a stray dog." This was what I heard Sánchez say.

"No, no. It was in the Göeses' house," said a strident German voice. *"We were all so drunk, and Friedrich said to me, look at Franz Johann, look at him . . ."*

". . . and that is exactly what happened. That bitch let Valdés die. She could have saved him, but she let him die—there's no doubt about it."

What bitch? I wondered. Isabella? The Moroccan maid? Mercedes? All I could do was silently curse Franz Johann and his friends.

". . . No, no, it wasn't the Göeses' house, I'm telling you for sure it was during the Graf Spee *thing. After that they threw her in the lake . . ."*

"Ja, ja, ja," said one of the two pairs of Bavarian legs.

"Ter-ri-ble," noted Franz Johann's friend. *"Ha, ha, ha."*

"But also, it's just so wretchedly simple. Nobody had to do anything, really, it was dumb luck. I mean, picture it: The guy is right there, dying in front of you, and you can either do something to stop it or not do anything at all. It's a split-second decision. One second, that's all you have. So what do you do?"

"Right, right." Franz Johann wouldn't let up.

At this point, all the chitchat—that of my Spanish friends as well as that of the Bavarians—was suddenly drowned out by laughter of varying degrees and pitch, a noise that sounded like yodels being yelled off the highest mountaintops. It went something like this:

". . . Ja, ja, ja he threw her in the pool . . . !"

". . . I mean it, listen to me, Bernardo . . ."

"Ahh." That was a sigh from the other pair of Bavarian legs.

"Very few times in life does one find oneself in this type of situation. Naturally, it is not the same as actually killing someone, because in fact it is much simpler and much easier to justify, even to oneself: 'How perfectly awful, I couldn't do anything to save him,' you tell yourself, totally bereft. But in the bottom of your heart you know the truth. And that, my friends, is human nature for you . . ."

Another yodel, this time in simultaneous falsettos and contraltos:

". . . Hee, hee, into that free-zing swimming pool, hee, hee, hee . . . !"

". . . All you really have to do is look the other way and let nature take care of the dirty work. Let's say that in this specific case Mercedes *did* call for an ambulance, and let's say they picked up the call, and then let's say, oh, that she was maybe a little vague about explaining how to get to the house . . . nobody would ever find out, right? Because she was the only other person in the room with Valdés at that moment. Very convenient, wouldn't you say?"

"Ja, ja . . . but wasn't it at the lake?" More yodels all around.

". . . And so now she's a widow . . ."

"Yes, yes, and the water was free-zing cold, you can't even imagine . . ."

". . . Which is a very bitter pill to swallow if you recall the kind of reputation Valdés had, plus the fact that everyone is now speculating that Isabella was caught up in it . . ."

"Ja, ja, right, Margaretha? You were there, too, weren't you . . . ?"

"... But you see, the catch, the real explanation is this: this lady was sick and tired of putting up with him, and so she took a lover. It's so obvious, trust me ..."

"... *I get shivers just thinking about it ... and I mean, we were so, so drunk that night ...*"

"... And since she has a lover, they probably agreed to meet here. I would bet any amount of money that this lady has come here for a little rendezvous with someone. We'll find out soon enough, don't you worry. And that, my friends, will be the conclusive proof that what I have said is one hundred percent true."

"... *nein, nein, Margaretha, you tell them what happened that night ...*"

Fortunately, Margaretha appeared to belong to one of the lighter species of those irritating insects; she was a far more delicate yodeler than her noisy friends. I watched her float toward the door to the restaurant, practically dragging the singing Bavarians amid a chorus of laughs and yodels until they finally disappeared from sight, leaving me absolutely exposed in front of the group I was trying so hard to study.

You see, I had been caught leaning forward into a kind of triangle, the most obtuse angle of which now hovered dangerously close to Sánchez's head. When the timid blonde suddenly looked over at me, I found myself forced to squeak out a very solicitous *"Gute nacht"* in the hopes that my Swiss boarding-school accent would work the miracle of convincing them that I had been listening in on the Bavarians' conversation and not theirs. An absurd situation no matter how you looked at it, one that I would have to address in the least embarrassing manner possible. And so I decided that the most sensible thing to do was to get up as quickly as possible and walk past my newfound Spanish friends, repeating my good night wishes in the most Germanic way I knew.

"Gute Nacht," I said, controlling the desire to click my heels to camouflage the words. They didn't even see me. As I walked out of

the restaurant, despite the fact that I now had all the time in the world to organize my thoughts, I could only think of one thing to add to the list that I had scrawled at lightning speed on Fernanda's fax. During dinner, I had jotted down the name "Habibi," followed by the words "stolen bracelet." And all I could think of to add were the words "Did SHE let him die" followed by a question mark. Really. It was all so terribly confusing.

Needlework

ONE SHOULD NEVER BE IDLE WHEN IT COMES TO REPAIRING any imperfection or flaw one may discover in one's attire. Needles can be our most faithful friends, because they can be responsible for breathing new life into our oldest (and perhaps most forgotten) items of clothing.

—Countess Drillard, *On Being Elegant,*
On Being Lovely, chapter on wardrobe

Pine Needles

You must believe me when I say that I did not drink a single drop of alcohol with my dinner. I think this is an important detail to mention, because what I am about to tell may sound as though Johnnie Walker or, perhaps more accurately, General Gordon (since I do prefer gin) was involved.

I had gone up to my room, which is on the second floor of L'Hirondelle, and turned on the light—not the overhead light but the side light, to avoid waking Gomez, who sleeps close to the window.

As I took off my jacket and tie I observed a very strange phenomenon, which I will now describe. On occasion I have read in some or other book a description of this type of occurrence: that of entering a room and suddenly feeling that one is the victim of a vast conspiracy. Inanimate objects, especially walls, begin to close in on you and your mind begins working overtime, digesting all sorts of unpleasant existential thoughts. Thoughts that somehow connect the present to the past, bringing you back to the most abominable childhood memories, awakening those memories from their tranquil slumber. And then, all of a sudden, these thoughts conspire with the astonishing movement of the walls, which threaten to close in on their victim in such a way that recalls the horrifying prophecy of the witches who once, long ago, sang the words, "Macbeth shall never vanquish'd be until / Great Birnam Wood, to high Dunsinane hill / Shall come against him." Or, in more practical terms, that "Molinet shall never fear that his past may conspire against him . . . until the walls of his bedroom begin to act like the Birnam Wood."

This phenomenon did not occur instantly. No, it materialized in the form of a claustrophobic shiver that came over me as I glanced toward the walls of my bedroom, covered entirely by needles. Yes, needles: needles that were conjured not by a bizarre curse or spell but rather by the hotel decorator, who had decided to line the walls in a pine-forest print. The walls, the bedspread, and the curtains, too, were covered in them: hundreds and hundreds of identical pine needles. At L'Hirondelle d'Or, you see, every room is decorated according to a different botanical motif, and mine happened to be that of pine needles. I haven't been able to admire the decor of any other room, but I discovered the flower-and-plant scheme by listening to the chambermaids. The room next to mine, for example, is the *chambre du muguet.* Next to that room, the *chambre pistache,* and a bit further down the hall, the *rose de thé.* The names are all in French, and always botanically oriented, perhaps to compensate for the fact that the hotel is located in the middle of a desert.

My room is very daintily called the "pine-needle room," the *chambre des aiguilles de pin*. And in honor of this, the room is upholstered in prints that bear the long, fine needles that tend to fall from evergreen trees and come in twos—those Siamese-twin pine needles joined at the head.

I removed my jacket and tie in the semi-darkness. Gomez was snoring away in his little corner, louder than I might have liked, but I didn't even notice him or the pine needles until I finished undressing. That was when I suddenly found myself covered in them— hundreds of identical pine needles, like the long legs of an endless chorus line or a lineup of pointing fingers. They were like hateful thorns pricking at my memory, making the past crash down on the present, precipitating a deluge of distant, long-forgotten experiences that had been buried, very well buried, but which suddenly reappeared, threatening to pounce and then close in on me like a fake forest. Now, I am perfectly aware that walls cannot move, not even walls covered in needles like these. That is why I want to make it very clear that I did not drink any alcohol whatsoever during dinner.

From the start I tried to ignore them. I wanted to think about the here and now, about things that had absolutely nothing to do with my past life, and so I turned off the light.

I decided to stave off the onslaught of sleep by thinking about the things I had heard that night at the restaurant: the different versions of the death of Jaime Valdés, who had been so present in my recent thoughts that I almost began to look upon him as I would a friend. "What a ridiculous story," I said to myself. First, there was the story that Fernanda had told me in London, and then the interpretations I had listened to here at the hotel: the same situation, the same characters, but depending on the storyteller, they sounded like two or three very different stories. This was really the ideal moment for putting all that disparate information in order, which is exactly what I began to do, eliminating hypotheses one by one.

Very well. I had all the time in the world and I gazed out the window and started to think back.

"How would you like to hear the story of a murderess?" That was how Fernanda had started her version of the facts: a man who choked to death in the company of his wife's very good friend, who, instead of helping him, ran off at the most compromising moment. This was, of course, where Fernanda's "murderess" bit came in. I smiled and then, to excuse my niece, I just said to myself:

Oh, she just got carried away, *mon cher,* a bit of exaggerated gossip. Fernanda doesn't think that Isabella actually killed anyone—she was just trying to tell the story as vividly as she knew how, to pass the time and brighten up a lunch date that would have otherwise been a total bore.

And it stood to reason that Fernanda's story was highly improbable, exceedingly illogical, and anything but realistic—after all, gossip is just supposed to be fun. Nothing but fun. Isn't that right?

I still do not understand how it happened: One single ray of moonlight somehow managed to fall very obliquely into my room. All the other moonbeams filtered through the darkness rather uniformly, but for some strange reason this one lone ray had managed to escape the crowd and illuminate, like a spotlight, a tiny corner of my room with an especially abundant pile of pine needles, and I swear that I could hear those needles shouting out at me:

Rafael Molinet, what the hell do you care about a story that has nothing to do with you, that involves a bunch of people you've never seen before in your life? What business do you have sniffing around like some kind of ridiculous old bloodhound? Why are you going to such trouble to connect a bunch of dots that will probably only lead you to the simplest, most typical of conclusions? Nobody killed this Valdés person. You know it better than anyone: He choked to death for a stupid, stupid reason. That's all . . .

As one might expect, I told myself, cutting off the pine needles' sudden monologue, trying to ignore what I had just heard, the more extended version of the story is that the guy died while making love to Isabella, and that is what adds a bit of spice to the story. That is the opinion of Ana, the timid blonde who seems to be such dear friends with the radio announcer. This explanation, moreover, coincides with Fernanda's story on all the basic points: a sudden, unexpected death at the most untimely moment—but then again, when is death ever timely?

The moonbeam was still there, casting its light on every last pine needle. Standing on the wall in vivid relief, they were like thousands and thousands of piercing memories determined to sew the past onto the present, to connect Valdés's story with another, far older story. But I didn't even look at them. Instead, I searched the landscape for the two lone palm trees I had noticed on the golf course, and I swear, I was truly amazed at the manner in which they followed my observations. They looked like movie-set palm trees, but they really did rustle and sway in silent and noble agreement with all that I had to say.

I felt very close to the palm trees and so very far from my bedroom. I tried hard to ascertain the real truth about the death of Jaime Valdés and to ignore the presence of those pine-needle memories. I realize that I heard Sánchez's explanation under extremely difficult circumstances, I said to myself. But it isn't hard to guess his theory: a rich, unscrupulous widow, a lover . . . and whether I believe this or not (what does my opinion matter, anyway?), the fact is that I now have a substantial amount of material that could easily be used to obtain a bit of spending money if I so desired . . .

Who are you going to blackmail now, Rafael Molinet?, the pine needles shouted out at me, grotesquely illuminated by the moon. *Lies, it's all lies. In all your life, when have you ever been able to take a situation and turn it to your advantage, and make money off someone else's sordid story? Admit it, Rafael Molinet, confess for once and for all, why the death of Jaime Valdés means so very much to you!*

At this, I turned on the light. Laugh if you must, but at that moment I went over to the closet to look for the tiny sewing box I had placed there so that I might occupy myself with a bit of useful activity, anything at all that might help me concentrate on the things I wanted to think about, not what those needles were urging me to remember. That was the best thing I could do, occupy myself with some practical domestic task, like darning a pair of socks.

And it worked, at first. As I threaded the needle, introduced a wooden egg into the first sock, and performed my first few stitches, the walls (or perhaps I should say, the memories) subsided and went back to where they had been before. And my head promptly began, once again, to try and organize the facts of a story that seemed to have very little to do with me.

Antonio Sánchez's story is even more idiotic than Fernanda's, I said to myself once again. And though his explanation had reached my ears through the high-volume chatter of the four Germans, I had little trouble weaving together the snippets of the radio announcer's story now that I had a bit of peace and quiet.

My hands continued working away.

The characters, obviously, are all the same, I reasoned. Valdés, the asphyxiated Don Juan; Mercedes, the widow; Isabella, the lover; and Steine, the hapless husband of Isabella. Plus Habibi, the Moroccan maid, though I haven't quite decided whether she belongs with the good guys or the bad guys. But that, of course, is the entire point of all this. This last thought made me pause for a moment to consider my fifth and final character.

Ana, the timid blonde, had mentioned Habibi with regard to a bracelet that disappeared the evening of Valdés's death. Fernanda had only referred to this detail in passing, which meant that if there was any truth to the story about Habibi and the lost bracelet (as the timid blonde insisted), then we were talking about a series of facts that had been obtained . . . oh, what had my niece called that bit about the household help? Ah, yes—the maid connection. No doubt this was the source of the timid blonde's version of the story. But then I never pay attention to the household help and their gossip.

Well, pay attention to them, Rafael Molinet, a cluster of pine needles seemed to scream at me from my bedspread. *Pay attention, for they are talking about a gold bracelet that disappeared precisely when the man died. Mercedes Algorta, down by the swimming pool, was wearing the same type of bracelet that Isabella wore in the photograph that Fernanda sent you. Are we talking about two different bracelets, or are they one and the same? Stop and think for a moment: What would it mean if those two bracelets were in fact the same? What does that little coincidence remind you of, Rafael Molinet? Perhaps another bad girl you once knew?*

"SÁNCHEZ'S VERSION," I said for the third time, aloud this time, in such a loud voice that Gomez gave a start, though thankfully he did not wake up. "Sánchez's version is even more idiotic than the others I have heard. According to him, Isabella did not callously leave her lover to die (as Fernanda claimed), nor had the guy dropped dead while having sex with his girlfriend (as Ana, the timid blonde claimed). No, no. Both versions were *très vulgaires comme petite histoire.* When someone like Antonio S. finds himself fascinated by a bit of common gossip, he will always try to turn it into something much more original than it really is. He will take the five characters as if they were five playing cards, shuffle them around a bit, and come up with the most shocking explanation for the same events we have already heard about: He turns the *wife* into the guilty party, the sinner. How? Simple: I believe the French call it *laissez-faire.* It means not getting involved, allowing things to run their course—in this case, letting someone die. From what I have been able to piece together, that is Sánchez's explanation."

Interesting theory, I said to myself, making sure that all my stitches were perfectly uniform. You might even call it the perfect crime. There are thousands of stories like it, with all sorts of variations. For example, I can recall a very similar case that took place in Argentina and involved a woman who was married to a very wealthy but tyrannical and insufferable man. It all happened on a sailboat, at night—nobody was on deck but the woman and her despicable husband. And suddenly the man fell into the water. Herein lies the dilemma: What did the wife do? Did she call for help? Throw him a life preserver? Or did she simply not interfere with destiny's handiwork? It was a split-second decision: In this case, the wife went down to their bedroom and began filing her nails instead of asking for help. It was the most perfect murder, with the most innocent weapon: Death by emery board is impossible, after all . . . except when it should have been in a night-table drawer while its mistress used her nails—and her hands—for more Samaritan purposes.

Clearly, Sánchez's theory suggested something along these lines despite the fact that the ingredients of his story are as hard to swallow as the ones in Fernanda's. The hypothesis that this Valdés character died as the result of a bit of *laissez-faire* is completely idiotic, I said to myself. We are not talking about someone who drowned on the high seas—yes, he choked to death, which is a similar affliction, but it is much more difficult to remedy unless one happens to be a medical doctor. What exactly was it that Mercedes should have done but didn't? According to Sánchez, she waited awhile before calling for help, and to support this hypothesis he claimed that she had taken a lover and finally saw a opportunity to be free—rich and free.

Oh, these elastic stitches are so difficult, I'm going to have to rip up the thread and start over again.

What kind of person could dream up this sort of madness? I asked myself. Because it is so, so obvious that . . . At this point I had to stop working on my sock, for I was sweating profusely. I wiped my brow, looked up from my darning, and once again found the pine needles staring back at me.

Why do you care so much about a story that is nothing but vulgar gossip, as you yourself say? Nothing but a bunch of conjecture about a very unfortunate accident . . .

It was them, all right. Yet again. This time they lunged at me from the wall near the window. I turned back to my sewing, talking to myself in such a loud voice that Gomez began to stir in his corner, but I didn't care if he woke up, because I had to try as hard as I could to focus on my sewing. "Could Mercedes have possibly wanted to kill her husband just because she had another man, a secret lover waiting in the wings? No! That is the most implausible story I have heard—not even Sánchez's hypnotic radio announcer's voice can make it believable. And it is implausible and unbelievable, because in this day and age, people hardly need resort to murder if they want to free themselves of husbands. Even if he was a womanizer and a cad, it is very hard to imagine that Mercedes would ever dream of doing something so risky and so very unnecessary. It takes a very curious—and very contradictory—sort of a person to pull something like that off . . ."

That, we know, is a lie. It is a split-second decision, scream the pine needles decorating the bedspread. *None of this was planned. That is why it all seems so accidental . . . so simple. All it takes is a little slip, an imperceptible delay in doing what should be done, and there it is: omission, the most perfect of crimes. Remember, Rafael Molinet, remember back to what happened that other time. That, too, was a split-second decision . . .*

"Don't be silly. A woman would never sit back and let her husband die when something as civilized as divorce exists. This is nothing but idle speculation, nothing more."

That was when I realized that the pine needles had no intention of leaving me in peace. They were there, waiting for me to be conquered by fatigue, but sleep can be very fickle: It takes its time when desired but assails us when we least wish to bring it on. And people think of such silly, silly things while in the dream state. I looked at

my watch: Two in the morning. I would have loved to have rumi-
nated on all this a bit longer, lingering on some or other fascinating
tidbit of the Mercedes Algorta saga. And there was, in fact, one thing
that I seemed to be stuck on, something all of them had mentioned
in passing:

"Solid gold, from Cartier . . ." That was what Fernanda had said
in her fax. I remembered it practically word for word: ". . . Mercedes
had spotted it at a Christie's auction, but Isabella beat her to the
punch and got old Papa Steine to give it to her as a Christmas
present . . . it was like an omen of sorts: the Isabellas of this world,
they start off stealing your bracelets and end up stealing your husband."

It was a stupid idea, but even the stupidest ideas in the world can
seem halfway reasonable when you are falling asleep, struggling to
keep your eyes open to stave off your sinister memories. That was
when, all of a sudden, I realized that if Mercedes was right here at
L'Hirondelle, and if I could ascertain that the bracelet I saw on her
wrist was in fact Isabella's . . . well, then, I might have good reason to
suspect that something fishy took place the night Valdés died. How
chilling to imagine Mercedes in the middle of that medical drama,
deciding to keep the bracelet as collateral or as revenge for her husband's betrayals. After all, Isabella would have to have a lot of nerve
to ask for it back . . . "Her hands should have been busy with more
Samaritan tasks," I repeated to myself, thinking of the story about
the husband who fell into the sea while his wife sat back and filed
her nails.

"Nonsense!" I cried aloud as a halo of common sense appeared
above my head. "Why, that is the craziest of all the ideas I have
heard, so crazy that not even Antonio Sánchez could have dreamed
it up, and his talent for sniffing out scandal is far better honed than
my own."

Pine needles, it seems, do not give up so easily, for they hastily
interrupted my thoughts:

Sánchez and his friends have not seen the bracelet on Mercedes's wrist—only you have, Rafael Molinet. What would you bet that she doesn't put it back on for the rest of her vacation at L'Hirondelle? Letting your husband die can be as easy—and as brazen—as keeping his lover's bracelet as a kind of trophy. It is all so easy. And that little item proves everything. Only you know the true story of Mercedes Algorta, just as only you know the true story of that other bad girl, long ago. Now that is the real reason you care so much about meddling in this affair: because of the strange resemblance between Mercedes and . . .

All right, enough. I am not meddling in anything—I was just curious, that's all, and bored after all those days with nothing to do. Curiosity and boredom, that's all. There was nothing at all strange about the way Valdés died. It's all just malicious conjecture. Gossip, simple and vulgar gossip . . .

Just like that other time, isn't that right? The gossip spread like wild-fire that other time, too, didn't it? But only you knew the truth. And now, almost forty years later, here you are again, the sole witness to a new series of facts. But what are you going to do with the facts this time around?

"What facts?" I ask. I am so gullible: One should never respond to questions as impertinent as these, even if they are posed by ancient memories that weigh heavily on the soul. I know nothing about these people—I can't even be sure if Mercedes's bracelet is the same as the one on Isabella's wrist in the fax Fernanda sent me, because it came out so blurry. I could ask my niece for a clearer photograph, but to do that I would have to *want to know,* and that is the furthest thing from my intentions—I don't want to know about any bracelet. I don't! I tell myself.

What are you going to do with these facts?

It was those damn pine needles again, questioning me, heeding none of my protests.

You claim to have taken an interest in Mercedes Algorta simply out of curiosity, but who are you kidding? Lies. There is nothing more fool-ish than a man who lies to himself, and you have been lying to yourself for . . . how many years now? Forty? Oh, just admit it, Molinet—after all, what does it matter at this stage in the game? You're already dead. Or are you going to tell us that you've also forgotten the reason you came to L'Hirondelle in the first place? Because we'll be glad to remind you: Two weeks and, then—ciao, au revoir, good-bye cruel world . . . Your entire stash of sleeping pills . . .

The entire stash? Yes, that's what the pine needles had said, with a remarkably southern sounding accent, a very old accent that had been lodged somewhere deep in my memory. That was when I realized I was half-asleep: Suddenly I was on another continent, in another country, in a very long-gone era. The pine needles were still there, though, staring at me from the walls, from the bedspread—so very formal and so very enigmatic, a diffuse canopy of leaves that was as thick as the goddamn Birnam wood that was prepared to ful-fill its prophecy. And I saw them on the walls, barely illuminated by the moon. They were quiet and still for the moment, but they didn't fool me, not for a minute.

Despite my best efforts, my eyes slowly began to fall closed and I was soon enveloped in slumber.

How to Behave
in Front of a Mirror

AS WE STUDY OUR MOVEMENTS WHILE STANDING IN FRONT OF a mirror, we must always remember that the elegant woman shall always aim to achieve a harmonious whole of her many disparate parts. Practice your smile before the mirror. Recite certain phrases that you employ in the hope of achieving a particular effect. There are some words that, when pronounced, make the movements of the mouth far more attractive and delightful.

—Countess Drillard, *On Being Elegant,*
On Being Lovely

With a Silver Mirror in Hand

Dreams, both the good and the bad kind, have a way of blurring everything. Even the cruelest ones, the ones we struggle so valiantly against, are never very sharply focused; their wretchedness may frighten their victims, but they never do any real harm; rather, they circle around and around their victim but never deliver the definitive blow. Why, it almost seems as if dreams wish to inspire curiosity as well as fear—a dose of sour followed by a dose of sweet, imposing fear and ambiguity all the way through.

I would have been far happier to have had an utterly cruel, crystal-clear dream, the searingly lucid kind that jolts you awake in a cold sweat, with your eyes popping out of your head, still seeing whatever ghastly vision made them open so wide in the first place. But, alas, that was not my dream; that was not my punishment.

It began, as I remember it, in a thunderous rather than a visual manner. In my dream, I suddenly found myself in Montevideo, on the first and last night that we would spend in the great house at El Prado, the estate that had belonged to my father's family and which had just been auctioned off for a miserly sum of money.

I never loved that house, because it had always felt so foreign to me. Only he could have loved it. Only Bertie could feel the loss of the house he'd been born in. Of course, in practical terms, he had spent very little time living there. Ever since marrying Mama he had moved around a lot, in Europe mostly. And as he played the role of the rich young dandy in places like Paris and London, the old family house had fallen into decline, swallowed up by the gardens that had once been beautiful but which had slowly degenerated into an overgrown tangle of burrs and thick tree branches that spread everywhere in a labyrinth of twists and knots, and wildflowers that covered everything in a kind of crazy natural blanket. There is nothing quite so brutal as nature gone mad. You could see how the bluebells fought against the grass to see who could do a better job of hiding the shape of the outer balconies and the stucco columns around the house. For this reason, by the time I laid eyes on the house, it was virtually impossible to tell what it had been like in its glory days, for the building had been swallowed up on all sides by all that rapacious foliage. Only the front door was visible, and that was only thanks to the efforts of my father's manservant, Gomez, who was as loyal as a puppy dog—though that was about the only thing that Gomez had in common with such a sweet animal. It was Gomez who had unleashed his machete on the dense underbrush and cleared a path to the front door. All of that, of course, was to indulge my father's dream of spending one last night in the place—yet another one of his extravagant fantasies that nobody dared protest. Through that very same door Bertie, Mama, and I were to leave the house the next day, never to come back to El Prado. The door had witnessed the exodus of the majority of the furniture, which, like the house itself, had been sold off at rock-bottom prices. Even the most ludicrous offers had been readily accepted. All that remained of the furniture—chairs, a table or two, some beds, and a grandfather clock—lay shrouded beneath sheets that had once been white, though by now they were nothing but rats' nests. And yet I saw none of this in my dream, for it began with sounds rather than images.

"Gomez, tell little Rafael that he will have to tend to the house and look after his mother for a few hours. Tell him that a boy of his age shouldn't be afraid of anything. He's fifteen years old now."

That was how Bertie always talked to me. He never spoke to me directly, even if I was standing right in front of him. One of his very few ideas that I actually agreed with.

"Tell him, Gomez," the voice thundered in the vestibule, and despite the chaotic nature of dreams that begin with sounds instead of images, I do think that I began to see myself there at the entrance to the house at El Prado, just to the left of the great grandfather clock whose tick-tock would survive everything that was about to happen. I believe I was hiding behind the stairway, trying in vain to insert my knee between two of the vertical bars that extended down beneath the banister, even though at fifteen I was clearly too old for such childish behavior. "And, Gomez. Be ready to leave at seven on the dot. We have a long trip ahead of us."

We have a long trip ahead of us. That was precisely the expression he used when he would gallivant around Europe, making up all those stories in which Gomez, faithful hound dog to the end, was used as an alibi, an accomplice, or a stupid excuse. And it was all so unnecessary, because my mother had long since stopped caring about where my father went in that dark suit and hat of his, just as he did that night, leaving a trace of cologne on the sheet-shrouded furniture, that scent of sophistication leaving its mark on a decrepit house that otherwise smelled of mold and rot.

From there the dream grows foggy again, and the events unfold in a jumbled manner. I do not see Bertie leave the house or get into his car with his usual officious air, as if instead of going to a whore-house he was paying a visit to a notary or a government minister. Gomez may be nodding his head laconically, as I have seen him do so many times before, sitting on the passenger's side. Yes, yes, his very dimwitted head bobs up and down like that of a great big dog.

The dream then jumps ahead, because that is what dreams do—they jump from here to there and back again until they land on something horrible that makes you see all the things you'd rather avoid. It is pitch-black in the house, because the electricity has gone out, and we have no choice but to light candles if we want to move around at all. For this reason my mother has gone to bed early. "Sleep well, Mama." "You too, darling, and please don't forget to blow out the candle. It frightens me, you know. What if you fall asleep? It could start a fire or . . ."

It must be dawn by the time my father returns home. I know this for sure thanks to the damn grandfather clock that chimes on the hour, the half-hour, even the quarter-hour, counting out the time in a way that makes it feel denser and longer—much, much longer. The clock has just struck four-thirty. I hear it from my bedroom one floor above. It has been hours now and I still can't seem to fall asleep—who could possibly fall asleep with that clock lying in wait, and those rats rustling about, so horribly close by? Sometimes you can hear their tiny claws scratching away at the wood, sickeningly soft little scrapes, and other times they moan in a way that is almost human-sounding, and it makes my hair stand on end. Two flights of stairs separate me from my father now. I can hear him below, in the vestibule at the bottom of the stairs. My mother has chosen to spend the night in a bedroom on the second floor, between me and my father. But I can tell that Bertie is not walking in that direction. No, he is heading further upstairs, to the floor where I have supposedly been sleeping for many hours now. But I am wide awake.

I can hear two other voices in addition to my father's. One of them is Gomez's. He's saying things like "Yeth thir, yeth thir," in that irritating lisp I always despised. The other voice, much sharper than Gomez's, grows louder and louder until it is eventually muffled by an admonishing, alcoholic "Shhh!," a masculine cackle that I know all too well.

The laughter rises. I can hear it coming my way. One of the people is a woman, and I don't know who she is, but it doesn't matter, for I have heard that same laugh so many times before, in so many different languages, and it's always the same: the sound of cheap liquor and seaport music, tinkling away like the sound of coins hastily shoved into a lady's cleavage, pressed tight inside a ratty bustier. The other laugh, the cackle I know so well, is probably buried in that abovementioned cleavage, because I can't hear it very clearly anymore. And Gomez, at his side, continues to bark "Yeth thir, yeth thir," and when I try to figure out what is going on, I begin to hear everything much more clearly: the tick-tock of the grandfather clock racing toward the next quarter-hour, followed by the laughter that once again is quickly stifled, and more words that I can hear easily now that they are coming from a room very close to my own, disrupting the silence. Only one flight of stairs separates them from my mother's room, and I pray to God that she is asleep, that she has somehow managed to drift off despite the moldy smell, despite the rats, despite everything.

And once again I hear my father's voice ring out: "We can't stay in this room, Gomez. Stay with the young lady here, I'll be back in a few minutes."

"Yeth, thir . . ."

"I have to find something more respectable than this. There must be a halfway decent room somewhere in this goddamn house." And the voice that sounds like tinkling coins repeats the phrase: "goddamn house." I think I detect a foreign accent, Polish perhaps, or maybe from somewhere else. It is an educated voice that is nonetheless betrayed by that tinkling, singsong laughter. My father's footsteps thump down the hallway, moving closer and closer. I pray that the lock on my door is not quite as rotted as the rest of the goddamn house, because I doubt Bertie remembers which room I decided to sleep in—why would he?—and I don't want him coming in here, for there are certain things he would be better off not seeing. And so I run toward the closet, to hide the things I've borrowed from the house. And I can hear my father's footsteps approaching.

"Aren't there any decent beds in this goddamn house?" A door very close to mine opens and then slams shut with a curse. "Nothing here, either, goddamnit. There's got to be some room . . ."

I can no longer hear the tinkling seaport laughter or Gomez's panting, either. What I do hear is the sound of Bertie's firm hand trying to open one door after another. Please, please, I beg silently. Just a few more minutes so that I can get myself out of these things.

What did they think I would do in a room full of trunks piled high with old clothes, crinoline petticoats, and lacy underthings, still bright white, and beautiful dresses from long ago? What did they think I would do in such a lonely house with so many treasures lying all around? I have almost managed to remove the dress. When the petticoats fall to my feet I am naked, completely exposed but for a lace garter belt that I can't quite manage to undo. This is what my father sees when he flings open the door, and this is what I see now in my jumbled dream: the half-open garter belt, with four ribbons dangling down. Garters that slap against my thighs like a cruel joke, concealing none of the things I wish to conceal. The very heavy silver mirror in my hand casts a glow of light from the left side of the dressing table all the way to the door, and I can see all of this in my dream, just as I can see my father's face, distorted from so much alcohol, unable to utter the one word that would make him feel so much better: "faggot." The word is stuck in his throat and sends a tremor through the candles illuminating the room but nevertheless, it does not emerge from his mouth. All he can do is rip the garter belt off my body, and as I watch it fall to the floor, I can hear Gomez cry out from two or three rooms away:

"I'm on my way, thir!" The word, that word Bertie cannot bring himself to say, remains stuck in his throat. In its place he unleashes a litany of curses, and then he calls out to Gomez:

"No, no, don't come here, goddamnit." And then, "Get that whore out of here!"

As Gomez escorts (or perhaps shoves) the lady from the seaport toward the front door, I can hear footsteps approaching. Meanwhile, I stupidly and idly wonder if the sound receding down the stairs is not the sound of coins clinking away in her cleavage but rather that of a bracelet. Yes, it must be a charm bracelet, I remember thinking to myself. What a time to be pondering such things. Then I hear Gomez and the whore reach the bottom of the stairs and the vestibule, though by now the sounds are nothing more than a very faint tinkling, accompanied by a frustrated sigh, for Gomez seems to be having trouble opening the locks on the front door. At that moment the door to my mother's room on the second floor flies open. Bertie is still upstairs with the garter belt in his hand and who knows how much cheap alcohol in his veins—the kind of alcohol that eats through a man's brain and drives him mad. Slowly he makes his way downstairs toward my mother. The whore, who can wait no longer for Gomez to open the front door, climbs out of a ground-floor window, unaware of the object that drops from her wrist and makes that dry tinkling sound as it hits the vestibule floor next to the grandfather clock. Alone now in the vestibule, Gomez looks up at Bertie and mouths a silent "Shall I go upthtairs, thir?" My father does not deign to even look at me as I stand a few yards away from him, so naked and so close. Bertie pushes me away and, running toward my mother, descends the stairs two at a time with that word still stuck in his throat. Other words, however, like "slut" and "whore," come out more easily, and my mother listens as she clings to the thick beams of the banister. Never before has she seen such a bizarre sight: a drunken man who clutches a garter belt as if it were a lethal weapon and then slaps it against her face, leaving the mark of four hooks on her cheek.

"Whore!" Bertie cries out, even though what he really wants to say is "faggot." "Whore, whore," he says, and my mother has to shove him away to keep him from striking her again. And where is Gomez? At first I think he must have gone away with the seaport whore, but the tick-tock of the grandfather clock forces me to look downstairs, and there he is, gasping for breath in the shadows, crouched down with his hands around his ears. Not his eyes but his ears, like a deaf ostrich, not doing a thing to stop his master from attacking Mama. I, however, know that I must do something, and I am still holding on to that heavy silver mirror. Brandishing it in my right hand, I begin to run downstairs. *Don't hurt her,* I think. *Don't touch her.* I'm almost there . . .

All of a sudden now, Bertie whirls around and runs toward me, as if the word caught in his throat has finally wrenched itself free, ready to jump out at me at any moment as he runs up the stairs to face me, naked and clutching the hand mirror, but he trips and now I see him fall backward down the stairs, and something that sounds like "faggot" finally comes out of his mouth. He said it! And then he tumbles down the staircase like an unstoppable giant ball, his head bouncing off the steps, one after the other, with sharp, dry thuds.

My mother starts to reach toward him, eyes wide open, to stop that massive body rolling past her. But then she hesitates.

"Step aside!" I want to scream out to her. "Let him tumble all the way down to hell!"

Another long second goes by, another moment of hesitation that lasts an eternity, and finally, as if she had heard my silent cry, I see Mama turn her head as the useless bulk rolls past her, thumping down the stairs until finally landing at the bottom. A dislocated wrist nestles amid the furniture shrouded in white bedsheets. And now I am the one who flies down the stairs in a single leap. Gomez is standing there by the clock, very close to me now, but his eyes are fixed on Mama as he covers his ears like someone fearing the onslaught of a bombing raid.

"Eeeeeooooh! I don't want to be here, I don't want to thee this," he cries as he turns his head toward the wall to avoid witnessing the spectacle. A minute can last such a long time, I think to myself. There's time enough for everything, everything. And there I am, standing next to Bertie, while my mother, still upstairs, calls out to me: "Dear God, dear God. Rafael darling, what have I done? What have I done?"

"Nothing, Mama, nothing at all, dear. Wait there, wait there, don't come down just yet."

Not even the rats dare come near me now, for they know when they should remain in the safety of their nests, in the squalor of their lairs.

I see and hear all of this during one long moment that lasts an eternity, until the clock chimes the hour, 4:45, drowning out one last beastly death rattle. It's over. It's all over. Yet before coming to a close, the dream flips over and jumps back out at me, gliding over detailed images like the precise position of Gomez, his eyes fluttering up toward Mama once again as he calls out, "Oh, madam!" Then he curls up into a little ball, like an orphaned dog, in a dark corner of the room. The dream does not bother to stop and focus on my mother, nor does it stop to focus on the cheap charm bracelet from the seaport lying next to the grandfather clock downstairs, because it has moved on, leaping over so many little details—forty years of lies and false accusations. The dream does, however, very tastelessly and noisily linger over certain idle conversations. "How would you like to hear the story of a very bad girl? Oh no, 'girl' is just a manner of speaking—we all know that little Elisa was already past forty when everything happened . . . but to me she'll always be a little girl. Now, how would you like to hear what they're saying around town? A very curious story about the death of Bertie Molinet. That night, one of the family servants was in the house . . . oh, what was his name? Sánchez or Gomez or something like that. Well, he saw everything, and as you might guess, he let a few details slip out here and there, to anyone who would listen. He swears that he was looking right at the staircase, at Bertie's body, at Elisa . . . yes, yes, I know they said it was an unfortunate accident, that he was very drunk and that there was nothing she could have done about it. That, at least, is what little Rafael said under oath, but nobody outside of the police believed a word of it, because that little queer simply adores his mother."

The dream leaps forward without further ado, and quickly lands in my little rented room in Tooting Bec, South London. That is when I hear my own voice: "Marvelous. What a marvelous idea to ingest all my sleeping pills in a fabulously expensive hotel that looks just like a movie set. That way, I can die like a gentleman. Excellent idea, Rafael Molinet, for that is the whole point, isn't it? To die exactly as you have lived, beyond your means. Oscar Wilde *dixit* . . ."

It is all so very confusing, as the worst nightmares always are, and for this reason I almost think that I am dead, not asleep—after all, don't they always say that our lives flash before our eyes like a wild and crazy dream just before we die? That is what is happening to me, without a doubt: Suddenly, my entire life is being replayed here in this hotel, blow by blow—an accident that nobody believes was really an accident and a woman declared guilty by a bunch of idle gossipers, because it is so much fun to turn a simple accident into cold-blooded murder. So much gossip, so much conjecture, so much speculation . . . Why, both stories involve a bracelet. How can it be? All the same ingredients are present. For this reason I try my hardest to retain all that I have dreamed, all that I have held back for so many years. I want to hold on to each and every detail as vividly as they appeared in my mind's eye just a few moments ago. And with the clarity of the inevitable, I suddenly sense that I will soon wake up and be overwhelmed by that precarious sensation that always follows the dream state, a feeling that will slowly dissipate as I try to cling to the things I have seen—images, sounds, comments, the tinkling sounds of laughter, a charm bracelet. But it will be useless, for everything will come apart and disappear without a trace into the drain of my conscious state.

When I awaken, all I know is that I have made some kind of strange connection between the deaths of my father, Bertie Molinet, and Jaime Valdés. But by the time I open my eyes, the memories have already retreated back to where they came from, and it is Mercedes Algorta who comes to mind. Nobody else.

The People One Meets at a Spa Hotel

1. Miss Guêpe

Miss Guêpe lives in a yellow room. The walls are yellow, as are the many fabrics used for curtains and sofa. The flower vases are reserved exclusively for narcissus. The stationery has a decidedly vanilla hue to it, and the framed pictures on the wall offer reproductions of camels, a few geese, desert dunes, and on occasion an image of a Mandarin Chinese in full traditional dress. All of these images, in any event, are very yellow.

Miss Guêpe feels very strongly about the importance of ambience, especially when it comes to the place where a person carries out his principal activities. A person who surrounds himself with various shades of blue, for example, is likely to become icy and distant. Green, on the other hand, tends to be calming—perhaps too calming, according to Miss Guêpe, who feels it may inspire excessive complacency. Yellow, however, combines joy with good taste, discretion with brio, character with conscientiousness. In short, yellow is the ideal color for the director and driving force behind the operations at L'Hirondelle d'Or.

For ten years now Miss Guêpe has been charting the destiny of LH'O, which is what she calls the hotel in the interest of verbal economy. They have not been easy years. When a respected chain of small luxury hotels called upon her to look after LH'O, nobody would have bet a dime on this type of vacation resort. The building was interesting—somewhat unusual and certainly not lacking in personality, but it was located in the middle of Nowhere, on the edge of a desert, which meant that its local clientele could only consist of jackals, vipers, or scavenger birds—and not in the metaphorical sense. Nevertheless, the executives of this hotel chain decided that the time had come to invest in a new kind of secret hideaway that, according to the very visionary, almost prophetic minds of the gurus of the hotel business, had the potential to become a very profitable venture indeed. All the trade publications seemed to suggest that the wealthy people of the world would soon become increasingly inclined to play down their fortunes and live as discreetly as possible— the opposite of what everyone did in the 1980s. Very soon, they predicted, chic vacationers would want to hide out like bunny rabbits in pleasant and exceedingly remote locations where the only people they saw were like-minded souls who had already caught on to this trend of reclusion and retreat from the world. "Where are you going for spring vacation?" They would ask one another. "Oh goodness, someplace in the middle of Nowhere where nobody can see us, where we can spend all day in flip-flops and ratty T-shirts. We just can't take all the craziness anymore . . ."

And so, Miss Guêpe accepted the challenge back in 1987, even though there would be more than a few kinks to iron out along the way. Not just because ostentation and exhibitionism still reigned supreme when it came to vacations, but also because two additional phenomena had yet to take place. Both would have a decisive role in the fate of L'Hirondelle d'Or. The first was a series of international scandals, misfortunes, and fiascos that drove many "important" types to "go undercover" when traveling. The attitude was something along the lines of "I don't want them to notice me or analyze me. I am sick and tired of the paparazzi trying to find out everything about me down to the price of my ties," and it was rampant. The second phenomenon was a fortuitous accident that occurred when L'Hirondelle was little more than a peaceful little hotel in an exotic corner of Morocco, with no particular claim to fame to grab the interest of the wealthy vacationing public. But then one day, shortly after putting the finishing touches on the hotel's luxurious yet understated décor, just after securing the services of an Algerian chef whose specialty was haute Middle Eastern cuisine, just when everything was in place for the first round of guests (perhaps not the most illustrious people, but certainly an acceptable lot), the water jets in the swimming pool began to cough up the foulest, ghastliest liquid, a stinking, red muck that recalled the very worst biblical curses. Miss Guêpe nearly had a nervous breakdown, for this horrific substance flowed out in thick, copious spurts, seeping into everything like a giant river of blood destined to tarnish the hotel's outstanding reputation forevermore. It was at this pivotal moment that Miss Guêpe decided to risk everything by implementing an extremely risky plan that would decide the fate of the establishment—and very possibly turn it into a most coveted vacation spot.

For three days the employees watched anxiously as the directrice shut herself off in her office, where she proceeded to communicate with them and the rest of the outside world exclusively by telephone. The employees with the most attuned ears would press the above-mentioned extremities against her door and listen as she talked, sometimes in German and very often in very hesitant English. Once, they actually heard her utter a curse in Italian. Through the door they also noted very long periods of silence, which seemed to suggest that the directrice was using these hours to carry out complicated calculations or research.

By the time she finally emerged from her self-imposed isolation, everything had changed. Word spread that her first move had been to place a phone call to a water expert in the city of Fez, since Fez was a very popular tourist destination, and he assured her that since time immemorial the red clay of the region was renowned for its high mineral content. As such, it was a magical remedy for the most diverse array of maladies—according to the man from Fez, the red muck was one of the wonders of the world, and he added that if the substance had indeed emanated from the ground beneath L'Hirondelle d'Or in such a spontaneous fashion, praise be to Allah. Evidently, this phenomenon had occurred for some very powerful reason that Miss Guêpe would be wise not to ignore.

Religious convictions aside, Miss Guêpe, a native of Switzerland raised in the strictest Calvinist tradition, who only considered herself moderately religious, did indeed take this as a kind of sign—from Allah, from God, or whoever looked over these details. And so she decided that the time had come to change direction, especially after her first and very faltering steps. She would now dedicate her energies to an entirely different kind of hotel venture.

To everyone's surprise, the very first thing she did was fire the Algerian chef specializing in haute Middle Eastern cuisine and hire a new culinary director, an expert in low-calorie, health-conscious fare. From her office, connected to the outside world by nothing but a single telephone and her superior hotel-management instincts, Miss Guêpe had ascertained that luck was on her side. She didn't have to be a rocket scientist to put two and two together—on the one hand, she had a thick red clay liquid spewing out from her beautiful gardens, and on the other hand, she knew that a hedonistic fervor was taking over the world—this, at least, was what she read in all the hotel-industry surveys she pored over so assiduously in her free time. Very well: She had never been much of a beauty, nor did she believe in nonsense like facial creams and youth serums, much less the wondrous powers of the sulfur waters bubbling out from her recently unveiled pool. But that didn't matter. Everyone else believed. People were willing to pay a small fortune for treatments that promised health and beauty, and they were even willing to travel to the edge of the desert to stay at an extravagant hotel like L'Hirondelle d'Or in order to avail themselves of these amenities.

And so this initially unwelcome discovery was what turned LH'O into a sanctuary of health and well-being, a well-oiled machine that ran according to such precise schedules that the guests had no choice but to forget about their frenetic lives in the city, for a few days at least, as they smeared their faces with muds of the deepest red and various other hues. The black mud, for example, was added a bit later on—and though it was not exactly authentic, it was certainly quite imaginatively created, formulated with truly superb products that Miss Guêpe purchased from a Swiss pharmaceutical company. And so, plastered from head to toe in these invigorating salts—and tightly controlled by a mealtime discipline that successfully married nutritional virtue and *cordon bleu* excellence—the guests lived in a state not dissimilar to bliss. Silence, routine, peace, and order: Miss Guêpe was there to take care of them.

Miss Guêpe's method, it should be noted, was radically different from that of the many other rigorously healthy spa hotels that had recently become so popular, especially in the United States. At the American spas, discipline was inflicted by smiling yet inflexible supervisors who directed the guests' activities with hands-on authority: First we go to the gym, then the massage room, and now, sir, a glass of carrot juice, and on and on like that. The guardian angels of L'Hirondelle, however, made themselves very wonderfully absent, being native residents who would never dream of interfering with the guests. As such, Miss Guêpe was able to avoid hiring energetic masseuses or chirpy restaurant hosts who recommended the fennel mousse over the cucumber puree. Miss Guêpe had eliminated all that blah-blah-blah, and replaced it with her long, invisible hand, taking care of everything behind the scenes. This very wise method was very clearly enumerated in a plaque of the hotel's ten commandments that Miss Guêpe had placed on a wall in her office the day

L'Hirondelle opened for business. No guest would ever have the occasion to see it, as it was located in a very restricted area of the hotel, and in any event, the decalogue could easily be whittled down to two basic golden rules. One: Do everything possible to ensure the full relaxation of the guest, since that is the reason he or she has paid such a fortune to come here. Two: Control every element of the hotel without ever allowing yourself to be seen.

They say that once she had perfected this unique strategy—the first of its kind in hotel history—Miss Guêpe rested. That was when she decided to reserve this sacred yellow room for her own use. From there, she would direct the establishment with serenity and moderation, a serious challenge at any hotel and even more so at L'Hirondelle, an oasis in the middle of Nowhere, a place where every so often the unexpected mishap could escape Miss Guêpe's stringent controls. Like today, for example: We find Miss Guêpe sitting at her desk, talking on the telephone, issuing the most detailed of commands to the hotel staff despite the fact that this very morning a most unfortunate incident has come to pass, threatening the very perfect Swiss machine that governs everything at L'Hirondelle. And now this most regrettable incident—if that is, in fact, what we can call it—is sitting on top of her desk wrapped up in a thick plastic case.

"Do you know what this is, Karim?" she asks as she hangs up the phone and turns to the young man in the gardener's uniform nervously standing at attention before her. He is young, perhaps twenty-five, his dark face cracked by the sun. His velvety eyes reveal the great anxiety he feels at this moment.

"Do you know what this is?"

"A bat, *madame.*"

"And do you know where this bat was found, Karim?"

Karim looks down at the animal, which is lying in a surgical-style metal tray covered by a film of plastic. Despite the plastic, he is able to distinguish some very unpleasant things about the creature, such as a set of extremely sharp teeth and a hairy ear standing up on end like an accusatory finger pointing straight at him, slender and as stiff as a board. Karim feels that Miss Guêpe has gone a tad too far by placing the witness of his sin on her table and displaying it in a metal box as an exhibition of sorts. But he says none of this. He simply looks at her.

"This bat, Karim, met its death in the winter pool of L'HO," says the directrice, making use of the verbal economy for which she is renowned. Short, terse sentences, the briefest interactions possible, including reprimands. She has always found this to be the most effective approach.

"Drowned in the winter pool, Karim. We found him floating in the water this morning. I believe you and I have discussed the issue of rats before, have we not?"

Karim remembers the moment all too well, though he would much rather forget it. Miss Guêpe, however, wants to make sure that Karim knows exactly what she means, for it is extremely important. To add a bit of realism to her bizarre spectacle, Miss Guêpe removes the plastic seal so that she and Karim may look directly at the bat lying in his metal box. Miss Guêpe prods the animal with a wooden stick that Karim believes was once attached to an ice cream pop, but he cannot be sure. It may very well be an instrument specifically designed for examining the bodies of dead animals. The defunct bat's stiff ear is pointing, once again, straight at Karim when Miss Guêpe says:

"The rat, Karim."

Karim implores her with his velvety eyes, but Miss Guêpe is immune to velvety eyes. "The last time the pool was emptied, an enormous rat was found in the drain pipe. You remember that, I know you do."

Silence.

"Sucked in by the water pump," she adds. To freshen Karim's memory, she takes her stick and prods the rigid bat, which flips over in the box. Karim indeed remembers.

Curiously enough, he does not think of the stiff, swollen rat that had gotten sucked in by the water pump and trapped in a pipe—he thinks of Miss Guêpe's foot, which, on that distant occasion, had flipped the gummy cadaver on its side once they had extricated it from the pipe and placed it on the ground. And he remembers how she said to him, over and over again, "Karim, Karim. This is repulsive. It must not happen again. But it was an accident. You did not place the yellow tape around the pool to alert the guests that we were draining it, did you?"

"Yes, *madame,* I did."

"For it would have been a very dangerous oversight—"

"It was in place, *madame.*"

"—because if the yellow tape was not in place, Karim," Miss Guêpe continued as if she hadn't heard a thing, "this dead rat might be a guest of the hotel, and you would be held responsible."

Karim does not understand how a guest could possibly fit into a drainage pipe, but as is his manner, he says nothing. Of the previous incident, all he really recalls is that it involved a disgusting rat. Not that he is especially squeamish about vermin—after all, he had seen plenty of dead rats in his life, but none had ever been quite like that one: as big as a rabbit, with four pink paws facing up toward the sky and a head that the water pressure and the contours of the drain pipe had molded into the shape of an egg and whose two eyes very nearly jumped out from their sockets like little marbles: a pair of bright white, useless eyes that stared up at Karim as Miss Guêpe had continued talking.

"No more accidents, Karim," she had said. "I don't want to see one more rat, bird, bat, or even the tiniest insect in that swimming pool. I hope you understand what I am saying." Just in case he hadn't, she had nudged the dead animal's swollen body a bit more with her foot, and Karim had looked on as the animal's damp fur grazed the tip of Miss Guêpe's very sober shoe for a fleeting moment.

And now, the memories come flooding back into Karim's mind,

prompted by the sight of this new, diminutive witness of his sins lying on the table before him.

"It will not occur again, *madame*. I promise you."

"It will not occur again," Miss Guêpe repeats. Then she reaches out for the telephone, a sign the gardener interprets as permission to finally leave the room.

"Just a moment, Karim."

"Yes, *madame*."

Verbal economy is one of Miss Guêpe's most admirable qualities, but for the moment she is still staring at the bat. In one hand she holds the telephone that Karim believes to be the instrument of his liberation and with the other hand she makes a vague gesture toward the vermin on her desk.

"Take this thing and dispose of it in the incinerator, please." She hands him the metal tray, along with the ice cream stick she had been using as a pointer.

"Thank you, *madame*," Karim says.

"Once you have disposed of him, and only after you have washed your hands *very* well, will you please do me the favor of going to the kitchen?"

"Yes, *madame*."

"And please tell the chef that I need to speak with him. That is all. You may go now, Karim."

Karim walks away with the evidence of his crime in his arms, and as he closes the door behind him, he takes a moment to breathe deeply and feel a twinge of pity for the chef, who, like himself, has been summoned to the yellow room. He stops for a moment before starting down the stairs, and using the ice cream stick, he bundles the dead creature in the plastic wrapper. If anyone right at that moment were to ask him why he is doing such a thing, Karim would swear in the name of Allah and his prophet that it is for reasons of hygiene, for he knows full well that cleanliness is paramount at L'Hirondelle. But the real reason is that he can no longer bear the sight of that dead bat's stiff ear pointing at him. He walks down the service stairs toward the incinerator, enters the furnace room, opens a small door, and finally throws the animal into the fire. Only then does Karim remember that he must go to the kitchen and speak to the chef at once, because a call from the yellow room can only mean that he has committed a dire breach of conduct, a blunder as un-forgivable as Karim's, because Miss Guêpe normally communicates with mortals by telephone. If she has summoned the head chef for a personal audience it must mean that she has a very serious matter to discuss with him.

"Perhaps he burned the lamb that is to be served at dinner," Karim ventured to guess. "Poor guy." The bat crackles in the flames and Karim stands there pondering these things for a few more min-utes until the highly unpleasant odor of scorched flesh spurs him back into action and he slams the incinerator door with resolve. For as long as he is the gardener at L'Hirondelle d'Or, never again will anyone find a dead rat, bat, or any other creature anywhere near the mud baths or the winter solarium, the home of L'Hirondelle's cov-ered pool.

Other People One Might Meet at a Spa Hotel

2. Sánchez

> *When two rats are trapped in a 50cm x 50cm maze, they will inevitably end up copulating, even if they are of the same sex.*
>
> *When four rats (or five at the most) are trapped in a box together, each one will keep his distance, trying not to invade the territory of the others.*
>
> *When six rats are placed together in a box, sooner or later they will begin to eat one another. This is a scientifically proven truth.*

Proven or not, it is too hot to pay much attention to the science section of the Spanish newspaper *El País*. Sánchez quickly flips through the pages until he arrives at the classified ads, one of his very favorite sections of the newspaper:

> *Zenda, your prisoner, sadist sanctuary, 284-1870.*
>
> *Paloma, submissive, Greek, golden shower, black kiss, 878-4580.*
>
> *Sexual smorgasbord, full of surprises . . . 885-8788.*

What on earth was it about the number eight that gave it such pre-dominance in the adult section of the newspaper? Perhaps it is the roundest, softest, most sinuous number? Antonio Sánchez López adores his daily trip through the sexual services offered in the news-paper, for that is where he gauges the level of misery humans have sunk to, an old habit acquired in the early days of his career as a scandalmonger.

Mature widow, generous bosom, 388-8864
Victor, real men only, 980-6899

Every day there is something new. He knows how very wildly the supply varies, for he has been poking his nose into lowlife habits like these for years now, and not because he is interested as a client. He is attracted strictly as a spectator of misfortune, and also because these pages often provide good material for his radio show. In the be-ginning, his stories were mostly about anonymous scandals, but not anymore—nowadays it is far more profitable to talk about politics and public life. People didn't care what he talked about as long as he made sure to dig up some dirt on the rich and powerful. That was the way things were now. Sánchez had changed considerably over the past few years, thanks to all his success, but his method was the same as ever. Every morning, after a relatively thorough perusal of the top stories in the newspaper, he would always save a few extra moments to revel in the detritus of his earliest radio career triumphs. By now it had become a kind of routine—he was like an old pan-handler so accustomed to eating cockroaches that he continued to fry them up even though he could easily afford caviar.

It is too hot for him to think much more, however, and his eyes wander from the printed word over to the calves of Ana Fernández de Bugambilla, who is lying beside him gleaming from head to toe with Ambre Solaire SPF 15. Her body still exudes the scent of their siesta-hour sex from a few minutes earlier, and Sánchez abandons his reading to caress his favorite contour, the smooth hollow where her lower back curves into her buttocks. She turns, submissively, a perfect little cat who knows just how to feign divine satisfaction:

"Daaarling . . ."

3. Ana

The latest bikinis are nothing but a nuisance when it comes to sun-bathing and swimming. At least this is what Ana Fernández de Bugambilla thinks. Perhaps Grace Kelly or Rita Hayworth—or any other woman from the days when women sacrificed all in the name of fashion—endured such discomfort without complaint, but not Ana. Wires are everywhere, digging into her ribs in a very admirable attempt to accentuate her nonexistent cleavage. Then, a bit further down, she wears a pair of micro-shorts covered by a tiny skirt, which takes years to dry when wet, threatening its mistress with, at best, a terrible cold and, at worst, an case of cystitis. The result, however, is stunning: luminous bikini, shapely legs, stomach, chest, neck (all held very tensely so as not to encourage the formation of wrinkles), and, finally, the face, which is hidden by a pair of extremely dark glasses that, if nothing else, prevent the outside world from reading her thoughts.

"Oh, the depths to which you have sunk, Ana," she tells herself with a newly acquired bitterness. "Good Lord, the things you do when you let your hair down," she would say to herself if she were to analyze all the unthinkable transgressions she has committed in the few months since her marriage dissolved. But philosophical analysis is not her style. She is far better off not thinking, not drawing any conclusions, because an explosion of thoughts might lead her to wonder something along the lines of:

"Good Lord, what on earth am I doing here at L'Hirondelle d'Or with a man like Antonio Sánchez?"

No, no. Too much thinking is an unpleasant and dangerous activity, as unpleasant and as dangerous as the exercise of trying to analyze oneself with the cold perspective of an outside observer. Because when we indulge in the audacity of philosophizing, we run the risk of looking at ourselves from the outside, of staring with shock at someone we never thought capable of such shameful behavior. This logic is precisely what keeps Ana from thinking about what has just happened only a few moments ago, during siesta time. Some things are better off forgotten. Like the image of two bodies writhing in a tangle of damp bed sheets and Ana telling herself, *Oh, it's so hot, it's so hot . . . don't look, Ana, don't look at that messy, sticky clump of hair, don't look at that drop of sweat rolling down his nose and hovering at the tip, threatening to fall off . . .*

Oh, gravity can be so very cruel to faces when they are distorted by desire, and the face that gazed down at her during siesta time was most definitely cruel and ghoulish: bulging lips, veins pulsating at the forehead, and then that droplet of sweat, poised less than an inch from her own lips. *I don't want to swallow it,* she had said to herself. *Good Lord, no. I must figure out some way to turn around, turn my face away . . .* After that, a change in position: Ana on all fours, Ana astride a greasy body: . . . *Oh, there must be some place for me to look. Maybe I should just shut my eyes so I don't have to see anything.* It just didn't seem possible—was that really Ana perched doggy-style, back arched, whispering silly things she must have heard in some movie? A couple of gasps (*Should I say this or that? Will that sound all right?*) followed by, "Oh, yes, yes, give me more, like that, like that! Yes, yes!" And then more gasps. Good Lord. Much better not to think, not to remember anything. And she remembers nothing, except for the one sentence that sums it all up:

"Oh, the depths to which you have sunk, Ana."

She and Sánchez are inside the solarium, where the mud baths are administered. As such, the Ambre Solaire SPF 15 isn't really necessary, nor is her haute couture bikini—any old rag would have done just fine for the solarium. In places like this, nobody ever stares at you. Nobody cares enough to check out their fellow hotel guests smeared with dark mud as they walk back to their lounge chairs, where they spread their arms and legs wide open, as per the instructions of the mud-treatment supervisors. A giant cupola, exactly like the glass dome that crowns the winter pool, protects the guests from the outside world. To the left sits a hot-water Jacuzzi, and to the right, thick bubbles of red clay come gushing out of a pool or a fountain of some sort. Ana wouldn't dream of going near the thing, for she has no desire to look like those Germans frolicking about like red-faced pigs in the mud, even if smearing yourself with mud is part of the ritual here. *Relax your body and mind, don't think about anything at all,* she tells herself. But it is so unbelievably hot, and the flickering reflection of the fountain dances above on the glass cupola, as do the rather odd-looking shadows of the people down below. First there is Antonio Sánchez, then Bernardo and Bea, and just a bit further away, Mercedes Algorta, who greeted them most amiably before settling down on a lounge chair at the other end of the solarium. Everyone is spread out, separated by the silence, and nobody says a word. Their shadows may come together on the ceiling, but not down here, thank God, Ana thinks as she looks upward, not daring to look down, left, or right, not even now, when it is all over. She has passed the siesta test with her lover, and she is finally free to relax in the mud room in her underwire bikini and her dark sunglasses that make her inscrutable to all. The moment is tranquil, but Ana still cannot bring herself to look toward her left, for she is deathly afraid of seeing Sánchez, of seeing his feet resting atop the lounge chair next to her, and especially of seeing that big toe of his. He has just slathered mud all over his body—not the red variety but the black mud, which is purifying, vitamin-enriched, and highly restorative. The pasty potion covers him from thigh to foot—all the parts that Ana does not want to see. The one thing, however, that has escaped the mud slick is his big toe (*Why?* she wonders. *For what disgusting reason?*). It is a tall, proud, naked protuberance. It is capped by a thick, dark toenail that hypnotizes Ana as it moves back and forth—for some reason she cannot tear her eyes away from the frighteningly hornlike nail that rises to attention as her lover (*My lover. Good Lord, this man is my lover*) turns the page of the newspaper he has been reading for over half an hour. Once again he stops at page 25, the science section, and he reads the item:

"When four rats (or five at the most) are trapped in a box together, each one will keep his distance, trying not to invade the territory of the others."

4. Bernardo

The lounge chairs are lined up along the perimeter of the mud baths, like the keys of a grand piano. The majority are white (that is, empty); only five are black (occupied). Every so often a waiter comes around in response to a request or to place a tray of honey-colored drinks garnished with a sprig of something—mint, possibly—on the low tables nearby. The silence is all-encompassing. One lounge chair is set apart from the rest. On it Mercedes Algorta flips through a magazine. A bit closer to Ana and Sánchez, Bea and Bernardo recline. Bea is currently executing a series of extremely challenging abdominal exercises. Next to her, Bernardo Salat snoozes away.

The heat doesn't do him justice. In colder weather, dressed in street clothes, Bernardo exudes a kind of dignity that the heat denies him. Now, his damp hair sticks to the back of his neck and there is a white, hairless region extending from his knees down to his ankles, revealing the merciless nature of knee socks—only the very best and most expensive kind have such a curious depilatory effect. The truth is, he looks an awful lot like a half-plucked chicken. But there he is dozing away, oblivious (or trying to remain oblivious) to the bathers and their flirtations. His sunglasses are reflected on the ceiling as two luminous, immobile blobs; he wishes his thoughts were as faint. After all, this isn't the time to think about anyone or anything outside of this place. No, no—nothing faraway; nothing related to work or family. He should just think boring, trivial thoughts. Yes, that is indeed the best antidote for all concerns, not to think. But not thinking proves practically impossible. He opens an eye to find one leg leaning at a sharp angle in one direction and the other stretched out in front of him, affording him a bird's eye view of his lower body. "Nice bathing suit," he says to himself. His suit is covered with zebras: red zebras, blue zebras, white zebras. He then thinks about how it was his wife who gave it to him the day before as he was leaving for the airport, but he avoids any further reflection on the topic because he recognizes the early formation of a nagging thought and wants to suppress it before it can evolve any further. "Items of clothing cannot speak," he assures himself. "They do not tattle, nor do they run around telling stories at random." Of course, it *does* make him feel guilty that he is using his wife's gift for a lover's tryst. It feels as if he is tempting fate.

Bernardo changes positions. That is the way nagging thoughts are when you try and relax. Just when you want to think about nothing but trivial things, they bombard you with the most inconvenient ideas.

Let's see: golf. That is a fine topic. Sánchez's putt, his drive, his swing . . . Bernardo needs to think about something completely irrelevant. Like teeing off with Sánchez—a pastime he doesn't particularly enjoy, confirmed once again earlier this morning out on the course. No, no, it doesn't entertain him in the least. Antonio S. is an important man, intelligent even, but as a golf partner he's a pain in the ass. "You can really tell," Bernardo said to himself, "that he's a newcomer to the sport, because he embraces it with the fanaticism of the recent convert. He is so tireless, so persistent, my God, it's enough to drive a person mad . . ."

This, as it turns out, is not a very pleasant thought, but it *is* something to occupy his head for a while.

"Now, remember. Above all, above everything else, no matter

what happens over these few days, you absolutely must tolerate this, Bernardo."

This is what he says to himself. And then, just as a pleasant wave of sluggishness washes over him, almost putting him to sleep, he is assailed by another stream of uncomfortable thoughts that have been waiting around for just this kind of defenseless moment. First thought: They picked the wrong hotel. That is problem number one. But it won't do them much good to turn around and leave, not at this point. Nor does it seem wise to concoct a bizarre story for the benefit of the casual and potentially nosy observer. *We are all stuck here together,* he thinks. After packing the zebra swimming trunks that his wife, Myriam, gave him, he comes all the way to this god-forsaken hotel with Bea, his lover, and the first person they run into is Mercedes Algorta, his wife's first cousin. How on earth will he be able to prevent her from mentioning the coincidence when she returns to Madrid? He can just picture it: "Guess who I ran into in Morocco? You'll never guess . . ." Shit. There is nothing worse than getting yourself exposed on account of an old, worn-out love affair, a passion that ended ages ago. Oh, Bernardo . . .

The African sun burns hot even in October, even though they are not in the great outdoors but rather inside a giant greenhouse, in a big glass box that has them all trapped inside: Sánchez, reading his newspaper; Ana, trying hard not to think; Mercedes, dozing away. All of them are just sitting around doing their own thing, which is one of the great advantages of visiting a spa hotel. Body-worshipping, Bernardo muses, is the only social activity that allows a person to say nothing, to feel no obligation to chatter away constantly. What a relief, he thinks, because it is so hot he can't bear the thought of having to talk to Sánchez about golf or Bea about much of anything. Unnecessary Bea. But undumpable as well. Love takes up where knowledge leaves off, someone once said, but Bernardo knows better. After several years of extramarital affairs, he has finally come to the conclusion that habit is what keeps things going between two people: habit, unfulfilled promises, and all the stupid sweet nothings people say in bed, sentiments that last no longer than an erection. Sentiments that he usually forgets by the time he gets into the shower. But they are so true, so heartfelt during that brief interlude when all romantic lies are true. *Real romantic love can only be true in fleeting moments,* he thinks. *I love you* now, *I need you* now . . . *it all happens in instants.* Who was the naïve person who came up with the idea that romantic feelings could produce eternal truths? A fool, no doubt.

Bernardo tries to peer out above his motionless body, toward the far end of the Jacuzzi, above the mud pools. Look, look at the multicolored zebras, he tells himself: Some of them are blue; others red. They seem so innocent all wrinkled up like that from the water. *What a lovely pair of bathing trunks,* he thinks.

5. Bea

Lying face-up in her lounge chair, her arms stretched out wide and her legs tense, Bea idly thinks of a friend she hasn't seen in ages, J. P. Bonilla. Physical exercise is so good for the mind: It organizes the thoughts, and butt-lifting repetitions help, with their very useful, military-style cadence: one, breathe in; two, breathe out. Very slowly now, once again: one, breathe in; two . . . As she does this, Bea thinks about J. P. Bonilla and his voice, which she heard on her answering machine just minutes before she left Madrid.

"Come on now, what's the big deal? It's just a goddamn telephone message," she tells herself, but she cannot deny the fact that she is definitely intrigued, because it has been no less than three years since she last heard that voice. And that can only mean one thing: money.

"Darling," the voice on the machine said. "Call me as soon as you get in. I've got something fabulous for you, something very important, a proposal I know you are going to love . . ." Breathe in, breathe out, breathe in, breathe out.

With the merciless eye of a livestock handler, Bea examines the skin on her forearm and then performs six or seven vigorous repetitions . . . five . . . six . . . seven. And she continues to think.

Back in the days when she acted as a kind of deep throat for a society columnist named Juan Pedro Bonilla, her muscles had not yet grown soft. She would tell him about absolutely everything—confidentially, of course—and he would publish the information in his column: illicit love affairs, forthcoming marital separations, the price tags of the costliest divorces, imminent scandals, blow-by-blow accounts of the private lives of public figures. Bonilla didn't pay much, but there was a kind of sweet revenge about selling out your friends for next to nothing. After all, it was the shallow nineties and people did pretty much whatever they wanted. So what if the fishbowl practically exploded as everyone madly whispered about who could possibly be the snake that had leaked such-and-such information to the press? Who was their informer? the exposed would wonder. "Oh my God!," they would cry. "Can you believe it? My private life all over the papers! What a nightmare. When is all this madness going to end?" Et cetera. It didn't matter much to her. Bea knew that nobody would ever find out that she had been the lady with the loose tongue, and in the end—shit, who the hell cared? Some people would say she was actually doing her VIP friends a favor—after all, they would do anything to get the paparazzi to pay attention to them. In those sweet old days you were a nobody if you didn't appear at least twice a week in a magazine.

Her chest. Her chest is the one thing that is still in tiptop shape, thanks to Mother Nature and a disciple of Dr. Pitanguy who has since moved on to more fertile and lucrative lands. Her breasts are a veritable gift from the gods. Nobody can tell they are fake, for they are round and only moderately stiff—all she has to do to soften them up a bit is give them a little squeeze: placing them between the palms, pressing hard, and then releasing, deep breath, hands on the elbows . . . that is the formula for achieving the perfect level of firmness. Truth to be told, however, her breasts haven't been put to much use lately, and as for J. P. Bonilla, she lost track of him a few years ago. More or less around the time he gave up his job as a greedy gossip hawker so that he could focus all his professional energies on a publishing house specializing in big commercial books. *They're all living like kings,* Bea thinks as she tightens her muscles. *The people who expose human misery, the scandal brokers, they're all kings. Just look at Antonio Sánchez, Juan Bonilla . . .* It must have been four or five years ago when her friend J.P. made the leap to respectability. And wasn't that the same year that he had asked her to marry him, the little sweetheart? Poor adorable J. P. Bonilla and his Armani suits—he had them in mustard yellow, leaf green, and a kind of drowned-mouse gray. Back then, of course, she would have had to be downright desperate to settle for a specimen like J.P., but of course that was before her flesh had begun to sag.

The calves are the most forgiving part of the body. A bit of pointing and flexing of the toes is all they require to maintain their shape: point-flex, point-flex, point-flex . . . someone recently told her that J. P. Bonilla is now considered quite the catch among her recently separated friends. Desperate is more like it, though. Desperado—it sounds almost respectable. Bea thinks about that group a lot. Recriminations aside (and she has certainly issued her share of them), she cannot deny that her ongoing affair with Bernardo Salat, which cannot even be considered a romance (too many years, too many hard feelings), has at least saved her from that dismal purgatory inhabited by recently separated women—the ever-growing legions of women without husbands whose numbers are somehow inversely proportional to the number of available men.

A little circle created by the feet, toes pointed as far as they can go, is all that is necessary to activate the circulation in the legs: twice to the right, twice to the left. She can't deny it—if it weren't for the fact that Bernardo trotted her out every so often, she too would belong to the club of the desperadoes, working all the cocktail parties and galas, condemned to attend even the most insignificant of social events. Those ubiquitous fortysomethings: Tuesday night, eight to nine-thirty, holding back yawns at some dreadful lecture. Thursday, dragging the heels to the latest it-girl's reading of her trashy novel. Monday, lunching at Guisando "to see who I bump into." Wednesday, opening night at the theater. Such a monumental effort, all in the hopes of securing the occasional invitation to a private party. But it pays off: Every so often you do end up getting invited to something. The method works: If you want to stay in circulation you have to be out there circulating.

Now it is time for the facial muscles, the most delicate of all. The face must first be coated with a generous layer of cream so as to protect the skin when one opens the mouth wide to form a giant but silent *A* followed by a giant but silent *O*. "Pa-va-rot-ti" was her favorite word for exercising her lips. Bea doesn't care if anyone caught her making these strange faces. After all, why would anyone bother looking at her? Everyone else here looks just as ridiculous as she does. She looks to her left and sees Antonio S. reading something about rodents. With difficulty she makes out the words: *"When six rats are placed together in a box, sooner or later they will begin to eat . . . one . . . another."*

Damn, she thinks. *I really am getting old. I can't see a goddamn thing.* She decides to turn away. Clearly, she is better off working on another useful word to keep those mouth muscles firm and youthful-looking: "U-til-i-tar-i-an" is extremely effective. The prolonged *u* syllable, the *til* that forces the contraction of the throat muscles, the *i* . . .

The door opens. Bea is unable to see who it is, because her facial exercises must be practiced in a supine position and she is lying on her back. But a fleeting reflection of light flashes through the rotunda, and two shadows are suddenly projected upon the glass ceiling. She easily recognizes the first shadow, for it is wearing a hat, and so it can only be the picturesque and solitary individual who wished them *Gute Nacht* the previous evening in the restaurant. The other shadow, however, is much bulkier, its movements agile and athletic. Bea completes her second "u-til-i-tar-i-an" and gets up to see who has cast such a promising shadow.

A very good omen, she thinks. *A new guest. Hopefully, an interesting one. There are so few of us in this little rats' nest, and we all know one another far too well.*

The Arrival of an Unexpected Guest

AN UNEXPECTED GUEST ARRIVING AT A SHOOTING SHOULD BE careful to observe the following simple rules:

1. Do not talk either at the firing point or when walking to your position.

2. Ask the person shooting where exactly he would like you to stand or sit (ideally it will be directly behind the gun and fairly near him).

3. After the shooting host and keepers alike will appreciate a guest who can say after a drive "There are so many in front and so many behind."

—Debrett's *Etiquette and Modern Manners*
(London, 1995)

The New Guest (as observed by Molinet and Bea)

PAPRIKA AND DILL
Cocktail parties, dinners and other social occasions
(Excellence Need Not Be Expensive)

Madrid, October 20

Dearest Uncle Rafael—

If memory serves me right, this will be my fifth fax to you in the last few days. My God, I haven't written this much since elementary school. Nowadays, all I ever seem to write are checks, and I suspect you can tell: I have a telegraphic writing style, impossible penmanship and an illegible signature.

But anyway . . . where were we? All right. Now you want some information on a man who turned up at the hotel a few days ago, and just as I have done in previous faxes (fax no. 1 on Valdés, Mercedes, etc., no. 2 on the four musketeers, Sánchez, Bea, Bernardo, Ana etc.), I will give you a bit of a profile on the new character (speaking of which, what the hell is going on in that hotel? It's like an outpost of the Gran Vía! If all of Madrid had agreed to spend a week losing weight and dropping dirhams in the same remote paradise, they couldn't have possibly planned it any better!). But anyway. To return to our new guest. If it is Santiago Arce (and I suspect it is, given the physical description), I will tell you this: The guy is (in this order):

    1. fabulously handsome,

    2. recently separated from an impossible woman, and

    3. a screenwriter for the movies,

something that until now was not especially glamorous, but given items 1 and 2, plus the fact that his movie got made

with next to no budget and turned out to be a giant and totally unexpected hit, he has become the boy wonder of the
moment. Photographed everywhere. We all have our fifteen minutes of fame, Rafamolinet, what can I tell you, and
I think Arce is ready to take full advantage of his. The
movie that catapulted him into the spotlight is called *Under
the Baobab*—I still haven't seen it, but even my stupidest
girlfriends tell me it is utterly marvelous and "makes you
feel like he's talking to you and only to you." The critics despise him, naturally—they don't say he's a bad moviemaker;
they just call him a "phenomenon of the masses," a slightly
strange way of saying, "All right, just maybe we'll forgive
you for being such a success." He, on the other hand, seems
just adorable. No matter who you ask, the answer is always
the same: "Santiago Arce? Darling, he is just adorable."

The truth is, I actually think they're right. He's the kind
of man everyone wants to protect—you want to wrap a big
scarf around his neck or knit him a sweater so he doesn't
catch cold. I don't know what the hell a baobab is, but I
must find out just in case I happen to run into him at a
party somewhere. Speaking of which, what do you think
he's doing all alone at a hotel in Morocco? Are you sure he
doesn't have some big-eyed blonde with him, or else some
BMW-driving intellectual babe to keep him company? It
just seems so odd. Maybe in your next fax you can fill me in
a little about what exactly is going on down there. To date
you have done nothing but squeeze me like a lemon for information, and I have had to write endless faxes providing
you with all sorts of details, and yet you haven't offered the
least little bit of gossip in exchange. For example, I would be
very interested in knowing various things about your four
players—first impressions, comments, and a bit of that observation you are clearly so very good at. For example:

A) At any moment have you seen Bea show contempt for Sánchez in public?

B) Has Bernardo spoken to Mercedes at all or does he avoid her like the plague? (He must have gotten quite a shock when he first saw her there, it must have been tremendous—the poor fool actually thinks nobody knows that he's been having an affair with Bea for the past seven years . . . anyway, as an Italian would say, *ma figurate*!)

C) I am also interested in knowing about Ana. How is she holding up? I feel terrible for her—she is going through the awful phase of being recently separated. And she has the brain of a mosquito and is sooo inexperienced . . . oh, the idiotic things people do in such circumstances! Oh! One other question: was the information I sent you in Faxes No. 3 and 4 useful in giving you an idea of each of them individually? You haven't said a thing, Uncle Rafael, and that is really unfair of you. Now, I want to hear some dish on Santiago Arce, everything he does and if he talks to anyone else and

DURING THE DAYS that followed Mr. Arce's arrival, life at L'Hirondelle had still been as dull as ever. Nothing happened. At least, nothing that Molinet had been able to observe from the outside. Of course, there was a bit of flurry for a moment or two that first morning when the moviemaker made his entrance in the mud bath area. The fishbowl was certainly rattled, and Molinet was on hand to take note of it all.

"Jesus Christ! Will you look who just walked in?"

"Santiago Arce! This is getting to be like a company Christmas party . . . Let me guess—he figured nobody in Madrid could have possibly ever heard of this place."

"Shit, join the club. God, I feel like we're in an Agatha Christie novel. I just hope we don't have a dead man on our hands at the end . . ."

Bit by bit, however, things return to their normal, tranquil state at L'Hirondelle, a hotel that has a way of anesthetizing its guests— could it be something in the mud? The 1,500 calories per day? The lack of human contact? Nothing at all happens here. Even Molinet is beginning to think that the very promising clash between the widow and the four musketeers has lost a bit of its sizzle. It has been a while since he last heard any caustic remarks; all everyone talks about is calories, Swiss chard, and the virtues of fennel. How is it possible that things have come to this?

In the long, deserted hallways of L'Hirondelle, where guests in terry-cloth robes occasionally emerge from the mud baths and walk among other guests in athletic clothes, no longer does anyone find it a nuisance to bump into other people at all hours of the day. Molinet has always felt that there is nothing quite so bothersome as an "acquaintance" at a hotel, a person with whom one feels obliged to chat all the time, but neither Bea nor Bernardo nor any of their friends seems to mind. They are all far too busy, and that, of course, is because their time here has been programmed down to the minute. And so, when they do run into one another on the way out of their morning workouts or their evening mud sessions, they just wave as everyone else at the hotel does, with the same deferential indifference.

Everything transpires in a very serene manner. Everyone does their own thing far from Molinet's ears, which are as alert as ever, although they haven't heard a damn thing lately. As such, Molinet has taken to observing his fellow guests from a certain window. Peering out over the multicolored vines, he can see the golf course, where he knows Bernardo and Antonio S. play every day at this hour.

Rafael Molinet keeps his distance from the golfers, preferring to observe them from his window. He feels tired just watching them leave so early in the morning, dressed up like two men on a holy mission. Instead of looking like two Tyroleans (thank God; it certainly would be the wrong moment for that), they wear brightly colored outfits, which makes it very easy for Molinet to locate them from any hotel window. Sometimes they are nothing but two dots—one red, one yellow—glowing on the horizon down at the far end of the course near a faraway palm tree.

Now, while some people keep busy playing golf, others use their time here to rest. Take Ana, for example, who lies down next to the Jacuzzi and forgets about everything. Behind her dark sunglasses, she puts all those torrid nights of passion out of her mind. Every so often she gets up a bit, but only to take a sip of Diet Coke in an effort to erase the taste of the repulsive kisses that still cling to the inside of her throat. And as many times as she can bear it—once, twice, a thousand times—she submerges her body in the clear waters of the Jacuzzi as if it were the Ganges and she were a very sinful Buddhist nun. What she does not like, however, are the mud baths. She feels there is something slightly obscene about the way the hotel guests wander around the area covered in all sorts of grotesquely colored mud—"from the days of the Romans" as claimed by a very large sign that she has read many times over out of pure boredom now that she has gone through all her reading material, including her gossip magazines and even the little leaflet inside the box containing her diet pills. She reads the sign yet again:

"The black muds are rich in zinc salts and are ideal for those with circulatory ailments," it explains. "They have also proven effective in cases of mild hair loss."

Could the case of Antonio Sánchez be described as mild? Could zinc possibly put a stop to the hair that seems intent on dwindling down to a little crown eternally beaded with little pearls of some greasy substance? At the very least, his head does look a bit more attractive with the coat of mud—it almost makes Ana want to take a healthy slab of the stuff and slather it on him one night to make his baldness (not his hair) disappear, like a Delilah reincarnate, silent and vengeful. Nevertheless, she remains where she is and takes a few more sips of Diet Coke.

Bea does not add any new activities to her boring routine today, either. For two days now she has been doing her exercises with significantly less brio than before—not because she has lost interest in her fitness regimen, but because she is afraid of being caught by surprise in an unorthodox pose. By the new guest, for example—a fascinating man whom Bea knows very little about, except that he writes screenplays and makes heartfelt movies that supposedly "make you feel like he's talking to you and only to you." At least that's what everyone says. Bea explains all of this to Ana, to fill her in a bit—Ana is always so clueless.

"An a-dorable boy," Bea adds, and it's true. All you have to do is look at him—he barely even looks like a writer. In her experience, writers are usually pasty-skinned weirdos who have phobias about traveling in elevators and who wear studiously wrinkled jackets, the type of men who yawn whenever they are not the topic of conversation. No, no—Arce is different. Bea can tell from all the photos she's seen of him in the magazines: Even the way he poses is different. Not once has she ever seen him photographed, like most writers, in front of a cluttered bookshelf or cradling his head with three fingers as if the wisdom contained in his brain was simply too heavy for his human neck to support. Santiago Arce looks more like an actor—an actor playing a writer. Not the usual actor who gets typecast as a novelist in the movies. He doesn't have any of Hugh Grant's wry cynicism or Anthony Hopkins's penetrating gaze, or Jeremy Irons's odd combination of sexy and sickly. Arce is strong, healthy, and innocent, and he has a square jaw and the kind of smile that reminds Bea of a cowboy from the Wild West. He is different, and original, and perhaps that is why she can't quite think of an exact comparison for him. All she can say is that he is adorable, adorable, a-dorable . . .

"And maybe," she says to herself, "just maybe he'll appear at my side and explain to me what the hell a baobab is."

But Santiago Arce does not appear. Not at the restaurant, not at the mud baths, and certainly not at the golf course or the tennis courts . . . It almost seems as if he's not there at all. Perhaps he is staying at L'Hirondelle d'Or à la Martin Amis, "finishing his latest novel in quiet solitude," as per the hotel promotional brochure.

Wanting to be discreet, Bea is lying facedown on her lounge chair, very close to the mud baths. She adores elusive celebrities, and she doesn't even care if Santiago Arce is playing hard-to-get, because he has now achieved the status of the divinely mysterious. In hotels, this type of guest is particularly fascinating—they are people who somehow manage to show up on everyone's radar. Because of them, people suddenly start sneaking constant peeks at all the doors so that they can catch a glimpse of the famous person as he or she walks into the room. And they wait, just as Bea is waiting now, for the right moment to approach the guest and say, "Oh, hello. Aren't you so-and-so? I loved your film." Or something of the sort.

And while Santiago Arce is elsewhere, either hiding or reading or smoking or writing screenplays, at least one pair of eyes (actually, two) remain very intently focused on his absence.

The other two eyes are those of Molinet, who is back in his room, far from the scene at the mud baths. Just a few minutes ago he put down Fernanda's latest fax, jolted to attention by what he thought was the sound of Arce's voice in the garden outside, which prompted him to drop everything and rush over to the window. He looks left and right but sees no one, and he hears nothing but the "uhu-uhu" of the birds. *I am going to have to figure out a new system if I want to find out what the devil is going on at L'Hirondelle,* he thinks, because all this long-distance snooping has proven utterly fruitless.

Molinet very quickly concludes that he most definitely needs to pursue a new line of investigation; if not, all his unanswered questions will simply fall between the cracks. He needs to talk, yes, but with whom? Well, the most loquacious of the group, obviously. That is usually the best tactic. And so he tells himself that in the next few days—perhaps tomorrow, or the day after at the latest—he will begin to question Bea or perhaps Ana, the timid blonde who seems awfully happy that Sánchez spends the greater part of his day playing golf, an activity that gives her plenty of time to surrender to the pleasures of her blank mind as she lies there by the mud baths or the winter pool. Molinet, meanwhile, remains at the window. Just when he is about to abandon his post and finish reading his niece's fax, he hears that "uhu-uhu" once again from somewhere else in the garden. And he almost doesn't even bother to look. "It's only the birds," he says to himself. "It may sound like people whispering, but it's just the birds." Nevertheless he stays there, peering out the window, and then, through the vine leaves he spies two human subjects that he had not noticed before.

Once he puts on his distance glasses, he very easily ascertains that the two figures are Mercedes and Santiago Arce, softly chatting in a remote corner of the garden.

The Story According to Mercedes, Part Two

NO LONGER WILL I TRY TO WRITE ABOUT GOOD MANNERS AS MY FRIEND J. P. Bonilla, the editor of Alfa Contemporary Editions, wants me to, nor will I continue jotting down my impressions of L'Hirondelle d'Or. I would be hard-pressed to do it now, you see, because the panorama has changed so radically. What was once a secret hideaway filled with only the most innocuous pleasure seekers, as L'Hirondelle was when I arrived (two Belgians, a group of Germans far too young to interest me, and that curious man who I like to call the Marquis de Cuevas), has become a neighborhood block party. Or a cocktail party. Or perhaps a masquerade ball is more like it. I am not one for exaggeration, but this is more or less the state of things here now.

It is also something of a disappointment to realize that the more you try to run from your ghosts, the more they pursue you. I had scarcely been here two days when I suddenly found myself face-to-face with the very incarnation of everything I wanted to leave behind me in Spain. Fate's cruel hand could not have picked out four more perfect representatives of what I least wanted to see: Bea, my elementary school classmate; Bernardo, her lover (everyone knows they are lovers, and everyone *knows* that everyone knows, except those directly involved, who prefer to keep up the charade, hiding out and making everything much more awkward for them and for the rest of us, who couldn't care less about their illicit affair). In addition to these two we also have a busybody radio-show host whose specialty is nosing into people's private lives, plus a dumb blonde—I don't know which is more dangerous.

I can only assume that the four of them were as annoyed as I was about the coincidence, which forces us into the typical awkward situation: We are all in relatively close quarters, which means we bump into one another at all hours of the day and night, and though I wouldn't go so far as to say we are friends, we definitely know one another well enough to make all the run-ins sufficiently uncomfortable. Sometimes I get nervous when I start thinking about what they must be thinking: the four of them over there, me here all alone . . . But then again that is the great advantage of coming to a spa hotel like this. We are all here on a holy mission to lose weight and eat properly, and that does get you out of a lot of things. We are not here, after all, to while away the time playing canasta—we're here to shed pounds, and every minute here is costing each of us a bloody fortune, so we are far better off using our time to lift weights and exercise. We don't even have to sit together at mealtime if we don't want to. We are all subjected to the same grilled fish, steamed vegetables, or lamb in broth, and the hotel staff recommends we take the same places at every meal. With such a practical hotel-mandated excuse, it's easy enough to decline any disingenuous offer of friendship. But what happens when we suddenly spot someone whom we *would* like to meet? It is still a bit too soon for me to say whether our recent arrival might interest me, but I do have to admit I was intrigued when I saw him walk into the solarium the other morning. I was in a corner by myself, well removed from the others, when Santiago Arce— that's his name—made his entrance at the very same time as the Marquis de Cuevas. At first I thought they had come in together, but when I saw that Cuevas was just looking for that dog of his, I realized that Arce had just come in for a look. We all turned around to check him out—I mean, so little happens in this damn place—and he looked at us, we looked at him . . . the look on his face was a cross between bewildered and wary, as if he was sizing things up, not quite knowing what to look for. The inquisitive look on his face, however, quickly turned into one of surprise (and I wouldn't say he was pleasantly surprised, either) when he realized that all of us in the mud bath area were from Madrid—with the exception of the Marquis de Cuevas, of course. And so we had no other choice but to wave hello, cough up a bit of awkward conversation, and crack a few smiles before Arce excused himself, saying he had to go up to his room to put on his bathing suit. But he didn't come back down after that. We didn't see him at dinnertime, either, or at breakfast the next day. For a little while, he seemed to have disappeared into thin air, it was as if the desert had swallowed him up—that is, until two days ago, which is when we ran into each other again.

It was Sunday morning. I remember because I decided to go down to the mud baths much earlier than usual. On Sundays people tend to get up late, and it never occurred to me that I might actually bump into someone, much less Bea, my old classmate. But there she was, already sitting at the door, in her yellow robe and with a very determined look on her face, anxious to get going with the daily round of activities, which begin at nine on the dot, in perfect British (or Swiss) punctuality.

Bea smoked. At that hour of the day there was no way I could imagine inhaling even the most innocuous light cigarette, much less a Gitane, which she offered me with a broad smile. Now, I am not one for judging people by the brand of cigarettes they smoke (and I in fact have my doubts about that method of analysis), but I have always felt that there are generally two categories of women who smoke unfiltered cigarettes: The first group is comprised of tough broads; women who aren't necessarily butchy but who speak with a gravelly voice and wear their hair and nails very short. The second category is a more indefinable sort, and Bea definitely belongs to the latter. Although I've known her since childhood, I have never quite managed to decide whether she is a good-girl type or if she is actually a little more perverse. For example, I don't know if she would ever be nice enough to do me a favor in the event I needed something. What I do know is that people have a pretty low opinion of her, possibly because she talks like a truck driver despite the fact that she looks like a Barbie doll. There is something about the very texture of her that is downright synthetic. I don't know how else to describe it.

She's indefinable, yes, and contradictory. We have run into each other just about every day this week, and Bea has been very friendly, though distant and tactful, which is ideal as far as I am concerned. And so I really have nothing to say about her aside from the fact that she smokes Gitanes from dawn to dusk. That is all. I have no opinion of her. Perhaps that is because I have been judged so often and so casually by so many people lately that I no longer dare attempt to judge anyone else. I can present my impressions of people and things, but I prefer to leave the interpretation to someone else.

The point is, there we were at the door to the spa, the two of us. The minutes ticked by, making me wonder about the hotel's very Swiss punctuality, and to pass the time Bea and I chatted a bit. The conversation, naturally, wound its way toward Santiago Arce—where he was, why he had disappeared from the action, et cetera . . . Bea was of the very romantic opinion that he had come here to hide out and write a screenplay about a hotel like L'Hirondelle d'Or, and we stood around for a few minutes talking about him until, finally, the door opened and we were able to go in for our morning mud bath session, along with a very friendly Belgian couple who had also risen early that Sunday morning.

I would love to meet the person who so very invisibly controls the destiny of the guests at L'Hirondelle d'Or, for I would love to congratulate him or her for how well everything functions. Apparently, this person is named Miss Guêpe, and from what I can tell she must be quite a character. I have never seen her in person, but all you have to do is take a quick look around the hotel to appreciate the huge difference between this place and other fancy spas. At other places, the staff makes you feel like a recruit at boot camp instead of a guest or a patient of some sort—and I know what I'm talking about, because my husband, Jaime, and I used to be frequent visitors at two or three spas. But that was another life, a very different life, and I should put it behind me. It's over, it's done with. I must forget about it already.

As I was saying, nobody was around that day to drag me from one place to the other—massage here, therapeutic Vichy baths there. I smeared my face and part of my chest with a very smelly, dark-colored paste, probably a mixture of seaweed and some kind of local clay. Then I started to wash my face, but decided to leave the black goo on from the neck down, since I have discovered it is amazingly effective for getting rid of freckles. In that state, I made my way to the dining room. I hadn't covered much ground when I spotted the Belgian couple striding a bit ahead of me, bundled up in their yellow terry-cloth robes. *Snap-snap* went the plastic yellow flip-flops that flipped on and off their heels with each step they took. My equally horrid flip-flops did the exact same thing, and we all flip-flopped down the hallway, all the way to the door that opened onto the garden, which is where the Sunday breakfast buffet is served.

"Good morning," said the Belgian gentleman, which was rather unnecessary, since we had already greeted each other earlier that day.

"Lovely day," commented the Belgian lady.

"Please, after you," I said, ever friendly.

"No, no, please. You must go first," she said, but I insisted, and followed them in, thinking about how early it was. We must have been the first ones to hit the buffet—three yellow ducks in flip-flops and terry-cloth robe. The two Belgians, of course, were sans mud, while I bore a frontal smear that peeked out above the neckline of my bathrobe, like the dark body hair of a macho man.

And then all of a sudden there he was: Santiago Arce, at a table underneath all the vines, not two steps away from me.

What bad luck, I thought. *What goddamn bad luck!* Had it been possible to do so unnoticed, I would have definitely beat a hasty retreat to the door so that I could return later, looking a bit more presentable. But there was nothing I could do about it. He got up to say hello and smiled as (I imagine) he assessed my rather idiosyncratic look, and I had no choice but to say hello, with the distant conviviality that is the norm here at L'Hirondelle. Then, despite the difficulty of walking in flip-flops without dragging my feet, I somehow made it over to my table and ordered a yogurt and a tea as gracefully as I could, given that I was covered from toes to neck in sulfurous black goo that smelled, I am afraid to say, a lot like sardines. I tried to sink a bit deeper into my robe and I cursed myself for not coming up with a wittier comment regarding my unsightly appearance, but embarrassment inspires witty, ironic remarks only on the rarest of occasions. Most of the time it just leaves you speechless, and there I was, silent as a mouse, trying to use my robe to hide the dark muck smeared across my chest—without much success, I'm afraid.

From where I was sitting, however, I was able to ascertain a number of things about Santiago Arce. Had I been slightly less flustered, I probably would have focused on something other than his pants, which were tan and well ironed; his shirt, which was a pale blue color I always find so flattering on men; and his book, which hid much of his face, thank goodness. Arce was reading *Les malheurs de Sophie.*

I have always been fascinated by what writers—or screenwriters, in this case—read, although I suppose their reading lists can't be considered too indicative of anything, given that as a group they must read a pretty wide variety of things. Nevertheless, I was

amused to see that Arce had borrowed the same book as I had
from the hotel library—the same book I had hidden behind on my
first evening dining alone at L'Hirondelle. I actually held on to that
book and kept reading it for the next two or three nights out of pure
inertia—my God, I would have read anything to pretend not to notice Bea and her friends, who sit very close to me in the dining room,
far too close if you ask me. Anyway, *Les malheurs de Sophie*—that is,
Sophie's Trials—is the last thing I would have expected to catch Santiago Arce reading—it was a child's book, and not a boy child's book,
either. It was definitely a book for a girl, purely female, and I found
it so funny that I must have sat there looking at him longer than I
should have, because after a little while I had forgotten all about my
silly look and was happily gazing up at the ivy and thinking that life
isn't half bad if you focus on the little things instead of the big ones:
the singsong of the birds, the flavor of spearmint tea . . . To make a
long story short, once I had fully surrendered to those enchanting,
nature-inspired thoughts, a dark cloud cast its shadow across my
table and said:

"Oh, excuse me, Mercedes."

At such close range, looking at him from the bottom up as I did
now, Santiago Arce was even more attractive than before. I am terrible in situations like this: Attractive men have a way of making me
extremely uncomfortable. It is horrible. Nobody would ever guess
that I am forty-two and the survivor of a long-term marriage as well
as a few innocent flirtations here and there, and yet . . . oh, anyway.
What I am trying to say is that I am hardly a schoolgirl, hardly the
kind of woman who should go spilling her spearmint tea all over the
place just because a good looking man says, "Oh, excuse me, Mercedes."

Luckily, I saved the tea from spilling all over the place but the
near mishap left me so jittery that for the rest of the conversation I
didn't dare lift my teacup for fear of being betrayed by my racing
heartbeat, which manifested itself through my nervous, trembling

9

wrist. It was a trivial conversation. I believe, in fact, that Sophie and her various travails were our primary topics because, after all, a book in common is such a perfect excuse for conversation and we couldn't just let it slip by. Maybe some people think it a cliché to engage in superficial conversations like that, but clichés are wonderful. They are so reassuring.

And so maybe it wasn't the most auspicious beginning. I looked appalling, which I always feel is a strike against a woman's intelligence—women say the stupidest things when they feel insecure about the way they look. But in any event it was a beginning. And from that day onward I started running into him everywhere. By now, thank God, we have gotten past that tedious phase of conversations like the first one we had:

"So what are you doing here, anyway?"

"I just got over the most awful experience, and I came here to forget about everything for a while. You?"

"Something along those lines, I guess."

"So you mean you're not writing a screenplay about spas? You've been missing for days, my friend, and I figured you were hidden somewhere in the bushes plotting some kind of movie about L'Hirondelle. I don't know, a murder mystery or something?"

"Murders? Screenplays? I don't want to see another piece of paper for the next six months. I just finished my last movie. You can't even imagine. All you want to do is figure out some way to murder everyone on the crew. One day you feel like killing the star, then the unit manager, then you could strangle the director [laugh, laugh]. No, no, I'm not working on any screenplay. But I wasn't hiding out, either. I got sick, actually. Montezuma's revenge, if you can believe it."

After that everything became easier, and a lot more interesting. Not just because I discovered that you could indeed pick up Montezuma's revenge on the continent of Africa, but because I have a very strong feeling that my relationship with Arce has become something of a topic around here. Ever since we started going on morning walks together, I swear I've seen more than a few people watching us. Not that it surprises me to catch Bea and her friends spying on me—my God, I can just imagine what they're thinking: *My, my, how quickly the little widow got over her mourning,* or something like it. What intrigues me far more is the quiet vigil of my Marquis de Cuevas.

Such a strange man. He has never said a word to me and yet I feel as if he knows every last detail of my life. But that would be impossible. *Nobody* knows—I have been very careful about that. I don't know what to think, and after all, there is really nothing to learn. I'm sure that if Cuevas (or whatever his real name is) ever did find out about my life he would probably think it terrifically boring. That's right—boring, despite all the things people have said about me. And in the end what does it matter? People always like to think the worst about you, don't they? Very well. They can say whatever they like, because in the end, what does anyone *really* know about my life?

It's odd. Before Jaime died I was always so worried about what other people thought of me, and now I simply don't care. It's actually a lot more fun to be thought of as a bad girl. I'm tired of being a good girl, and that's what I was for far too many years. The Marquis de Cuevas is not the only person I've caught spying on me, either—there are plenty of others. They size me up from far away, and though they hide it slightly better than the Marquis, I can tell just the same—you pick up on this kind of thing pretty fast in hotels. Plus, it's so easy to get caught up in the lives of those around you. Take that Antonio Sánchez, for example. I am absolutely sure that he is watching me like a hawk. In his case it's probably just an occupational hazard—he happens to be a very well known radio announcer—but still, every time I catch him looking at me it sends a shiver up my spine. The worst part of it all is that his room is right next door to mine, and we run into each other far too often. Of course, we don't talk much, and if we do it's usually about vitamins or health food, nothing very significant, but I can tell he is dying to know what the hell I am doing here alone in this hotel. "Hello, darling," he always says when we cross paths in the hall, and I watch him as he plays with the key to his room, which is called *Rose de Thé*. Such a pretty name, so sweet. *Antonio SSSSS in Rose de Thé* . . . Why, it sounds like a snake hiding in a box of bonbons. Oh, stop it, stop it. I shouldn't say such things about someone I know nothing about aside from what other people have told me. It's not right, and anyway, I really do despise speculation.

How to Use the Secret Language of Flowers

Rose de Thé

Hotel rooms have a remarkable way of assuming the characteristics
of their inhabitants, transient as they may be. The room adapts and
conforms to the guests at hand until, after a short while, it seems as
if it belongs to them.

The room known as Rose de Thé, the third room off the stairs, is a happy room, illuminated by weak rays of sunlight that dance on the ochre-hued fabrics until they turn deep orange. The furniture is neutral and simple and the mattresses are perfect, with no personality whatsoever—they simply sit waiting for the next guest to come and warm them up. During these empty hours, the room tends to smell like a combination of Pledge furniture polish and a very excellent soap product called Saponetta Macaccini that Miss Guêpe special-orders from Italy. A gentle aroma, a tranquil atmosphere, and a spotless environment: That is how Rose de Thé may be described— but only when it is free of guests.

At the present moment, the Rose de Thé room is very different: Over the past several days, a variety of extremely personal odors have invaded it, effectively banishing the scent of Macaccini and Pledge. Nevertheless, a hint of its former scent can still be detected in the folds of a white piqué robe lying on the bed, as well as in the bathroom, where the soap product emanates a bit more intensely from a tiny glass jar nestled among the various cosmetics products lined up next to the sink: a light-pink lipstick, a jar of hypoallergenic foundation, creams, tubes, and an odd assortment of medicines. And C'est la Vie by Christian Lacroix, a very feminine-smelling perfume. C'est la vie!

Another highly personal scent is discernible on a number of clothing items littered about the room—you can smell it, for example, on a polo shirt, slightly damp with perspiration, that has been tossed upon an easy chair. There are other items thrown about the room that also exude this second odor. The tight runners' briefs, for example, which lie just beneath the television set. Or the still-wet bathing suit that proudly displays its pink mesh lining on top of the bidet. And a pair of short, thin black socks. Every last item smells to high heaven of that most masculine essence, that oily perfume by Chanel, Egoïste. Its master: Antonio Sánchez.

In addition, there is one more spot in the room where we may observe, even more patently, the evidence of each guest's imposition. That spot is the desk. Upon arrival, perhaps Sánchez and Ana agreed to share it ("This side is mine. That side is yours if you're a good girl and don't hog too much space."). But as the days wear on, one side begins to encroach upon the other in a slow but implacable onslaught, with the determination of a Panzer and the agility of a chinook. The last bit of territory Ana Fernández de Bugambilla has managed to hang on to is not difficult to identify: It is very clearly at the far side of the desk and covers no more than one fifth of the entire surface area. It should be duly noted, however, that she has done an excellent job of maximizing her space, occupying it with a teetering pile of four fashion magazines, a Nintendo Game Boy, two jars of American pain relievers, and one bottle of Milk of Magnesia.

The rest of the table belongs to Sánchez. On the right-hand side, a pile of newspapers sits alongside a Sony VAIO laptop, while the left-hand side is occupied by a dictionary of modern slang, six well-sharpened pencils, six Pilot Razor Point pens, one cellular phone in its leather case, and a shiny new pair of crescent-shaped sunglasses, everything arranged as if for a magazine layout.

If it were any hour other than four o'clock in the afternoon right now, Rose de Thé would exhibit a bit more activity on the part of its occupants. Early in the mornings, for example, this very elegantly named room has borne witness to a ritual that has been faithfully observed every day since the guests' arrival. A shrill alarm clock puts the ceremony into motion: Antonio S. jumps up from the bed, with a determined spirit and messy hair, while Ana Fernández de Bugambilla (who tries to avoid looking at him so early in the morning) vacillates between horror ("Good Lord, I survived another night. Only five left to go.") and delight at the thought of having the entire room to herself for a considerable portion of the day. Still, it will be a full half-hour before Sánchez disappears from sight: First he will take his time darting about the room, going in and out of the bathroom. Then she will have to wait patiently as he makes his forty-five minutes' worth of phone calls to Madrid so that he can catch up on the latest news and scandals. And then, once his mission is accomplished, his teeth brushed, his belly emptied, his bald spot shiny from the coat of Vaseline he has applied, Sánchez will finally leave the room clad in robe and yellow flip-flops and go downstairs not to the thermal baths like the rest of the world but to the winter pool, which is always deserted at that hour of the day. And there, he will begin his daily athletic regime: forty laps, fifteen of breaststroke and the remaining twenty-five divided between freestyle and backstroke, as well as a prolonged period underwater for respiratory endurance training. He does all of this long before he changes into his clothes for his second athletic date of the day: golf with Bernardo Salat. And off they go, driving their little cart beyond the palm trees at the edge of the hotel property.

These, then, are the hours when Rose de Thé bears witness to an entirely different array of activities, for these are the hours when Ana takes over the room—oh, they are delicious hours, between ten o'clock and noontime, followed by the brief spell before lunch when she goes down to the pool to find Bea. Then, unfortunately, the afternoon rolls around, dragging her slowly through siesta time, the frightful hour when Ana must have sex with Antonio, an activity she has managed to avoid for the last two days thanks to heavy doses of pain relievers and old heartfelt excuses like "I'm sorry, Antonio, I have the worst headache. You can't imagine, it's just awful. I think I'd rather just go for a walk . . ." This is followed by the hour that is just about to materialize, heralded once again by the shrill sounds of the alarm clock. Four-thirty.

This is the time of day when Sánchez usually returns to Rose de Thé to take care of a bit of professional business, which normally involves jotting down a number of unrelated thoughts that he might be able to use on his radio show. This afternoon, however, Antonio S. has a slightly more taxing task at hand: He has been asked to write forty lines for a newspaper spread. *Shit,* he thinks. This is the last thing he wants to do, but there is no way he can get out of it, since he did give the paper his word. The assignment—one of those supposedly innovative projects dreamed up at newspaper editorial meetings—is for a special issue of a very important Sunday supplement in which twenty important public figures—writers, politicians, actors, businessmen, and famous radio personalities such as himself—are to write about their perception of the state of contemporary Spanish society. Something meaningful, something fresh and new. *As if there is anything new to write about,* Sánchez thinks. *The more a society advances, the less it is capable of ever truly changing.* That is what the great Sánchez believes, even though he probably shouldn't say so, for it sounds old-fashioned and unworthy of a man as astute and perceptive as he. "Everything must change in order for things to stay the same," he very mistakenly quotes, taking a deep breath. He then decides to shelve the philosophical ruminations for the moment so that he can focus on his forty lines. There is nothing better than lashing out at a few politicians, he thinks.

Sánchez sits at the desk, but before settling in he casts a disapproving glance at the corner piled high with Ana Fernández de Bugambilla's belongings, most specifically her Nintendo Game Boy. *Doesn't this child have anything better to do with her mind than occupy it with machines that take her to nonexistent worlds? Poor fool,* he thinks.

"What a bore. Words, real words, spoken words are what I am good at, not letters printed on a page . . ." he sighs. "All right, let's see what I come up with this time. It can't be that hard."

He opens his Sony VAIO, 29 by 20 centimeters of pure technology. This, he tells himself, was designed to serve the mind—not vice versa, as in the case of the Nintendo Game Boy that belongs to his "poor fool." For a fleeting moment he thinks of her legs which, he must admit, are truly divine and that, in the end, is all that matters. She can addle her brain with Nintendo all she wants for all he cares, as long as she keeps those goddesslike legs of hers in tiptop shape. Sánchez hits the power button on his laptop; the ten seconds of boot-up time allow him to perform a kind of warm-up exercise in which he and his body prepare themselves for the art of creation. How amazing it is to feel his thoughts come into alignment, forming a miracle, his mind achieving a kind of astral convergence with his Sony. As he prepares for what is to come, Sánchez cracks his knuckles like a pianist preparing to attack a polonaise. Wait. Pause. The program logo appears on the screen, the anti-virus program runs through its routine, and by the time the Start menu has finally appeared, Sánchez has already decided what he will write about today: a son-of-a-bitch congresswoman who, just yesterday, had the gall to snub her party by casting the decisive ballot in favor of the government in a congressional vote. The witch. Sánchez hopes that forty lines will be enough to create something dense and complex, evocative of the lucid prose of the most acidic political columnist. A difficult task, admittedly, and for this reason he has turned to his dictionary of modern slang, which is now open to page 125, where he has highlighted the word "dick."

He creates a new document and immediately saves it with a single-word title: "whore." Using only one word is the best way to remain focused on the topic at hand. Whore. He cracks his knuckles again as he conjures up the image of that turncoat congresswoman who deserves all the derision he can dish out, a blonde with an ample bosom and extremely abundant backside. *Fucking traitor,* he thinks. *Lying bitch.*

Despite the very vulgar nature of the media nowadays, Antonio S. still holds on to *some* scruples: He knows that it would be in extremely poor taste, for example, to make a crack about a lady's physical attributes in a newspaper article. Such a shame. One of his greatest talents on the airwaves, back in the days when he commented on general-interest issues rather than politics, was the masterful manner in which he wove people's most obvious physical traits into his very convincing sermons. Nowadays, however, he is more than just a mere radio announcer—he is a Journalist with a capital *J,* and he does not feel it appropriate for a Journalist to exploit a woman's physical appearance in a politically oriented article that will be read by thousands—no matter how much the woman deserves it.

"Dicking everyone around, that's what our little congresswoman has been doing to her electorate. Careful, careful, sweetheart, you wouldn't want to fall on your face like Burt Lancaster did in the movie *Trapeze.* But that doesn't matter much now, because one thing is crystal-clear: You're in free fall, lady . . ."

Now, Rose de Thé is not the aggressive sort of room with walls that close in on its occupants, attacking them with inopportune, long-forgotten memories. But for some reason, these last few words (or perhaps it was the image of Burt Lancaster) prompt Sánchez to pause for a moment. He raises his eyes from the computer screen.

He is scarcely five lines into his article, and although he finds the topic perfectly serviceable, his eyes have strayed over to the wall, where his gaze settles on a bouquet of yellow roses. He has lost his train of thought while staring at that flowered wallpaper, damnit. It was as if some sort of imaginary wall suddenly came between him and his thoughts about the traitorous congresswoman.

His eyes return to the screen and he rereads what he has written. The piece isn't half bad, he tells himself, and that last bit about Burt Lancaster is pretty sharp. Now, with renewed energy, Sánchez decides to delete the last two lines, but after a brief pause he rewrites them exactly as they were: "to fall on your face like Burt Lancaster did in the movie *Trapeze* . . ." He continues clicking away on the keyboard for a few more minutes, coming up with two more very convincing paragraphs, and then . . .

He is certain now. It is those two words, "Burt Lancaster," that have begun to create interference on the VAIO. Every single time he types in the name Burt Lancaster he suddenly feels a surge of word association—or perhaps "idea association" would more accurately describe the phenomenon that has somehow led him to confuse that fine actor's square jaw with another, very similar jaw that has been tickling the subconscious of Antonio S., radio announcer to the masses, for the past few days.

At first that angular mandible appears in his mind as a shadow and then it becomes an outline, then a sketch, and now, all of a sudden, amid the yellow-flowered wallpaper reflected on his computer screen, he sees not just the jaw but the entire face of one of his fellow hotel guests: the screenwriter Santiago Arce. This truly startling mental process makes Sánchez turn around and actually look for the man, even though he knows it is preposterous—what on earth could Arce be doing nestled among the flowers on his wallpaper? He duly confirms that there is no one there, but the incident is enough to interrupt his train of thought again, and his eyes travel aimlessly over the folds of the curtains, dappled with tea roses. Of course, the flowers have nothing to do with his loss of inspiration, just as Santiago Arce has nothing to do with the newspaper article he is presently writing.

One angular jaw can be very similar to another, no doubt about it. And a keen mind like that of Antonio Sánchez can be expected to draw unforeseen connections between the two. Burt Lancaster and Santiago Arce. Yes . . . maybe there is a certain resemblance around the jaw area, but nothing more. Sánchez knows that he has to get back on topic. The treacherous congresswoman is the one and only thing that should occupy his thoughts right now.

"Come on, come on, it's starting to look like you can't do this, come on. Shit, it's forty lines, forty lines that will be published alongside the opinions of the most important minds in the country. Come on, man . . ."

Antonio waits, and the screen flickers. But not one single idea flashes through his head. He racks his brains to come up with some explanation for this writer's block. Sánchez is a man with a fertile imagination, and so it takes him less than two seconds. The problem, the reason for all this interference, is ridiculously simple: The topic of the traitorous congresswoman is a dreadful bore.

His inspiration floats back to Santiago Arce, and it does not settle on the topic of his jawline but rather on that of his love life and the attraction he very clearly feels for Mercedes Algorta. There's dirt here, he can feel it. And now nothing can stop his fingers, which seem to have developed, in conjunction with the Sony VAIO, a mind of their own.

What is a person to do in a situation like this? Should he allow his inspiration to take over? His ideas—or perhaps his fingers—crackle and hum now that he has let them loose on the keyboard. Very well, they are free now . . . let us see where these ideas go. But what if they cannot be used for the article he has been asked to write about the current state of Spanish society? After all, he has a reputation to consider, one that should not be sullied by frivolous topics, boudoir gossip. Oh, it doesn't matter, he tells himself. He will find some way to turn it into a terribly important issue—a metaphor for all the sins of his nation, something like that. Yes, what a magnificent idea: He shall illustrate the sins of his nation by way of a little love story that is taking place before his very eyes here at L'Hirondelle d'Or.

The ingredients are all there: Following the very odd death of her husband, a rich widow plans a rendezvous with her lover in a remote corner of Morocco. Now, why have they decided to travel such a great distance? Do they have something to hide? What is their real sin? Ah, what a superb topic—a story that illustrates the moral and ethical decline of the nation. Much more tantalizing than that little story about the congresswoman, no doubt about it. People are sick to death of politicians, but they just love stories about illicit lovers.

His fingers fly freely across the keyboard; nothing can stop them now. All Sánchez has to do is lean back and watch his magical fingers take over, unstoppable and lightning-fast. And soon the screen of his Sony VAIO comes to life with something far more intriguing than what he was writing before:

"Crime doesn't pay." *Not a bad opener,* he thinks. *Looks promising. Let's see where it goes.*

Little by little, an entire paragraph of sparkling prose emerges on the screen. He writes:

"Crime does not pay. Crime is an art. An enlightened method for changing the course of Destiny. But nobody, not even the most deranged criminal, is immune to the despicable feeling of guilt."

A bit moralistic perhaps? Not worthy of Hemingway. Perhaps, but wait . . . let us see how Sánchez gets himself out of this one.

"Guilt," Sánchez types, "is like an old, nearsighted exhibitionist . . ."

Nearsighted exhibitionist? That sounds a bit farfetched. Perhaps he should interrupt this stream of consciousness and stop his index and middle fingers as they race across the keyboard. They couldn't possibly have meant to write "nearsighted." That must have been a mistake. But no. Sánchez lets his fingers do the talking, and he continues to read as they type away:

"Yes, that's right. Guilt is like a dirty old man, nearsighted as all hell, who hides out in parks and leers at all the pretty blond girls with ribbons in their hair. A man who never dares to step out into the light until one day. The day of his big event. And oh does he make a scene, in the worst possible place. No longer able to contain his urge to let everything hang out, this bold but nearsighted exhibitionist waves his cane up and down, left and right, until he finally reaches a deep, dark place. Far from everything. And there, this unrepentant criminal grows aroused . . . very, very aroused. What he does not realize, however, is that the deep, dark place he has chosen to exhibit his ignominy is the metro station at Callao. A public location like this, naturally, is teeming with cops. Big, tall, brawny cops, the six-foot-four type. Ballbusters."

This very long introduction, which presents the notion of guilt in the guise of an old nearsighted exhibitionist, will serve as a lead-in to the revelations that he now prepares to deliver. As he types away, Sánchez watches as his prose slowly evolves into a far simpler writing style:

"This is a story for our times, a story that reveals the utter lack of backbone and moral values in modern Spanish society. And yet there is something even more troubling here. Consider this: Mercedes Algorta, a prominent figure of Madrid society, has just been widowed. How did it happen?, we may ask ourselves. Was her husband's death a setup? These stories about rich girls are always so fraught with contradiction, with lies. Let us suppose for a moment that her newfound freedom is in fact the result of a terrible accident. And yet, now, with her husband's body still warm in his grave, Mercedes Algorta has just made the same mistake as the nearsighted exhibitionist in the Callao metro station."

If a professor of language and literature were watching Sánchez's fingers galloping across his Sony VAIO keyboard, he might wonder how the great radio announcer planned to connect the dots between the blind exhibitionist and Mercedes Algorta. Suffice it to say that after devoting six or seven lines to the topic of his first day at L'Hirondelle, Sánchez (who is such a keen observer of people) notes that two guests in particular caught his eye and raised his suspicions the minute he laid eyes on them.

"There is something serious going on between Mercedes and Arce here," he writes. "But they made a big mistake, an uncharacter-istically idiotic mistake for two such intelligent people, when they selected L'Hirondelle d'Or as their rendezvous point scarcely two months after the rather questionable death of the lady's husband. Both Algorta and Arce are sophisticated—they should have known that the golden rule of illicit lovers (and perhaps accomplices to an unspeakable crime—who knows?) is to never ever pick a remote hideaway as a meeting place. How stupid, how nearsighted of them to have even thought of coming here. A date in a bustling, popular location always comes off as much more innocent—but then again, guilt is a nearsighted exhibitionist, exposing its ignominy in the least appropriate place."

The words that Antonio Sánchez now types into his computer have an intense, suffocating quality to them. On the surface the prose is simple, but inside it is rotten to the core—his words seem to evoke the Puritans (or witch-hunters, to be more precise) of Salem, the sins that beg for punishment, the sound of wicked flesh burning at the stake as people cry "Guilty! Guilty!" and other zealous accusations. This is even more remarkable since Sánchez has never heard of Nathaniel Hawthorne or his masterpiece *The Scarlet Letter.* Even so, the same themes are all there in black and white:

"The general public—an exceedingly wise group when it comes to these matters—has begun to point its fingers at Mercedes Algorta as the potential culprit of this very abominable crime. How did she do it? How did she lead her husband so definitively to death's door? Simple: She didn't do a thing. That is what all of Madrid is whispering these days—and please remember that I am merely presenting the information that I have in my possession. They say that on that fateful night, our lady friend found her husband gasping for breath, and she very simply did nothing to help him. What could be easier? Or more innocent? And yet what crime is more despicable than the crime—the sin—of omission? An omission that kills, an omission that looks on impassively at the agony of another human being, an omission that watches on as a dying man turns to the one person he believes can save him and looks up to see nothing but an icy smile . . ."

At this point, Sánchez's fingers pound out their electric phrases and crude images at full blast:

"Poor Valdés, breathing his last breath, watches as Mercedes coolly closes the door to the room, as if to say that life exists outside that room, as does the woman Valdés almost made love to a few minutes earlier—Isabella, his impossible love, his desire. Inside the room, he has only his ruthless wife, who so cruelly and ironically sits beside him and pretends to loosen his tie despite the fact that death, procuress of so many unspeakable infamies, has already come to call on her husband."

How his fingers sail across the keyboard now! The article, no doubt, is slightly erratic and far too long, but he is not concerned, for there will be plenty of time to edit it later. Naturally, it will have to be written in another style—not because what he has written is untrue, of course. What he has written is as true as life itself. And the proof is right there under everyone's nose: The two lovers are right here at the hotel, which must mean that Mercedes Algorta killed her husband. Case closed. When he reworks the article he will have to tighten it up a bit, throw in a few shocking tidbits, the kind he uses to spice up his radio programs. Still, all that can wait. For the moment, our great man is content to sit back and see what other brilliant ideas find their way out his fingertips and into this magic machine.

Sánchez runs a very admiring finger across the top of his Sony VAIO. "How grand it is to be so very talented," he says to himself, certain that this sort of thing never happens to anyone but bona fide geniuses. Talent always seems so elusive, and then it creeps up on you just like that! All right, he tells himself, let's see what I come up with now. *Click, click, click* go his fingers across the keyboard. As he rereads the next paragraph he pounds out, he notes with satisfaction that it has a delicious gossip-magazine tone, with a dash of malice thrown in, Elsa Maxwell–style this time:

"The angular jaw of screenwriter-of-the-moment Santiago Arce, an attractive man drooled over by women of all ages, would have dropped a full four inches had its master dared express his feelings out loud: 'What a colossal, irrevocable mistake!' he would say. And he would be right. After pulling off the most perfect crime with his lover, bumping off Mercedes Algorta's husband—*this* was the very worst mistake he could have possibly made."

Sánchez is very pleased by the *in crescendo* tone, for his fingers have finally asserted that the two of them, Mercedes and Arce, killed her husband together. Bravo, bravo! Now it is a homicidal duo he is dealing with, not just one little murderess. Of course, when he uses these notes to write the final version of the article, he obviously cannot spell it out quite so clearly, but there are plenty of ways to allude to certain things—after all, allusions can be far more effective than straightforward factual statements. What about the truth? you might ask. What if it turns out that the husband did in fact choke to death before anyone could get to him? What if it turns out that the little tête-à-tête between Mercedes and Arce is entirely coincidental and that they never even laid eyes on each other before coinciding at L'Hirondelle d'Or? In that case . . . the story would be of no interest to anyone. Elsa Maxwell was fully aware of this in her day too, but she was a master of her craft, and never allowed real life to get in the way of a good story. Sánchez feels precisely the same. Faithful to his mission, he allows his fingers to click away:

"In reality, ladies and gentlemen, everyone in Madrid suspected she was guilty of this sin. People were buzzing about it in living rooms all over town. And the lovers would have gotten away with it had it not been for one minor detail. A truly unfortunate detail, one that has proven time and again to foil even the most perfect crimes. After pulling off their great effort, criminals all too often make the mistake of toasting each other with champagne or dancing a rumba over the dead man's grave. When they do this, they commit acts not of sacrilege but of mortal stupidity. No, my friends, our fair Arce and his divine lover did not commit the specific post-mortem gaffe mentioned above. But there are many ways to drink champagne or dance a rumba on a dead man's grave, and theirs was as follows: Once they had completed their abominable deed, they made the very idiotic decision to take off for a vacation at a luxurious Moroccan hotel to celebrate their despicable success. Criminals, you see, are often too impatient to lie low for an appropriate period of time after committing their crime.

"Uncovered! Exposed!

"It is a real shame, but destiny has no mercy on impatient murderers. An unfortunate ending for an otherwise perfect crime, I'm afraid, because this couple will face a bitter finale to their wayward adventures. A few days later, free as birds, so very vulnerable in their belief that they are safe and sound in their golden hideaway, Arce and the lovely Mercedes suddenly bump into the one person capable of exposing their little sham to the rest of the world. And that *one* person is, of course . . ."

Sánchez's fingers would have written something like "this humble servant," but "servant" doesn't really go with the Elsa Maxwell bit. For this reason his fingers stop short precisely when they are about to finish off the story by explaining how their master (that is, Antonio Sánchez López himself) discovered the truth about Mercedes Algorta, a mousy little Nobody from a good family who turned herself into a merry widow and wealthy heiress. *What a delicious story,* thinks Antonio Sánchez. It has all the ingredients—some real, others not so real, but who cares? Anything goes, as they say.

Sánchez rereads his text, breathless. It's so odd, so unfamiliar, slightly incoherent too, perhaps—but that is what you get with stream of consciousness. It is unpredictable, anarchical . . . and brilliant. He scrolls back up to the first line:

"Crime doesn't pay."

What an uncanny beginning. Until this moment, he hadn't fully realized the magnitude of journalistic possibilities presented by Mercedes Algorta's story. For the moment, he plans to tell it without mentioning any names, for that will serve to add intrigue. "Who can it be?" everyone will whisper. Magnificent idea, yes, that is exactly what he will do, and he'll look for a good title, something like "Crimes of the Rich" or "Days of Wine, Roses and Treachery"—yes,

yes, something like that. Perfect. Of course, he has much more material than he can actually use; his notes are endless. But he is in no rush, for he doesn't have to hand the thing in until next week, which gives him plenty of time to perfect it. Although, no, his day's work isn't quite done yet. He still has one more detail to take care of, one that some people might find irrelevant, but he believes it to be paramount, for it is the key to his success. Ever since his earliest days on the airwaves, Antonio Sánchez has always practiced his sermons. Someone, an ordinary person who more or less represents the average man (someone pretty dense, in Sánchez's opinion), must listen to Sánchez recite his spiel out loud and in person. That is the very best way to make it perfect. Only by reading his material out loud can he determine both the strong points (which he will later accentuate) and the weak points (which he will later eliminate). This little method also happens to work like a charm with written articles. As such, what he needs right now is a standard run-of-the-mill set of ears, those of an average person. And all of a sudden it hits him. *What a stroke of luck,* he thinks. For goodness' sake—I have the perfect specimen right under my nose.

He looks at his watch. Six o'clock in the evening. More than an hour to kill before dinner, which is very convenient, for that will be just enough time to recount the whole story to Ana Fernández de Bugambilla as she gets dressed for dinner.

"How would you like to hear the story of a real bitch, darling?"

Let's see . . . that opener is definitely out, for he already used it as an introduction to a previous conversation, and Antonio Sánchez is not a man to recycle conversation starters. No. The prelude will be different this time around—much simpler, something like "Sit down, darling." And then he will launch into his story while caressing the contours of her neck or one of her divine calves.

Sánchez sits up, saves what he has written, and before closing his word-processing program he thinks: *Fuck the fat congresswoman.* And he thinks this because he no longer has the slightest doubt that

the piece he has been asked to write for the special Sunday supplement will be a hell of a lot more successful if he sticks with the story
of high-society infidelity and murder.

"I feel sorry for you, but you fucked up, Santiago Arce and company," he says as he closes his laptop. "You really fucked up."

Sports

CAREFUL! TO PLAY PADDLE TENNIS, DON'T EVEN *THINK* OF wearing tennis clothes, for that would be terribly gauche. Men will look perfectly fine in a pair of old cutoffs that land right about mid-thigh level (shorter shorts are only for French backpackers who frequent campsites) or a simple pair of bathing trunks with a T-shirt (if possible, as well-worn as the cutoffs). Oddly enough, an unspoken rule seems to dictate that the best players are always those with the most ragged, disheveled appearance.

—Carmen de Posadas, *Yuppies, jet set, la movida y otras especies* (Yuppies, jet-set, the movida and other species, 1987)

Paddle Tennis, Cellular Telephones, and Sneakers
(*Two Days Later*)

The Muguet bedroom at L'Hirondelle, occupied by Bea and Bernardo, pays homage to its name even in the tiniest of details. Lilies of the valley decorate the porcelain in the bathrooms, the subtle wallpaper is dotted with faint petals and stalks, and lovely little flower buds cover the bedspread. Bea stops to admire these little flowers, alternately wrinkling and smoothing them as she chats with J. P. Bonilla, whom she has just telephoned in response to the message he left on her machine.

"I can hardly hear you, J.P. Please tell me you're not in a restaurant because, I might remind you, it is the height of bad taste to sit there talking into your Nokia unless you are eating alone, and I doubt you are, given how terribly popular you say you have become."

Bonilla assures her that, no, he is playing paddle tennis at the moment. He does not, however, wish to waste his one hour of athletic activity by talking to Bea and so he quickly explains the reason for the message he left her. As it turns out, he wants to offer her a little assignment, one that he claims is tailor-made for her.

"It's a real cushy job," he says. "You are going to absolutely love it—it's easy, well paid, a real deal. Look, for someone who's well connected, speaks English, and knows how to be a guardian angel it's a breeze."

Bea raises her hand—not to indicate enthusiasm for such a hearty pitch, but to search for the pack of Gitanes she has left somewhere on the bedspread. She locates it and lights a cigarette, despite the fact that such strong tobacco hardly jibes with the delicate *muguet* decor of the bedroom. And she listens.

"Are you familiar with Harpic Arvhaubi, darling?" asks J.P.

"No. I don't think I could even pronounce the name, matter of fact. Someone important?"

"Darling, darling, come back to planet Earth. She's in all the newspapers. Harpic Arvhaubi is the writer everyone's talking about these days, or haven't you heard?"

The smoke from her Gitanes wafts across the *muguet* wall, forming a rather uninteresting hieroglyphic.

"What? Did she win some kind of prize, or something?"

"She doesn't need it. Her book has already hit the *New York Times* bestseller list—didn't you see the photo of her with Condoleezza Rice at the White House? She is a victim of intolerance, a woman who has been silenced."

"Good writer?" Bea asks, thinking about how much this call is going to cost Bernardo.

"Darling, I am telling you that this is a writer who has been silenced, censored. A political refugee from Borrioboola-Gha. You've read Dickens, haven't you?"

"I don't think I made it past the back cover . . ."

"Well it's a shame, because if you had, you might understand a little more about the plight of certain faraway, primitive countries like Borrioboola-Gha," Bonilla replies. "Now, come on. Don't tell me you've never seen a photo of Harpic Arvhaubi. Thirtysomething, stocky, she's been all over the world promoting her book—a titillating novel, erotic and scandalous."

"No. What's the big deal? There's thousands, millions of books like that out there . . ."

"Right. But none of them were written in Borrioboola-Gha," J.P. replies. "And that, my dear, has brought her plenty of trouble and more than a few personal inconveniences. You know what it's like out there, darling—it's a jungle, a godforsaken jungle. But anyway. The point is, this lady is going to be in Madrid at the end of the month, and I want to know if you would be interested in being her guardian angel, her hostess—take her under your wing, go wherever she goes, make sure she gets invited to your friends' parties—you know the friends I mean, the ones who are so allergic to the paparazzi. What I want is for you to be her interpreter and her friend. Harpic Arvhaubi, you see, has chosen Spain for the European launch of *The Blue Midriff*."

"Why blue?"

J.P.'s paddle-tennis teacher, José Carlos Fernández Santabárbara, has begun to practice a special forehand, which appears to require considerable agility of the elbow. Like Bea, he has never heard of Borrioboola-Gha. Nor does he understand the complexities of literary marketing, the lengths to which one must go in order to promote a book, or the great significance of Harpic Arvhaubi's decision to launch the Spanish edition of her book in Madrid, a book which is currently number one on the *New York Times* bestseller list. And since José Carlos Fernández Santabárbara only reads the sports pages, he is also unaware of the fact that a group of anti-feminist fanatics have raised holy hell over the publication of *The Blue Midriff,* creating a scandal that has rocked the world—all the way from Borrioboola-Gha, thanks to CNN. Fernández Santabárbara couldn't possibly locate Borrioboola-Gha on a map, nor does he have any reason to know that following the publication of the novel, its instantly famous author was forced to flee her native country and travel to a number of faraway places, including New York, Paris, and London, in the interest of averting the imminent danger she suddenly faced in her own homeland, where, they say, a group of fanatics have burned every last copy of her book—all three hundred of them. The Western world, of course, has rallied to her defense, calling the threats "barbaric," since all she did was write a slightly shocking erotic novel. And J. P. Bonilla has managed to bring her to Madrid, where the heavily bodyguarded authoress has demanded the services of a guardian angel—a woman, a friend who might put her up and introduce her to important people.

FAR AWAY, in her bedroom at L'Hirondelle d'Or, Bea has taken note of all the information, including the very tempting fee Bonilla has proposed. After a quick bit of calculation carried out on the flowered wallpaper, Bea can safely say that this three-day affair will earn her more than most people make in a month.

"What do you say, sweetheart? I have to get back to my paddle-tennis class. If you want, I can call you back in half an hour. Give me the number."

Bea and Bonilla agree to talk later on. They both need a brief respite—to save the battery power on Bonilla's Nokia and to let Bea mull over the offer. After a bit of pondering, Bea decides that a little extra cash would definitely come in handy, because it has become increasingly difficult to support herself as a single woman without jeopardizing her social status. By the time she stubs out her Gitanes the decision is already made: She will accept the offer, partly for the money and partly because it sounds like an interesting new experience.

Writers are so odd, Bea thinks. *Such mysterious people, so fascinating.* And now, as she waits around for Bonilla to call her back so that she can tell him she will be delighted to accept the assignment, her mind wanders back to another writer—a screenwriter, to be more precise. Right now he is somewhere on the grounds of this hotel—right downstairs, perhaps, or maybe in the garden. And suddenly she thinks of how lovely it would have been if J.P. had asked her to be the guardian angel and social ambassador to Santiago Arce. But of course people like Santiago Arce never need guardian angels or ambassadors of any sort.

"Back to reality," Bea tells herself. "You're lucky he asked you to take care of a writer from . . . wherever the hell that lady is from. After all, God only knows who will ever read an erotic novel by someone from a country like that." The phone, however, does not ring, and time passes very slowly as Bea's thoughts wander back to Santiago Arce. Strange, she hasn't thought of him at all in the past few days. What good would it do, anyway? She has already given up any hope of becoming chummy with him. No longer does she dawdle at the mud baths, waiting for the moment to ask him the meaning of the word "baobab." They may say hello in the hallways, of course, but she'd have to be an idiot not to realize that Arce has already taken an interest in someone else—Mercedes Algorta, obviously. She can tell it from a mile off, and she both understands and accepts this fact. She lights another Gitanes. Smoking is terrible for the skin, but she, as Scarlett O'Hara would say, will think about that tomorrow. For the moment, she smokes, thinks, and congratulates herself on knowing how to be such a good loser. Yes, she certainly knows how to lose with style—that has always been one of her great gifts.

Perhaps this is not the moment to analyze her past losses, but she does. Bea has lost many times in her life. She lost, for example, when she separated from her husband almost nine—nine!—years ago. She lost when she had to give him custody of their children, because when you fall in love with a ski instructor at Baqueira Beret and decide to go off and live on a mountaintop, it isn't very fair of you to expect your kids to want to move in with you and grow up like a couple of characters out of *Heidi.* Her children were twelve and fourteen at the time, old enough to have an opinion about such a thing. Bea also knew how to lose when Rafa, her ski instructor, fell in love with an American heiress who for some bizarre reason was skiing in the Spanish Pyrenees when everyone in the world knows that all rich American girls ski in Vail and Aspen. But facts are facts, and seven years ago this past December, Kate Goldsmith decided to go skiing at Baqueira Beret and not Vail, where, incidentally, Rafa now lives, the part owner of a sensational restaurant called Ralph & Kate's Den.

With Bernardo Salat, Bea has always been the loser. She always knew that he would never leave his wife, but at least he offers her a pleasant sort of a life—that much she has to admit. Nevertheless, every so often Bea does find it necessary to make him feel just a little guilty for all the promises he has made and never kept. But Bea is no longer thinking of Bernardo Salat or J. P. Bonilla, because her thoughts have turned back to Santiago Arce, whom she has seen sidling up to Mercedes, slowly and cautiously. It was a foregone conclusion, that relationship: two people, both alone, at the same hotel in the middle of Nowhere. Both of them attractive, wealthy, and single . . . Bea smiles.

Now it is Antonio Sánchez who comes to mind, reminding her of a rather incongruous story that her friend Ana Fernández de Bugambilla told her by the pool earlier that morning. She hadn't paid much attention, because Ana has such a convoluted way of telling stories, but according to her, Sánchez was now spending several hours of his free time writing an article about Mercedes and Arce. What was this all about? What kind of a job was he going to do on them? Apparently, Sánchez was writing about what he thought was a perfect example of modern society's lack of morality, and he supposedly had a true story to back up his claims: a rich widow, the object of much idle gossip, recently vacationing at a remote hotel in Morocco and cozying up to an attractive, fascinating, and highly popular writer. With these ingredients mixed together Sánchez-style, the result could only be . . . trash, most likely. Bea smokes her cigarette, and the smoke curls its way around a ray of light that falls in through the window. How boring. Her thoughts, as voluminous as the smoke from her Gitanes, continue down their spiraling path. *Sánchez has always been irresistibly drawn to stories of infidelity,* she thinks. *He can't help it. Tales from the boudoir, adultery, especially if they involve what he calls Beautiful People. So what if he is the star of a radio show whose purpose, he claims, is to serve the* truth? *Sánchez is one of those people who talks himself blue in the face about upholding the truth.*

Bullshit, Bea thinks. *A leopard never changes his spots. Stories of blood and semen are what really turn him on, even though he may try and dress them up as serious news.* And Bea begins to recall all the sordid bedroom tales that Antonio Sánchez and his ilk have unearthed and transformed into issues of national concern: duchesses caught with their panties down, marital infidelities that have shaken the foundations of some or other financial empire, courtly maidens married, divorced, and remarried to the delight of the housewives who idolize them. Sex and money; sex and power. Bea yawns. Only someone as unsophisticated as Sánchez could possibly be capable of, or interested in, shaking that beehive of raw passion and turning people's private matters into nationwide scandals. But the truth, Bea recognizes, is that he has done it. Somehow he has managed to turn the entire country into one giant, gossipy block party.

And Mercedes Algorta? As far as Bea is concerned, her story doesn't have even half the sizzle of many other seamy tales that have been dredged up before. But who cares? Rich, beautiful, and famous: Those are all the ingredients necessary for cooking up a juicy article or radio show. Naturally, her friend Ana Fernández de Bugambilla fell for Sánchez's version, and she wouldn't be the only one to buy it, either. The more complicated the intrigue, the more people go for it. The idea that Valdés died as the result of a stupid accident is a bore—it's much more fun to think him the victim of some evil plot. And then the idea that Arce and Mercedes bumped into each other at L'Hirondelle d'Or completely by accident—even more of a bore. Sánchez will dress it up a little and say that the two of them are lovers and that they agreed to meet here to begin their new and exciting, sexy life together with the dead guy's money. It all fits so well, except for one thing: It's a lie.

"If I didn't smoke so much, I'd be a genius," Bea says to herself, as if she had replaced her Gitanes with some kind of opiate, the kind that kills thousands of brain cells per minute. The point is, Bea considers herself pretty savvy—or at least not stupid enough to fall for Antonio Sánchez's story, which is just a variation on the same theme of intrigue and unbelievable coincidences. He should be writing Venezuelan soap operas, for God's sake. Bea doesn't believe the radio announcer, not for a second, because his script is all wrong. Life can be a lot of things—crappy, ironic, bitter, whatever—but the script is never contrived. For this reason Bea is absolutely certain that Mercedes and Arce have never met before. Because aside from being a very good loser, Bea has another important virtue—a rather useless one, in the end, but a virtue all the same. Bea happens to be an expert at identifying the faces of people who have just met for the first time. It is a talent she has honed over the years, through a multitude of personal affairs that gave her plenty of experience in what one might call *beginnings*. Middles and ends she usually messes up, but beginnings are definitely her forte. She has savored thousands of incipient romances, and she can spot the signs from a mile off. She doesn't need to hear a single word of what two newfound lovers might actually be saying to each other. The eyes of an expert like Bea need rely on nothing more than the faces of her subjects. And she has read volumes in the eyes of Mercedes and Arce—like last night, for example, when she bumped into the two of them before dinner. Or this morning, when she caught them in the hall talking about nothing in particular. Bea knows that their faces, not their words, are what count, and in their faces Bea has seen all the telltale signs of a romance just beginning to blossom. She can see it in their smiles, just a bit too elastic, as they widen with glee at the least little remark; their pensive expressions as they listen to each other's first few confidences; the false security in their eyes as if they were sculpted in granite; their fleeting gazes; and their mouths that barely crack open as if to say, "Should I smile now or just separate my lips to form a little *o*, or should I run my tongue over them?" She sees the winks, the almost imperceptible trembling—she sees all the things that give them away, for faces take a long time to settle into the serenity of long-term relationships. Faces are like calendars to Bea.

Bea stops thinking about Mercedes and Arce for a moment. *For God's sake,* she scolds herself. Why am I wasting so much time on them when I ought to be thinking about that writer from Borrioboola-Gha?

She thinks about how kind it is of Bonilla to think of her after so much time, how sweet of him to offer her such a simple, well-paid, glamorous little job that any one of her desperado women friends would die for. Because in addition to the handsome fee, it could be very interesting to be the hostess of a famous fat lady writer—the "fat" part is Bea's way of interpreting Bonilla's use of the word "stocky" to describe Harpic Arvhaubi. And suddenly she conjures up an image of the authoress enveloped in a giant sari that covers her head but reveals the rolls of coppery-colored fat around her waist. No doubt she is the spunky type, probably with a gold tooth stuck in there somewhere, emphatic body language, and rapid-fire English—the kind spoken by Pakistanis who sell gum and trinkets in markets all over the world: *Nicetomeetyou, miss, yesyes indeed* . . . Next, Bea pictures herself holding on to Harpic's arm, introducing her to absolutely everyone at a party somewhere. Then she envisions herself standing next to the lady writer at the cocktail reception at the Hotel Villa Magna following the launch of *The Blue Midriff*. And then she pictures herself as she rapidly, seamlessly translates everything Harpic says in her English accent. "The world needs more women like her," Bea muses. "Brave, because you have to have a serious pair of ovaries to write a book like that in a Muslim country." Finally, Bea pictures herself waving good-bye at the airport as Harpic thanks J. P. Bonilla for all the hard work he has done promoting the book. There they are, kissing one another on either cheek: *muuua,* right, *muuua,* left . . . Then all of a sudden Bea hears, not in her imagination but in the here and now, something that she has heard so many times at L'Hirondelle d'Or: a call to prayer. It must be coming from some unwitting sound conductor in the room, because there is no mosque or muezzin anywhere near the hotel that might be the source of the chant she now knows by heart, thanks to one of the hotel waiters, who translated it for her. And she also knows that according to the rules of Islam, the muezzin is to repeat the verse five times: *"Allah akbar; God is the greatest . . ."*

"Allah akbar, Allah akbar . . ."

Bea is now on her third Gitanes. Suddenly it occurs to her that maybe Bonilla is playing a joke on her or that he hasn't told her the full story on Harpic. Because, let's see, what exactly does this job entail? She will have to provide lodging for the authoress from Borrioboola-Gha, escort her to a number of parties, and act as her interpreter during her afternoon of glory at the Hotel Villa Magna, where she will address the women of Spain and dedicate *The Blue Midriff* to them? And what about the evenings? And the rest of the time she has to spend with this Harpic? "Guardian angel" is how Bonilla put it. "Go wherever she goes" was mentioned as well. Suddenly the Harpic assignment has completely lost its appeal.

"Allah akbar . . ."

Ring, ring, ring . . .

Bea has no intention of answering the phone. This is the time of day she usually goes down to the solarium to take her mud bath, but today she just doesn't feel like it. She just doesn't feel like going into that hermetically sealed chamber where nobody talks, where the mud is like a warm, soft muzzle on all conversation—a very pleasant muzzle, no doubt, but a muzzle all the same. If she is to go to the mud baths, total silence and introspection are what the next few hours will hold for her.

The telephone rings again. Bonilla can go to hell for all she cares—she's not picking up that phone. She gets up and smooths out the flowered bedspread, telling herself that she has most definitely decided. This afternoon she will skip out on the mud baths and see where the afternoon takes her. Perhaps she will go for a walk, sit on the terrace, get drunk, talk to the stucco columns on the balcony—damnit, anything but lie around with the other guests, as silent and somber as Egyptian mummies, covered in mud or bandages like a bunch of escapees in the Tintin adventure *The Cigars of the Pharaoh*.

Just as she opens the door to the Muguet, before she steps out

into the hall, the phone rings once again and Bea allows herself one
last moment to reflect, not very favorably, upon her friend in Madrid.

"Goddamn con artist," she whispers, and for some reason this
makes her think of Antonio Sánchez and his article about love and
infidelity, and then the infidelity part suddenly makes her think of
Bernardo. Her hand continues to rest on the doorknob, but she is not
sure anymore if she wants to leave the room. And then Bea thinks of
Santiago Arce, who is so attractive, so off-limits, so immune to her
charms.

Men, she thinks. *It's always the same old story.*

Given her current mood, what she needs right now is some nice
person she can chat with, but who? Where? And, most importantly
and most specifically, about what?

Bea turns the doorknob. As she closes the door behind her, it
slams with unnecessary force, a movement that sounds like a complaint, as if to say, "Shit. Of all things . . ."

Golf

GOLF . . . GOLF. THE GREAT MYSTERY, IN WHICH THE LOWEST scorer wins; which, like haggis, comes from Scotland; like cancer, eats into the soul; like death, levels.

—P. G. Wodehouse, *The Heart of a Goof*

A Conversation While Watching Golf. Or, the Story According to Rafael Molinet: how he learned of all the events that transpired in the previous chapters and how he plans to put such information to use

"So, what do you think? I mean, can you just picture Antonio Sánchez locked up in his room, writing and rewriting some shocking exposé about the vices of modern society? Balls, it takes balls. When my friend Ana told me what he was up to, I practically died laughing: the son of a bitch! And everything else, what do you make of it? J. P. Bonilla and his paddle-tennis game. Hilarious, huh? But wait, wait . . . don't go away. I'm out of cigarettes. Let me run up to my room. I'll be right back down—there's plenty more to tell, Mr. Moulinex."

I despise it when people call me Mr. Molinete, Mr. Molina, or, as on this particular occasion, Mr. Moulinex. But this was not the moment to waste time complaining about people's manners, for we had been talking for a good two hours, and I was fascinated by all the stories the blond Bea regaled me with. First she told me all about her friends and what they were doing at the hotel, and then she launched into a detailed explanation of what Ana Fernández de Bugambilla had told her, something about the journalistic endeavors of this Mr. Sánchez.

"Sánchez," she said to me, "is one of those people who always knows everyone's secrets. And if he doesn't know them, he just makes them up." I wish I could have added something—anything— to our little chat to make it seem more of a dialogue, but the blonde was on a roll and did not seem interested in banter. After that, she went on to tell me about another, much more recent telephone conversation with someone by the name of Bonilla, just a few minutes before we met, and everything—I mean everything—she told me before running upstairs for more cigarettes was absolutely captivating, not to mention informative and useful. With a bit of patience and an ear for confessions, a person can really get quite a comprehensive picture of the things that go on behind closed doors.

Bea and I ran into each other on the north balcony facing the golf course. I must say, it is the very best spot in the hotel for exchanging confidences. Nobody ever goes up there, because of the strong winds on that side of the building. And of course we all know how these things happen: When you find yourself in the presence of someone who wants to talk, you should never pass up the opportunity to listen. I would have held out against anything from a strong breeze to a desert *simoom* just to listen to all the information I have so joyously described to you over the past few chapters. Have you ever noticed how simple it is to get people to divulge their deepest,

darkest secrets when you are an innocent bystander? Oh yes, perhaps I did do my part to encourage the confessions on this occasion, but Bea probably would have spilled the beans on her own.
And, anyway, I happen to be a bit of a magnet for this type of situation. After all, I am a loner, a detached listener, so absolutely foreign
to many people, and those are just the qualities that make me the
ideal candidate for listening to people's life stories. But no other confession has ever been quite as interesting as this one. Or as useful.

There I was one October afternoon on the north balcony at
L'Hirondelle d'Or at the exact same moment as Bea. All I had to do
was prick up my ears. I learned so many things from Bea that day—
things that would change the outcome of this story, in fact.

I TOOK ADVANTAGE of Bea's brief cigarette run to gaze out at the golf
course, but she didn't take long. In less than five minutes she reappeared, pack of cigarettes in hand—barely enough time for me to
spot Sánchez and his friend Bernardo down below, very doggedly
chasing a little white ball around the green. Before sitting down at
my side, Bea squinted out at them and waved—how many times
had we all done that in the course of a day? And then, as if our conversation hadn't been interrupted at all, she plunged right back into
her tale. Now, the one problem with these spontaneous confidences
is that they do tend to get terribly off-track. They start out swell, ter-
rific, full of all sorts of interesting details, but after a while the storyteller starts to sound like a mechanical toy, yapping away, and all
that brio and intrigue become monotonous. And so, after divulging
copious amounts of information about her friends, Bea lit a cigarette
(number seven, I think, *bon Dieu*) and began to digress, meander-
ing to other topics—personal travails, details about her life that
didn't interest me in the least. At that point I closed up shop, so to
speak—I stopped paying such close attention to her and let my mind
wander. Every so often, naturally, I would lift my eyes off the green

hills of the golf course and look at her, nodding as if I were fascinated by all that she had to say, but to tell the truth, I haven't the faintest recollection of all that she told me about her life in Madrid, because minutes later something happened—something important, which would dramatically change my train of thought.

The golf course at L'Hirondelle d'Or is very small. As they play, the golfers move closer to and farther away from the main building depending on the whims of the greens. Stage one of my conversation with Bea had gone on so long, what with everything she had to say about Sánchez alone in his room with his computer and so on, that Bernardo and Antonio S. must have walked past us at least three times, like horses running around and around a racetrack. First they headed away from the hotel to tee off. Then they came back toward us, en route to hole five and then, a bit later on, they passed in front of us again on their way to hole seven. As such my eyes began to follow them, and I waited anxiously for the right moment to bid farewell to the blond Bea and to get the hell out of there in the most amiable manner possible. In the meantime, however, I had no choice but to sit there like a fool watching the golfers flit about.

Each time they approached the balcony, the four of us would all call out a greeting, like a bunch of wind-up toys: "Hello," "Hell-oo again," we said, over and over again. It was all rather ridiculous, but those mechanical, repetitive social rituals were what allowed us all to go on doing what we were doing: Bea talked and talked; I pretended to listen to her; and the two men tallied up their points out on the green, I suppose.

"Are you listening to me, Mr. Moulinex?"

"Yes, dear. I'm following you, absolutely. Go on, please."

Bea went on and on, all right—something about her eldest son, I believe, but I just couldn't bring myself to pay attention. None of what she said mattered to me, because an idea was now floating around in my head—although it wasn't quite a full-fledged idea, not yet. More than anything it was a feeling that *something,* some nugget of information, had begun to take shape in my mind. But since I couldn't quite put my finger on it, the uncertainty fluttered about in my stomach like a bad case of indigestion.

As Bea went on about her family or whoever, I whiled away the time observing the golfers as they approached us now for greeting number four. On this occasion, however, they came to a halt at a shady corner just beneath our balcony, where a water fountain bubbled away—such a refreshing, pleasant sound at that particular hour of the afternoon. It was all so *Thousand and One Nights,* if you can imagine it.

Boredom can be such a strange state of mind—and often I think it is the state of mind that has the virtue of unlocking our most unexpected feelings. Yes, I truly believe there is a great deal of truth to the things one discovers when one is bored to distraction.

Sánchez was now directly beneath our balcony, just a few yards away from where Bea and I were sitting, standing with his back to us. All of a sudden I found myself staring at his bald spot in that intense, distracted manner of someone feigning interest in a dull conversation. Intense, distracted, and meticulous, too—not unlike the way we would stare at the person sitting in front of us at church when we were children.

His was a pink, precise little crown: Sánchez's bald spot, I mean. It was a scant few yards beneath my foot, but, no, I didn't feel like stepping on it—not for the moment, at least. I was so close and yet so very far away. I was upstairs, he was downstairs, and the hair that cradled his bald spot shone more than it should have and the bubbling fountain was like music and the afternoon was clear and perfect. Everything was perfect . . . everything except for that bald spot, which loomed even larger when its master bent down to take a sip of water.

Is it possible that Sánchez anoints his crown with some or other oil-based product? I wondered. *Vaseline, perhaps? Some type of ointment to prevent sunburn?* Fortunately, I have managed to hold on to my hair, but even if I were bald as a billiard ball, I would never stoop to smearing my skin with such a disgustingly greasy substance—*que c'est dégueulasse!*

". . . And ever since that fateful day, my older son has failed all his university entrance exams. But I can't blame myself for that as well, can I, Mr. Moulinex?"

Molinet, my dear. Mo-li-net! That is what I wanted to shout at that woman; she was so very dense when it came to names. But I refrained yet again. Thanks to her, I now knew so many of the deep, dark secrets and undercurrents that united her friends in the most mysterious ways. But then, inevitably, I had to ask myself: Why the hell had I been spying on them for the past six or seven days? Of what use was it to me?

"You are absolutely right, my dear. One cannot blame oneself for what other people think."

"*Think,* Mr. Moulinex? What do you mean, what other people *think*? Have you been listening to me at all?"

"Absolutely. Every last word, dear."

"Well, let me continue," she said. And, in effect, she continued.

At that moment, not more than two or three yards beneath my foot, I saw how Sánchez's bald head began to wrinkle into a series of pink folds, just like that first night in the dining room. Beads of perspiration, thousands of them, quivered atop that brilliant surface. I almost took off my eyeglasses—I am rather blind without them, and removing them would have alleviated my horror somewhat, but the grotesque can often be every bit as compelling as the beautiful, so I kept staring. To make matters worse, Sánchez then ran his hand over his head in an attempt to reposition a damp lock of hair that had been displaced as he bent down for a drink of water. His buttocks faced the sky as he bent over the fountain, hunched his back, and pursed his lips as if to plant a kiss on the cascading water. There was something in that *glub, glub, glub* . . . a kind of screech that escaped his lips as he slurped the water. I don't know quite how to describe the sound. It was like the noise made by a sink drain but infinitely sharper—more like the sound of chalk on a blackboard, a kind of *eeewwweeeewwwyyy,* the kind of screech that runs through the spine and threatens to explode from under one's fingernails. Yes, that is what it was: first, the *glub glub* and then, oh Lord: *eeewwweeeewwwyyy . . . glub.* Followed by a shudder. And then once again that feeling came over me again, the feeling that something dreadful was gnawing at me, though I couldn't quite place it: *eeewwweeeewwwyyy . . . glubglubglub.*

How repugnant, I thought as I peered down at Sánchez. *What truly unbearable noises.* The afternoon was so calm, so placid, and yet that sound—once again, *eeewwweeeewwwyyy . . . glubglubglub—* rose up through my inner ear, so very relentlessly. Surely you understand what I mean about those calm, lazy afternoons: The least little sound can acquire the most disturbing intensity and insolence, like an obscenity breaking through silent air. And Sánchez just slurped away as if he intended to go on *glub-glubbing* for all eternity, occasionally throwing in a few *eeeewwwees,* like a cat meowing.

When will this agony end? I asked myself. I could strangle him. *Mais quelle horreur.* If only I could . . . oh, it just makes you want to . . . —*glubglubglub*—slit the man's throat in tiny slices, drown him like a rat and shut him up forever . . .

THAT WAS the moment I realized I was going to kill Antonio Sánchez.

THERE ARE certain revelations in life that make a person feel like new: brand-new. I don't know what Archimedes felt just before he ran out shouting "Eureka!" but I feel certain that it must have been something like the emotion I felt the minute I resolved to commit murder. Of course, when the great man from Syracuse made his discovery, it is entirely possible that he only had an *inkling* of his extraordinary breakthrough—very likely it was something he couldn't quite identify, because in the beginning, every brilliant *eureka!* is nothing more than an elusive gust, wink, or spark of some sort. The point is, we all *know* when we have hit upon something important, but sometimes we don't know quite what it is. In these cases, we have no choice but to sit down and mold that fantastic *thing* that has been revealed to us by a rapid thunderbolt of intuition. For this reason, I would bet that Archimedes just went home and, not bothering to get dressed or do anything (because I believe he went around in the nude), got to work on a series of calculations and diagrams, which would help him get to the root of the spark that had just gone off in his head. And that is precisely what I did that afternoon. I wrapped my mind around the idea that had suddenly entered my mind. And the first thing that occurred to me was to laugh—to myself and only myself, of course.

Other than that, I did not move a muscle. I stayed right where I was, for the air was clear and the afternoon seemed to encourage contemplation. What about the woman at my side? you might ask. Wasn't it difficult to organize my thoughts with someone droning on and on in the chair next to me? No, not really. You will see why. Killing Sánchez: What a discovery! Suddenly I felt certain ideas become clearer, more focused. And the terrible irritation that had been plaguing me all but evaporated. Now I just had to figure out why the idea filled me with such unbridled joy.

The Art of Conversation

Sánchez looked up at me, but only for an instant. He raised his head, which was still poised over the fountain, and looked at me.

"Your friend is quite charming," I said to the blond Bea, who had halted her soliloquy and turned to stare at me, perplexed.

"Do you mean Antonio Sánchez?"

"Excuse me, dear, I didn't mean to interrupt you. Please, go on, go on. You were saying . . . ?"

I learned many things that afternoon. First, that it is exceedingly easy to neutralize the chitchat of a compulsive talker. All one has to do is shuffle the deck of actors in the scene at hand. This blond chatterbox was determined to tell me her life story chapter by chapter, and that was fine with me. But no way was she going to stop me from assimilating the many fascinating but still disjointed ideas that were presently running through my head. Let me explain: Naturally, I had no intention of revealing my thoughts to her, at least not out loud. But, you see, I did find it useful to have a sparring partner close at hand, a person with whom I might share some of the ideas going around in my mind, ideas that were still very much muddled. Most loners are probably pretty familiar with this trick, which consists of superimposing an imaginary, private conversation on top of a real one. I, of course, am a loner through and through, and this is only one of the many techniques I have developed in the course of my life.

I leaned back in my chair: This was going to be fun. I commenced to ask the first question—in my mind, of course.

Let's see, darling. What would you say if I told you that I was planning to kill your friend Sánchez because he has such an insufferable way of drinking water from a fountain?

The blond Bea lit another cigarette and exhaled the smoke as if to say, "Come on, Mr. Moulinex." Good Lord! This proper-name issue had to be rectified, at the very least in this imaginary dialogue. So, please, as long as the blonde is speaking within the bounds of this mental sparring, forgive me for having her call me Mr. Molinet for once and for all.

Now, Mr. Molinet, you may be a perfect stranger to me, but you don't seem abnormally mad. You know what I think? I think that someone who feels driven to kill a man on the basis of something so insignificant— the way someone slurps his soup or sticks his fingernail between his teeth in an attempt to dislodge a piece of food, for example—must harbor a far deeper, darker reason for wanting to commit murder.

What an intelligent girl. Two points. Two points.

"Tell me, Mr. Moulinex, do you think complex problems can be solved with simple solutions?"

This question was real—I mean to say that the blond Bea actually asked me this—probably to see if I was really listening to her droning. And I very amiably replied:

"My dear, in my experience, the things that seem the simplest in life often have the most surprising explanations. The most obvious situations are rarely what they seem to be. Wouldn't you agree?"

The blonde was delighted with my response. And though I hadn't the faintest idea of what she was talking about, I was pleased that my answer seemed to fit in with her monologue. Meanwhile, I went on with my own:

You are absolutely right. When one is inspired to murder a man for an insignificant reason, it can only mean that another, deeper, reason lies behind that urge. My story presents an additional twist, however, though I doubt you would ever be able to guess what it is. Do you know why I have suddenly decided to kill your friend? Very well, the reason may not be obvious but it is indeed simple. I am going to put an end to that Mr. Sánchez (and, no, I don't know him at all, nor has he ever done a thing to me), simply because I can. And therein lies the difference between me and the rest of the mortal world . . .

I looked at Bea for a moment. Naturally, there was no answer forthcoming. She continued blabbering on, but the curls of smoke from her cigarette seemed to demand a more convincing argument, so I clarified my position in the following manner:

I don't think you quite understand, madame, but that is to be expected. Please forgive me, for I should have explained before that I find myself in a rather curious situation. Finis, *get it?* Kaput. *Over. I have come to this exorbitantly expensive spa with the sole intention of vacationing for two delicious weeks and then swallowing a treasure trove of sleeping pills, all at once.*

At this, I believe the blonde interrupted her soliloquy to grace me with a most admiring glance, but that might have been a mirage of some sort—after all, we *were* in the desert.

And since I came here with that objective, absolutely nothing will stop me from committing one tiny, arbitrary act. I will not have to go to jail for killing a man who annoys me, nor will I be held accountable for my actions, because I will be completely off-limits. Can you appreciate

*what an ideal situation it is? I can afford myself the indulgence of fulfill-
ing one of those abominable desires that all of us have felt at some time
or another. Yes, yes, darling, you too. Come now, don't lie, despicable
thoughts like these occur to everyone, even the sanest of us—the difference is that I can actually make them real because I am finished, do you
understand? End of the line: Rafael Molinet is dead.*

As I said this, I felt as if twenty or thirty pieces of a very complicated puzzle had suddenly fallen into place all on their own, creating
a panorama that perhaps I didn't fully understand but could see in
my mind's eye, and it was very promising indeed. What an incredible process. These mental jousts are so useful—at first I often feel a
bit foolish imagining this verbal tug-of-war with someone who, in
reality, cannot hear a word I say, but the method is infallible and ultimately very logical, especially in light of what I mentioned before:
even when we find ourselves surrounded by willing ears and sympathetic lips, we all speak exclusively for our own benefit. Isn't that so?

*The delicious, creative, and unique impunity of a dead man. That
pretty much sums up my current situation, and you needn't be particularly clever to know that when a man is about to die, he can permit himself the luxury of committing arbitrary acts of will. But there is something
else as well, something far more disturbing. A man in my position has an
opportunity to put things in their place, and if he wants, he can add a little twist to the destiny of others as well. Don't you see? A dead man (or
better yet, an almost-dead man) is a lot like God. Of course he is,* ma
chère, *and a god has the power to change the course of worldly events and
deliver justice in his own particular way. What a sublime revelation!*

"YOU ARE SO sweet, so patient, to listen to me like this, Mr. Moulinex.
You don't know how grateful I am for our little chat."

"As am I, dear. And you'll see, that great big jumble of thoughts
in your head will become remarkably clear once you've gotten it all
off your chest. Now, where were we . . . ?" Good God, it was going

to take a miracle for me to keep track of my own thoughts with all these interruptions. Yes, yes, let's get a move-on . . .

Thanks to a very simple discovery, many things became clearer for me. I had been at L'Hirondelle d'Or, such a blessed haven, so blissfully removed from the rest of the world, for just over a week, entertaining myself as many solo travelers often do—by observing my fellow vacationers. It had been an amusing diversion to play the role of the gossipy old man, sniffing about the private lives of other people, but . . . for *what*? I had to ask myself. At first it was out of sheer boredom, obviously, and then it was because one of them, Mercedes Algorta, reminded me of Mama and the very strange manner in which she was widowed. Very well, until this point everything was rational, normal. Now, however, I was beginning to realize that all the information I had culled over the course of the week were like the pieces of a puzzle: one woman who resembled someone very important to me, two similar accidental deaths, separated by forty years of my own life. But how did the other guests fit into this picture? Antonio Sánchez? Ana, the timid blonde? Everyone else? And what in God's name had made me decide that Sánchez was so abominable when Bea told me about the article he was planning to write about Mercedes? All these questions were like a prelude to a great discovery, the most interesting revelation of all: since the two stories were indeed so similar, perhaps I might intercede and change the ending of the second one, given that I am dead—and a dead man is omnipotent and immune to everything, as is God.

Listen, darling. As we just mentioned a few minutes ago, there is always some kind of logical explanation behind every, shall we say, atypical action. Now, would you like to know exactly what is behind my desire to murder Antonio Sánchez?

Absolutely, the imaginary blonde said. The real one, on the other hand, was blabbering on ad nauseam about something, though I had no idea what.

Very well. I will begin by telling you a very old story—not the whole story, though, for it would take me too long to get to the important part. The winds are so disagreeable here, don't you agree?

At that point I believe I heard the real blonde say something like "son of a bitch," but I don't think she was referring to the desert winds.

In short, my dear, all this business regarding Mercedes Algorta and that gossipmonger Sánchez is very oddly connected to my past. Now, don't go and get Freudian on me—we're not there yet. Right now I want you to think back to what I said about how the simplest, most obvious situations very often have the most surprising explanations. The present situation, you see, reminds me of a very old story, which I will very quickly explain. During my childhood, an accident occurred. My father, a man named Bertie Molinet, arrived home one evening with a prostitute, both of them extremely drunk. When I say "home," I don't mean our home in Europe—that night we were in South America, in a rambling old, abandoned house that belonged to my family. That was the first and only night we would ever spend there, though, because the property had been sold and the house was in a state of total disarray. Practically no furniture, no electricity . . . a mess. Very well, the house had a number of abandoned bedrooms, one of which was to be mine for the night. To me it was fascinating, unexplored terrain, filled with marvelous treasures: trunks with exquisite clothes from bygone eras, lacy underthings, and crinoline petticoats. On a table—do take note—there was a hand mirror with a silver handle. Now, if you put these elements together, do you think you can imagine what happened next, my dear?

An arabesque of Bea's dark, dense tobacco smoke curled up before my eyes into a giant question mark.

Now, let me give you a general idea of all the things people claimed happened that night. I then told my sparring partner of how Bertie found me in one of the bedrooms clad in nothing but a lady's garter belt and clinging to the mirror with the silver handle, and I went on to describe the various violent incidents that ensued, which sent Bertie tumbling down the stairs as my mother stood by, doing nothing to break his fall. I also took a moment to mention how Gomez, my father's majordomo, watched from the bottom of the stairs as my father fell and how my mother stood as still as a marble statue as Bertie's head hit the stairs . . . twenty-one, twenty-two . . . Twenty-two steps leading down to hell. I also told the blonde about how Gomez, useless fool that he was, had cowered in a corner of the vestibule, covering his ears, crouched down low like a frightened ostrich, acting even more moronic than usual. I re-enacted his reaction for the benefit of the blonde, screeching as he did:

"Ooooooooooooeeeee! I don't want to thee this," he shrieked in his lisp. "I don't want to thee it." This was absurd, you see, because the idiot in reality was covering his ears so as not to hear anything. And Bertie's head hit a total of thirty-two, thirty-three, thirty-four steps in all before he finally landed with a thud at the bottom of the staircase. At that very moment, I raced down the two flights of stairs separating us until finally I arrived at my father's side. My mother, up on the second floor, did not move at all:

"My God, Rafael, my God!" she cried. "What have I done?" To which I responded:

"Nothing, Mama, nothing, my dear. Wait, wait—don't come down just yet." And as I said this, Gomez looked at neither my mother nor myself, for he had turned his head to the wall to say this time,

"I don't thee anything, I don't hear anything at all . . ."

I went on to tell the blonde about all the things people had speculated about that dreadful event, and of how the gossipers wasted no time disseminating the hypothesis that Bertie's death was the result not of an accident but rather an . . . omission on the part of my mother. Such genteel people, speaking of "omissions"—how very Christian of them. The only thing left to tell, now, was what became of our lives—specifically, my mother's life—after that day. In my mind, I told Bea all about the shadows of doubt, rumor, and conjecture that hung over us, all of it so intense that my mother isolated herself from everyone, turning herself into a kind of voluntary exile.

I made very certain to explain to the blonde that all of this is what people *said* happened. It was *their* version of the story, built around everything Gomez went around saying, that clumsy oaf who stood there covering his ears all the while.

So much speculation, so many hypotheses . . . a veritable legend was constructed on the basis of one arbitrary fact—just as in the case of Mercedes Algorta. And because of that, I know exactly what will happen to that girl if Sánchez publishes his article: two unfaithful husbands who die in what seem to be ambiguous circumstances, two identical events forty years apart. Can't you see why I am so bothered by the likes of such rumor scavengers?

Bea continued smoking incessantly, which was a tremendous help. Her next mouthful of smoke seemed to say:

Fabulous, Mr. Molinet. Fa-bu-lous. You don't have to say another word; I understand perfectly. Because you are practically dead yourself, you can permit yourself the luxury that the rest of us cannot: You can finally settle an old debt. Two identical stories. How incredible!

Would you like me to describe some of the despicable things that certain charitable souls said about my mother?

I can only imagine—more or less the same type of wild accusations that people have made regarding Mercedes Algorta. Your plan is nothing less than an attempt to thwart destiny: you have seen Mercedes Algorta suffer many of the same accusations that were directed at your mother. And Sánchez is now going to add even more grist to the rumor mill, and we all know what happens to rumors when someone puts them in writing. There is something so very sacrosanct about the printed word . . . people tend to believe everything they read, even if it is utter nonsense. But . . .

The blond Bea smoked, doubtful about something.

Let us be frank: One fact remains, and I don't mean to quibble over details, mind you, but you do understand. Both your mother and Mercedes—of course, I can only speculate about Mercedes; I have no way of knowing for sure—took advantage of, oh, how shall I put it? They took advantage of a very crucial moment in which a circumstance was served to them on a silver platter—excuse the expression, but I do think it appropriate. A circumstance that would permit them to send their respective cheating husbands to hell. Of course, believe me, I am not one to cast the first stone. Maybe I would have done the same. And my friends? Oh, don't get me started on them, who knows what they would have done. The point is: Almost all the husbands and wives I know, at some time, have dreamt of such an ideal situation—to be scot-free of their spouses, without having to move a finger!

My dear, how could you possibly think . . .

Oh, how romantic, Mr. Molinet!

A semicircle of smoke that the blonde has just traced with the cigarette in her left hand interrupted my thoughts.

How romantic. Now I understand all of this even better. You are going to take revenge for both of them—not because they are innocent, but rather despite their guilt.

That is where you are mistaken.

Oh?

Both women are innocent.

But you just told me that your mother allowed Bertie to tumble down a staircase right under her nose.

Darling, you haven't listened to a word I have said. I just told you what the gossipmongers *were saying about my mother. A tumble down a flight of stairs, three people present, plus one non–family member, who told all sorts of tales about what he saw. But that doesn't mean the story is true. Not necessarily. The facts that seem most incontrovertible, the ones people rattle off with such ease and certainty, are precisely the most disconcerting elements of the story. That is the reason I want to put things in their place. Please forgive me. I am as repetitive as uncooked garlic—*quelle horreur—*I realize this, but things that seem utterly obvious always have the most surprising explanations. As such, I have decided to*

*take care of Mr. Sánchez in my own way. First, because I am a dead man
and I can allow myself to do so. And second, because I am certain that
Mercedes is every bit as innocent as Mama.*

*But what do you know? Nobody really knows what happened the
night Valdés died. There has been no consensus whatsoever, so really.
There is no way . . .*

*Darling, believe me, I don't need to know a thing. The story is iden-
tical to that of my mother.*

*And that is enough for you to decide that Mercedes is innocent as
well?*

*Don't be a bore, dear, or is it that you prefer the simplistic interpre-
tation of our friend Sánchez, who says that two plus two always equals
four, and a widow who happens to coincide with an attractive man at a
remote hotel is necessarily guilty of an atrocious murder?*

Bea looked offended, and the smoke from her cigarette reflected
this as it curled into another, far more unpleasant arabesque.

*Of course not, Mr. Molinet. I do not have the soul of a soap opera ac-
tress. Nor do I need to possess the sour grapes of someone like Sánchez to
deduce that simply because they are both here at this hotel, Mercedes and
Arce are lovers and guilty of murdering Valdés. But the fact that our little couple met only two days ago—and I am certain of this—does not
necessarily imply that Mercedes did not take advantage of that situation
that was served to her on such a silver platter. You can't rule that out.*

The air blew colder and colder. I could not allow my mental
sparring to continue down such an unsettling path. I repeated once
again:

*Believe me, dear, the story is just like my mother's: two philandering
husbands, two stories that have provided endless fodder for the rumor
mill—identical, I tell you. Mercedes n'a rien fait . . . And I will prove it.
Listen carefully now, because this is the really interesting part.*

"Am I boring you, Mr. Moulinex?" *C'est la blonde qui parle, bien
sûr,* I thought.

"What on earth do you mean, my dear?"

"Well, it's just that you've been staring at the golf course with the most intense look in your eyes and there isn't anyone out there. Our friends stopped playing a long time ago. It's just the two of us here."

"Just the two of us, darling. How right you are. And, believe me, I am delighted. It's been years since I've had such a fascinating conversation. Please, do go on."

The blonde launched right back into her monologue as I resumed my own.

If you can believe it, darling, I am about to tell you what really happened the night my father died. And this is the real story of a bad, bad girl. I paused, though I don't quite know why. Perhaps I needed to ask my imaginary conversation partner one of those stupid questions people always ask, the question we all want to ask, everyone's favorite: "Tell me, dear, I must ask you: what do you think of me?" Now, isn't that the one question we would all love to ask? Yes, yes, it is . . . don't lie. What do you think of me? Wouldn't we all love to know. On this occasion, however, the narcissistic query was in fact quite crucial, and my sparring partner, the chain-smoking blonde, rushed to respond, but I intercepted her with another, even more specific, question:

Now that I have told you that I intend to kill a man simply to halt a rumor, tell me: What do you think of me? Am I an indulgent man? Someone who, in the twilight of his life, finally figures out a way to avenge all the suffering his mother endured? And then, if you want to apply a bit of pop psychology, might you say that I am a homosexual who has lived in the shadow of my mother for years, adoring her and plunging into a deep depression upon her death? Am I mistaken?

The blonde stopped smoking, which made it harder to maintain our imaginary conversation without her realizing, but I took the risk anyway:

Is that how you see me? Come now, dear, don't underestimate me now. Do you really think me so . . . simple? Simple enough to avenge the memory of my beloved mother by helping another person who looks quite a bit like her? It sounds so romantic, and don't get me wrong—I adored my mother. I would have done anything for her. But once again I must remind you that things are not always what they seem. There are certain debts in life that are far more compelling than those of affection, and bonds far stronger than those of love—secrets, for example. Don't tell me it didn't occur to you that I might have omitted a fact or two from my story? Of course the fact to which I refer is something you couldn't possibly have inferred on your own, and so I will tell it to you. I have a debt to my mother—this much is true, though it is not the one you imagine. As I have said before, I am no saint, but if there is one thing I am proud of, it is that I was able to keep a secret up until the day she died. Now, things are different. Sadly, the one person who cared about that secret no longer exists, and finally I am free to act as I see fit, even if it is forty years overdue. Do you understand now?

The smoke from another of Bea's Gitanes (number ten?) did not understand a thing, which prompted me to make a special effort to explain my motives.

It's odd. Suddenly, after many, many years, a person can decide to confess something he has always kept hidden, a detail about which he has never spoken, and yet, just when he is ready to utter it, it sounds so false. It almost feels as if in one's effort to grasp the truth, the truth becomes unreal, as if the thing that has never been uttered or thought does not exist in the end. Perhaps that is why, as I relived my encounter with Bea on the north balcony of L'Hirondelle d'Or, I was once again surprised at how hollow my confession sounded, even if nobody really heard it. As far as the blond Bea was concerned, I was just a silent conversation companion staring out at a distant point on the golf course. Yet there is always something rather indecent about confessions, even those that fall on imaginary ears, and I had to turn away for a moment as I said:

My father did not die from a simple spill down a flight of stairs.

It was so odd to hear myself say something out loud that I had never even allowed myself to think.

Neither the fall nor my mother's "sin of omission" was what killed Bertie. Those are lies, although I imagine you might be rather shocked to know that my mother actually preferred that version. Are you scandalized, darling? Well, it is true. Even with all the rumors flying around town and people whispering on and on about how the "accident" had really occurred, Mama kept her mouth shut and simply nodded her head. With imperious authority, legions of venom-filled souls said things like, "Oh, there was a witness," or else they would wonder, "Who is that man, that Gomez character who described everything he saw that night?," or else they would say things like, "No—really? You mean you don't know the real story about little Elisa? It is a far cry from the official version, let me tell you. Yes, yes, I know they declared it an unfortunate accident brought on by alcohol, and that she couldn't have prevented him from falling—at least that is what Rafaelito swore under oath—but nobody except the police believed a single word that came out of that faggot's mouth. He adores his mother." The more the rumors flew, the less she talked. So what do you think now? Would you say that she was stupid, that she should have at least defended the official version instead of letting people imagine the worst? My mother did the exact opposite: Her silence almost seemed to encourage the speculation. Come now, dear, don't look at me that way. I think you are going to learn a great deal about human nature this afternoon. Now, pay close attention, for we have almost reached the very surprising finale. As I told you, it is a lie. My father did not die the way everyone said. But he did not die accidentally, either. The Berties of this world, my dear, are very tough nuts to crack.

Suddenly, I felt an urge to burst out laughing. I suspect I may have actually done this, because the blond Bea looked over at me and said, "Do you find the things I have just said amusing, Mr. Moulinex? Maybe we should leave the conversation for another time, it's starting to get cold."

"Oh, one last cigarette, dear," I insisted. And it was upon this last smoky volute that I made my final confession.

After a tragedy occurs, you cannot even imagine how long the minutes take to tick by, the amount of time you have on your hands when things are in complete and total pandemonium. Just picture it: My father, flat out on the vestibule floor, the grandfather clock against the wall advancing toward 4:50 in the morning and Mama standing completely still at the top of the staircase. Gomez stood there staring at her while I leaped downstairs to see what had happened. Until then, everything makes sense, does it not? Tick-tock, tick-tock, went the clock, slowly and precisely, but still so much faster than real time, which has a way of stretching out into eternity at a moment like that one.

"I don't want to thee, I don't want to be here," cried Gomez before turning his face toward the wall. That, you see, is why he did not see me reach the ground floor, where I quickly and efficiently made sure that my father would never open his eyes again. It was so easy. A good hand mirror has so many different uses. There we were, in that darkened mansion, my mother upstairs, Gomez facing the wall like an orphaned puppy, his hands still covering his ears, assuming that the inevitable had already occurred. Of course, in point of fact the inevitable occurred just a little later, when nobody was looking. Now, what do you think of that, my dear?

Satisfied with the confession I made to my imaginary sparring partner, I thought that perhaps I might be able to confess it, blow by blow, to the widow I have so closely observed over the past few days, so that she too might see that nothing is quite what it seems. And why not? That way she would learn the story of a real bad girl, straight from the horse's mouth. A person unlike herself, whom I believe to be innocent of the things Sánchez believes her to be guilty of. Unlike my mother as well, whose only crime was being paralyzed by fear at a terribly tragic moment. No, no—I speak of another bad girl, one who came to life that night in the house at El Prado . . .

You do see who the real "bad girl" is, don't you, dear? Of course you do. The real "bad girl" is the one who was caught by surprise in a dark bedroom filled with old clothing, lacy things and crinoline petticoats. And now tell me: What do you really think of me?

The blond chain smoker's curls of smoke laughed no more. I saw quite clearly that I seemed not fabulous but rather quite terrible to her now, because those curls of smoke now called out to me:

How could you, Molinet? How could you have kept that secret for so long? Why didn't you at least tell your mother, so that she wouldn't have to live all those years filled with such unnecessary guilt? And what about the gossip she had to endure, all the conjecture about what she might have done? Oh, Mr. Molinet, how could you have hidden your guilt for so long? Didn't it matter to you that people blamed your mother for his death? People talk so much. They talk and they talk . . .

At this point, I ended my little conversation with my blond friend's smoke curls. Nobody understands anything—of course they don't. I suppose it is a good thing I never told this story to anyone, for very few people would understand what she always knew. My mother always knew that it had been another blow, final and definitive, that had killed Bertie Molinet, that a fifteen-year-old child had been responsible for his death. What, then, had Gomez seen? Nothing, obviously. The stunned eyes of Bertie Molinet, however, most definitely saw the mirror with the silver handle rise above his body and the reflection of its glass face bounce off the ceiling, illuminating my mother's countenance for an instant before it came crashing down upon him in a single, sharp thud. Just one hit. That was enough. Words were unnecessary, for that moment of fleeting light was enough to make Mama realize what had happened. And *I* knew that *she* knew, even though she never allowed us to mention it. Oh, those stupid curls of smoke simply couldn't understand that there are times in life when it is easier for a person to bear the burden of gossip and suspicion than to admit, even to herself, the far more appalling guilt of a person she loves more than anyone else.

That which is not spoken does not exist, and as such, a secret untold has a way of disappearing in the end. The fact that I killed

Bertie was *her* secret, not mine. Can you understand that? I would have preferred, a thousand times over, to have been able to confess my guilt to someone—even to Dr. Pertini, that distinguished London psychiatrist to whom I am grateful for having prescribed me the three vials of sleeping pills which will come very much in handy over the next few days. But foolish Dr. Pertini would never have guessed the truth, and I could never have told him, because one cannot go around divulging other people's secrets, especially when there is no reason for it. Now, however, things are different. She is dead, and I have since come across a real-life story that is identical to hers. How could I waste the opportunity to set the record straight this time?

"Mr. Moulinex . . ."

. . . Silent for so many years, unable to do a thing as everyone else told lie upon lie.

"Are you listening to me, Mr. Moulinex?"

I would say that this is a most singular circumstance.

"I would say that it is as cold as an icebox out here. This breeze has turned gale-force. Don't you think we ought to go in?"

I looked at her, I'm afraid, as if she were an extraterrestrial. Bea, the blond clone, remained exactly where she was, which I found extraordinary—so very many ideas had been racing through my head over the past few minutes that I could scarcely believe I was still sitting there facing this woman, listening (so to speak) to the very long-winded story of her life, or her children's lives, or whoever's life she was presently concerned about. I turned to her and smiled attentively as she thanked me profusely for my patience and for the time I had devoted to her confidences. Yet another example of how things are *never* what they seem.

"Your advice has been such a help to me," she said.

Advice? I had barely opened my mouth.

"You are an awfully perceptive person, Mr. Moulinex," she added.

I really couldn't understand how on earth she could possibly think I was a perceptive person and not a complete lummox based on the two or three words that I had spoken to her. But we all know, don't we, that people have a way of confusing things, and of believing a seemingly sympathetic ear to be the sign of great intelligence. Such a typical mistake.

"It has been so wonderful to have been able to share this conversation with you," she said.

"Likewise, *madame.* You can't imagine how much it means to me," I replied with the same attentive airs I had been feigning as she told me her story.

I took her hand and bid her farewell with a few more gallantries: "Good-bye, my darling. You really are a truly lovely young lady."

Kill Sánchez! That was it, I had to stop him from spreading false suspicion!

"Do take care to cover up, *madame,* it is quite nippy out here."

Forty! It's been forty years! I'll set things straight soon enough.

"Allow me to help you up."

Mama would have preferred silence. But things are so different now . . .

"My God, Mr. Moulinex. It's so windy you've sprouted tears!"

"Really, dear?"

"Yes—come, come in with me, let's go back inside."

Preparations for a Demise

THIS, I MUST SAY, IS A TERRIBLY SAD CHAPTER, FOR NOBODY IN the world escapes death, and etiquette, which does not shirk its responsibility under any circumstance, must dictate the manner in which grief is to be experienced, or at least demonstrated.

—Baroness Staffe, *Usages du monde*

Five Bluebottles

Twenty-one, twenty-two, twenty-three . . . how many sleeping pills must a suicidal man ingest if he wants to be certain of achieving his goal? Twenty-four, twenty-five, twenty-six . . . how many sleeping pills must a murderer administer if he wants to be certain of killing his victim? These are the kinds of highly delicate questions that arise when one finds oneself at the edge of the desert, many miles from civilization. Not a single pharmacy in a fifty-mile radius, no way to increase my supply . . . Forty-seven, forty-eight, and . . . forty-nine pills of a highly effective substance for battling insomnia stared out at me from the inside of three childproof vials sitting on the bed-spread.

It was early in the morning on October 22. A day and a half, ac-cording to my calculations, before Sánchez and his friends were to return to Madrid. And there I was, measuring pills like a shipwreck victim on a deserted island counting his ration of fresh water. Forty-nine pills to be split between two people: twenty-five to kill Sánchez and the rest for me. Would it be enough? Naturally, I knew that it was in my interest to err on the side of excess, and as such I could not allow myself the luxury of wasting even half a tablet to help me fall asleep that night. Which meant that I would die of exhaustion and a bloody inconvenient case of insomnia as well.

It must have been around four-thirty in the morning. Gomez slept peacefully next to my bed, as he always seemed to do whenever I was assaulted by my most troubling thoughts. Ungrateful mutt. His ears, flapping out like soft wings on either side of his head, al-ways made me so maddeningly jealous, for they were so innocent, so oblivious to everything around him—completely oblivious, no doubt, to the plots I had been hatching over the past twenty-four hours.

I have spent those hours planning the murder. And, believe me, it is not easy to figure out the proper way to finish off an individual at a hotel like L'Hirondelle d'Or. I suppose I have already mentioned that the location comprises a large redbrick building that is quite grandiose but, unfortunately, free of any masonry detailing. The fa-cade of this stout building is extremely smooth, with scarcely more than one or two plants in the immediate vicinity. As such, I had to rule out all the classic accidents, like a calamitous fall from a dizzy-ing height, such a simple method for eliminating an undesirable subject. Even the idea of bopping the victim on the head with a blunt object launched from a nearby window did not seem terrifically promising: First I would have to locate an object heavy enough for my purposes—an alabaster vase, or else a hefty chunk of molding, neither of which was available. And second, my firing skills would have to be similar to those of William Tell, so I need not bother going into the futility of that idea. The one and only thing I have in common with such a skillful hero is that I, too, despise apples.

Given that I do not particularly favor unnecessary violence, I also had to eliminate the more, shall we say, dirty instruments of murder, such as large butcher's knives or certain gardening tools . . . although I must admit that I was tempted by a scythe I found resting against the garden wall—but only for a few moments. The inspiration owed more to allegorical reasons (e.g., the Grim Reaper) than practical ones.

Speaking of practicality, I should clarify that I was not hindered by any of the factors that typical assassins, at least those with a bit of foresight, generally must take into consideration. For example, I had no need to contemplate logistical issues such as: Will they find out it was me?, Will I be able to make my escape?, and Will they throw me in jail? Given the circumstances, I did not have to waste a single minute on these concerns, but on the other hand there were certain aesthetic issues to consider. And murder, like everything else in life, should be carried out according to a plan that is, if not elegant, at the very least imaginative. I had to find a way to dispose of Sánchez that was slightly more elegant than administering an overdose of sleeping pills. But I couldn't come up with a single idea, not even after an entire day of strategizing. The hours went by, the sky darkened, and the day dwindled away, as did my hopes of finding a solution. It seemed that sleeping pills were my only choice. How many would I need to send the two of us—him first, then me—to the land of eternal rest? Movies never seem to explain the means of suicide in proper detail, and a good explanation certainly would have come in handy right then. Would a half dozen pills do the trick? I had no idea. If so, I could easily reward myself with half a tablet that night. But no. I couldn't take such a risk, given the delicate matter at hand: When you decide to commit an act of this nature, you have to keep as many odds as possible on your side. No exceptions. For that reason, at 4 A.M. on the morning of October 22, I found myself sitting in my room at L'Hirondelle as wide awake as an owl, with three vials of sleeping pills on my bedspread.

The night sky was clear, and the moon illuminated the broad land that spilled out before my eyes. I couldn't quite see the mud baths, which were set in a very deep hollow, but I was able to see the left-hand side of the garden. The light was so abundant and crisp that had my lazy fingers been willing to reach for my eyeglasses, I surely would have been able to see the winter pool and even the surface of the water. The winter pool of L'Hirondelle d'Or, extravagant hotel that it is, is always illuminated at night for the visual appreciation of the guests.

What a peaceful evening, I thought. *So utterly uneventful.* As uneventful as the past twenty-four hours I had spent performing my logistical research. In fact, the only fruitful moment of the day had been at breakfast, when I observed the various characters I had been spying on with renewed interest. An interest that was scientific, you might say, and somewhat capricious, not unlike the intense fascination of a little boy studying a handful of bluebottle flies he has trapped in a glass jar. There they are, five or six in all, and the little boy gazes at them through the glass jar, observing their every move. Picture, if you will, one of the flies trying to take flight inside the jar. "Silly," the little boy says, smiling. "Soon you won't have any wings at all." And he slides a finger into the jar, scaring the fly, which tries to flutter its wings ever so briefly. He spots another fly cowering in a corner, and he watches it, pressing his face against the jar and declaring: "Don't worry, little one, you'll make it out, because I like that little spot on your right wing." It is all so very arbitrary, so deliciously . . . divine. Yes, that is what it is: divine, in the most literal sense of the word.

Now that sleep was out of the question, I decided to mentally replay the early hours of the day. I had walked downstairs to breakfast

very early, just before eight-thirty. Breakfast is a splendid time for
observation, for people are truly themselves at such an early hour.
Our social façades are generally not in place at breakfast time. As
such, the stupefied, unrecognizable faces reflecting back at us through
our morning tea or coffee are often the very mirror of our souls.

This was an especially promising morning in terms of the number of people. Rarely does everyone converge on the dining room at
the same time, but yesterday (yesterday? Of course, October 21 is
now over and another day will soon begin) I found a select group of
guests parading in and out of the dining room, much to my surprise
and delight. There they all were, either loitering by the garden door
or the vestibule. And then, when the garden door opened again, I
found the blond Bea and Bernardo Salat advancing toward me.

"Good morning, good morning, *Mr. Moulinex*!" she cried out as
she strode past my table. Even more irritating than that, however,
was the cloud of smoke that descended upon me half a second later.
That woman really does smoke too much. I had grown slightly fond
of her since our conversation out on the balcony—it had been so
lovely to chat out in the open air—but there in the dining room, the
smoke was just too much, and on such a lovely morning at that.
I didn't want her anywhere near me. Luckily, they found a table
by the door with a nice view of the garden, well enough away from
my own. The window was open, the birds were singing, and the
rosy early-morning light created the sharpest, clearest silhouettes of
everyone, leaving me discreetly in the background. Perfect. As they
served me my tea with milk, I took a moment to study Bernardo
Salat. Like every morning, he was dressed for golf: a green polo shirt
and a pair of stone-colored pants. What little hair he had was slightly
mussed, which made me think that perhaps he had already stepped
outside for a quick, routine inspection of the weather, the typical
golfer's weather check. Golfers always stick their heads outside before embarking on a round so they can sniff at the breeze, lick their

expert finger, and hold it up in the air to test the direction or the intensity of the morning wind.

I surmised that Bernardo Salat had already performed this ritual before breakfast. A bit unnecessary, I thought—it wasn't even eight forty-five, and I know for a fact that neither he nor Antonio Sánchez has ever started playing golf before ten. Impossible: The great radio announcer always uses that early hour to take advantage of the winter pool, to swim a few laps at his leisure and warm up his muscles. I exhaled deeply. I had ordered fried eggs with bacon, which no doubt would have horrified a more fastidious group of waiters than the friendly team at L'Hirondelle d'Or, and I made a mental toast to Sánchez as I savored the glorious scent of crispy bacon, the smooth delicacy of my perfectly fried egg—not too dry, not too raw. And as I looked over at the garden door where Sánchez usually entered the dining room after his morning exercise, I thought about how exhausting life must be for people who are so concerned about maintaining their youth and elasticity. For the moment, however, he was nowhere in sight and I envisioned him intently plowing through the waters with all the discipline and energy he could muster: twenty laps of crawl, another thirty, say, of backstroke, ten laps of butterfly—good Lord, what hell! Followed by, perhaps, a healthy spell underwater, and finished off by a series of water calisthenics for strengthening pectorals, abductors, and groin muscles. *That poor soul, what useless nonsense,* I thought, almost laughing out loud—not unlike the little boy watching one of his bluebottles very foolishly try to fly from one end of the jar to the other. *Exhausting,* I thought. Not to mention stupid, unnecessary, and useless—because by tomorrow, he would be dead.

In this silent paradise, *Le Monde* is the only newspaper that we receive at the breakfast hour, and its format offers the perfect cover for hiding. It isn't too large like some papers, or too small, like the tabloids—not that I ever would have allowed myself to flip through such trash, of course, not even to disguise my surveillance of Bea and Bernardo. As I was saying, *Le Monde* has the ideal dimensions for this sort of spying, and so I killed some time waiting for Sánchez to arrive—oh, how I would enjoy watching the biggest and bluest of my bluebottles up close! Perhaps by spying on him I would hit on some brilliant idea for sending him into the great beyond.

At that moment, a very distinct feeling suddenly came over me, reminding me of the days when I was more of a participant in life, caught in the throes of some love affair or fling. It hit me right when I turned to observe Bea and Bernardo at their table by the window. Occasionally—perhaps more frequently than occasionally—it can be a painful anticlimax to eat breakfast in the company of someone with whom we have just slept. Sometimes my eyes would grow suspicious, and then I would suddenly ask myself how those hands could have possibly caressed me, good God, just a few hours earlier. It's interesting how our fingers seem to have been tailor-made for lovemaking: fingers so tender as they travel across our willing flesh, so skillful at discovering hidden pleasure spots, wet fingers that embark on consummately intimate explorations; divine fingers that elicit such infinite joy . . . And then all of a sudden, with the very same appetite, we find our fingers dedicating their efforts to . . . a piece of rye toast! They are still the same fingers, no doubt, but they betray us now as they brazenly stalk their way across the tablecloth in search of the salt shaker or as they ruthlessly smear that pat of butter on the toast. Such disingenuous hands and fingers. Like the mouth. Every bit as deceitful. Look at it, look at the mouth curling into the form of a kiss as it preys upon a straw stuck in some beverage. Even more humiliating is the sight of those same lips, just as wet as they were before, suddenly coming together to suck away lasciviously at a teaspoon. Everything is demystified at breakfast.

There are, however, far lovelier breakfast scenes to be had, the kind that inspire genuine, spontaneous smiles instead of frozen facial masks, smiles that emerge unconsciously after a night of love in

its earliest phase. Such was the case, for example, at the breakfast
table to my right, occupied by a couple I find consummately fascinating. Mercedes Algorta and Santiago Arce had chosen a table by the
door, a fair distance from the other guests. Their tender gazes as they
passed the coffeepot or creamer and the slow caresses that slid back
and forth across a teacup spoke volumes about what was happening
between them. And just as in the case of Bernardo and Bea, the fingers now preoccupied with breakfast were the same fingers that had
caressed the most intimate contours and stroked the ruffled folds of
love. The only difference between the two couples was that the fingers and lips of Mercedes and Arce seemed to continue to lavish one
another with caresses. When they licked their teaspoons, they appeared to be actually licking something else, perhaps the soft nape of
their respective necks. And the marmalade recalled something else,
too—something sweet, like a kiss. Lovers need not touch or even devour each other with their eyes, because the coffeepot, the cups, and
even the forks and knives are all there for them, for their pleasure, as
are the sausages, the smooth butter, and the honey, too: "Ooh, ooh—
drink this, drink a bit of this. It's about to overflow . . ."

Ever since I made my decision to kill Sánchez, Mercedes Algorta and Santiago Arce have become my most intriguing subjects of
observation. Especially Mercedes. I have watched her move around
the hotel, and I have admired the very well educated way she avoids
all contact with the other Spanish guests. I have always been fascinated by the kind of women who know how to be present without
actively drawing attention to themselves. It is an intelligent and, I
believe, exclusively feminine virtue—after all, have you ever come
across a single male who would ever *choose* to go unnoticed? Of
course not.

Mercedes, on the other hand, is both here and not here. I have
observed her steadily over the past few days, and have watched how
she so discreetly began her affair with Arce, without a single external gesture, all of it so private. And when I say private I don't mean

to suggest that they are trying to hide anything—not at all, because they are not hiding from anyone.

Three days, I thought. *It has been three days since their romance began. They are in the most marvelous phase of their relationship, and if all goes well . . .*

If all goes well, they can thank me for it. That is what I thought, still feeling like that little boy with his glass jar full of bluebottles. And I was very satisfied with myself. What an odd position to be in, but what sublime delight this position provided. To be the master of that glass jar, to be there and not fully there at the same time. Would you believe me if I told you that I have not exchanged a single word with that woman beyond the terse greetings we all murmur so many times a day here at L'Hirondelle d'Or? It is true, my friends, and it is something I am extremely proud of. Mercedes is my creation. I don't know who this woman is; all I know is that her story is too similar to that of my mother, and for that reason I believe her to be innocent of all the nonsense they say about her. As I say this I watch her pour a second cup of tea with a firm hand, and I gaze at her shapely, strong arms, bare to just above her elbow. She is a vision, a true lady serving her tea, a ritual that Mama performed with equal elegance.

That was when I remembered the bracelet. Yes: that thick, ostentatious bracelet Mercedes Algorta had been wearing regularly, even to go to the swimming pool, before the throng of Madrileños arrived on the scene at L'Hirondelle d'Or. She hadn't put it back on since their arrival, a detail which troubled me somewhat for a time—specifically, just after I received that fax from Fernanda with the fuzzy photograph of Isabella wearing a very similar bracelet. To keep a piece of jewelry as a token of vengeance while one's own husband is on his deathbed is . . . All of this came rushing uncontrollably into my head right then. And at that very moment, two tables away from me, Mercedes's bare arms rapidly flew up to her face to banish an annoying fly that had suddenly started buzzing around her.

Oh, the ridiculous things a person thinks of at this hour of the morning, I thought. *Here I am thinking about nonexistent bracelets when I really should be thinking about the cleanest way to finish off old Sánchez. Sánchez the gossipmonger, the author of that malicious article about Mercedes Algorta that he plans to publish when he returns to Madrid so that he can illustrate "the vices of modern society," as he puts it. People can be so capricious when they decide to put someone else's life in jeopardy.*

My widow had such lovely hands. I was able to admire them up close as she and Arce walked past my table after finishing their breakfast.

"Bye-bye. Lovely morning, isn't it?"

My lovely couple smiled as they walked away—even their backs smiled, despite the fact that we all know backs can't very well smile, nor can intertwined arms or two bodies that are slowly growing accustomed to each other's contours. Arce and Mercedes, Mercedes and Arce . . . what would they do on this sunny morning? Frolic in the indoor pool, perhaps, play a game of tennis . . . My day, on the other hand, was sure to be grim: I had twenty-four hours to come up with an imaginative way of killing Antonio Sánchez.

To make a long story short regarding my various failures in this endeavor, allow me to summarize my activities as follows: I wasted the rest of the day inspecting the hotel and the surrounding area from top to bottom in search of . . . well, I don't know what I was searching for, exactly. And I found the afternoon upon me.

Hmmm, I thought during the quiet serenity inspired by the afternoon siesta. *There must be some way to locate a bit of rat poison in this elegant hotel. For that, I will have to explore the kitchen, or perhaps the boiler room . . .* By nightfall, I was racked by the most complete sense of failure. Dinner was a sterile affair, and then I retired to my room.

*   *   *

AT THE present moment I find myself counting pills in my pine-needle room, not allowing myself to waste a single tablet on my own insomnia even though it is five in the morning. Now I know for sure that I will have no choice but to use the pills as my lethal weapon. In the next few hours, I will somehow have to make Sánchez swallow them, because he and his companions are planning to leave the day after tomorrow.

What is the proper moment for such a thing?

Perhaps breakfast, or during the period when everyone lays out by the mud baths . . . Who knows? There must be some way to get him to ingest twenty-five (twenty-five? *Ciel, quelle besogne*) pills dissolved in . . . what? That repulsive carrot juice that seems to be L'Hirondelle's specialty cocktail? So much pureed vegetable must taste repulsive—and that might be just the trick for disguising my little green pills. Yes, why not? It is certainly a viable method for disposing of Sánchez—perhaps not the most brilliant method, I admit, but it is certainly plausible and easy enough to carry out. Very well. Decision made. That is how it will be done.

The first light of this tremulous daybreak emerges on the horizon, gaining intensity bit by bit, but for the moment it is still just a thin red line far away in the distance. Every time Bertie Molinet spied a horizon line like that one, he always said the same thing, in his magnificent Oxonian accent, *bien sûr:* "Red in the morning, traveler's warning; red in the night, traveler's delight."

And I repeat the refrain, suppressing a cackle. Red in the morning is dangerous for the traveler, true enough. And red in the night promises only good things for those very same travelers. Hmm . . . I know of one traveler in particular who would do well to heed the warning of such an ominous dawn, but for the moment he is dreaming away in what will be his last night of sleep.

I, on the other hand, have not slept a wink, and at about five forty-five I get up to stretch my legs. Except for the glow of the horizon line, it is still dark outside, even darker than it was a few moments ago, with the moon now hidden behind the hills on the golf course. Perhaps because the darkness is so intense, I am startled to discover a bright beam of light that briefly but very clearly illuminates the hotel before bending its way across the garden and then shining down through the glass house that protects the winter pool. I am all but blind without my glasses, but I could swear that I see someone down there, carrying a very bulky object. Just a moment, just a moment . . . I reach out toward my night table in search of my glasses, and when the light from what appears to be a flashlight ricochets off the glass walls, I am able to make out the figure of the very attractive hotel gardener I have seen tending to the pool, making sure it is immaculate, free of leaves or any stray insect that may have drowned in the water. He is such a conscientious worker.

I know him . . . what is his name? Ah yes, Karim. I have exchanged a few words with him from time to time, a most handsome young man with eyes black as coal . . . he reminds me of Reza, my neighbor in London. Of course, I can't distinguish all of these details right now through the darkness. All I can manage to make out is the very large roll of tape bundled under his arm, shining in the oddest way, like a giant green snake. He has left the glass door open, which makes it much easier to watch him as he winds the tape around the perimeter of the pool. I can even see how he wraps the tape around four posts, one at each corner, and from my position I would say it is similar to the fluorescent tape policemen use to prevent onlookers from sticking their noses into an accident site. *Do not cross; police line. Do not cross; danger zone.* Oh, how attractive he is, that gardener, how early he rises to begin the day's work, how carefully he winds the tape around the pool before emptying it—because, of course, why else would he wind that phosphorescent snake around the pool area? Obviously, it is because he is emptying it. It takes a bloody long time to empty a pool—it takes a bloody long time to even *notice* that a pool is being emptied, and as such it is extremely important to place very clear indicators to this effect, a green snake whose job is to warn all those *très sportive* types who like to use the pool early in the mornings when no one else is around: twenty laps of the crawl, a few laps of backstroke, who knows how many lengths of the butterfly. You know, those very athletic types who head downstairs and dive in without even looking. The swimmers, after all, must be warned: AT-TENTION: BATHING PROHIBITED. ATTENTION: DANGER. The tape is crucial, because people are so idiotically accident prone at hotels. Even at L'Hirondelle d'Or, a seemingly very tranquil establishment where nothing ever seems to happen . . . My God. My God—what a magnificent idea!

Meanwhile, the Sun Rises

(A SILENT JOURNEY THROUGH THE HOTEL)

1. The Yellow Room

The fine red line marking the beginning of a new day filters into the room through a tiny crevice.

Miss Guêpe is a staunch believer in ventilation, she feels it is an indispensable measure for ensuring proper sleep, and for this reason she sleeps with the window open. The blinds, however, are another story. She did not discover this sublime Mediterranean invention until rather late in life, due to her strict Calvinist upbringing, and she thinks the world of blinds, for they make it possible to air out a room without allowing a single ray of sunlight to assault the retina. And so Miss Guêpe sleeps away, tucked beneath a yellow duvet dotted with little yellow daisies—a well-deserved rest for the secret force behind L'Hirondelle, whose alarm clock rings out at 6:45 on the dot each day.

At this moment, the second hand slowly advances toward 6:10 and Miss Guêpe's dream life continues to transport her through a series of immaculate, pleasure-filled subconscious experiences. A very good sign—whenever Miss Guêpe dreams in an orderly fashion, all will be perfect the following day, and her tidy little dream is responsible for the serene smile gracing her face as she sleeps.

She sees a mountain of towels: large towels, small towels, towels for the bidet, towels for the bath, almost all of them yellow, soft towels piled up in the giant, glass-enclosed precinct of the winter pool. The air is warmed by the early morning sun, and Miss Guêpe envisions someone wrapped in the immense fluffiness of a giant towel. It is the silhouette of a male figure, small but well toned, with tight, wet pectoral muscles and strong legs covered in the finest layer of masculine fuzz. The man is lying face-up, practically nude, and Miss Guêpe suddenly feels the need to approach him—to cover him, of course, for what else could she possibly want to do to him? And then a mental click suddenly erases the entire scene—not because it was an unpleasant vision, of course. But there are certain mental clicks that are hardwired into the subconscious, protecting the dreamer from certain visions. The dreams continue, and they are generous dreams, for they present their mistress with yet another welcome vision. Now she sees the pool filled with people. There is animated conversation, a bit of *blah-blah-blah,* women in bathing suits and straw hats and men in golf attire who have forgotten to take off their shoes with cleats. This last detail is a minor flaw in an otherwise perfect dream, for cleats absolutely destroy the clay tiles surrounding the pool. Even so, Miss Guêpe still finds the dream very pleasing. Just last night she told Karim, the gardener, to empty the winter pool as quickly as possible, using the water pump at maximum power. Speed is of the essence, because Miss Guêpe wishes to refill the pool in the afternoon and then mix in a special product she has just received from Zurich—a delicious, vaguely aquamarine-colored substance that she hopes will encourage the guests to take advantage of the pool early in the day, because it has been seriously underutilized in the morning hours and this error must be remedied as soon as possible. The dream clearly indicates that the guests will respond positively to her maneuver—that is why so many people are gathered around the pool, chatting away in such a lively fashion. Perfect. This is exactly what she was hoping for. After all, she is a master when it comes to gently modifying the habits of her guests through subtle persuasion, almost undetectable schemes. These are the classic methods of our good Miss Guêpe, now sleeping peacefully, comforted by her very promising dream. It is 6:40.

2. Pistache and Muguet

The Pistache and Muguet rooms face each other; both are free of bothersome alarm clocks that threaten to go off at any given moment. The first room faces east, while the other room faces west. One room receives the morning sunlight that rises in varying shades of red, while the other room remains shrouded in penumbra. The bed in this second room is large, super–king size, and the two bodies sleeping in it, their breathing perfectly synchronized, are enveloped in inky darkness, making them almost invisible to the naked eye. They reach out for each other, searching for the contours that have grown familiar from years and years of spending such early morning hours together. Bea and Bernardo breathe in unison. Bernardo's pajama top, with its embroidered monogram on the left breast pocket, rises and falls in time with its master's breathing, as does his companion's short nightgown. His arm rests upon her thighs. Up and down goes the peaceful slumber of a lazy morning, and in the darkness Bea's skin seems to blend into Bernardo's. Even their faces have similar expressions. They move and breathe identically, too. It's a good thing we cannot watch ourselves while we sleep, for we might be very surprised indeed by the sight. We might discover, for example, that sleep has played a terrible practical joke on us—by separating two bodies that, when awake, want only to passionately devour each other, or by creating an intimate cuddle between two people who, in their more rational state, act as if they no longer need each other.

At this moment, Bea and Bernardo are unknowingly locked in an embrace, still dwelling in the kingdom of sleep. Soon enough, consciousness will arrive with its retribution. It is just before 7:30.

In the Pistache room, on the other hand, things are much easier to discern. Its occupants' faces are greeted by the sun as the day commences. The red line on the horizon is now a yellowish sliver and easily filters into the room, happily revealing a woman's arm flung across the pillow and pointing very clearly toward the temples of one Santiago Arce, the man of the moment, the moviemaker everyone so admires. He faces the light source directly, but his eyelids are closed and so he does not see the bright red reflections, nor is he conscious of the pressure exerted upon his temple by Mercedes Algorta's index finger. Their bodies are nude but separated, one behind the other, both facing the light that grows more intense with each passing minute. They are like two strangers on a train.

Last night, in the flurry of their lovemaking, they must have forgotten to close the blinds, because a strong glow now burns down on them, so persistently that Mercedes must open her eyes for a few moments. Arce opens his eyes as well, but only to look at his watch:

"God, it's early."

Now the two bodies move closer together, seeking each other out, coming together in new caresses.

"What do you say we stay in bed a little longer? It's so nice snuggled up here, isn't it, baby?"

"I've never been better, Santi. You know I adore you, don't you?" It isn't quite seven-thirty.

3. The Garden Shed

Hello, my name is Karim. I come from Morocco.
Hello, my tailor is rich. My mother is in the kitchen.

Seven forty-five in the morning usually finds Karim in the tool shed, surrounded by gardening implements. As he cleans and sharpens his tools, Karim often sings a few choice suras with the help of a little book *English in 20 Lessons*.

My brother is tall. Is your brother very tall?

Yes, very tall, and very fat too.

There are days, and today is one of them, when Karim gets up before sunrise so that he can take care of certain things early on so that he may dedicate the rest of his workday to more important tasks. This morning, for example, he was to empty the winter pool and block it off very visibly with fluorescent green tape. Very good: mission accomplished. One task done. Now he can focus on more pleasant duties.

Karim begins sharpening a set of rose clippers. He continues reading:

Do you like bananas? No, but my sister likes bananas very much.

Young Karim dreams of prosperity. For this reason he makes a great effort at work, and tries hard to perform all his tasks to perfection. With a bit of luck, he will soon have a good command of English and then, who knows? Perhaps the hotel chain affiliated with L'Hirondelle might recommend him for a position in another country, perhaps in Europe.

Does your uncle like bananas, too?

Yes, but my uncle is a tailor.

A hotel in Europe would be a very important step. Karim has a cousin who lives in Liverpool. From gardener in a Casablanca hotel to dishwasher in a very famous London hotel, and now he is the owner of his own laundromat in Liverpool. That is exactly how he made the leap. So smart, that Mohammed. Mohammed of Liverpool.

Yes, madam, my uncle is a tailor and my tailor is rich.

Karim selects a scraper from among his pile of tools and gets to work cleaning the small hoe and the boxwood clipper. He still has fifty-five minutes before he must return to the pool for a quick checkup, a routine inspection to make sure that the water is still draining and that everything else is functioning properly, like the extraction pump and the grating on the drain on the pool floor. He must also double-check that the green tape is still in place around the perimeter of the pool with the very visible warning, ATTENTION: DANGER. ATTENTION: SWIMMING PROHIBITED. Karim scrapes away at the blade on the hedge clipper, still practicing his English.

> *Hello, what time is it?*
> *It is eight o'clock.*
> It is eight o'clock on the dot.

4. At the Winter Pool

Waking up at the crack of dawn is so unpleasant. Interrupting one's slumber at such an unnatural moment feels like the slow, excruciating removal of a Band-Aid that rips off a field of innocent hairs in its wake. This, at least, is how Rafael Molinet feels. This laborious, annoying, and agonizing moment inevitably puts a man in the foulest of moods.

Staying awake for an entire night, however, does present a person with a variety of other, far less odious sensations. True, the insomniac may feel languid and lethargic, but he does acquire a kind of detached clarity about what is going on around him: everything becomes crystal-clear and yet distant at the same time. This is exactly what Molinet is experiencing right now as he observes the tips of his caramel-colored moccasins. They seem so far away to him, a thousand miles away down there at the base of his legs, which are stretched out on one of the lounge chairs by the winter pool. His torso rests lightly against the back of the chair, but his feet seem so far away, down past most of his body, which is enveloped in one of his best caftans, the whitest one of them all.

Gomez rests at his side, having selected a choice patch of terrain warmed by the oblique, early-morning sunlight that has entered

through the glass walls and illuminated the tile-covered vicinity surrounding the pool. His ears are spread out like the wings of a bi-
plane, and his jaw rests atop his crisscrossed paws, thick and heavy.
Such an innocent creature, sleeping away as he always does through
life's most critical junctures. Molinet looks out onto the water. Nobody would ever guess that the pool is being emptied—not just because the fluorescent tape with the "swimming prohibited" sign has
been removed, but because the water level seems to be exactly the
same as it was when the draining process began. The only signs of
today's pool maintenance are a faint burbling near the water's surface and a very wide, almost imperceptible swirl of bubbles by the
far end of the pool where the drain is located, indicating that the
pump is indeed extracting the water. How big can the hatchway be?
Ten by ten inches? Fifteen by fifteen? Molinet is unable to see that
corner very well, but he knows that a dark, almost invisible hole
beckons just a few feet further down at the bottom of the pool, its
mouth wide open.

Fifteen laps of the crawl and several more laps of various other
styles. This, Molinet knows, is Antonio Sánchez López's morning
exercise routine, kicked off by a sporty, confident first lap of vigorous, masculine strokes that begins with a dive, head first, from the
north end of the pool.

Molinet hunkers down in his lounge chair. Sleepless nights give
the insomniac such a special kind of clarity. Right now he is not
wearing his wristwatch, for it doesn't go well with his caftan, but
there is a very visible clock mounted on the wall that reads 8:15. A
splendid hour: Nobody but Antonio Sánchez would ever dream of
coming down here so early. How convenient that the great man has
such an original early morning routine, because with a bit of luck
there will be a *petit accident* and in all probability Molinet will have
enough time to put the fluorescent tape back in place around the
perimeter of the pool, just as it was before he removed it. The
minute hand of the big wall clock advances in slow jumps: 8:20. Per-

fect. If Antonio Sánchez comes down according to schedule, there will be plenty of time left to leave everything in its proper place, because it wouldn't be right for that hardworking young Karim to be blamed for whatever might happen. A few minutes go by and the second hand jumps again: 8:30 on the dot and . . . *Le voilà!*, Molinet says to himself as he sees the figure of Antonio Sánchez emerge from the foliage like Tarzan of the Apes.

What admirable punctuality, observes Rafael Molinet Rojas, who has always been a true enthusiast of this particular virtue.

"Good morning, Mr. Sánchez."

"Good morning."

"Good morning," Molinet repeats as he stands up and approaches the edge of the pool, where the swimmer prepares to begin his exercise routine. "Do you mind if I watch?" he asks.

Sánchez is slightly taken aback at this. One brief greeting is the extent of the morning ritual at L'Hirondelle d'Or. After that, people steer clear of their fellow guests and their activities. *Oh, who cares?* Sánchez thinks. If this eccentric old fart wants to watch him take his morning swim, so be it.

"A bit of a swim, eh?"

What a perfectly idiotic question, thinks Sánchez as he removes his yellow robe and begins to warm up his arms by swinging them across his chest and back.

"That's right, a little morning swim."

"And do you like to swim on the surface, or underwater?"

Sánchez continues his arm swinging, more energetically now. *Good Lord,* he thinks. What could that decrepit old man possibly know about staying in shape? He looks at Molinet; he's clearly not a very athletic looking type, but then again you can never tell—perhaps he is a swimmer himself. Appearances can be so deceiving at these hotels, so who knows . . . ?

"Both," replies Antonio S. "Today I will begin with a few laps of the crawl, then some backstroke, then butterfly and I think I'll finish up with a half-length underwater."

"Ah ... of course. The pool is too large to do an entire lap underwater, isn't it? Fifteen meters is quite a lot, and after all that exercise your lungs must be exhausted. Of course, of course ... if you did it the other way around—the underwater part first and then the other strokes, I would wager that you could do two entire laps."

More arm exercises. In two quick movements, Sánchez removes his yellow flip-flops.

"Well, as a matter of fact, I sometimes do it that way—in that order, I mean. Sometimes I like to start off underwater. It helps open the lungs."

"Me, I just love the crawl—swimming underwater makes me nervous. After all, a person can only go so long without breathing, and this pool is massive, plus at such an early hour ... all that time underwater. And then of course there is the matter of the dive. Because underwater swimming calls for a special kind of dive. A very deep dive. Very difficult to execute."

Sánchez's toes now curl around the edge of the pool.

"A pike dive," Molinet says knowingly. "Bent at the waist, knees bent at first, hands by the toes, and then arms up, straighten the legs and dive straight into the water until you reach the bottom. Oh, excuse me. I know I'm an old fool talking on and on. It's just that you remind me so much of myself, many years ago of course. Swimming was never really my forte, but diving—ah, nobody did the pike better than I. The idea, you see, is to glide as far as you can underwater, although it isn't absolutely necessary, technically speaking."

Perhaps it is the chitchat, perhaps Sánchez is simply growing tired of Molinet, for the knuckles on his toes, which are presently gripping the edge of the pool, have begun to turn white.

"If you don't mind, it's getting a bit late, and I've got my activities here timed down to the minute. So if you don't mind ..."

Sánchez stretches his arms out in preparation for a conventional plunge, the kind used to kick off an ordinary, commonplace swim. He is just about to dive in when . . . Perhaps it is the minor glory of being in the presence of an expert in pike dives. Perhaps it is the warmth of the morning sun. Or perhaps it is simply that he now wishes to start off his morning swim with a long stretch underwater. The point is, at the very last moment Sánchez turns to Molinet and says:

"You want a pike? I'll show you a pike!"

Off he goes. Sánchez's body soars up and executes the movement to perfection: bent at the waist, knees bent, hands by the toes, and then arms up, knees straight and . . . there! Straight into the water. Perfect. For a moment the water engulfs him, and he is invisible to Molinet. What will come next? Will he emerge or won't he? Will he rise to the surface or will he push off and swim underwater toward the other edge of the pool, gliding just above the pool floor? Antonio Sánchez López does not come up to the surface, and Molinet congratulates the blue figure underwater that now glides toward the deep end of the pool, the deep end, where he will never hear Molinet's exclamation:

"What a splendid *plongeon,* Mr. Sánchez. Truly *mag-ni-fique!*"
It is 8:45.

100 Percent Terry Cloth

"PEOPLE CAN BE SO INCREDIBLY STUPID," SAYS MISS GUÊPE. "NOT TO mention utterly thoughtless when it comes to others," she says as she settles in for a very lengthy telephone conversation, conducted almost entirely in French.

"There were no witnesses?" asks the voice at the other end of the line.

"Witnesses, *monsieur*? Had there been a witness, don't you think he or she would have told the guest that he would have to be mad to try swimming in a pool as it is being emptied—a pool that has been cordoned off with fluorescent tape which has been secured to posts at all four corners. All four corners!" Miss Guêpe does not usually repeat herself like that, but for goodness' sake, there are times when verbal economy is not the order of the day. "Fluorescent tape that very clearly reads DANGER: NO SWIMMING."

Silence at the other end of the line.

"That is what I am trying to tell you, Monsieur Pitou. Aside from being complete idiots, people have absolutely no consideration for others. I mean, to think of the situation we are in now!"

Monsieur Pitou smokes a cigarette at his end of the telephone line. Perhaps smoking is a rather unusual practice for the general manager of an international hotel chain based in New York, but that is precisely what Monsieur Pitou is doing at this moment.

"Who found him?" he asks after a few moments. "One of the guests?"

"No, thank goodness," Miss Guêpe replies with a sigh of relief. "It was Karim, an excellent employee, whom I trained myself. And by the way, I recommend him wholeheartedly in the event you need someone of his qualifications. He was the person in charge of emptying the pool according to procedure. He went back to check exactly when he was supposed to, and at first when he spotted the man underwater, he thought he was swimming, because how on earth would anyone imagine that a guest would be held there—sucked, *monsieur*! Sucked and immobilized by the force of the water draining out. My God, he drowned like a . . . like a . . ." Miss Guêpe, recalling the previous pool incident, is on the verge of saying the word "rat," but she refrains from making the comparison out loud. The Monsieur Pitous of the world need not know such gruesome and pointless details.

"He died quickly, at least," reflects Pitou. Miss Guêpe decides to steer the conversation toward the rapid, efficient manner in which the well-trained hotel staff responded to this challenging situation.

"Karim, the young man I mentioned to you before, reacted immediately, and following the organization's instructions on how to proceed in this type of emergency, he shut off the water pump right away. Then he located two of his co-workers and with a bit of difficulty they pulled the guest out of the water. Karim then came to alert me while his two co-workers tried to revive the man at the edge of the pool. But it was too late, I'm afraid."

Miss Guêpe quickly explains to Monsieur Pitou how she and Karim went straight to the pool area with a large number of towels of all sizes—small, large, all of them 100 percent of the highest-quality terry cloth, the same ones used by the guest. Miss Guêpe always speaks of "the guest," in precisely that manner. "The guest" this, "the guest" that, she says as she tells Monsieur Pitou how they wrapped Sánchez up in a huge yellow towel.

"He still looked remarkably athletic," Miss Guêpe cannot help but comment, thinking back to the very solid condition of the guest's pectoral muscles. And she feels honor-bound to admit that despite her best efforts, it was impossible to prevent the other guests from discovering what had happened. By the time they wrapped the towel around the guest's body, people began to gather around the winter pool—women in bathing suits and wide-brimmed hats and men who, given the level of distress, had entered the pool area with their golf shoes on, all of them talking on and on about what had just happened.

"Very unpleasant," says Pitou. "But at least it was very clear that our organization was in no way responsible for the accident. A guest who ignores the security barriers, very clearly marked danger signs, cannot possibly expect . . ." He trails off.

Pitou quickly stubs out his cigarette, pulls out a legal pad, and begins scribbling notes as to how the press release should be written. He continues: "Serenity, my dear. Above all else, serenity. I will take care of all the external details. Within the hotel property, however, I will be counting on you to make sure that this terrible incident goes as unnoticed as possible. Now, what-do-we-do-in-cases-like-this?" he asks, as if reading straight from the hotel-executive bible.

"Normality," replies Miss Guêpe, in the same tone of voice. "Everything must go on just as it did before. I will take care of everything, Monsieur Pitou. In a short while, the guests at L'Hirondelle will forget that anything ever happened. That is one of the great virtues of our establishment, I promise you. Nothing ever happens at this hotel."

"Except, of course, to the friends of our 'guest,' " Pitou counters.

"We will take care of all the necessary arrangements so that they may leave as soon as possible," Miss Guêpe assures him, and almost adds that they will probably be thrilled to leave in the most discreet manner. But her instinct for verbal economy tells her not to bother explaining that the guest's friends have their own, rather complicated personal situations, which will induce them to disappear without too much of a fuss. The three of them will be back in Madrid on the double, no fear.

"I put L'Hirondelle d'Or in your hands, Miss Guêpe," says Monsieur Pitou.

"I will take care of everything," she replies, looking out the window of her yellow office, serenely and peacefully as always.

The Story According to Mercedes, Part Three

IT WAS EXACTLY TEN DAYS AGO. I REMEMBER IT PERFECTLY BECAUSE there I was, in this very lounge chair by the winter pool, trying to jot down a few ideas in this notebook. On the other side of the pool, just as he is now, was that strange individual I have come to think of as the Marquis de Cuevas, accompanied by that odd little dog I foolishly tried to befriend by offering him the slice of cucumber floating in my Pimm's cocktail. Now, thanks to Bea, I know that the Marquis's name is in fact Moulinex and that his dog, Gomez, is not interested in anything other than taking long siestas in the sun. I also know that despite the veneer of tranquility, many things have happened here at this hotel—some very tragic things, although you would never guess it to look around. Neither the decor nor the ambience nor the behavior of the guests has changed in the slightest. L'Hirondelle d'Or continues to be synonymous with two things: silence and discretion. Everything is fine; we are all on vacation.

The pool area is completely empty except for Mr. Moulinex, his dog, and myself. I am presently drinking a Pimm's number 3, the cocktail of the house, so to speak: Pimm's and plenty of ginger ale. Everything is just as it was the day I arrived, totally and completely tranquil. I still have about twenty minutes before another one of my daily mud sessions, which are proving to be quite effective. I have already lost five pounds, an entire inch off my waistline, and almost all the freckles on my chest, which is nothing short of a miracle, since I have always despised them, that ugly proliferation of stains which proclaim—or, rather, proclaim*ed*—to all the world that I am in my forties. Jaime used to chide me about things like that, telling me that my outlook on life was infuriating and that I was in denial of everything I found unattractive. "You lie to yourself. Even the way you think about things is a form of denial. You can't own up to your problems—you just avoid them, whenever and however you can. How do you ever plan to take control of your life? You always let things happen to you. You let yourself get carried away with the first thing that crosses your mind . . ."

That was what my poor Jaime used to say, but he's dead now. And I'm the one sitting here drinking a Pimm's with ginger ale at L'Hirondelle d'Or.

"Good morning! Good morning!" I call out to Mr. Moulinex. "Did you sleep well?"

"Like an angel, darling. How is your charming friend Mr. Arce?"

Given that we are together all day, every day, those of us who have stayed on at L'Hirondelle d'Or have naturally broadened our repertoire of banal conversation somewhat. Now we actually exchange full sentences, although most require no response, much in the way the English chirp their ritual questions: *How do you do? How are you?* etc. Who answers that kind of question? Nobody, because the answers are irrelevant. And this is exactly the way it is at our hotel. I know, for example, that Mr. Moulinex would be flabbergasted if right now I were to walk over to the other side of the pool and give him a blow-by-blow report of the activities of my attractive new friend Santiago Arce. It would be extremely incongruous for me to get up from my lounge chair and say something like "Listen,

Mr. Moulinex. Santi, with whom I have shared a magnificent night of passion—you cannot begin to imagine it: the trembling, the ecstasy—has rented a car and gone off to Fez. We are so content together that Santi has decided to change his return ticket and stay on with me here for a few extra days, probably until sometime next week. He isn't due back from Fez until the evening, so I have decided to enjoy my day alone down here by the pool. And aren't you simply amazed at the diligence of the hotel staff? Look at the water. Lovely color, isn't it? Well, that's thanks to a new, turquoise-colored emollient that Miss Guêpe mixed into the pool water after Antonio Sánchez died."

No, no. Mr. Moulinex obviously does not expect me to tell him any of that. Nor does he expect the two of us to sit around gabbing away like a couple of old scullery maids about the grisly accident that took place only yesterday, for Moulinex is a man of few words. Even yesterday, in all the commotion that broke out after they found Sánchez dead in the pool, he had only one thing to say to me and it was in passing, something he whispered in my ear like a secret:

"Don't take it too hard, darling. It's just one of those things, one of those terrible accidents that happens. There's nothing anyone could have done. Just look the other way and be happy."

I don't know why he said that to me, for I don't consider myself to be the kind of person who likes to gossip about morbid things like that. In fact, I have never been able to understand the way a lot of people behave when an accident occurs—on the highway, for example, when all the cars slow down to see the mutilated bodies that some charitable person has covered up with a jacket or a shirt and then those pools of blood and the shoes lying on the road alongside some bloody leg. Perhaps some people find death fascinating, but I prefer to avoid it entirely. I always try not to see anything—after all, what good does it do? For that very reason, I didn't even try to go near the winter pool yesterday like all the other guests did. Instead, I went straight to the garden, which is where I found Mr. Moulinex, very doggedly searching for a sprig of mint to adorn his white caftan. That was when he made that strange comment. "Look the other way and be happy," he said. In the middle of all that chaos, people running around like mad, Bea smoking like a chimney, Bernardo talking nonstop on his cell phone, and Ana Fernández de Bugambilla leaning against one of the columns sobbing inconsolably, even though it does seem rather odd that she would cry so desperately over the loss of such a recent lover. In the middle of all this, Moulinex just strolled his way through the garden in his white caftan with that little dog that follows him around everywhere and stopped to whisper his little comment to me. As he did this, he looked over at Arce, who was with all the other guests, and then he looked at me, as if he were some kind of endearing old maiden aunt who had just given me the most wonderful gift, an old family heirloom, a cameo or something. Although . . . better yet, I would say that Moulinex looked at me with an artistic air. Yes, that's it—like a sculptor admiring one of his own works. It was so unbelievably bizarre, really, it just made no sense at all. Although, I don't know, maybe it's not such a big deal—after all, it was an extremely tense moment and people say and do strange things in difficult circumstances. That might very well have been the case with Moulinex. He certainly is an amiable old man, but in the end he is still a complete stranger to me and my life. All I know is that he said the same thing to me twice in the middle of all that uproar and all those people coming and going— nervous guests, Moroccan policemen with big mustaches, et cetera. The general atmosphere was so stressful and harried that it took the talented Miss Guêpe and her able staff quite a while to calm everyone down.

Today, thank goodness, things are quiet again. It is a spectacular morning, and we are once again the same group that we were the day I arrived at L'Hirondelle in the hopes of putting things behind me (Jaime and his unfortunate death, for one) and getting some distance from all the gossip in Madrid. Once again I feel that soothing sensation of solitude that comes from being surrounded by total strangers—not even Santi Arce is here now. My "charming friend Santiago Arce," as Mr. Moulinex calls him. I still haven't really figured out our . . . romance? Is that what I should call it? I've never been one to exaggerate, for I've always thought exaggeration brings bad luck, and I really have no idea what will happen with us. For the moment, it's fair to say that we have laughed a lot together, we have become lovers, and we do plan on seeing one another when we get back to Madrid. But he is so very attractive, and I know what it is like to live with a man whom women adore and who adores women, perhaps too much . . . Oh, come on, Mercedes! Are you forgetting what you said? The first promise I made to myself when I got here was not to think about the past—it's finished, story over . . . I can't tell if it's the Pimm's I'm drinking or if it's the peaceful atmosphere at this hotel, but I feel so content here—I have no desire whatsoever to get back to Madrid. I wish time could stop right now, at this very moment, because there are so many things I still have to think about—calmly, quietly, just as I am doing right now, spelling things out for myself. That, I suppose, is the luxury of being far away. Distance has the same effect as time. It makes everything seem so far away, almost irrelevant, and I like it that way. My poor Jaime used to say that I am not in control of my own life, that I let myself get carried away—and at my age, my God. But really. What did he know? I haven't made out too badly with my system: Going wherever destiny takes me, doing nothing at all, waiting and seeing what happens. My relationship with Santiago Arce, for example. I didn't plan it, it just happened—or, rather, it is just beginning to happen. So why should I sit here looking back when the future has so many things—much more interesting things—in store for me? Over the past few days, I feel as if I have finally learned to enjoy my freedom. Of course, the surroundings don't hurt—here nobody interferes in anyone else's life, and I hope I can take that lesson home with me to Madrid so that I will remember to simply ignore the things people say about me and to approach my life a bit differently than I might have otherwise. Thanks to this trip, I do believe I will be a lot calmer about things. For example: this past week I finally realized that being a widow actually has certain advantages—as long as one is rich and young, of course. Oh, how awful! How can I even allow myself to think such things? All I do is brag about how I hate to exaggerate, and the minute I drink half a Pimm's with ginger ale, I act as if I couldn't care less about my husband's death and everything that went along with it. Why, you'd think I took life and all the emotions wrapped up in it to be some kind of joke. Oh, I'm not like other people. Other people are so much more consistent with their feelings of grief, of love . . .

And Arce? Where does he fit in the middle of all this chaotic hypothesizing? Santi is adorable and successful and attractive, but I've been married to a man like that, and I know the price that comes with someone like him. Conclusion—Pimm's in hand, the winter pool in the background, the Marquis de Cuevas my only company: Life is short, Mercedes; don't fool yourself. You're better off taking the good, only the good—the passion but not the commitment, the cream but not the milk. What I need is love with no strings attached—no more "Darling, this soup is cold," "Darling, don't wait up for me tonight; I'm going to have to work late." Enough. I am through with all of that. Enough. It's amazing how much a person can learn in an isolated hotel, where it seems that nothing at all ever happens, with so much dead time, so much time to think.

In the end, then, was Jaime right when he said that I lie to myself even in the way I think about things–or, rather, the way I choose *not* to think about things? If so, then I would do well to take a few minutes to contemplate the death of poor Antonio Sánchez, for I feel I may have banished the event from my thoughts rather unjustly. What happened to him was perfectly terrible—after all, nobody ever expects to die while on vacation, much less while on vacation with a woman other than one's wife. Oh, come now . . . don't forget what we said, Mercedes: No looking back.

Very well. All I will say, then, is that the whole incident has been very unpleasant. I actually find it kind of incredible that these sorts of awful things really happen. Not that I knew him very well. Before running into him and his friends here, I had heard of Sánchez, of course, who hasn't? He is a well-known man with a very influential radio show; everyone's always talking about him. Now, if I were a person who really lied to herself, I would say that I am sorry he died, that I feel his pain—after all, the situation is very similar to the one I recently went through. But I don't. It would be a lie, because I don't feel sorry at all. I was appalled by the accident, for it was truly horrific and it affected all of us here in some way, but the commotion that ensued has actually been very convenient for me, wretched as it may sound. You see, when I return to Madrid, everything will be different. By then nobody will even remember Jaime; we will be nothing but old news. Good-bye to the thousand and one versions of what happened the night he died; good-bye to all the hypotheses, all the speculation, all the conjecture; good-bye. It's over, and what a relief it is. The old *tam-tam* of the jungle no longer beats to the sound of my name.

The *tam-tam* of the jungle. That is how my friend Fernanda refers to it—all the gossiping and chitchat, especially the kind that revolves around one event in particular, the one event that is on everyone's lips: the "I swear, I swear, I heard it from a very good source." I am talking, of course, about the Gossip of the Moment, the gossip that will spice up so many conversations over the next few days, months, or however much time it takes for another, more outrageous scandal to surface. Not so long ago, the *tam-tam* was about us, and people said such stupid things. Now, however, the drums will beat for Sánchez.

What will they say? It isn't too hard to guess. They will say everything, they won't speak of anything else, because the great advantage of this *tam-tam* business is that it can only handle one scandal at a time. *One* sin, *one* unforgivable crime, *one* tale of marital infidelity—whatever it is, there can only be *one* of it, and the *tam-tam*'s new rhythm drowns out the old one. And the one that beats for Antonio Sánchez will drum up plenty of whispers indeed. What will the gossips say when they hear the news? I don't know because I am here at L'Hirondelle d'Or savoring a Pimm's with ginger ale as the drums beat away—the smoke must be coming out of their ears by now from all the effort. And they're not gossiping about *how* the poor man died, either. Because his accidental death, in the end, as spectacular as it was, could have happened to the most exemplary of husbands. They are all probably gossiping about the "where" and "with whom" aspect of the story. That is the other dismal thing about death, the one thing everyone always forgets about: Death is like a photograph that freezes reality at one specific moment, and there are some realities that a person would rather not see frozen in time—such as the one that existed here at L'Hirondelle between Antonio Sánchez, Bea, Bernardo, Ana. For the dead person the moment is frozen, but for the survivors it has a way of becoming an indelible stain. This will be the case, no doubt, of Ana Fernández de Bugambilla, poor thing. Not that she was a saint—but even if she were, even if this had been her very first time as the "other woman," they would nevertheless look upon her forevermore as the weekend mistress. Death has that quality, that uncanny way of turning happenstance into something solid and permanent.

Then there is the matter of Bea and Bernardo. Another delicacy for the most frenetic of the *tam-tam*mers. Now, this is not new information—Bea and Bernardo's love affair has been vox populi for years, six or seven at least. Everyone in Madrid knows about them. But it's one thing when "everyone knows," and another thing entirely when a sudden and unexpected death has left you—as Bea herself would say it—with your goddamn pants down.

With your goddamn pants down . . . Call me a complete idiot, but I am always shocked when I see, time and again, how people summarily decide to call something a "scandal" even though everyone in the world has known about it for years and years. And that moment, the very moment the game is exposed and not an instant earlier, is when all the well-mannered souls will turn their back on the sinner and stick it to them where it hurts. Not to incriminate them for their errors or sins (because everyone already knew about their errors and sins), but to say, "Go rot in hell! I don't even remember your name, because you were stupid enough to get caught."

Mr. Moulinex is looking at me. Contrary to his usual habits, it seems that he has actually asked the waiter to bring him a drink. I suppose it will be a Pimm's. I don't know him well, but he looks like the type who would observe the worldly rituals of this place—and, anyway, what else would one drink at this hour at L'Hirondelle? A Pimm's, I am sure of it. What else? Now, let's wait for the waiter to come around to see if I am right. I would even lay money on it. Pimm's, Pimm's . . .

The people I really feel sorry for in all this are Ana and Bea, especially Bea. This is what suddenly runs through my mind as I look over at Mr. Moulinex. What a dismal situation for them, and I don't just mean the accident—I mean the way all three of them had to leave so quickly, so suddenly. Before dinner, even. I did, however, have time to stop by Bea's room to talk to her for a moment. In the end, she was my one friend in that group and I wanted to tell her how badly I felt, and I meant it, because I know what everyone will be saying about her relationship with Bernardo. And Bea just laughed. She always laughs, whether or not she's smoking at the same time.

"Oh, who knows, honey?" she said, as if shrugging her shoulders about the whole thing. "Who knows? Men never get divorced once they start having a real affair, not even when they fall in love. But now that the whole thing is going to go so public, maybe

Bernardo's wife will summon up her pride, threaten him with divorce, put his suitcases at the front door, and then, who knows? Maybe I'll finally get my chance. 'It was scandal that brought them together.' Isn't there a movie by that name? Yes, *United by Scandal,* something like that," she said, with a cackle that came out sounding a lot more like a cry for help.

I like Bea, and I think Mr. Moulinex does, too. I didn't manage to catch what they said to each other last night just before Bea and her friends left, but I did see Mr. Moulinex very ceremoniously kiss her hand. Then he pulled her close and gave her the closest thing to a hug that a person like him was capable of. Perhaps he said the same thing to her that he said to me in the garden. "Be happy, darling." What a strange man, that Mr. Moulinex. He speaks to us as if he actually knows us. Perhaps he was able to get to know Bea a bit more, chat about this or that. I, on the other hand, have exchanged nothing but a handful of pleasantries with him. And yet somehow I feel as if he knows my life story . . . oh how stupid. Nobody knows my story. Nobody at all. Impossible. It isn't worth a second of my time to go worrying about that. *Silence,* I tell myself. Ah, but look at this. If it isn't Mr. Moulinex's little dog trotting over to me now, just as he trotted over to me that first morning.

"Come here, sweetie, I'm not going to give you anything to eat today. I just want to tickle your ears, that's all . . . Come now, don't be scared."

Dry Martini

TO PROVOKE, OR SUSTAIN, A REVERIE IN A BAR, YOU HAVE TO drink English gin, especially in the form of a dry martini. . . . Connoisseurs who like their martinis very dry suggest simply allowing a ray of sunlight to shine through a bottle of Noilly Prat before it hits the bottle of gin. Another crucial recommendation is that the ice be so cold and hard that it won't melt, since nothing's worse than a watery martini. For those who are still with me, let me give you my personal recipe, the fruit of long experimentation and guaranteed to produce perfect results. The day before your guests arrive, put all the ingredients— glasses, gin, and shaker—in the refrigerator. Use a thermometer to make sure the ice is about twenty degrees below zero (centigrade). Don't take anything out until your friends arrive; then pour a few drops of Noilly Prat and half a demitasse spoon of Angostura bitters over the ice. Shake it, then pour it out, keeping only the ice, which retains a faint taste of both. Then pour straight gin over the ice, shake it again, and serve.

—Luis Buñuel, *My Last Sigh*

Dry Martini

A few yards away from Mercedes, Rafael Molinet has just sat up in his chair to address a rather nervous young waiter standing above him with a cocktail shaker in hand.

"No, no. *Pas du tout!* Dispose of that disaster, Hassam, please. Throw it to the ants, let the salamanders get drunk on it—that is what this rank brew deserves. We must start from scratch. For the love of God, get it out of my sight and come back here with a notepad. We are going to write down the recipe step by step, and this time you will pay much closer attention, Hassam. Please, now."

The bewildered young waiter retreats as Molinet leans back against his lounge chair, smooths out his white caftan so that it is perfectly stretched over his body, and places the tips of his fingers together as if he is about to tell a very long story. This is what he has to say:

AS YOU CAN see, this story ends exactly where it began. At the winter pool of L'Hirondelle d'Or, ten days after the morning I first laid eyes on Mercedes Algorta. And now, all that remains to be told is the finale.

Had you arrived here two minutes earlier, just two tiny minutes, you would have witnessed a scene identical to the one played out here on October 13: Gomez and I were comfortably ensconced in the warmest corner of the solarium, Gomez was napping and I was studying my little widow at the other side of the pool as if I knew nothing about her, as if this were the first time I ever laid eyes on her broad face, her very subtly highlighted blond hair, and that indefinable quality that made me think, as I did even back then: A widow is the very best thing a woman can be.

Of course, since you have arrived two minutes later, the scene is not quite the same as it was on the thirteenth. Yes, the two of us are the only ones in the solarium, and, yes, Mercedes is on the other side of the pool—although not terribly far away—caught up in what looks like some very serious philosophical meditation. Just like the first day, of course, it is terribly hot and she is very slowly sipping away at some type of beverage, an activity which forces her to raise her arm every so often to lift the drink to her lips. I watch her, for I wish to study certain details of her appearance—specifically, something that gleams brightly on her wrist. At that very moment, however—and herein lies the difference between today and our first encounter—Hassam comes by and ruins everything. First by rousing Gomez, who, quite annoyed, decides to trot over to the other side of the pool. And second by bringing me, after a very long wait, an abominable concoction that he claims is a dry martini.

This is the moment at which you have found me, and thus begins the final chapter of the story of a bad girl, the tale I promised to tell you ten days ago. Here we are, just the two of us: Mercedes, ruminating on who knows what just a few yards away, and I, lifting my eyes to observe her every so often. There is something God-like about knowing that you have done a good deed for someone without their knowing it. But that is not what I think about right now. I do not think about the delight I certainly feel at having settled an old debt with my past, nor do I think about the magnificent *plongeon* of my friend Sánchez, who to my great satisfaction has suffered a terrible accident. No. None of these reflections interest me in the least. The one thing I care about right now is my favorite cocktail.

This is an important point, mind you. Do not take it as a flight of frivolity on my part. Today is October 23—all I have left here at L'Hirondelle d'Or is a day and a half. Two weeks is what I decided. No more, no less. That was always the plan, from the beginning. And then, if you remember correctly, it was to be *adieu, ciao, au revoir,* and all those other euphemisms I like to use when I speak of my decision to gaze out at this marvelous Moroccan landscape as I swallow the three vials of pills that Dr. Pertini prescribed me. That is precisely what I still plan to do, believe me, but there are certain details that mustn't be overlooked, details which should be addressed with clarity and plenty of time. For this reason, just a short while ago, as I dozed away here by the pool, it suddenly occurred to me that a magnificent dry martini would be the ideal beverage to accompany Dr. Pertini's pills. And for that reason I asked the waiter to prepare a sample—a first rehearsal of sorts, for my general plan is still rather rough around the edges. This waiter, for example, is very attentive and may have the loveliest eyes, but he is a zero in the cocktail department. We still have plenty of time to perfect the recipe, though, so I tell myself to be patient; everything will come out just fine. Here comes the waiter now, bearing a notepad to take down my instructions, just as I requested. Very well. I am willing to test his cocktails all morning if I have to—after all, there isn't much else to do here.

"All right, Hassam. Now you must pay very close attention to what I tell you. Take notes and repeat after me: To make a good dry martini, we need, in this order; one part gin, Beefeater if possible."

"One paht gin, Beefeatah if possible," Hassam repeats. "Very good, sir."

I would be very disappointed if you, the readers who have been with me since the beginning of this story, were to think me careless or disrespectful and as such I want you to know that before I end my life (martini and Pertini, in large doses), I will take the time to go over a few more significant details, just as one finds in all great stories of suicide. To start with, I will amuse myself by telling you two or three insignificant points that nevertheless must be raised in order to complete the story properly, and then I will have to write a note explaining my decision to the hotel supervisor. I have not yet written this note, but I am sure it will be a masterpiece of simplicity and grace. In the end, a suicide note or epitaph is the most transcendent thing a man can write, is it not?

"Now, write this down, Hassam. We need a few drops of dry vermouth. Very dry."

"A few drops of dry vermouth, very dry."

When contemplating a letter of this nature, one inevitably feels that it must be sublime. I don't know how I will frame it, exactly, but I do know that it will be extremely conventional and that it will be addressed to Miss Guêpe. The classic approach, I suppose, is always the best for cases such as this, so it will probably sound something like this:

"My dear Miss Guêpe . . . please do not blame anyone for my death . . ." Now that I think of it, I will have no choice but to add something with respect to Antonio Sánchez. Of course I must—that is the right thing to do. I know that his death was regarded by one and all as an accident, but this *would* be a perfect opportunity to clear up any doubts that might still linger. Two deaths, one right after the other—so many dead bodies all of a sudden at one charming hotel. No, this is not going to help the reputation of L'Hirondelle one bit, and so I think it better if the letter reads something like this:

"My dear Miss Guêpe, please do not blame anyone for my death, for it was entirely my own wish. In addition, I must take full responsibility for the death of . . ." Or should I use the word "murder"? Yes, yes, very well: ". . . the murder of Antonio Sánchez López." Perfect. This is a fine start. This way the situation will remain absolutely clear.

"Now we will need a glass cocktail shaker."

"Let me write this down," says Hassam. "Transparent glass cocktail shaker."

It would also be nice if I added a few words of praise for this magnificent hotel—just before I apologize for stiffing them. *Ce n'est pas très gentil* on my part, and of course it is the least I can do. What I do not plan on explaining, however, is my reason for killing Sánchez. I am sorry, but no. Under no circumstances.

"Do you have it all down, Hassam? Very well. Now, you don't have to repeat this next bit back to me, just take it all down. First, fill the cocktail shaker with a fair amount of ice. Have you got that? All right, you will then bless the ice cubes with a drop—one drop, Hassam!—of vermouth and then you shall add the gin. Then—and this is extremely important, Hassam. Don't try and be original, please—the liquid shall be *shaken,* not *stirred.* Is that clear? After that, all you have to do is pour it, making sure that no ice cubes fall into the glass. A good dry martini, Hassam, is a difficult thing to achieve, although I am sure that if you follow my instructions point by point . . ."

Yes, it is the very least I can do for this spectacular hotel—the explanatory note, I mean. But one thing is for sure: I will not devote a single word to the reason I decided to murder Sánchez. I glance up at Mercedes and smile at her. There she is, all alone, just like on the first day, with that defenseless yet determined air about her—the kind of person that you can very instinctively understand, without even trying to read her thoughts. Just like Mama.

For the moment, however, here we are, Mercedes and I, just as we were the first day, alone and silent, minding our own business. Mercedes drinks a cocktail and thinks thoughts that are completely foreign to my humble person, and I sit here recounting my final observations on all that has come to pass at L'Hirondelle d'Or in between my attempts to get this dimwitted waiter to mix a perfect martini.

"Ah! There you are, Hassam, finally! Let's see how you made out this time around."

I test out the martini, though I will save you the gory details. Once again, the experiment has been a disaster.

Just as we are going into round three—that is, my third semi-martini—someone approaches me with a bulky fax from my niece Fernanda. Perhaps it is the early morning alcohol clouding my mind, but the fax looks absolutely endless. Miles and miles of paper. It looks like one of the Dead Sea scrolls, with drawings, huge amounts of text, and a few pasted-in clippings that I can't quite distinguish.

I don't believe, of course, that my three semi-martinis have had such an astounding effect on me, but I do feel as if time has suddenly grown elastic somehow. The minutes stretch out like a piece of gum, giving me time to do two, or even three things at a time. First I chide Hassam about his cocktail mixing, then I look up every now and then to gaze tenderly at Mercedes, who will never know what I did for her. And in the middle of all that I am still able to peruse the fax Fernanda sent me. Although, to tell the truth, I have no desire whatsoever to read the thing, so many pages of nonsense. A few lines are enough to give me a general idea of what she's written: questions, questions, lots and lots of *blah, blah, blah.* Herein lies a sample:

> *But, Uncle—how can this be? You were there when the accident happened. My God, you must tell me everything. I'm desperate for details. I can hardly believe it. When I heard the news I practically fell flat on my face: Antonio Sánchez, our hero, the same Antonio Sánchez I have been telling you about in all my faxes—dead! And in such a compromising position, wouldn't you say? Antonio S! A great man like him, a pillar of the Western world, a . . .*

Some nervous scribbling covers the "a" which is replaced by "the."

> *. . . the champion of the truth, sucked to death by a drainpipe! Just when he was cheating on the saint of a woman he has lived with for God knows how many years! You cannot even begin to imagine the things people are saying around here. We are all absolutely transfixed by the gossip. What a colossal . . .*

That is more or less how Fernanda's fax starts off. For this reason, after skipping over the first two or three paragraphs, I am extremely

surprised to find something completely unrelated to the Sánchez affair: an article from one of those English gossip rags that Fernanda
has cut out and pasted onto the page. It reads as follows:

> *Drones, the famous restaurant, the symbol of an entire era in
> London, has changed owners. Worrall Thompson is the man
> who will be responsible for breathing new life into the establish-
> ment. The legendary kitschy decor and the walls lined with
> childhood photographs of Hollywood stars (tasteless, according
> to many), will be replaced with a cool Latin emporium look.*

I continue reading. There will be time enough later on to lament the
demise of one of my very favorite restaurants—that is how life goes,
alas—because right now I have hit on something far more interesting to focus on. I am taking care to keep the pages organized so as
not to create a logistical nightmare later on, when suddenly, ten or
twelve miles ahead in the document, I see that Fernanda has stopped
to make a few observations on the fallout from Sánchez's death.

> *. . . I know, Uncle, that you have little sympathy for people who
> externalize their feelings—I know you find it lowbrow to lose
> control, to sob out loud and cry hysterically at funerals, but you
> should have seen the woman that was Sánchez's . . . (should I say
> romantic companion? I'm not really up to speed on hip, modern
> slang for this sort of thing: companion, longtime lover, I don't
> know what you would call Sánchez's girlfriend. Because, and
> don't go calling me old-fashioned, they were technically not
> married). But anyway. My point is that you cannot begin to
> imagine the state his girlfriend was in at the funeral. My own
> philosophical conclusion is that either the girl was crushed at the
> thought of losing all those "sponsors" that Antonio helped her
> get for her "artistic" jewelry business or as the old Spanish song
> goes, "la vida te da sorpresas, sorpresas te da la vida"—that*

is, life is filled with surprises, and surprises fill your life, and you can never tell how a woman will react to the death of the man she lives with. This poor, poor woman just fell to pieces, and I think it was for real. Not to compare or anything, but Mercedes sure was cool as a cucumber at Jaime Valdés's funeral; not a single strand of hair out of place. I told you about all that before— she was so composed, so elegant, that some people believed she was completely indifferent about what had happened.

Just like Mama at Bertie's funeral, I think back with pride. Nobody saw tears fall from her eyes either—and she did have such lovely lilac eyes. Nor did people ever catch her avoiding them, despite everything she had been through and all the despicable things they so openly said about her.

"I will toast to that!" I call out, raising my glass in the direction of Hassam so that he will serve me a bit more of that pox he calls a dry martini. As I do this, my eyes cannot help but stray over to the other side of the pool, to the little widow who never shed a tear, according to all the gossipers. And as she sees me raise my martini high in the air, she returns the friendly gesture by raising her own.

"To your health, Mr. Moulinex," I hear her say, for my ears are in far better condition than my eyes. At that very moment a beam of sunlight bounces off her wrist, making it sparkle a bit more brightly than it should. This of course must be due to that thick bracelet she wears, the one that seems so out of place at a country hotel, the one she stopped wearing after that first day we bumped into each other down here by the pool.

"How odd," I say to myself, though for the moment it is just a passing thought, because without my distance glasses I cannot see a bloody thing from so far away. I am blind as a bat. Anyway, I really must get back to Fernanda's fax.

Why are long letters such a bother to read? I must admit that Fernanda's rambling is often quite entertaining, but in this case I

find myself skipping over various sections until my eyes suddenly
come across a familiar word, "Borrioboola-Gha," which makes me
backtrack a paragraph or so. I read:

> And since I am much more generous than you when it comes to
> divulging information about certain people we know, I should
> warn you that there is a fresh batch of news regarding Isabella
> Steine and I must *tell you about it blow by blow. Because her
> situation—my God, it makes you want to do voodoo on her.*

Bon Dieu. I pray the blows are brief ones. I have come to live in fear
of Fernanda's treatises on Isabella Steine. She has a way of ripping *la
petite* Isabella to shreds.

> *Here's the latest, Uncle. It appears that our Isabella (I assume
> you remember her, even though you are a total disaster when it
> comes to names. She is the gorgeous woman we ran into at
> Drones, the woman who sparked our entire conversation about
> Mercedes and Jaime Valdés) has gotten over the death of her ex-
> lover incredibly fast because she already has a new boyfriend,
> and he is quite a little dreamboat. She seems to think he is the* ne
> plus ultra *because he is absolutely everywhere, always getting
> invited to this event and that event, they're literally fighting over
> him at parties—I mean, there are so few eligible bachelors in
> Madrid that the women here would duke it out over a donkey,
> but the point is, the man in question is named J. P. Bonilla and,
> believe me, you would die if you ever checked him out.*

I have to confess that I skipped over the J. P. Bonilla description—
but my memory for names is not quite as bad as Fernanda believes,
for I do happen to remember a very long story about this Bonilla
character from my recent chat with Bea on the north balcony of the
hotel. From what I could tell, a very *réussi* editor—one of those dis-

ciples of American-style marketing who always knows how to take the tiniest little bits of trivia about his authors and turn them into major news. According to Bea, Bonilla is a very cheeky man who very recently tried to convince her to do a job that sounded like some kind of scam. If memory serves me correctly, it involved the author of an erotic novel entitled *The Blue Midriff*—he wanted Bea to throw her parties, get her photographed, and basically go everywhere with this woman, a native of a place called Borrioboola-Gha—wherever *that* is. And speaking of geography, I cannot help but feel that the world is so very small and Madrid even smaller. My God, to think that here, without moving an inch from L'Hirondelle, I have come to know *tout le monde*: Bonilla, Isabella, Bea, and then some. Of course, I can't say that I am very surprised, because all the tightly knit, insular societies of the world are so very small in the end. High society everywhere is made up of about four or five fat cats, and everyone always knows everyone else. As such, I skip over one or two *Who's Who*-type paragraphs and continue reading a bit further down in Fernanda's fax:

> As you know, I couldn't care less about Isabella's love life—she can shack up with all the J. P. Bonillas on Earth for all I care. My problem with that little two-faced darling is that her meddling has left me without a job that Bonilla had originally promised me. You see, he had been scouting around for a woman friend to do a little job for him, a really cushy assignment given my circumstances. You know how things are for me and Alvaro financially—it is so hard to make any money these days. Anyway, Bonilla had picked me for this project—a fabulous project; it even had a bit of cultural cachet to it. Believe it or not, the idea was that I was supposed to accompany this very famous Borrioboolian writer named Harpic or Sidol or, oh, I don't know—some name that sounds like a bathroom cleanser, but it doesn't matter—she's incredibly famous, that is what I am get-

ting at. The idea totally appealed to me, because it meant that for a few days we would be invited around everywhere, we would get covered in ¡Hola!, *which is always fun . . . but all of that is beside the point, really. The point is, what really got me was that Bonilla was going to pay me a fortune for about three days' worth of work. I have no idea why he decided to be generous, because let me tell you, any one of my friends would have been thrilled to do it for free. It sounded fun. You'd meet all sorts of interesting people, go to all sorts of parties. You know what I mean. It would have been so glamorous—which is exactly what Isabella must have thought, too, because in the wink of an eye I was left* sans Harpic, sans *photo spread in* ¡Hola!, sans *cushy job, because of Isabella, who is already loaded. Life is so unfair, Uncle Rafael.*

Borrioboola-Gha, I think. Isabella, unwittingly involved in the Borrioboola-Gha mess. Not bad. Maybe life is not as unfair as Fernanda thinks. Of course I know she wouldn't agree, because two or three paragraphs down I come across another tale of what Fernanda calls "the stony-faced Isabella Steine."

. . . All right, now. I promise to stop talking about that witch, but I can't resist showing you one more little thing—proof positive of what tacky, tacky people Bonilla and Isabella really are.

I flip to the next page of this eternal fax and find Fernanda, once again, in top form:

To give you an idea of what I'm talking about, take a look at this article and photo I clipped from a gossip magazine. It states that "the renowned and beautiful Isabella Steine" blah, blah, blah, "will act as escort and hostess to a famous author from Borrioboola-Gha" whose name, as I told you before, sounds like some kind of toilet cleaner. As you can see, the photo from the press release is not new. It was taken the same day as the other photo I sent you a few days ago—you remember, don't you? The shot of Valdés (may he rest in peace) at a party with Mercedes and Isabella. How do I know this, you ask? Darling, a person who devours gossip magazines like you do shouldn't even have to ask. Can't you see the girl is dressed exactly the same as in the other photo? She's even wearing the same Cartier heirloom bracelet that Mercedes spotted in a Christie's catalogue and Isabella got old Papa Steine to give her for Christmas. Obviously they used an old photo, but it goes so perfectly with the article— it's a close-up from the waist up, perfect for catching every little detail of our darling Isabella's features. Look at her. Her posture is so perfect, and it almost seems as if she predicted the whole thing, because she even has a kind of intellectual look on her face, the hand resting on the jaw as if she were just waiting *to* read The Blue Midriff, *that little fraud. The only thing that doesn't fit the intellectual look is the bracelet—a bit too much, wouldn't you say? Look at that leopard-printed gold, top-of-the-line Cartier.—Did it come out in the fax? I tried to enlarge it a bit this time, because I know how much you love these little details. After all, you're such a snob, Uncle Rafael!*

Cheap & Chic

WHAT IS A PERSON TO DO WHEN HE BELIEVES HE HAS FINISHED TELLING the story of a bad girl, a story whose elements fit together as perfectly as the pieces of a puzzle? A story that has no bad girl at all, as the reader discovers in the end? Perhaps the less-conscientious reader must be told that there *was* one bad girl, a very long time ago—a bad girl who wasn't even a member of the female sex and who one night took a silver-handled mirror, committed a crime, and never felt the slightest twinge of guilt. As far as the other characters in the story are concerned, the ones you have met at L'Hirondelle d'Or, we all know that following a *petit accident,* the good girl is redeemed and absolved of all guilt and the bad man pays dearly for his lies. And finally, as for the third man (that is, yours truly, me, Rafael Molinet), a man with an old debt to settle, well, after forty long years he finally takes his tiny but very delicious bit of revenge on the gossipmongers of the world. But what is a man to do, I ask, when he believes he has finished telling the most perfect, most complete story . . . and then suddenly realizes that there is a fly in the ointment? He drinks another martini, obviously.

"Hassam, before you go back, dear, leave the cocktail shaker on the table here, please."

"Did you like the last one, sir?"

"It is as dreadful as all the rest, Hassam, but I am afraid I will be needing it. This one, and two or three more, I fear."

All because of a devilishly clear photo in Fernanda's fax.

Ever since this story began, ten days ago in this very spot, I have made quite a big deal about the fact that I have told everything exactly as it unfolded before my eyes, as if I were a spectator at the theater. I have even gone so far as to proudly assert that I would intersperse the various situations, combining more recent ones with older ones, mixing in Fernanda's information with some of my own conclusions . . . after all, isn't that what writers do? They are so very devilish. And I can do it just as well as they do. The writer always has the upper hand, after all, because he knows the ending of his story. And I too know how this story ends, which makes it easy for me to make all the pieces fit, every last one . . . Every last one! That was true up until a few seconds ago, when Fernanda's fax had to go and ruin everything.

I look down at the fax again and there it is: the photo of Isabella, clear as a bell, down to the most unpleasant details; no room for a single doubt. Now, don't go thinking that I would have purposely avoided mentioning the one discordant fact in the story of Valdés's death—meaning the Cartier bracelet that has appeared three or four times in the course of this tale. But, well, it just seemed like an incidental fact that was impossible to verify one way or the other. Now, however, Isabella's image in the photo Fernanda faxed me is so clear that it seems to be crying out at me, "Look! Look!" Nobody ever wants the incongruous elements of a story to come jumping back to haunt them especially when everything else fits so perfectly. But sometimes they do.

An utterly unmistakable Cartier bracelet . . . a bracelet that disappeared the night Valdés died. A bracelet that, as such, could only have been saved as a token or as a bit of revenge by someone who should have been occupied with more Samaritan tasks at that moment. Yes, this bracelet has popped up several times throughout the course of my story, almost as if it were trying to disrupt the harmony between the story of my mother and the story of Mercedes Algorta. Yet I disregarded it, thinking it superfluous, and perhaps I did that on purpose. In the end, on that distant day—the night Bertie Molinet died, I mean—there was a bracelet, useless and inconsequential, that ended up on the floor next to the grandfather clock in the vestibule. It was a tiny, misleading little chord on my part, I suppose. A writer's trick—or perhaps it was more like a violinist's trick, the perfect dissonant note clashing against the magical harmony of the rest of the story, ruining the loveliest piece of music.

I say this because I am enchanted by the soothing notion that our lives possess a kind of musical harmony, a mirroring of sorts, not unlike the echo that follows the sound of every bell that tolls if one listens closely enough: two identical stories; two philandering husbands; two innocent wives unfairly accused. And so, many years later, I take an action to prevent a gossip broker from disseminating lies. Sweet revenge.

I take a long sip of my martini, which is actually beginning to seem drinkable. Now, what would happen if I were suddenly to question the innocence of one of my good girls—and I am referring to my little widow, who reminds me so much of Mama. What would happen if she was not innocent but guilty, as Sánchez intended to claim?

This calls for another gulp of my martini. And the gin, such a wise liquor, successfully calms the two or three vital organs that have suddenly begun to palpitate at this new thought. No wonder all those tough guys, all the detectives in those police novels, are always drinking gimlets and martinis, for they are such rational cocktails. The first horrible notion diminished by this gin is that your very own

Philip Marlowe has unjustly sent the noble Mr. Sánchez straight to hell precisely when he was on the brink of publishing not a calumny but rather the awful, awful truth about Mercedes Algorta. Nevertheless, this amiable liquid very quickly reminds me of a very handy trick for vanquishing this fear.

"Listen, darling," the gin seems to tell me. "Don't waste your time worrying. In this topsy-turvy life of ours, even a broken clock is right twice a day." Nice quote, isn't it? And, no, it was not uttered by Philip Marlowe or James Bond or any other famous gin drinker, although it could have been. It was said by Mama. She said it a lot, in fact, and it is nothing short of gospel to my ears. Sánchez was preparing to expose Mercedes not because he knew of anything specific—as I do, for example, thanks to that damn bracelet—but because he *felt* like it. He was all set to write a scandalous article based on two or three stupid coincidences, and while a broken clock may be right twice a day, that doesn't mean you shouldn't toss it into the garbage.

I look at the photograph of Isabella again. In effect, I can see every last detail of that Cartier bracelet: a wide band of gold with a flamboyant leopard motif, fat, with big black spots, one of the most celebrated symbols of this jewelry house. Is it the same one that Mercedes is wearing this morning, now that we are alone, now that nobody from Madrid is here to identify it? It would be so easy to stroll over to the other side of the pool, put on my eyeglasses, look her in the eye, and say, "Excuse me, darling, would you mind if I took a look at that exquisite bracelet you are wearing?" It would be so easy to confirm, for once and for all, that the bracelet gleaming on Mercedes Algorta's wrist has nothing whatsoever to do with the bracelet that disappeared the night Jaime Valdés died. Even so, I wouldn't dream of doing it. They are just silly fears of mine, nonsense. It must be all the gin . . .

The bad thing about doubts, however, is that they inevitably lead to more doubts. Two identical stories separated in time, the bell tolling, then the echo . . . and two good girls unjustly accused. Yes, that is how it shall be: everything identical. That is how it *must* be, because if not, it might mean that Mama . . .

Bon dieu, I think as I pray that Mercedes hasn't chosen this moment to come over here. From above my little piece of lemon rind on the edge of my glass, I can see her walking on the other side of the pool. No! Do not come over here. Do not even think of approaching me with that glittering wrist, that bracelet. Stay where you are, for I—like all civilized human beings—always choose doubt over certainty, at least in this case.

Two identical stories, two identical women. I repeat this to myself over and over again. I have repeated it so many times that it has started to get annoying, even after all the dry martinis I have consumed this morning. The old and the new . . . the bell and its echo . . . that is how it shall be, everything symmetrical. And if not, I am better off not finding out . . . like what Mama did after everything that happened in the house at El Prado that night. That is the inopportune comparison I have drawn. Of course, Mama did see me as I ran down the stairs to my father's side. And she also saw how the reflection from the mirror ricocheted off the ceiling. A quick, sharp blow, and that was it. Bertie Molinet was over, but we never spoke of it—why would we? Certain truths are better off shrouded by doubt.

Unfortunately for me, the bracelet of that woman on the other side of the pool has caught a ray of sunlight, causing it to sparkle indecently, and I think: *What if things didn't happen the way I thought? And if the reflection of the mirror on the ceiling went unnoticed in all the confusion that night?*

In that case, I tell myself, with the lemon rind suspended in front of my eyes, a lot of things don't fit. Mercedes Algorta is right there, as is Gomez—both of them are presently teetering just above this fragile lemon rind. There she is, rummaging about, picking up her things, looking for her slippers and her hat as if she's getting ready to leave. I am hoping she won't find a reason to come over here, to deliver me my dog or something. Plus, she doesn't have to pass by me in order to leave the pool area. Walk by, walk by for God's sake, just as you do every day . . . "Of course everything fits," I tell myself, and the martini makes me repeat, with the crystal-clear memory of the inebriated, the very same words I used to explain my story to Bea that afternoon we spent looking out onto the golf course. ". . . From the very first moment my mother knew that another blow, final and definitive, was what killed Bertie Molinet, that a fifteen-year-old child had been responsible for his death. Are you scandalized, darling? Well, it is true. Even with all the rumors flying around town, when people whispered on and on about how the 'accident' had really occurred, she kept her mouth shut and simply nodded her head . . . Come now, dear, don't look at me that way. I think you are going to learn a great deal about human nature this afternoon, because there are times in life when it is easier for a person to bear the burden of gossip and suspicion than to admit, even to herself, the far more appalling guilt of a person she loves above all others."

It's true: that is how it happened. Thanks to the reflection of that mirror on the ceiling, Mama immediately knew what I had done. She knew it and she chose to overlook it. And that is why she remained silent for all those years. This thought makes me feel better, but still . . .

The *click-click* of Gomez's nails against the clay tiles of the solarium floor makes me lose my train of thought. Oh, that inconvenient mutt. I can see him over there, next to Mercedes, shaking his ears as if he's about to trot off.

But then doubt strikes again.

What if I am fooling myself? In the end, how can I be sure if Mama saw it? We never discussed it.

At this moment the alcohol (not such a friendly substance) brings to mind another fleeting moment of that dark night: Bertie is sprawled across the floor of the vestibule, and I approach him at the foot of the stairs as my mother, observing the two of us from above, shouts out: "Dear God, dear God. Rafael darling, what have I done?"

"Impossible," I counter. "What nonsense. It can't be. Mama did nothing wrong—I was the one who, seconds later, with a silver-handled mirror . . . I am convinced of what I say here. There is no way two people can be guilty of the same crime. There is no way two parallel stories can be true at the same time. She *knew* . . ."

But then . . . what if Mama did not see the reflection from the mirror that night and, as such, did not know of my sin? And what if she remained silent all those years, in fact, for reasons other than those I believed, for facts I knew nothing of, for an act that was not of my own doing? Impossible. Unthinkable. And in any event this is irrelevant at this stage in the game. It's always better not to know.

Mercedes Algorta has put on her hat. Women always put their hats on as they leave pools, which is so ridiculous. Hats should be put on before, not after lying in the sun. She is now ready to leave. Oh, she won't come over here, will she? This isn't the shortest route out of the solarium, after all, and yet . . . *Click, click, click.* Even without raising my eyes I can tell when Gomez is approaching from the sound his nails make as they scrape against the solarium floor.

"That which is not spoken does not exist. As such, a secret untold has a way of disappearing in the end." That was our anthem for all those years during which Mama and I never discussed what occurred that night. But what was it, then, that she did not want to discuss? Two identical women, two twin situations. The echo has to sound exactly the same as the bell that rang out the first time around. Both women are innocent.

Mercedes Algorta has put on her hat. For the love of God, please don't come over here!

The image of a gentleman my age carefully studying a piece of lemon rind is, no doubt, a rather eccentric sight. Nevertheless, this is what I do to avoid looking anywhere else. I will not lift my eyes; I will not look anywhere—for God's sake, doesn't the credo of this hotel state that the guests are supposed to talk as little as possible to one another? This woman should be leaving, not walking over to me with that smile I can see coming over her face. Now that the very worst has happened, I will remove my eyeglasses. Without them I cannot see a thing, I cannot see anything at all in detail.

"May I?"

"What? What did you say, dear?" I ask as I remove my glasses.

"Just a few minutes ago I made a little bet with myself and I want to see if I was right. Let me see: that cocktail you are drinking, is it a Pimm's by any chance?"

She is standing in front of me. Gomez, too. His nails against the clay tiles have made their way back to my lounge chair, much to my dismay.

"What's that, my dear?"

"Oh, I'm so stupid! I should have known from the glass. You're drinking a martini, not a Pimm's. Would you mind if I took a sip?"

There are moments in life when, rather unwittingly, one finds oneself standing in plain sight of an incontrovertible fact. The woman stretches out her arm, not waiting for a response, and a blurry but excessively sparkly wrist, dotted with turquoise, red, and green stones, flashes before my eyes.

"I always love a good dry martini, though they are strictly off-limits here—diets, you know. But then suddenly as I was about to leave the pool, I saw you and . . . oh, may I?"

Turquoise, red, and green stones. This can't possibly be a Cartier leopard-motif bracelet . . . impossible. Doubt. *Maintain the doubt at all times,* I tell myself, *for it is far more ambiguous, far more soothing than the truth.* If I were to put my glasses on, of course, I would be certain for once and for all. I am almost sure, those little colored brilliants . . . oh, what a relief. No, it cannot be. It cannot be the thing I feared.

She has now served herself the remains of the martini, just like that, as if we've been friends all our lives. As she raises her arm, her wrist sparkles yet again, and then I do something I have never done in my entire life.

"Cartier, my dear?" I ask her. I have not put on my glasses. There is still a tiny bit of room for doubt if I want to seek refuge there once I hear the answer.

She laughs. Once again she raises her hand and her sparkling wrist to take a sip of the martini.

"Cartier?" she exclaims. "Are you kidding? Cheap and Chic— not exactly the same league. You mean this trashy thing?"

I smile.

"Of course," I reply, exhaling deeply. "You see, I'm not wearing my glasses, and when I spotted it from far away, well, your wrist was sparkling so brightly that I imagined it might be one of those wide bracelets, you know, 1940s-style, with a leopard or something . . . very Cartier. Oh how silly of me!"

She takes another sip of the drink. The dry martini has another very special quality, and though I can't confirm this with my eyes, I am sure it has taken effect: the dry martini has a way of bringing out the sparkle in the eyes of its drinker.

"I'm sorry to disappoint you, but it is no Cartier. It's one of those cheap Moschino pieces. Nothing but a fantasy, I'm afraid, Mr. Mouli- nex."

"Molinet, my dear. My name is Rafael Molinet."

"Oh. Excuse me."

"It's all the same. And I mean that. It is all exactly the same. We all make mistakes . . . luckily."

Once again she laughs, and once again she raises her arm, mak- ing those divinely fake stones sparkle in the light. That marvelous bit of costume jewelry banishes all my doubts, and the world is once again perfect: The sound of the bell and its echo are one and the same; the discordant note of my fears proves to be nothing more than the work of an able violinist. I lean back against my lounge chair with the tranquility that comes from knowing that I have just made a silly, foolish mistake. And that is when I hear her say:

"Such ideas you have, Mr. Molinet. Cartier, and with a leopard no less—here? At this hour of the day? It would be so out of place, downright tacky if you ask me. You can't possibly think that I would wear that sort of bracelet to come down to the pool . . . even if I had it. Right, Mr. Molinet?"

About the Author

CARMEN POSADAS was born in Montevideo and is the daughter of a Uruguayan diplomat. She lived for some years in London, where her father was ambassador, and also in Buenos Aires and Moscow. Her novel *Little Indiscretions,* first published as *Pequeñas infamias,* won the coveted 1998 Planeta Prize in Barcelona, and her books have been translated into twenty-one languages. Also a prizewinning children's author and cowriter for film and television, Posadas now lives in Madrid.

About the Type

This book was set in Granjon, a modern recutting of a typeface produced under the direction of George W. Jones, who based Granjon's design upon the letter forms of Claude Garamond (1480–1561). The name was given to the typeface as a tribute to the typographic designer Robert Granjon.